Sunny
stays at the
Shetland
hotel

Erin Green was born and raised in Warwickshire. An avid reader since childhood, her imagination was instinctively drawn to creative writing as she grew older. Erin has two Hons degrees: BA English literature and another BSc Psychology – her previous careers have ranged from part-time waitress, the retail industry, fitness industry and education.

She has an obsession about time, owns several tortoises and an infectious laugh! Erin writes contemporary novels focusing on love, life and laughter. Erin is an active member of the Romantic Novelists' Association and was delighted to be awarded The Katie Fforde Bursary in 2017. An ideal day for Erin involves writing, people watching and drinking copious amounts of tea.

For more information about Erin, visit her website: **www.ErinGreenAuthor.co.uk,** find her on Facebook **www.facebook.com/ErinGreenAuthor** or follow her on Twitter **@ErinGreenAuthor**.

Sunny stays at the Shetland hotel

ERIN GREEN

REVIEW

First published in 2022
by HEADLINE REVIEW
An imprint of HEADLINE PUBLISHING GROUP

1

Cataloguing in Publication Data is available from the British Library

ISBN 978 1 4722 9500 2

Typeset in Sabon by CC Book Production

Printed and bound in Great Britain by
Clays Ltd, Elcograf S.p.A.

Headline's policy is to use papers that are natural, renewable and recyclable
products and made from wood grown in well-managed forests and other
controlled sources. The logging and manufacturing processes are expected
to conform to the environmental regulations of the country of origin.

HEADLINE PUBLISHING GROUP
An Hachette UK Company
Carmelite House
50 Victoria Embankment
London EC4Y 0DZ

www.headline.co.uk
www.hachette.co.uk

To those pesky imperfections we each have,
which make us unique and fabulous!

Wherever there is sunshine, shadow must fall.

ANON

Shetland Glossary

Peerie – small/little

Daa – grandfather

Crabbit – bad-tempered

Yamse – greedy

Chapter One

Tuesday 1 February

Dottie's diary
That peerie duck has walked mud throughout the tiled hallway! Housekeeping are overseeing the cleaning duties for the guests – scrubbing, mainly. Thankfully, my dusting duties are assigned purely to the Campbells' private quarters. It's lovely to hear laughter and chatter return to the old place, it reminds me of bygone days.

Pippa

I'm nervous standing here upon the cobbled yard in the low afternoon sunshine. That jittery expectation of fight or flight irks me as we await the big reveal for Lerwick Manor's latest venture. I shouldn't be nervous – after all, the Campbells seem to have enjoyed the Midas touch with their previous projects – but I am. For unlike the adjoining Lerwick Manor Allotment Association, which dates back aeons, or The Stables arts and crafts gallery, which has been a booming success since last autumn, and even their newly refurbished hotel, which occupies several floors of their stately home, this eagerly awaited project involves me. I'll be at the helm, in the driving seat, so to speak! I have every faith in their vision, their ethos and business acumen, but something deep down inside is niggling away at me. And that unnerves me immensely.

'Pippa! Pippa! Has anyone seen her?' calls Ned, craning his neck towards The Orangery, failing to see me hiding amongst the crowd of artists lining the gallery's cobbled yard.

At twenty-seven years of age, I don't know whether to laugh or cry, so I stand stock-still, peering over the artists' shoulders at the monstrosity trundling through the stone archway. I can make out Levi's frame through the tinted windscreen, as he proudly draws the vehicle to a halt centre stage, before killing the ignition.

I can't remember what I had in mind when the initial plans were explained to me, but this . . . this wasn't it! When I volunteered for my new job, I thought I had realistic expectations of what was required of me. My big boss, Ned, is a stickler for a job well done and his wife, Jemima – my older cousin by just two years – is pretty savvy when it comes to creative ideas and ingenuity. But this is a sodding joke! I'll be the laughing stock of Shetland, driving this bulky wagon between the rural communities. And what for? All in the name of . . . I peer at the swirly script decorating the nearest side panel: 'The Artisan Bread Basket – straight from our ovens to your doorstep!' Well, that figures. The bulbous curves of the metalwork, with its gleaming new paint job in beige and brown, make it looks like a crusty loaf on wheels. I must be short of a loaf or two to even contemplate switching from being head waitress in the gallery's artisan coffee shop, to belittling myself by driving that thing around.

'There you are! What do you think, Pippa?' asks Ned, an expression of delight plastered across his strongly defined features.

I don't answer. He tilts his head, awaiting an answer. Flecks of grey nestle attractively amongst the darker brown of his temples.

He might have married into our family, but still I need to lie. I must lie. I can lie; I have before.

'It's g-great!' I stutter, sounding the least convincing of any moment of my entire life.

'Pleased?' he continues, beckoning me forward from the huddled crowd.

'Y-yeah. Pleased.' I'm not, which I think is clearly obvious. Or rather, it might be to Jemima, if she were present; despite our strained family ties, I suspect her female intuition would detect my disappointment instantly.

Ned hastily strides to the driver's door where Levi, the local taxi driver and dear friend of my cousin, hands over the keys and swiftly departs in the direction of the manor.

'This way, Pippa ... come and have a look what's inside. I think you'll be impressed,' says Ned, indicating for me to follow him to the rear of the vehicle.

He unlocks the double doors while I stand waiting, like a petulant child refused sweets. My sulky words slip from my mouth before I put my brain into gear.

'Given the shape, I assume it was an ambulance?'

'It certainly was. We got her for a bargain price, removed the interior to create more space, and –' Ned wrenches open the rear doors and pins them back to reveal the new interior – 'now she's fully functional, with storage racks, a serving counter and cupboard space!'

My mouth falls open. I simply stare. Mute.

Metal racks line both sides, from floor to ceiling. Sturdy wicker bread trays sit neatly upon each shelf, with a gleaming lip of metal securing each one in place – clearly to prevent mayhem whilst driving. A wooden counter, with many drawers and cupboards, is positioned behind the driver's padded seat, completing the refurb. Metal hooks and carabiner clips hang from the ceiling struts, providing easy access and storage for paper bags, serving gloves and metal bread tongs.

'There's even a tiny sink with running water,' says Ned proudly, pointing at a set of taps protruding from the countertop. His words fill the growing silence but, sadly, only serve to highlight my lack of enthusiasm.

'Well. At least ...' I'm desperately trying to find something productive to say, as there's no way I can stall any further. 'I can't wait to get started,' I lie.

'Great! That's the spirit, Pippa! We were thinking as soon as tomorrow morning . . . out and about, advertising and possibly taste-testing,' says Ned, passing me the keys.

'Great,' I repeat, but without Ned's enthusiastic tone. I suspect that the assembled artists are expecting me to deliver a witty line of appreciation. I'm not impressed. Surely they've got things to do, to make or create, rather than wasting precious time watching this tragedy unfold?

The conversion job was entrusted to the MacDonald lads, a local trio of brothers on whom everyone relies when a favour is needed. I'm grateful that they've removed the blue lights from the roof, the trolley ramp and the colourful Battenberg stripes. They've done a decent job – but still, this simply isn't me.

Wouldn't it have been lovely to drive a custom-built bread van of which I could be proud? Instead I'm presented with a second-hand ambulance, resurrected from retirement, in which I presume some folk may have died and others could possibly have been born.

'It's come all the way from the mainland,' says Ned knowingly.

I wish Jemima was showing me around instead. I could be honest, say what I truly think. She'll understand my disappointment, or possibly remember the root cause. Being the youngest of three girl cousins, I rarely got anything new. Callie and Jemima were both careful with their clothes, their childhood toys and belongings; our parents thought they were being thrifty passing on bin liners bulging with outgrown clothes. Being the youngest, guess who always had the final wear? And now I'm lumbered with this cast-off from an NHS ambulance depot. Ned's expecting me to show delight, so just like with those pre-owned clothes of yesteryear, I'll fake a smile and dream of alternatives. I could ask Jemima if Aileen still wants the job. At the time, I was miffed when she eagerly volunteered, but now I think Aileen is more capable of making a success of this new venture than I am. I'll happily give her a chance at promotion from being a waitress in the artisan coffee shop – I know she hates wiping tables as much as I do. If she wants to prove her true worth, she could start tomorrow. Label that as 'personal development' in the next round of appraisals – mine, not hers.

'Where's Jemima?' I ask.

'She'll be along in a while. She's settling new guests into their rooms,' Ned says, his dark eyes twinkling as his gaze roves about the vehicle's reconditioned interior.

I'm stuck. Lumbered with this monstrosity until I speak to Jemima.

Autumn

'Dottie, please. You frighten me when you gallop down the staircase at such a pace. What'll happen if you fall and injure yourself?' I enter the reception area of the newly converted Lerwick Manor Hotel to find the spritely octogenarian dashing through the hallway clutching her favourite feather duster.

'I've run down that grand staircase more times than you've eaten haggis, Autumn. My days of light dusting are over when I can't choose my own gear speed,' she says, her watery blue gaze intent upon mine. She wafts past me, heading for the rear kitchens. 'Don't you forget, Ned said I could do as much or as little cleaning as I please round here, now we're open.'

'I haven't forgotten, Dottie.' Though I don't know what I'll say to Jemima or Ned if she breaks a hip – it doesn't bear thinking about. I've only been here a week, and I thought she'd heed my warning after daily reminders, but no, I suppose old habits die hard. I'm aware that Dottie knows this manor house like the back of her hand, but the ground floor plus the next two floors have all been refurbished to accommodate paying guests. So there are definitely more bodies, obstacles and trip hazards lining these once-silent corridors. I can do without an emergency occurring on what's supposed to be a quiet midweek opening.

A collection of suitcases and holdalls are lined up on the hallway's classical black-and-white tiled floor. I'm hoping each is clearly labelled, ensuring swift delivery to the assigned suite; there isn't anything nicer than entering your suite to find your luggage awaits you. There are plenty of staff on hand, prepped and ready to assist, eager to iron out any unexpected niggles; nothing's ever perfect until it is up and running, despite the Campbells' meticulous planning.

The shuttle bus from Sumburgh Airport delivered our first group of guests, travel-weary and hungry, some ten minutes ago. Jemima quickly ushered them through to the library for a warm buffet lunch and a brief introduction, while I prepare the necessary paperwork. I don't suppose this will happen every time but I understand her attention to detail; it provides me with some breathing space, ensuring their luggage is delivered correctly.

I'm excited that today has actually arrived. After much anticipation and effort I'm fully prepared, but slightly nervous in case things don't go as smoothly as planned. But that's all part and parcel of a front of house role in a top-class establishment – you need to think on your feet and be able to pull a rabbit out of a hat, when necessary. My current position is an amalgamation of roles; the Campbells are calling me the General Manager, on account of my responsibilities and daily duties, but I also have shifts on reception. I'm certain my role will change as the establishment develops over time.

Amongst the rows of luggage, two in particular grab my attention. A couple of identical hessian duffel bags, standard army issue in khaki, complete with drawstring and metal eyelets. The second pile, a set of seven designer cases, decreasing in size, accessorised with bulging buckles and straps, in a taupe colour.

It's a silly game, but old habits linger from my previous employment working in hospitality on cruise liners. I'm yet to meet any of our residents but their luggage speaks volumes about their personality. The cruise ship's gangway would still be in place and we'd be waging daft bets on who's who and what's what – a bit of fun that made arrivals day less monotonous for the staff.

'Autumn, are the keys ready?' asks Levi, entering from the rear kitchen door, through which Dottie had disappeared just minutes ago. He's full of energy, his blond hair sticking up at his crown.

'Perfect timing. I was just assigning their suites.' I indicate my prepared booking sheet and gesture towards the wall-mounted key cupboard. 'Is Ned happy with his new bread van?'

'Mmmm, he is. I'm not so sure it's to Pippa's liking.' He joins me at the reception desk. 'Knowing Pippa, there's bound to be a drama before too long.'

I can't comment; I know her by sight from the local area but we're yet to be fully acquainted. I believe she has the room opposite mine in the refurbished servants' quarters up on the fourth floor, which partially extend above the Campbells' private quarters below. Every night this last week, I've climbed the old wooden staircase at an ungodly hour to fall into bed, ready for an early start in the morning – much like I did on board ship, when I hunkered down in my tiny cabin.

It takes me a matter of minutes to attach a suite label to each guest's luggage before Levi swiftly collects suitcases and carries them up the grand staircase. He might be moonlighting from his main taxi job to help out for today – filling in for the lack of applications for the advertised bellboy/waiter role – but Jemima assures me Levi's a legend. There's nothing more rewarding than being surrounded by willing, pleasant staff who take pride in doing their job well. That's one of the things I'll miss about the cruise liners; nothing was too much trouble if it pleased our guests. Be it a special request for an anniversary meal, or arranging excursion trips ahead of disembarking at a port, or locating a member of staff who could serenade a proposal, perform a magic trick or walk an elderly guest to their seat. But a long career spent at sea has left me hankering for roots on land since my fortieth birthday. And, dare I confess, a smaller, more homely establishment to organise instead of being responsible for an entire deck of cabins. The long working hours and lengthy absence from family takes its toll in the end, regardless of how organised and dedicated you are.

I linger at the reception desk and admire the swathes of Black Watch tartan and elaborate tapestries which decorate the high ceiling, encircling the impressive crystal chandelier which plunges into the vast hallway. Generations of family portraits watch the proceedings from their gilt-edged frames, high above our heads. I wonder what they'd make of the Campbell family being confined to the third-floor landing as their private residence?

The Lerwick Manor Hotel may be a newly refurbished establishment but the standards are incredibly high, the facilities plush, and the family history provides an ambience to die for. I'm impressed. My two-piece uniform of dark navy is teamed with a silver satin blouse, which wasn't of my choosing, but it looks rather fetching against my mature complexion and auburn hair. The staff radio hanging from my slender belt feels bulky as I walk, but I'll get used to it. I'd much prefer to rely on my mobile, which remains in my pocket throughout my shift.

'Does Levi need a hand taking the luggage up?' asks Mungo, appearing from nowhere and gesturing towards the many suitcases. He strokes his greying beard as he crosses the hallway. I've sussed that he's Dottie's companion but I know from growing up in Lerwick that he lives at the end of her road.

'I'm sure he'd appreciate it – and if he doesn't, I certainly do. Thank you, Mungo. The hessian holdalls are for the Whalsay Suite on the first floor.' Each suite has a geographical name based on the local area. I pass him the assigned key before he bundles the luggage up the grand staircase.

It's a pity there's no lift facility yet, but guests are informed prior to booking; luckily, that isn't a concern for our current crop. Of the twelve available bedrooms, just eight have been refurbished to accommodate paying guests, with all mod cons and stylish en-suite bathrooms. The Campbells have created many new ventures in recent months: The Stables gallery, The Orangery, and now, a plush hotel. Being locals, my family can't believe how a manor house can lie dormant for decades, with hardly anyone seen about the premises, only to become a thriving estate brought to life with guests and gallery customers in a matter of six months. I keep telling them, that's what happens when the right two people get it together in life and work as a duo; anything is possible. My sister reckons the Campbells weren't even dating this time last year, which I find hard to believe.

'The large set of cases is for which suite?' asks Levi, returning from his first delivery.

I quickly check my booking list. 'The Unst Suite on the first floor. Though I believe the occupant didn't arrive on the shuttle bus. She's gone sightseeing in Lerwick and will be checking in later tonight.'

Levi collects the largest two cases before saying, 'Can you send Mungo up with the lighter ones? I'll return for the heavier suitcases.'

'Sure. I appreciate your consideration, Levi,' I say, attempting to fix a stray strand of hair which has escaped from my low bun.

'The old bugger's as fit as a fiddle, but he needs to pace himself.'

'Aye, the same goes for Dottie.'

'You've more hope of curbing Mungo's antics than hers,' chides Levi, with a chuckle, before grabbing two taupe cases and ascending the staircase.

Chapter Two

Pippa

'Hello, Pippa, come on up. Ned said you wanted a word,' says Jemima, leaning over the banister of the third-floor landing and viewing my ascent. Her dark flowing locks fall forward, enveloping her olive skin. We're first cousins, our mothers were sisters, though you wouldn't know it. I take after the Quinn family in appearance: the Scandinavian blonde colouring with piercing blue eyes. Sometimes it would be nice to be as unique as our Jemima, but that's thanks to her father's side.

'Please. A quiet word,' I say, not wanting to chat in the stairwell for fear that Ned might overhear and assume I'm being ungrateful.

'Sure. We'll use the office as Ned's just gone out to visit a tenant farmer.'

I climb the remainder of the grand staircase under the watchful gaze of Ned's descendants, honoured within decorative gilt frames, before reaching the only modern landing in the manor, complete with its row of skylights, leading to a minimalistic office. Jemima waits patiently in the open doorway; I know she's sussing me out as I draw closer. She probably senses what I'm about to say before I explain. We might be blood relatives but there's a world of difference between us since her recent good fortune in meeting, marrying and moving up in the world, becoming joint owner of this place. Not that I'm jealous: I'm certainly not. But name any single woman you know who wouldn't give her right arm for her dreams to come true in literally two seasons? Exactly. I don't know anyone who'd say 'no, thanks' to the good fortune that's been bestowed upon my cousin.

Having embarked on a sabbatical, spent mostly on Granddad's allotment, Jemima quit her role at the local tourist office, before suggesting and setting up The Stables gallery, providing me with much-needed employment and an escape route from a boring admin job, proving that blood is thicker than water. I'm grateful to her, especially as we haven't always been the closest of relations. Waitressing in The Orangery, reporting to Isla as my boss, I confess I was jealous of her dedication and talent for baking. I definitely became lazier and slapdash when I realised I couldn't compete with Isla's skillset. I don't blame her for reporting back to Jemima and Ned, I'd have done the same in her shoes. Five months on, they encouraged my interest in their new mobile delivery venture. Though now, having seen the actual vehicle, I'm not too sure.

Jemima gestures for me to enter the office and I settle at the meeting table. I rarely come up here, but I know Isla attends daily meetings to report on The Orangery's previous day's sales.

My cousin settles opposite me, her elbows resting on the white table, an expectant look in her eye.

'I don't want the delivery role for the Bread Basket,' I say. I feel incredibly guilty, but there's no point beating around the bush. She might be my boss, but I should be able to say what I want to family. 'I'm sorry for wasting your time.'

'O . . . K . . .' Jemima slides her elbows from the table and sits back. 'And you didn't think to mention this to Ned while he was giving you a tour of the vehicle a matter of thirty minutes ago?'

I shake my head, biting my lower lip. I wasn't expecting her to be happy at my announcement, but she seems shocked.

'So the account he relayed to me of a smiling, excited Pippa wasn't actually the truth?'

I shake my head again. 'Remember when you were little and all you wanted for Christmas was a lovely big doll's house filled with lots of tiny furniture and pretty objects?'

'Yeah, I had one like that when I was about eight. I loved it.'

'I remember it well, I wanted one just like it . . . but I received a skateboard instead!'

Jemima grimaces, as I knew she would.

I swiftly continue, 'I didn't ask for a skateboard, but it's what I was given, as it was the popular craze at the time. That was a definite "smile and be grateful" moment on Christmas morning.'

'You loved that skateboard – you were forever doing tricks and stunts. And if I remember correctly, didn't my mum give you my doll's house years later?'

'She did; that's precisely why my parents wouldn't buy me an identical one. Am I always to receive second best in this world, then grin and bear it, regardless of what I want or how hard I try?'

She averts her gaze, before giving a hefty sigh.

I wait for her to speak; I'm not about to trip over my own apology by making whimsical excuses purely to satisfy my cousin.

'Pippa, Ned is hoping to hit the road with this new venture tomorrow. He isn't going to be impressed to learn that he's . . . we've . . . forked out for a conversion job, only to find we have no driver.'

'I had an image of actually enjoying what I do each day. No more wiping tables, fetching coffee or clearing dirty trays, but taking sole responsibility for the enterprise,' I say. I want to add, it's amazing how your enthusiasm dies when reality doesn't live up to expectations, but I don't.

Jemima doesn't look best pleased.

I change tack. 'Look, I wasn't expecting anything state of the art – or even posh – but I never imagined I'd be a laughing stock by the end of day one in a converted ambulance. I'd prefer to be wiping tables and making umpteen lattes than driving that thing.'

'Oh, Pippa!' grumbles Jemima, her eyes pleading with me.

'Ask Aileen,' I urge. 'She'll be up for the job at the drop of a hat. She wanted it initially, before you awarded it to me. There'll be no chance of her refusing the opportunity, if you pitch it right.'

'If I pitch it right?' Jemima's furrowed brow returns.

'You know . . . explain that there was an issue with my driving licence . . . or that I failed my written assessment for the health and safety certificate . . .' I pause.

She's listening intently and doesn't appear amused by my solution. 'So the long and the short of it is that you want to bail out because you're embarrassed by the second-hand vehicle we've purchased, yet you'll freely volunteer Aileen as your replacement without speaking to her.'

'It makes sense,' I mutter, feeling less confident now.

'No, Pippa. What would make sense is that you honour the task you were assigned after you volunteered. That you step up to the plate with the venture you said you wanted. You said, and I quote here, "I want to be on the open road, being my own boss." You were excited at the prospect of spreading the word about the gallery and making deliveries to the smaller villages and the isolated communities. Or is that something that I've made up?'

'Err, not quite. I doubt I said "the open road".'

'OK. I might be ad-libbing slightly, but words to that effect?'

I nod gingerly, feeling bad for voicing the truth. She's not a happy bunny. Ned will be even less amused when he hears.

'And I suppose I'm the one who's to deliver this news flash to Ned upon his return, am I?'

'Err yeah, you're the other half of the management team.'

Jemima's jaw drops. That last phrase came out slightly wrong. I give a fleeting shrug, not trusting myself to speak for fear of annoying her further.

'Can I ask what you are choosing to do instead?'

It's my turn to frown. Surely that's obvious.

'I'll continue to waitress in The Orangery and work alongside Isla.'

Jemima purses her lips. 'And if I were to say we've already lined up a replacement with immediate effect, given that you were to begin preparing "your project" for trading.'

'Oh.' The realisation dawns; I hadn't thought of that. 'Can't she replace Aileen instead? I'll happily train her up in the role, if it helps.'

'If it helps?' Jemima shakes her head – in disbelief, I think. She has a habit of repeating phrases when a quick-fix solution fails to spring to mind.

'Sorry, just trying to be honest. Surely a happy workforce makes for a productive team!'

Jemima offers me an exasperated look; she clearly thinks I'm a waste of space.

Natalia

I didn't think I'd be this anxious at the thought of seeing him again, after months of silence. No doubt he'll portray his usual cool exterior, while my senses are spinning into orbit, but I'm used to that. Ned's a man of few words, but deep down he cares immensely. I've always suspected his mannerisms were moulded by upbringing, family duty and a deep sense of tradition. Thankfully, I know the other side of his nature: his tenderness towards me, his gentle encouragement on each visit, and our intimate pillow talk. I sense this is the right time for us; as long as I don't mess up like last September. I'm trying to steer clear of calling this my 'last chance saloon', but the notion certainly fits.

I've made every effort to ensure my arrival is a complete

surprise. Ned hates surprises; I think they keep life interesting. I refused the shuttle bus from the airport, opting for a taxi ride into Lerwick and a few hours to browse the quaint shops. I've enjoyed a manicure, a fresh pedicure and a very nice afternoon tea overlooking the busy harbour.

My blonde hair is discreetly swept up beneath a woollen peaked cap, which will hide my face, if needed, and my bulky winter coat and large designer sunglasses complete my disguise. I've no fear of bumping into Ned. It's early evening, so there's only one place he'll be: in his third-floor office, shouldering his daily worries as lord of the manor. It's the locals who might rumble me – the Dotties of this world.

I'm taken aback by the refurbishment of the manor's hallway, which includes a stylish reception area situated to the right of the grand entrance. The elegant wooden counter encircles the entrance to what was once a disued parlour in which Ned housed his old estate accounts and dusty box files, but which now appears to be a fully functioning rear office.

'Your luggage has been delivered to your suite, Ms Muir,' says the receptionist – or Autumn, as her name badge declares – who's being extremely efficient with the paperwork and my keys. 'If I could ask for a quick signature here, here and here.' She indicates each place marked with tiny crosses. I oblige with a squiggle; I doubt room service will be checking my signature against each order, come the morning.

The past few months have been taken up with non-stop modelling assignments for high-end cosmetics or beauty products. I realise that others outside the industry think the work is easy money, labelling it as 'pose and pout', but having jetted here, there and everywhere to please the agency bosses and photographers alike, I'm exhausted; which is why this little excursion comes as a welcome break. I may not have reached the heady heights of the catwalk queens but my face, hands and flowing locks have featured in many glossy magazines. I've yet to sign my latest contract with the modelling agency; I'm unsure if another three-year commitment is where my heart truly lies. Who knows? Ned might surprise me with a suggestion that will encourage me to put down roots sooner than I imagined.

Nobody interrupts or appears during the check-in process. I knew arriving at this hour would reduce the chances of bumping into anyone before reaching my room. Society believes it embraces a modern lifestyle 24/7, with the time of day no longer dictating people's activities, but they're so wrong; certain parameters still exist. Most hotel guests check in early, making the most of their first night, either in the bar or restaurant, which means corridors and staircases are free from guests, staff or a watchful proprietor. There's usually a hive of activity in kitchens or dining rooms, with no one paying attention to the final check-in of the day: the solo traveller.

The Unst Suite is unchanged in many ways from my previous visits, apart from the new name. This large airy room was never the bedroom of my choice, but usually the one which Dottie assigned me after her cleaning duties. She knew perfectly well that I adored the larger bedroom, two doors along, on this floor. His mother's old room, I believe, though now renamed the Sumburgh Suite. A stunning room with the same prospect, overlooking the manor's grounds and stables, but being the corner room of the building, the layout provides a true suite comprised of a dressing room and connecting boudoir, complete with a four-poster bed suggesting an extravagance which this, the Unst Suite, despite being luxurious, simply can't emulate. The decoration is to a high spec, the mocha and beige colour scheme tranquil, while the solid traditional furniture is tastefully arranged. A quick glance around the facilities confirms I'll be comfortable during my stay. How could I not be? In all honesty, I'll probably be switching rooms by the morning – either enjoying the four-poster boudoir or, better still, Ned's private quarters on the third floor. Fingers crossed, I'll be here for longer than my planned two weeks.

As the door softly clicks shut, I breathe calmly for what seems like the first time today. I stride to the huge window, whipping the lacy voile aside to view the manor's grounds below. In the dusky light, it looks gorgeous, as always. A vast cobbled courtyard with mellow light spilling from the open doorways, the sweeping gravel driveway, decorated with ornate gates and an expanse of luscious greenery on either side. I assume the galleries' artists have finished for the day . . . and now to have established stylish accommodation too – business must be looking up for Ned Campbell.

How many times have I enjoyed this view and dreamt of my future happiness? It seems so long since last September. I acted like a fool, back then, dropping in unannounced for the allotment's annual festival. I didn't even stay for a night or two, as I'd planned. Instead, I handled things badly, then lost my head, dashing off into the night. I shot back to that tiny B&B, disgruntled as hell, and flew back to Edinburgh the very next day. Hardly a successful trip! We hadn't seen each other for near on nine months, but it wouldn't have taken much to rekindle the fires between us; it never does.

This time, I'll play it cool; show Ned how much I've grown in recent months, and plant the little seeds regarding our future together.

I traipse back and forth between the bedroom and en-suite, filling each glass shelf with my delicate tiny bottles, toiletries and make-up. I've purposely packed many of the gifts which Ned has bought me over the years – whether it be an expensive cream, discreet earrings or a designer necklace – each will pose as a little reminder of days gone by. My intention is to settle in this evening, recover and freshen up from my travels, before popping upstairs for a nightcap. Boy, will he be surprised. It's taken more courage than I care to admit for me to book a room, take a flight and arrive here to see if we can reconnect. I need to be brutally honest with Ned and ask him how he feels. Scarier still, tell him how I feel. The years are ticking by, neither of us is getting any younger, and I want to settle down together and create solid plans for our future. I've enjoyed a longer stint than most in modelling, but everything must come to an end at some point.

I'm as anxious as I am excited. This stay is going to mark the beginning of the rest of my life. I hope.

Chapter Three

Wednesday 2 February

Autumn

The cobbled courtyard is a hive of activity, with early customers sauntering leisurely from stable to stable enjoying the sights and sounds offered by the various artists. The Artisan Bread Basket van is parked in the centre; it looks out of place, but I suppose it's free advertising.

'Morning, Nessie, how are you?' I ask, tentatively entering the forge to be greeted with a wall of heat and the sound of rhythmical hammering. The blacksmith immediately stands tall, stretching out her shoulders from her bent position at the far end, hammer silenced, and removes her protective goggles.

'Hello, Autumn, how's it going?'

Her shock of pink hair makes me smile; it was vibrant blue only last week. I was never the hair-dyeing teenager that my girlfriends morphed into. They opted for a range of grungy, daring and outlandish makeovers, ensuring I looked a complete oddball hanging around with them, until they reverted to my more conventional style in later years.

'Very well, thanks. I thought I'd drop by to say hi, as I've been dashing about in recent days,' I say, making my way to her end of the forge. 'No . . .?' I gesture towards the empty workbench that belongs to her companion Isaac, the glass blower.

'Not yet, he's out and about quoting for a commission piece,' says Nessie, putting down her tools.

'I hear you pair are getting along very nicely,' I say, giving her a smile.

'We are. Boy, news certainly travels fast – you've only been here a week,' says Nessie, a deep blush spreading across her cheeks. 'Are you enjoying it so far?'

'I am. Hospitality is what I know – although it's a bit of a switch from the cruise liners.' I note her change of subject and assume it's early days for their relationship. I'm pleased for them, so respect her privacy.

'Exciting to be part of a new venture, isn't it?' she says, with enthusiasm. 'It reminds me of our first days here in the gallery. I thought I'd have gone under by now, but hey ho, I'm still here, pounding the metal.'

'Exactly. Amazing how popular it's become with the tourists and locals alike,' I say, glancing at her display of wrought-iron products. Immediately, I spy the layer of gritty dust on the display cabinet. I imagine this place is difficult to keep clean.

I've always been ridiculously organised since childhood. My dolls were always sitting up straight, lined up alongside teddy bears and other cuddly toys. I love a crease-free duvet, squarely aligned to the frilly valance, topping a hidden flat sheet displaying hospital corners. I'm a perfectionist: be it fluff on the carpet, a stray hair on your collar, or a nick out of a china tea cup – I'll spot it a mile off. Some folk are people persons, and some people are goal setters. Me, I'm a perfectionist, through and through; if a job's worth doing, it's worth getting every detail right. In the hospitality industry, every detail counts and is noticed by others. I've learnt that from years on the cruise liners – though that can bring issues of its own, if I allow it. I don't search for imperfections; they wave at me from across a crowded room, making their presence known.

'And to think it was only a matter of a few months ago that I attended your masterclass workshop – my sister is still using the toasting fork I made.' I was on annual leave at the time, but I don't mention my sickness leave which immediately followed it, nor my resignation from the cruise liners shortly afterwards. Not that I'm embarrassed; switching careers will help me to find a work–life balance, allowing me to spend more time with my family, whilst living in staff quarters will give me a level of independence.

'Is she?' Nessie gives a hearty laugh. 'You'll have to come across on a day off and make her a poker to go alongside it.'

I join in with her laughter, which slowly fades as I remember the accident which occurred.

'Did the lady's burnt hand heal?'

'Who, Mavis? Yeah, it took a while, given the depth of the burns, but she's fine now. She regularly drops by, asking when I'm organising another course. Between you and me, I keep putting her off for fear of it happening again.' Nessie gives a shudder at the memory.

'That's good to hear, but yeah, I'm with you. I'd be scared to death – though I loved trying my hand at a new craft.'

'You're welcome to drop by any time for a cuppa and a chat, Autumn.'

'Thank you. I'd best get back before I'm missed – the kitchens are still serving the last of the breakfasts.' I give her a fleeting wave and make for the door, before adding, 'Who'd have thought I'd be back as an employee rather than an eager craft person?'

Nessie swiftly returns to her work, bent double, goggles in place, creating another fabulous piece while I traipse back towards the main entrance via the stone archway.

In the coming weeks, if I'm not consumed by long hours at the hotel, I might try a new hobby in an attempt to broaden my horizons – enjoy a new experience, meet like-minded people.

Which goes some way to explaining why I work in the hospitality industry; I simply wish to delight guests by providing the highest standard of care and attention while they are with us. It might seem lowly to some, namely my family and friends, who insist that I am at the beck and call of strangers. Worse still, I often find myself working for little more than the minimum wage, but money has never been my thing. Whereas true satisfaction is. I'll happily create a delicious basket of fruit for room service, organise a special table for two, or tend to the cut flowers for a requested buttonhole. Seeing the delight in someone's face when their loved one is surprised by the tiniest of details during a stay means the world to me. That one moment lives on in their memories, long after they've left our establishment. Autumn Halcrow, General Manager, is always at your service. A first-in-and-last-clocking-out kind of gal who is willing and very able to roll her sleeves up and attend to any job. Whether it's unblocking a sink unit, serving afternoon tea, or checking in an entire coach party with missing luggage – I'm your person.

The Campbells have entrusted me with their general manager/receptionist role – which I see as being a pivotal role in their new hotel. And that, my family frequently tells me, is my downfall. The whopping big clanger in my personality; I wish to please others before I please myself. I've heard the same comments, time and time again, from every generation of my clan. This time, it'll be different. I'm not going to allow this job to take over my life. I promise to make time for myself and have a personal life away from work. I will delegate tasks to the appropriate staff members, ensuring our standards are higher than expected and delivered more swiftly than our guests could ever have imagined. This time, I'll manage my own time as expertly as I manage the front of house duties. I can't allow my striving for perfection to be my Achilles heel. I know full well that, over time, it'll slowly undermine my happiness and achievements – just as it did, that very first time way back in sixth form, when I crashed and burnt under my self-imposed pressure. Broadening my friendship group, staying close to my family ties and taking time for myself will enable me to have a life outside my work.

This is a new start.

Pippa

'Jump up and I'll show you what's what,' says Levi, climbing into the passenger seat. He's trying to be helpful but unwittingly playing into Ned and Jemima's hands by doing so.

I reluctantly settle into the driver's seat – not a place I wish to be, but he's not to know that. I'm surprised that Jemima hasn't worked her magic by now and relayed our conversation to both Ned and Aileen. I'll go with the flow for now, then act surprised when I'm pulled aside by Ned.

'So, you've got the norms on the fascia but the MacDonald guys have removed and covered many of the obsolete switches and buttons when stripping it out for the conversion. These blank panels are nothing to be concerned about, OK?' says Levi, eagerly pointing to the moulded dashboard.

I nod, purely for effect, but I'm not really interested; he'll be performing this demo again, tomorrow morning, with Aileen.

He rapidly continues, 'Though, between you and me – and Ned's not to know this – the guys did say they'd forgotten to disconnect this switch here.' Levi's finger hovers over a metal flick switch. 'The next time the vehicle returns to their workshop for maintenance and servicing, they'll remove it then. So best keep schtum for now.'

'What's it for?' I ask, intrigued that the MacDonald trio have slipped up on a task; very unusual for them. Be it heavy lifting, a day's hard graft, or the installation of a sculpture or two, the locals always call on the brothers to fulfil the brief and deliver the goods – but obviously not, this time.

I stare at the tiny switch.

Levi eyes me cautiously.

'Come on, man, spill the beans,' I urge, sensing its importance.

He wavers before answering. 'You know the front grille . . .'

I nod, but I don't. I didn't bother looking at every feature on this ridiculous vehicle.

'They forgot to remove the emergency light which sits behind it. They each thought the other had disconnected the wiring, so it got ticked off on their 'To-do' list, and they only realised later . . . but no worries, it's a simple task. They didn't want to keep Ned waiting for her, and delay the big reveal he'd been planning for you.'

I'm shocked that people expected me to become giddy with excitement on viewing this vehicle. They couldn't have been more wrong.

'It's a her?' I mutter, unsure if I'm feigning interest enough.

'Yeah, don't you think?'

I screw up my face in answer.

'You're the odd one out then – even the MacDonald guys call her "her" . And they've put hours into bringing her up to scratch, to meet Ned's requirements.'

I fall silent. I've no come-back on this subject. It's a converted ambulance which fails to live up to my expectations.

A wave of guilt floods my veins. I hate to disappoint folk, but I want to be happy doing what I do for eight hours a day. I need to be my own person and not the Pippa who simply puts up and shuts up, goes with the flow and accepts the cast-offs of life. Trouble is, I've done it for so long, I appear blasé about most things but, deep down, it matters . . . it truly matters to me that others start seeing my worth. Most families unwittingly label their members: the clever one, the musical one, the sporty one, the quiet one, the talented one – or in my case, the proverbial black sheep of the family. There was never anything I did that my cousins hadn't done first, be it schooling, driving tests, passing exams or choosing careers. I've always been trailing in their wake, dragging up the rear. I've made plenty of silly mistakes, trying to fight the labels and trying to cover up how I feel, not wanting to step out of line compared to my two cousins. But no longer. I'm me, and others shouldn't assume they know me based purely on reputation or family stories. People need to start asking why I do the things I do.

'Anyway, strap yourself in and we'll take her for a spin.' Levi twists about, grappling with his seat belt, dragging it around his frame and securing it.

'No, thanks, I'm fine. Honest,' I protest, reaching for the door handle to escape. It's one thing to waste five minutes of his time running through a dashboard console, but I can't feign interest any longer.

'Seriously. She runs like a dream machine. It's best you have a go now, rather than wait for Ned to show you the ropes. As well-mannered and pleasant as the guy is, he'll expect you to handle her like a pro on the first outing. Whereas me, taxiing around day and night, I'm aware how nerve-racking a test drive can be. Come on, you can stall her as many times as you like; I won't criticise your errors.'

'I wouldn't wish to take up your time,' I say.

Levi looks at me with the expectant expression of a puppy eager to please.

'I'm sure you've better things to be doing on your day off,' I continue, before quickly adding, 'I'll be better without a co-pilot witnessing my reversing, thanks.'

None of my excuses wash with Levi; he remains steadfastly determined to force me on to the road. Unless I want to utterly embarrass myself by explaining my misdemeanour and change of heart, I have no choice but to turn the ignition over.

I sigh heavily, stalling for time.

The green-painted door of the manor's side entrance opens and Jemima appears, crossing the cobbled courtyard heading for The Orangery. Maybe she's going over to chat with Aileen about the sudden change of plans. She glances in my direction and our eyes meet. In a heartbeat, without word or gesture, I can see her disappointment in me. Ned wanted me out on the road today, offering tasty samples to eager customers. She'd better not think I'm scared of driving this contraption. I'm not. I've simply changed my mind.

Jemima continues to stare as she reaches the door to The Orangery, heaving it open.

She thinks I'm chicken. Cousin or no cousin, boss or no boss, I'll show her, though I'm still rejecting the role. My hand drops from the steering wheel and I turn the ignition key in a defiant manner. When I say I've changed my mind, it is purely that and nothing more. I'll show her and Ned; I'm not yellow-bellied. I'll test drive this pile of junk, if I choose to. And it doesn't mean I'll be driving it tomorrow.

The ignition fires. A robust rumble fills the air as the engine roars into life and The Orangery door shuts behind Jemima's slender figure. She'll have heard it, even if she has other more important things to discuss. When she exits the café, this vehicle won't be here. That'll be enough to convince her that I've thought this through, I mean what I say.

'Atta girl! That's the attitude!' says Levi, who I've forgotten is seated beside me. 'Where's it to be?'

'Along the driveway and back,' I quickly say, reaching over my shoulder and feeling for my seat belt.

Levi pulls a quizzical face.

'I, err . . . I won't be needing any longer. I just need to prove I can move this baby.'

'Fair do, though you'll probably need to practise parking and such like if you're going to hit the open road alone. A quick look under the bonnet to locate the screenwash bottle, oil dipstick – and maybe a practice run for changing a tyre?' suggests Levi.

I shake my head, before adjusting the interior mirror.

There's not a hope in hell Levi's instructions will ever be needed, as this is the one and only time my backside will be leaving an imprint on this driver's seat.

From tomorrow, she's Aileen's concern.

Chapter Four

Natalia

It didn't take long to unpack my suitcases last night. It'll be time wasted if I need to swiftly repack this morning, though I'll hardly complain at the prospect of moving into Ned's private quarters. Last night, I had every intention of showering, changing and reapplying my make-up before heading to the third floor for a late-night surprise visit, but the weariness of travelling took over and I must have fallen asleep.

Now, with the morning sunshine illuminating the curtains, I lie back and take delight in the joys ahead. I'm glad I fell asleep; today's meeting will be exhilarating now I'm refreshed and perky, more like the woman he knows. Rushing such a meeting could end in disaster; I need him to recall memories of our nights spent together, the laughter we've shared and, most importantly, see if I can arouse a realisation that he doesn't wish to see me leave his side.

Staying in this suite isn't too shabby, but the thought of gracing the manor house as Ned's private guest will be quite something. I'd never abuse his goodwill but surely the staff will wish to please his special guest. Ned doesn't flaunt his status, but he has always spoilt me with the luxuries of life, which he knows I adore. Chilled champagne on the terrace, the little gifts of jewellery left on my pillow – and even, on one occasion, when he employed a local chef to indulge us with a glorious meal in the sumptuous dining room. Not something Dottie approved of; she was overly frosty and obsessed, as ever, with his every move.

It's one thing to have a legal guardian when you're growing up, but surely Ned has outgrown her self-imposed role. No adult man needs someone like Dottie. She's not going to be happy when she spies me. Oh well, I'm not going to let that worry me. I know how I feel about Ned; always have, always will.

I have no intention of holding back, this time. We can venture out on those coastline hikes and wildlife expeditions he always talks about. It'll be idyllic, with his two dogs pounding at our heels, a picnic basket, and plenty of time to reconnect with each other. I might even attempt to get him on horseback – now that *will* be fun.

During this stay, if Ned invites me to accompany him on his work around the estate and visit the tenant farmers, I'll jump at the chance; he was always eager to introduce me, but I avoided estate business. I should have found my own niche in which to flourish and broaden my interests alongside his daily routine. Much like he's doing now, though it must be killing him to shoulder the responsibility of the new hotel venture single-handed. I'll show willing and make a conscious effort to embrace his lifestyle, take an interest in those around him – even Dottie, if I must.

I leap from beneath the covers and raid the printed literature lying on the dressing table, searching for the room service menu as I'm famished, before darting back to the bed. I'll enjoy a leisurely breakfast, then shower and dress, biding my time before I climb to the third floor and visit Ned. I can imagine his expression when he sees me standing in the doorway. I won't make a fuss, I'll allow him to take in my presence and get over the shock before I speak, otherwise he'll be deaf to my explanations. A bubble of excitement lifts within me at the very thought.

It feels like only yesterday that I was last here. I'd chosen to wear that slinky little two-piece number in pastel silk – it cost me a small fortune. Ned couldn't keep his gaze from drifting downwards from my eyes . . . to my chin . . . to my décolletage. I wasn't brazen enough to make a move, though his invite to partake in a brandy should have been my cue. I won't be making the same mistake today.

Typical Ned, everyone else was enjoying the annual allotment festival and he was holed up in his office, consumed by paperwork.

That was before *she* knocked on the door and entered without being invited: such a frumpy little girl, muttering something about pumpkins.

I remember smiling politely as she bumbled her way through an introduction; hadn't I even extended my hand to formally introduce myself? I can't quite recall, but I do remember her 'rabbit caught in the headlights' expression, which blindsided me for a moment. And Ned, the manner in which Ned spoke to her, his gentle tone encouraging her to continue with her stuttering compliment when I'd have dismissed her instantly. He could have explained that he was otherwise engaged at present, it really wasn't a convenient moment, allowing us to return to the private chat we'd been enjoying before her unwelcome interruption. But that's Ned; it's in his breeding.

Weren't we talking about our Christmas plans? I'm sure we were, though we never returned to the subject once she'd scurried from his office.

'Hardly your type,' I'd muttered, in a nonchalant tone, my attempt to dispel the green-eyed monster failing miserably. Ned hadn't answered at first, merely inclined his head, but that twitch of the eyebrows had said more than it was supposed to.

'She's actually a lovely woman. She's very creative, has an acumen for business and works like a Trojan.'

'On second thoughts . . . definitely your type,' I scoffed. I'll never forget his expression as he whipped about to face me; his expression said it all. An instant reaction, like a knight in shining armour; every inch of his being was on guard to defend her.

I'd ruined my chances with those remarks, but I've learnt my lesson.

The sharp rap on the door to the suite sounds within thirty minutes – a little longer than I was expecting, but I suppose everyone is new to their roles. I answer the door with a bright smile, having freshened up, and welcome the young woman carrying the large wooden tray laden with a silver cloche and a coffee pot.

'Good morning, madam, your breakfast,' she says, as I step aside and hold the door wide. She busies herself depositing the breakfast tray on the small dining table and laying out my cutlery and napkin. There's hardly a passing heartbeat before she offers me the padded wallet to sign on the dotted line. 'Will there be anything else?'

'No. Thank you.' I scrawl my initials, before adding, 'Can I ask, is Ned Campbell usually about in the mornings?'

'Yes, though Mrs Campbell is usually the first point of call at this time of day.'

Strike me down! That can't possibly be right! I must have misheard her.

'Sorry?' I murmur, slowly returning her pen and wallet.

'Mr Campbell is present, but it's Mrs Campbell who oversees the manor's guests,' replies the young woman, her ponytailed hair gently swinging as she speaks. 'If you need a word about your suite, simply call reception and Autumn will make the necessary arrangements.'

My heart plummets to my stomach. It's on the tip of my tongue to quiz her further, but that wouldn't be correct or polite.

'That won't be necessary,' I say, turning away to stare at a table laden with food, for which I've suddenly lost my appetite.

Pippa

'Take her up a gear, Pippa. That squealing noise is the engine calling on you to take action,' encourages Levi, a look of concern etched across his kind features.

I grab the gear lever and take her up a notch. My movement is clunky, forcing the lever into place and causing the vehicle to judder, but I manage the gear change eventually. Levi visibly relaxes as I complete the action.

'The engine purrs when she's happy, listen.' He cocks his head, as if the vehicle were alive and breathing. I humour him by smiling. Seriously, what planet does he think I've fallen from? No woman I know can get excited by the sound of an engine – not unless she's trying to appease a guy.

The open road is before us. I had every intention of halting at the entrance gate to Lerwick Manor, having navigated the driveway without disaster, but after my ungainly attempt at reversing in the courtyard, witnessed by half a dozen artists, I thought I'd better disappear off site. It'll prove to Ned and Jemima that I have given it a shot but am still sticking to my guns by refusing this new role.

'Have you a name for her?' asks Levi, settling back into his seat.

It's now my turn to pull a quizzical face.

'Come on, she needs a name.'

'You're telling me your taxi has a name?'

'Yep. She's Gloria. I talk to her all the time when we're out working alone.'

'Are you feeling alright?' I ask, unsure if Levi is usually this chatty or open. He's always pleasant and polite when he comes into The Orangery for coffee with Mungo, but I hardly know him, other than as the local taxi driver. I trust him because Jemima thinks so highly of him; he's like the brother she never had. I believe they only met through Granddad's allotment plot, less than a year ago.

'My Gloria is honoured to deliver folk home after a good night out.'

'It's a bread van, Levi. Hardly the be-all and end-all of someone's day.'

'You never know. If you can't cook or eat, and this baby turns up at the end of your street, it can make all the difference between a rumbling belly or a satisfying ploughman's.'

'Huh! I think not.'

'What's it to be?'

'I'm not naming a sodding ex-ambulance,' I retort.

'OK, then I will. How do you like Rowena?'

I grimace.

'Edwina?'

My foot presses hard on the accelerator at the irksome thought.

'No. What then?'

'Rolly, and I believe it's a he!' Who knows where that came from?

'Rolly? Sorry, but you're going to have to explain that one.'

'Beige paintwork, bulbous curves, and delivers fresh bread rolls, so Rolly,' I quip, quickly adding, 'unless you can think of another bread-related name which is male.' Not that I'm keeping this wagon for any longer than is necessary after this brief road trip, but Levi doesn't need to know.

A lengthy silence fills the cab.

'Take the next right,' instructs Levi, admiring the passing scenery as we meander along the lane.

'I'm not on a sodding driving test, you know?'

'I know. But you need to feel confident about hills, tight turns – and maybe an emergency stop?'

'Hardly! If you bang the dashboard, I swear to God I'll bundle you out and make you walk back to the manor.'

'Fair enough. If I were you—'

'But you're not me, Levi. *I'm* me, and I'm happy doing what I'm doing.'

Levi shrugs.

What is it with the folk at the gallery – actually, more specifically, the folk from the allotments? They always feel the need to tell you what you should be doing, when you didn't invite their opinion in the first place. Not that I ever ask for anyone's opinion. But still, they give it so freely.

'Is there a radio?' I ask, attempting to fill our awkward silence.

'No. But no doubt you'll sing to yourself between stops.'

'I won't.'

'What . . . never?'

'Never!'

'Phuh!'

'What?'

'Sorry, but I fail to believe you don't sing to yourself whilst driving.'

'Do you?'

'Yeah, all the time. I've performed many imaginary concerts at the Hydro, the Royal Concert Hall, even the Edinburgh Corn Exchange, if the mood takes me whilst I'm on the road.'

I'm not sure whether to believe him; not that I know him too well. But when you've grown up in Lerwick, the taxi drivers are familiar faces, renowned in the local community, even if it's only on nodding terms.

'Get away with you, everyone does it!'

'I can assure you they don't.'

'Why not?' he asks.

'I can't sing.'

'Everyone can sing.'

I shake my head. This argument is futile; I'm not about to prove another point this morning.

'They might not be able to sing tunefully, but what does it matter? I bet you can sing just as well as the next person.'

'OK, let's define it as "not to a pleasant level".'

'Ah, well that's different. Though on your own, who cares?'

'Me. I care.'

Levi offers me a fleeting glance. 'Well, you shouldn't. If no one can hear, you should just let rip and enjoy your own company instead of being . . .' He stops talking, falters and abruptly stares out of the side window.

'Being what?'

'Nothing.'

'Levi?'

He turns to stare at my profile as I refocus on the road ahead.

'No offence meant, but you're hardly easy-going, are you? You can be a bit uptight at times, and not singing to yourself purely confirms it. Now me . . . well, I find myself utterly ridiculous several times a day, yet I can sing to my heart's content between taxiing customers, and still laugh at my antics for the best part of the day. I'm chilled, but you're . . .'

'What?'

'Intense.'

'Intense?' I mouth.

'Yeah. There, I've said it. Either throw a hissy fit or forget it, one or the other, but don't go holding it against me for ever and a day!'

'What are you on about, man?' He's pushing my buttons now.

'You and your grudges.'

'Grudges?' Is this another label I'm supposed to accept? No need to take the time and effort to get to know me, simply read the label and be done!

'You're renowned for holding a grudge against Jemima for getting her grandpop's legacy and his allotment plot. Didn't your other cousin receive an engagement ring or something? Not that you wanted it, and yet ...'

'Hang on a minute, you seem to know an awful lot about this subject.'

Levi eyes me warily. 'Mmmm, just an observation ... but you're pretty vocal, and you never hesitate to give your opinions, OK. I've overheard you once or twice, whilst visiting The Orangery.'

I'm open-mouthed. Cheeky git! I fall silent. There's much, much more to that story, yet no one ever asks, which makes it painful to hear Levi's summing up. That's the story of my life, right there!

'Do you disagree?' he says.

'Yes!' I say instantly, realising how ironic my answer seems.

Levi's mouth twitches on hearing my immediate response.

I scowl.

'And now you're sulking?'

'No, I'm not!' I snap, weaving between two parked vehicles and just missing each by a hair's breadth.

'Whoa! I'm surprised you squeezed through without scratching fresh go-fast stripes upon their paintwork,' says Levi, simultaneously grabbing the edge of his seat and the door frame. 'Take it steady, Pippa.'

'Relax. I could have driven a tank through there with room to rattle it.'

A fog of silence descends, proving how vital a radio is in every vehicle.

'Make yourself useful then. Sing,' I say half-heartedly, to lighten the atmosphere.

Levi immediately begins to sing 'Suspicious Minds', filling the cab with the richest, deepest voice I have ever heard.

I gasp at his unexpected talent, turning to look at him, nearly crashing the ambulance into the nearest garden wall.

If I wasn't driving, and if I closed my eyes, I'd be convinced that Elvis was fit, healthy and alive, sitting beside me.

I don't know what I expected, but not this. It's like a real-life Susan Boyle moment, though without the panel of stunned judges and a thousand-strong audience providing a standing ovation.

'Where did that voice come from?' I utter in astonishment, swiftly navigating various obstacles to regain full control of the vehicle despite the Bread Basket becoming a one-man mobile musical box.

He delivers a sidelong glance, before finishing a chorus to say, 'I'm prepared to reveal the private side of my character whilst others rarely are.' Without waiting for my answer he returns to his lyrics, barely missing a beat.

It takes thirty minutes of driving for Levi to deliver his full repertoire, whilst I ponder his remark. In the meantime, regardless of my intentions, I prove myself more than capable of handling the refurbished ambulance before returning to Lerwick Manor. I only hope Jemima duly notices as I carefully park the vehicle in the courtyard's central spot.

On bidding farewell to the mobile Bread Basket, I have a definite spring in my step, thanks to Levi's good company and musical talents, though I'll answer his remark about the private side of my character another time.

I've done what was asked of me; my test drive is over, and now I can resume my regular duties of waitressing. I assume that Jemima has spoken to Aileen in my absence, so I'm expecting to be summoned for a conversation at any moment.

'Hi, Aileen,' I say chirpily, finding her clearing the nearest table of its dirty crockery.

'Hi, Pippa. Good drive?'

'Actually, yes. He corners well, responds to a firm hand on the

steering wheel, and is surprisingly comfy,' I explain, attempting
to sell the new job to her subtly.

'Wow! You must be delighted,' says Aileen, grabbing a damp
cloth from beneath the countertop and returning to wipe over
the cleared table.

'Me? Why would I be delighted?' I say.

'Well, you couldn't wish for better, could you?'

I tilt my head and squint; not the response I wanted to hear.
Where is her jubilation at having been offered a new role? Or
her delight that this will be her final shift waitressing?

'Are you alright?' asks Aileen, disposing of the damp cloth.

I don't know what to say. I can't let the cat out of the bag
before Jemima speaks to her, but on the other hand . . . maybe I
should. I turn to look out at the cobbled yard beyond the plate
glass, and spot Levi standing in front of the manor looking up
at the building. I edge nearer to gain a full view. Levi is staring
up to a third-floor window where Jemima's head and shoulders
are visible, leaning from Ned's office window. Is Levi giving a
thumbs-up gesture? Why is Jemima grinning broadly and gesturing too?

Interesting.

'Aileen, has Jemima spoken to you today about anything
important?'

'Nope. But I'll tell you who has been in – you've just missed
her . . . your cousin, Callie.'

Chapter Five

Autumn

I'm bone tired as I climb the rear staircase to the fourth floor. I can't believe it's been exactly a week since Jemima galloped up this wooden flight dragging one of my suitcases, as I followed a few steps behind hauling another. The days and nights have merged into a blur of activity and a never-ending task list, now the hotel is open for business. After a lengthy shift, all I want is a shower and a warm bed. I'm grateful that the servants' corridor is home to just two of us: Pippa and me. She's been sociable in passing, but not overly familiar, which I like. I can't be doing with people who are nosy in the name of friendship. I might appear to be anti-social but I'm not a 'girly' girl who relies on others to keep me on track and balanced. On a practical note, there's only room for five occupants on this floor, as each refurbished bedroom enjoys an en-suite. It means I have a huge bathroom; when I recall some of the staff quarters I've occupied over the years whilst at sea, this is sheer bliss. My previous experience has been of tiny cabins, broken furnishings, and noisy colleagues who thought nothing of partying all night and feigning sickness the next day.

I'm satisfied with my day's work; in addition to my basic duties, I've tackled everything that's come my way, from ordering fresh flowers for the library, to arranging advertising for the bellboy vacancy, and addressing an issue with the supplier of vegetables for the hotel's kitchens. I can't wait to fall into my warm bed; my aching feet burn with each step I take. I'm feeling every one of my forty years tonight! I check my phone screen as I return to my room: there are four missed calls from my older sister, Sienna. Damn it, I did promise her I'd call her today. It's too late now, I'll call her first thing tomorrow for a chat.

The staff corridor is pristine, thanks to freshly painted walls and sanded floorboards. The atmosphere is cosy and homely, not claustrophobic or oppressive as you'd expect high up in the eaves of the manor. If I'm off duty at the right time I get to enjoy the most amazing sunsets from my bedroom window, not to mention the surrounding views of rural Shetland.

I unlock the door of Room 2, walk in and immediately kick off my shoes after a long and tiring shift. I dart around the room, flicking on various lamps which give a mellow warmth to the colour scheme – instantly, the place feels like home. I might be living above my work, but once I've showered, changed and snuggled up for the night, the hotel could be a million miles away. That feeling alone tells me I've made the right choice in coming here, as long as I can maintain a sense of distance after finishing my shifts. There were many times on the cruises when I felt overwhelmed, simply trapped, by the demands of being in the same environment for every minute of every day. Stupidly, I worked around the clock, trying to please everyone.

Working here, I'm a stone's throw from my sister, Sienna, and her husband, Amos – which will be precious family time, especially as we no longer have our parents, just each other. I'm looking forward to plenty of visits, and being able to enjoy vital support and a true sense of 'home', in the community in which I was raised.

I empty my pockets of the debris I always pick up during the day as I move around, inspecting here and there, as I go. I drop the knot of loose threads, rolled-up balls of silver paper, paper-clips, an orange Tic Tac and torn price tags into my waste bin. A ridiculous habit, but one which has become second nature; there's never a shift when I haven't a pocket full of litter and debris.

Rat-a-tat-tat.

I exhale sharply. I hope this isn't an emergency call to return to reception and attend to a guest's urgent query; it would be ironic, given my previous moment of self-awareness.

Smile in place, I answer my door to find Pippa, looking sheepish. She's clearly had the evening off work as her blonde hair is freshly washed and she's sporting her usual civvies of jeans and a skinny top.

'Hi, I was wondering if you fancied company?'

Urgh!

'To be honest, I'm whacked. It's been a long day. I'm dying for an early night and . . .' The words are barely out of my mouth before her smile fades and she's apologising for interrupting me. I feel awful for being so dismissive, but I have to be honest. 'Maybe another night. We could go into town or have a quiet drink here?'

'Sure. Sounds good. Night.' Pippa turns and, in a single stride, disappears behind the hastily closed door of Room 1. I hear her door lock click. I feel wretched; her first attempt to be sociable, and I refused. I hesitate. Now what should I do? Knock on her door and agree to a quick drink, or look after myself? If I knock on her door, I can wave goodbye to my quiet night; I know from experience a quick drink will turn into an entire evening of drinking, leading to a late night. I've got an early shift tomorrow morning – I can do without a hangover or lack of sleep.

I quietly close my door, vowing to pay Pippa a little extra attention tomorrow – and I'll definitely agree to her next invite.

I lie in bed, staring at the eaves of the room, and wonder who the previous occupant might have been, all those decades ago. Probably a local girl, delighted to have joined the household as a kitchen or scullery maid, in the days when the manor house was buzzing with serving staff waiting upon dignitaries. I glance towards the opposite wall and imagine a second bed tucked behind the door, making the room incredibly cramped. It's ideal for me; I've few possessions and little need for clutter. If only these walls could talk. I bet the staff had some laughs after a hard day's work. And I bet Dottie will remember those times, if I ask her.

Sleep draws near as I listen to the sounds of the manor house – the erratic creaking, the rattling windows and the occasional thump or bump on the floor below. Like a giant doll's house, it's hard to imagine there are people in each suite; it's a decent occupancy rate for this first week of opening. I begin running through the guest list, each face magically appearing before me. The first floor has Mr Drummond, who is here for a month-long stay. He's a corporate guest, with his hessian holdalls, and has spent the day exploring the coastal wildlife. Then there's Miss Muir, also on the first floor . . . I haven't actually seen her today, as she's stayed in her suite and called room service for each meal, which is never a good sign. Not what I expected at check-in. I seriously thought she was a celebrity after one look at her dark shades and peaked cap. A soft chuckle escapes me as I recall how I Googled her name, expecting a high-profile result, but found nothing.

Mmmm, tomorrow I'll make a point of speaking to Pippa. And I'll look out for Miss Muir.

Natalia

I can't sleep. Having spent all day hiding in my suite, I've wound myself into a coiled spring. My mind is firing on all cylinders. The young woman's words keep replaying inside my head. 'Mrs Campbell oversees the manor's guests.' She said it so casually, without a care or a second thought, and yet the words slipped from her lips obliterating my world. And now, here I am lying in the darkness, inside a manor which I used to grace as Ned's unofficial girlfriend, though everyone knew it was simply a matter of time before he proposed to me. Me, the successful model, who couldn't settle down any earlier because of my commitments to the major brands who were key clients of the agency.

What was I supposed to do? Throw in the towel on my career, before having a chance to shine, purely to move here – virtually at the top of the world – and spend a lifetime nesting and producing a brood of children to populate the next generation? How was that fair? Now I arrive to find Ned Campbell's gone and got married!

I don't believe it for one minute, seriously I don't! The man works twenty-four hours a day, keeps constant company with his two grumpy hounds, and converses the most with old Dottie. I pull the duvet up to my chin for comfort. Who the hell he'd impetuously choose as a wife is beyond me – unless I was spot on about the pumpkin girl from the neighbouring allotments! It was very wrong of me to judge her. Ned was understandably miffed when I allowed my disdain to show.

I fling back the duvet, stretching my long bare legs over the edge of the mattress before I retrieve my robe from the nearest chair. I might have spent the entire day attempting to read, washing and re-drying my hair or applying make-up, but my mind still hasn't freed me from the object of my desire: Ned.

I need answers. I need to know who and why?

I swiftly knot the belt around my waist, grab my mobile from the nightstand and collect my door key. It might be half eleven, but I know Ned better than anyone. I bet he's upstairs, sitting at his desk with a cold mug of coffee at his elbow, scrutinising estate accounts and planning for the coming day. Why not go and brighten his workload with a little hello from me? Who knows, I might be able to clear up this misunderstanding.

I scan the corridor and check the coast is clear before leaving my room. I lean over the polished banister, not to admire Dottie's handiwork in the mellow gleam, but to crane my neck as far as possible: the hallway appears empty. I half expected to see a solitary security guard on a hard-backed chair. I wasn't listening properly when the receptionist reeled off details during check-in. But I can't afford to cause a commotion at this time of night. Worst-case scenario would be CCTV on the stairway capturing my every move.

I quickly walk the length of the landing, each footstep sinking into the plush pile of the carpet, cautiously flatten myself against the wall, then slide my body around the curved banister and run up to the second floor. I have no idea but I assume that behind each wooden door now sits a refurbished and occupied bedroom suite. I repeat my actions to gain access to the third floor. Ned's floor.

His private quarters span the length of this corridor. I want to giggle at the number of times we scrambled half-naked from his private lounge and headed along this landing, past his office and that old ceramic jardinière, and dived into his bedroom for hours of enjoyment. I always feared the watchful gaze of Dottie. Boy, those were the days!

I was always nervous when he invited me to stay, anticipating the big question. A single girl can't play it too cool when it comes to matters of the heart. I never intended to chase him, begging for his attention, or push too hard during my previous stays. Maybe if I had, we'd have made our relationship official and this would now be my permanent home. Foolish woman. I didn't know which side my bread was buttered, did I? I certainly know now, after being apart for a further five months.

Glancing ahead along the landing, I'm immediately thrown; there's no light showing from beneath his office door. He must have moved offices. I tiptoe past the silent rooms, my gaze glued intently to each door, willing Ned to throw it open and appear. He doesn't.

I pause for a second before returning to his office and turning the doorknob. I purposely don't knock; I don't wish to announce my arrival and ruin the surprise. I take several deep breaths, smooth down my silk robe and ensure that I'm appropriately covered for the big moment. With a quick roll of my shoulders and a shake of my hair, I intend to be tension free before entering, but I'm not. I'm as nervous as a kitten.

On autopilot, I stride in ... to be greeted by darkness. Not the view I expected; I've never walked into this room without finding Ned hunched over his paper-stacked desk, pen in hand and a neglected cup of coffee cooling at his elbow. The office is empty. You could knock me down with a feather.

I close the door behind me, carefully navigating the room with outstretched arms to switch on his large desk lamp. The halo of light picks out the usual scene: a medley of papers, files and account books alongside his abandoned coffee mug. His desk chair is pushed out at the angle from which he left. What I wouldn't give for him to be sitting there now! I'd contentedly settle beside his desk, as I used to do, and bring him up to date with the latest developments in my career.

If I'd played my cards right last autumn, we could have been one step nearer to our happy ever after by now. But no, I chased him, yelled, ranted about the locals and stormed off. Did I expect him to follow and talk me round? Yeah, of course. Though when he didn't, I should have retraced my steps, rather than driving the short distance to my B&B and letting the bad mood fester.

Nothing looks out of place in Ned's office, except his empty chair.

I open and close each of his desk drawers, peering at the contents. I have no idea what I'm searching for, but a wrapped package – preferably a ring box, with my name clearly labelled – would be the highlight of my year.

There's nothing of interest here.

I glance around the room: the meeting table, the sofa and armchair combination positioned before the grand mantelpiece, and . . . my gaze zaps back to the offending object, balanced upon the mantel – the photo frame. Even from this distance I recognise the colouring, height and stance of the man in the smiling couple. I can't miss the white dress and bouquet either.

I snatch the decorative photo frame from its position and take a closer look. It's him. My Ned. Smiling, happy, married . . . alongside her, the allotment woman. Palpitations squeeze my heart; my hands start to shake and tiny beads of panic stand out on my pale skin. Mr and Mrs Campbell! The room service woman wasn't lying!

Instantly, I feel sick. A rising tide of panic takes over my body as I begin to tremble from head to foot; my hands are still visibly shaking as I clutch the wedding photo. I quickly attempt to thrust the frame back in its rightful position on the decorative mantelpiece, turn and dash from the office with my hand clasped across my mouth.

Chapter Six

Thursday 3 February

Autumn

'Autumn, has Dottie arrived?' asks Jemima, descending the staircase as I replace the telephone's handset.

'Not that I know of.'

'Can you tell her that Ned would like a word as soon she does?' she asks, turning towards the rear kitchens.

'Sure. Anything I can help with?' I offer, seeing her furrowed brow.

Jemima stops dead and turns, her features relaxing for a moment. 'Actually, yes. Any chance you could take a dustpan and brush up to the office? There's been a mishap and there's broken glass by the mantelpiece. I'm trying to do three jobs at once and getting nowhere fast.'

'Sure.' I'm eager to stretch my legs after being seated for too long. I've been attempting to secure Mr Drummond, the hessian holdall owner, a local music lesson; a simple request via room service which is proving to be difficult to orchestrate. I cross to Dottie's cleaning cupboard, which she refuses to give up or share with the new housekeeping team, citing her length of service. I know there'll be a dustpan to hand; it's probably the poshest understairs cupboard in the Northern hemisphere, given its manorial surroundings, but she'll not hear of her beeswax and polish cans being moved elsewhere. On opening the door to her domain, I find it immaculate and clean. There's a pristine pan set hanging from a wall nail. I'm impressed – not that I expected anything else from Dottie, she's my sort. Well, maybe not quite, but near enough.

I swiftly ascend the staircase, dustpan and brush in hand, while Jemima continues through towards the kitchens. I'm sure there are numerous jobs that she and Ned are juggling between them, but which could easily be delegated to other staff members. They've employed a small army of locals to wait tables in the dining room, numerous chefs to create gourmet meals, and that's in addition to all the volunteers, such as Levi and Mungo, who lend a helping hand when necessary. Given the pace of work in recent months, I expect they've got into the habit of doing as much as they can themselves; maybe they'll relax a little when life settles into a routine. It can't be easy juggling all their enterprises. At the minute, they both seem to be functioning at top speed, in fifth gear, every time I see them; it's not a healthy way to live.

I reach the first landing, spy a tiny ball of silver paper lying beside the skirting board, and bend to retrieve it. I can't break the habit of a lifetime; I don't understand how others can ignore it. It sounds harsh, but I've seen them on many occasions walk past the same blemish, a piece of litter or a dirty utensil, countless times before it's pointed out to them. Only to have them roll their eyes, sigh heavily and then pointedly clean or dispose of the offending object.

I reach the third landing, slightly breathless but happy that my en-route inspection hasn't thrown up any other anomalies needing my attention. I do love it when things are organised and perfect.

I rap on the office door and wait to be summoned. It's customary for me, given my years in the industry. I don't find it belittling or subservient, simply good manners.

'Come in!' calls Ned, in muffled tones.

'Good morning. Jemima asked if I'd dispose of some broken glass . . . by the mantelpiece, I believe.'

I enter to find Ned seated at his desk, amidst a forest of piled papers and accounting books. It gives me the shivers to look at it; one afternoon of sorting and tidying, I'm sure I could create a better filing system in no time.

'Ah yes, good morning, Autumn.' He gestures towards the fireplace. 'Lord knows how it happened, but I found our wedding frame smashed on the hearth when I opened the office.' He looks quizzically at me.

'I'm sorry for the damage, but I don't enter this room unless called,' I assure him.

'It's not as if the mantel is narrow, and yet . . .' He's still looking puzzled. 'Well, that's that. I suppose Jemima will purchase a new frame.'

I'm halfway across the room as he speaks. The now glassless frame has been repositioned in its usual spot.

'Would you like me to organise a replacement?' I kneel down, swiftly brushing at the splintered glass which lies in a near-perfect oblong despite being fractured.

'I think Jemima has that in hand, but thank you all the same.'

'Quite right, she'll want to choose the frame herself.' I could kick myself for my automatic response. It's their wedding photo, not some generic photo frame accidentally broken by a paying guest. I need to curb my trait of volunteering every time a task presents itself; that's precisely how I become bogged down with unnecessary chores which are of no concern to me. Just look at me now, crouched before a fireplace sweeping up shards of broken glass which I didn't break! My knuckles look particularly dry this morning. I'll dig out my hand cream once I return to my desk; I can do without my skin flaring up and looking unsightly.

I'm thorough with my handwashing routine. Turning the 'Hot' tap on, I'll sigh with relief and delight as a stream of scalding water gushes into the white ceramic basin before swirling towards the open plughole. I won't flinch at the piping-hot temperature; I'm used to it. I don't rush but systemically dab each hand beneath the tap, wetting it sufficiently, then depress the hand soap dispenser: one, two, even three blobs, before sweeping my palms together and creating a rich lather. I'll happily spend time creating a rolling ball action. With each movement, lather patterns form and disappear before I interlace my open fingers, one hand on top of the other, and glide them back and forth. Making a fist, I scrub firmly around each thumb, before circling each wrist in a twisting motion. I don't recite a poem, a prayer or count. I cease only when it feels right; when I believe my hands are perfectly clean. If that's two, five or ten minutes, so be it! In a fluid cupping action, moving side to side, I rinse meticulously beneath the running tap, allowing every bubble and soapsud to disappear. Gone. For good. For ever! Be it germs, grimy dirt, ink stains, fluff or a sticky residue.

Freshly washed, sweet-smelling hands are the final act on completion of a task. They symbolise perfection to me: job done.

I shake my head and return my attention to the present moment. 'Was the breakage discovered this morning?' I ask over my shoulder.

'Jemima noticed it, ten minutes ago. I wondered if Dottie had arrived early for her dusting duties and dislodged it, that's all.'

'She'll be gutted if she thought she'd caused it to tumble,' I say, picking up the final few slivers of glass twinkling on the hearth rug.

'Another reason why I asked you – I wouldn't want her fretting over a breakage.'

Personally, I can't imagine Dottie not speaking up if she'd dropped or nudged the photo frame whilst dusting. Her relationship with the Campbells is second to none. They are like one big happy family – which is sweet, as each of them appears to have an absence of close family members.

'There, all done!' I announce, standing tall. 'If I see Dottie, I'll send her up.'

'Thank you, Autumn. I'd appreciate that,' Ned answers without looking up from his paperwork. I can see he's busy so I make a swift exit, pleased that I've been able to help out.

I angle the dustpan, allowing the broken glass to nestle safely, as I descend the grand staircase. I'd have my work cut out to find the shards in this carpet pile if I scattered them as I went.

'There you are!' cries Dottie, busily tying her pinny around her waist, as I turn to descend the final flight. 'I was wondering where yee were, lassie.'

'Upstairs, helping out.'

'Aye, had a little accident, have you?'

'No. Just helping out.' I reach the bottom step as Dottie closes her cleaning cupboard door, her face expectant and staring at the dustpan and brush in my hands.

'Helping who?'

I raise my eyebrows; there's no getting by this one, is there? She's as cute as they come, despite her age.

'Simply assisting where I can.' I keep walking; if I hesitate in disposing of this broken glass she'll wheedle every detail out of me, and then Ned will think I'm a snitch if he finds out I told Dottie before he could have a quiet word with her. I simply pass on his message. 'Ned wants to see you in his office.'

'Me?' Her delicate brow furrows deeply. 'Nah, get away with you, lassie. Ned Campbell has never called me up these stairs in his entire life. There's not a chance in hell he's asked for a word with me. Not a chance!' Her frail bird-like frame straightens as her shoulders ease back and her chin lifts.

I reach the kitchen corridor while Dottie remains fixed to the spot in front of her closed cupboard, staring at me.

'Seriously, I'm not joking. He asked me to pass on his message—'

'Lassie, you've misunderstood, because there is one thing that doesn't happen around these parts . . . and that's Dorothy Nesbit being summoned to Ned Campbell's office. I won't be having it, not now . . . not ever!' Her tone is calm but steely; her eyes glisten like diamonds.

'Dottie, he's not angry or anything. It's a simple request.'

'Request? Pull the other one, it's got bells on it!'

'Dottie, you've misunderstood me.' This conversation has quickly soured. I'm reluctant to leave the scene and dispose of the broken glass for fear she doesn't head upstairs.

'I've not misunderstood!' she says, shaking her head vigorously.

How do I put this right without breaking Ned's confidence? I watch her fiercely rooted pride engulf her entire being. She must have been a feisty one when she was younger.

'Dottie, don't shoot the messenger . . . Ned simply remarked that he'd like a word, it wasn't an order or command,' I urge, gesturing for her to go up to the third floor.

That takes the wind out of her sails; her shoulders relax, her chin drops slightly.

'I might pop in when . . . *if* I clean that third-floor landing,' she says reluctantly, traipsing up the staircase at the slowest pace I've ever seen her move.

'Right you are . . . at least I've passed his message on.' I give her a beaming smile and head towards the kitchens to dispose of the splintered glass.

Boy, oh boy, that's a lesson in life; Dottie doesn't take orders from anyone, not even Ned Campbell.

Natalia

I didn't sleep a wink last night but lay awake weeping, sobbing and staring into the darkness until the morning light crept through the curtains to reveal my view of the high ceiling.

How could Ned do this to me, after all our years together? The whole 'will we, won't we' scenario developed while I was patiently waiting, never pushing for commitment. I realise that to my friends and family our set-up seemed strange, unconnected and somewhat distant. What mattered was that we had an understanding, we respected our exclusive status, like an agreement or vow based on our unique connection. It might not have been conventional, but it worked for us. We both had demanding careers, personal commitments to loved ones – and never once did I moan about the travelling required to spend time here in Shetland.

Yet to find he's moved on, without a backward glance or a word of warning, after four years . . . it hurts like hell – certainly more than any fling or casual affair. Admittedly, he hasn't been in touch since the autumn, but that's nothing new; we've never lived in each other's pockets whilst apart. I've got my work; Ned has his. I never questioned his motives, I accepted what we shared together. It's like the unwritten life rules of Natalia and Ned: always there for each other, regardless of the months spent apart, then pick up where we left off, and never demand anything of the other in between. Independence, we called it. Those were the unwritten guidelines and we've survived numerous dramas by sticking to those ground rules. I've seen too many couples rush to commit, complying with the social norms simply to please their parents, when what we had was a deeper mutual understanding. A genuine connection, which seems rare, but right.

I always assumed it was his upbringing; the gentry appear to stick with their traditional lifestyle and time-honoured ways. Society people rarely announce the details of their private lives; they work hard and yet, behind the scenes, there's a particular flame, biding her time, proving herself worthy of the prestige into which her intended husband was born. Then suddenly, when the time is right, as if out of nowhere, big announcements are made. It always appears to be a whirlwind romance, but everyone in the know is aware that their relationship has been conducted away from the public eye and has been slowly developing for years. That's the world in which Ned was raised; I wasn't, but he was, so I never questioned him. I learnt to live within the boundaries imposed by his upbringing and status. I placed my faith in Ned, and I believed he did likewise with me. I refused other men's advances, knowing Ned was my one true love. Knowing that, one day, our announcement would surprise others, much as other couples had previously surprised me.

I hate using the term 'soul mate' – it sounds so tacky after being overused by dating apps and TV shows – but the bottom line is, we were. Admittedly, we blew hot and cold, with late-night phone calls full of affection when we were good, and long-distance silences when we hit a tricky patch. Like now, or rather last September. Periodically, I'd fly here for a long weekend during a stopover between international flights or modelling assignments. Ours was never a conventional love story, but still it worked for us ... or rather, it did.

I turn over, burying my head in the fluffy pillow. This is unbelievable. And to think my arrival here was an attempt to surprise him, please him by showing interest in his latest project, and maybe even seal the deal on us! What an utter joke!

Now what do I do? Stay and speak to Ned, confirming the situation, or pack my bags and slink out of here under cover of darkness?

I glance around my suite. It's comfortable and spacious, I can easily stay in my room and survive the next few hours, but what then?

I reach for the bedside telephone, dial zero for reception.

'Good morning, Ms Muir, how can I help you?' comes the perky voice.

Instantly, I recognise it as belonging to Autumn, the attractive woman who checked me in on Tuesday.

'Morning. The Unst Suite here. I'd like to order orange juice, a pot of tea and toast, please. Wholemeal bread.'

She repeats my breakfast order before warning me of a twenty-minute wait.

I stumble into the shower on autopilot. I've been here before, knocked back and emotionally spent, many times in my life. It comes with the territory of a chosen career in such a bloodthirsty dog-eat-dog world, where there's constant pressure to be perfect on the outside, however you are feeling inside. But every knock-back creates a tougher cookie who always bounces back. As a child, I dreamt of becoming the next supermodel striding along the catwalks of London, Paris or Milan. Given my height, slender frame and perfect complexion, securing 'top model' status seemed within easy reach. The reality was different: harsh rejections from the countless agencies I approached. Over time, I lowered my sights and accepted the cosmetics assignments instead. Sure, it was modelling, but despite my carefully observed routines regarding diet, alcohol, exercise and physical grooming, I've never been able to aspire to the fashion modelling I desperately craved.

I haven't chosen an easy lifestyle – a nomadic existence punctuated by early get-ups, late-night hotel check-ins, and endless hours spent waiting while photographers and make-up artists decide 'the look'. I've forfeited a sense of normality, be it missing my family and important occasions whilst travelling, jetting in and out of Edinburgh without time to recover from the last trip, or my unconventional romance with Ned. I'll get through this latest setback slowly but surely, one step at a time, or one task at a time. It's like those photo shoot assignments where I don't like the chosen make-up, the location and, worst still, the photographer assigned to the job. Life is much easier when it goes your way, the brief is a joy, and the assignment a breeze to complete; it hardly feels like work on days such as that. But there are crap days, when every detail is against me, I wish to be anywhere but posing on the edge of a diving board, reclining on a sun-kissed beach or cavorting through a summer meadow. I've landed many prestigious shots with top-name photographers, but I still had to bide my time in the early days, with nothing but hand modelling for nail varnish or hand cream. Now, I'm assigned a range of high-end cosmetics, such as shampoo adverts, lipsticks or skin products.

It's so much easier when you're enjoying the shoot. Otherwise it feels like an arduous slog, when you focus on the actual task purely to get you through to completion. This morning's routine feels like that. I'm showering, cleansing and drying my hair and body in a step-by-step sequence, without thought or feeling, while my mind mulls over last night's revelation. After all these years, you'd think Ned could have dropped me a quick line, spared a few words over the phone – as a heads-up, if nothing more. Or is this how his society works? Which gives rise to the question: how have I not heard the news on the grapevine? Admittedly, Ned and I don't share friendship groups, but even so, I occasionally bump into his circle of old university faithfuls whilst passing through Edinburgh, yet no one has said anything, despite them being present when we first met. But again, I don't truly belong to their world or their inner circle, do I? They probably view me as a bit of fun he entertained in his younger days, when I was naïve and gullible. Or has Ned sworn them to secrecy? Lost touch totally? Or is he too embarrassed to say he's married a local woman? Obviously they didn't have an extravagant society wedding, otherwise he wouldn't have been able to quash the news. Or did they elope and no one in his circle actually knows? Surely, any proud bridegroom wants to show off his new wife. He wouldn't have needed a quiet wedding if it had been us. How dreadful to break with the long traditions within such a fine family.

Instantly, I feel sorry for Ned; that's the level of my devotion.

What has actually happened? Is there a reason behind this furtive wedding? And more importantly, is there any way I can help him?

I swiftly dry, comb out and tie back my hair, knowing my breakfast will be arriving soon. I need to prepare myself; I don't want to overstep the mark by quizzing the room service staff. Worse still, raise their suspicions or have them question my stay. At present, the staff I've met accept me purely as a solo traveller booked in for fourteen nights. It needs to stay that way until I decide otherwise. I don't want to draw attention to myself and have Ned spy my details in the register. On second thoughts, bumping into Dottie might be the worst possible scenario. She'll be sniffing around, demanding answers and running off to Ned quicker than a jack rabbit after a mate. In fact, that should become my primary aim for today – steer clear of Dottie Nesbit and her inquisitive nature.

A sudden rap on my door brings me back from my internal rant: breakfast has arrived.

Chapter Seven

Pippa

'Have you got everything you need?' asks Jemima, escorting me to the driver's door. I wish she'd bugger off, to be honest, but she's lingering like a bad smell, probably nervous that I'll change my mind again, forcing the delivery van to remain in situ for another day. I can assure her there's no fear of that happening; I'll happily embrace my new role after yesterday's news.

'For the umpteenth time, I have everything I need, thank you. I've checked and double-checked. And do you know why?' I stare at my cousin intently, as I settle into the driver's seat and secure my seat belt.

Jemima has the decency to blush despite her underhand tactics of yesterday. Namely persuading Levi to remove me from The Orangery for a test drive, meanwhile enabling Callie, our older cousin, to have an interview and guided tour.

Despite my previous misgivings about the Bread Basket, the alternative doesn't bear thinking about. Simply put, there's not a cat in hell's chance I want to waitress alongside our Callie, so I've chosen the lesser of two evils. Today, me and Rolly begin our travels – and together, we're going to make this mobile venture a booming success, despite our outward appearances and being unfairly labelled in life. We're in this together.

'Call me if you have any difficulties,' adds Jemima, stepping aside.

I close the door with a firm slam, then lower the window to finish the conversation; it would be rude not to.

'I have all I need, thanks.' I indicate the laminated map which Ned has dutifully supplied. I'm grateful that he's done the research on my behalf, but I would have liked to participate in outlining my actual route. But fear not, I'll make alterations where needed.

If Jemima and Callie wish to become as thick as thieves, well ... let them. It won't be me who comes unstuck. It's not as if they've ever been close as cousins but, when needs must, I suppose blood is thicker than water.

'I'll let you know how I get along,' I say, bidding Jemima a swift goodbye, eager to be alone and on my way.

I slowly reverse under her watchful gaze. She gives a weak smile. I sense she's triumphantly thinking *that worked*. Though Jemima needn't have any more bright ideas; if push comes to shove, I'd sooner return to my old job in admin than settle for a role alongside our Callie. Though the thought of returning to a solitary desk job, filing invoices and chasing queries for a builders' merchants, fills me with dread. At least with waitressing, I might remain on a basic wage, but I'll have some social inter-action – and Isla's a decent sort to work alongside.

I'm relieved that we get to hit the open road together, Rolly and me, without prying eyes watching our every move. Techni-cally, from today, I'm my own boss, with full responsibility for generating sales and ensuring our customers' full satisfaction. This venture is truly mine. And I'm determined that, for once in my life, no one – be it parents, uncle or my older cousins – is going to utter those fateful words, 'Pippa strikes again!' or label my efforts as a failure.

I quickly check all my mirrors in case that pesky pet duck of Jemima's is waddling aimlessly about. I doubt she'd laugh if I accidentally squashed the little blighter! Once the coast is clear, I put Rolly into first gear and slowly draw away, embarking on what I hope will be a successful opening day.

As Rolly trundles under the stone archway, I spy Dottie

sweeping the front steps of the manor. I raise my hand in a hearty wave and she returns the gesture. Her beaming smile brightens anyone's day. Not that we haven't had our moments in the past. I cringe with embarrassment, knowing I was particularly snappy and rude towards her at the annual festival, when we had a run-in over a bunch of allotment keys, which now seems unbelievable, given her sweet nature. Since working here, I've managed to sidestep our previous issues, and hopefully she views me in a different light.

I exit the wrought-iron gates and turn on to the main road, put my foot down, sliding through the gears as swiftly as possible, and embrace a sense of freedom.

I've memorised Ned's planned route. But should I wish to drive across country, taking a slight diversion, clocking up the miles and heading towards an additional village or two worthy of my time, then I fully intend to. Ned will never know.

I'm on the A970 in a matter of minutes, seeking the nearest layby in preparation for my big day ahead. I should have addressed this task before leaving the courtyard but I couldn't bear to have an audience questioning my actions. It might seem like unnecessary homework, but it's essential to serving my first customer.

Within a mile, I'm indicating and pulling off the main road to steady my nerves. I need today to be a success, otherwise I risk hearing the same old remarks: 'What did you expect, she never gives it her all!', 'Pippa's hardly one of life's doers, is she?' or worse, 'Typical Pippa, just look at her track record – nothing ever works out.' I jump down from my driver's seat, attempting to banish the negative voices in my head, and stride to the rear of the van, opening each door and pinning it wide using the special elbow hinges. The tantalising smell of fresh bakes tickles my nose. I'm hoping the aroma lasts for the duration of my journey; customers won't be able to resist it.

I need to view the products with fresh eyes, purely to remind myself of the stock. The interior of the van is laden with large wicker trays, each holding various goodies and pastries. I did listen as Isla ran through the stock earlier, but I want to be sure. As always, Isla was too efficient in helping me to carry each bread tray from The Orangery's back room and slide them into place in the van's racking system. If a customer asks me for a couple of bannocks, a Hufsie cake and a wholemeal loaf, I'll die with embarrassment if I select and charge them for a couple of crusty cobs, a carrot cake and a large rye bread. It's not that I wasn't paying attention, I was simply distracted by nerves, self-doubt and a reputation for failure.

It feels foolish parking in the middle of nowhere, but now I can take my time and view today's bakes. Not that I'm particularly knowledgeable about the artisan bread market, but I've learnt so much from Isla. She might be fairly young, but she's got the know-how on this baking business. Her gran's precious recipe book has certainly provided the backbone to the gallery café, and subsequently this mobile delivery scheme.

There's no bending or crouching necessary, as there's plenty of height inside this vehicle. I might not appreciate its previous life as much as others appear to, but I'm grateful for the head room.

I pull each bread tray forward on its runners to view the assortment of breads, cakes and pastries lying on neatly folded sheets of parchment paper. Every item has been freshly baked this morning by Isla's fair hand. It simply boggles me that she can start work at six o'clock, though the compensation is an early finishing time. She'll get the entire afternoon to herself. The knock-on effect means the other waitresses have to cash up and close the café at the end of the day.

That's probably the reason why the Campbells have invited Callie on board ... that, and her being family; I sense Jemima likes employing family.

Callie won't last; she never does. She's too set in her ways; somewhat superior and haughty in her manner towards me and Jemima. Yeah, Callie's too materialistic for my liking. She's always made out she's doing well as a qualified beautician, so I'm surprised she's come cap in hand asking Jemima for a job.

On hearing the news that Callie had dropped by for a little chat with Jemima, followed by a quick introduction to Isla and a tour of the gallery, I knew what was going on. I'm not as green as I am cabbage-looking. The added knowledge that Levi was thumbs-upping Jemima, straight after our test drive, simply confirmed my suspicions. Though I'm still impressed with his hidden talent for singing Elvis. He showed a patient and observant side to his nature, in addition to the always helpful, always obliging Levi who I serve each day. It helped not having Mungo hanging around him, which is usually the case when he pops in for a quick coffee. I don't get their relationship; they are more like father and son than best friends. Apparently, they aren't even related, unlike many of the folk who live in Shetland.

My countertop is furnished with a tiny cash till and a mini card payment machine – that, in itself, was enough to give me palpitations; I don't do electronics. Hanging from a ceiling hook is my logoed tabard, which Jemima proudly presented to me. She wanted an apron-style garment – I simply grimaced when she showed me the catalogue photo, prior to ordering. Not that I think I'm a tabard kind of person, but anything is better than a waitress's pinny. I've paper, pencils and brown paper bags decorated with the gallery's seasonal logo, all lying alongside serving tongs and serrated cake slicers.

On inspection, I'm happier and more confident. Tomorrow, I'll probably write down a stock list as Isla fills each tray. But for now, I'm ready.

I climb down the steps and slam the rear doors closed. There's nothing more to do, so I'd best drive to my first location, the quiet village of Gulberwick. See what interest I can create amongst the locals whilst parked on the A970, a little way along from their local bus stop. Ned said I can amend the route in a few weeks, but for now he wants his bread route followed to the letter. I'll make notes on the number of customers and any requested orders; statistics and data will prove handy during our discussions. I know Isla does that with her waste and sales book. I intend this venture to be a success, because I'm eager to prove my worth when given a chance. If I'm doing this, I'll do it properly – unlike Callie waitressing in The Orangery. I bet she calls in sick today, this being her first morning shadowing Aileen.

I wait at the designated spot for ten minutes without a single customer. I'm conscious of Ned's instructions, but in order to drum up regular custom, our presence needs announcing or advertising; otherwise this is a wasted stop.

'Come on, Rolly, my decision is made – I'll defend it if I must!' Having secured the rear doors, I turn the ignition and away we go in search of customers.

I feel very conspicuous turning off the A970 and entering the Hillside estate. Much like the Child Catcher in *Chitty Chitty Bang Bang*, I feel the eyes of all the residents are on me, whether they're peering around a drawn curtain, through a slatted blind or twitching a lacy drape. It would be great if they spotted me driving by and nipped out to purchase their goods, unlike the ten minutes I spent parked on the main road without a sale. I have Ned's printed timetables to hand out with each purchase; next week should be easier, with customers waiting along his designated route.

I park in the first accessible spot, a little way from a hotel. Jumping down from the driver's seat, I begin my set-up routine: double doors pinned open, tabard on and poppers secure, pen and pencil pushed into the large pouch pocket. Waiting inside the van at my countertop, I've got a great view of the village framed by the vehicle's interior metalwork, but nothing else. Ideally, there'd be a flurry of locals, with purses and wallets, drifting from the houses to make an orderly queue and await my service. Nothing and no one. I'll wait, I won't be hasty and dash off. I run through the bakes in my head, like a child playing a memory game: 'Mrs MacCrouch went to the Artisan Bread Basket and bought . . .' I add an item each time before attempting to recall my own crafted list.

I check my watch: five minutes.

I stand and wait. I can't wipe down the surfaces as there are no crumbs, can't restock from the storage units as there is no free space, and I can't make small talk as there are no customers. Yet. There are no customers yet.

I recheck my watch: ten minutes.

Still nothing or nobody appears.

Well, this is bloody great. I'll pitch up at each designated spot and return to The Orangery with the exact same stock I left with this morning. I instinctively know what Isla will say about reselling each item tomorrow – that'll not be to her liking! Not a great start to my working day. Though I did spot Levi driving by on a taxi run – our passing wave reminded me of truckers on a highway, which made me smile.

I might as well get a breath of fresh air whilst waiting. I climb down the rear steps on to the tarmacked road and, hey presto, a line of five customers has quietly formed against the side of the Bread Basket, all awaiting my attention.

'S-sorry. I didn't realise anyone w-was h-here,' I stammer, shocked out of my skin.

'You open, lass?' asks one elderly dear, her aged hands clutching her purse.

'Of course. Today, I have . . .' It takes a few minutes to reel off the bakery list but my customers are all ears, which is lovely.

I need a chalkboard secured to the inside of the rear door panel titled 'Makes and Bakes'. Listing the goods will save customers' time – and my voice.

'Any spoils?' asks a young mum, with a wriggling toddler in her arms.

'Not today, maybe next week,' I answer, noting the little one's gummy smile, before swiftly selecting a couple of lemon muffins from the nearest tray and handing her the paper bag, free of charge. I'll note them down in my 'waste book' later, just like Isla does with Dottie's freebie cake slices. 'Here. Enjoy these as a treat.'

Her eyes widen in surprise, before she stammers, 'Th-thank you. I'll see you another week.'

It takes all of ten minutes to serve, chat and wave a hearty goodbye to my first queue. I'm overjoyed by their enthusiasm when I handed each a scheduled timetable.

I jump down the steps, slam and secure the rear doors before climbing back into my driver's seat to return to the designated route via the A970.

'Come on, Rolly, we've got our first sales under our belt – it's onwards and upwards from here!' I'm buoyant, brimming with excitement, eager to pitch up at my next stop: the almost desolate village of Quarff.

Chapter Eight

Natalia

I can't decide whether I'm enduring a self-imposed house arrest or staging a one-gal sit-in – either way, I can think of worse places to be confined than a plush suite. I hate to think how much my room service bill will be.

It's baffling to think that Ned has successfully transformed a series of old-fashioned stately bedrooms into luxurious hotel rooms in a matter of months. He's not one for flashing the cash, but in recent months he's certainly been forking out the readies, if you include the stable conversion.

I can't pretend that I'm not intrigued to glean anything I can from the vantage point of my padded window seat, which is a new addition to this room. From early this morning I've watched a steady flow of customers milling around the cobbled courtyard. I've watched numerous artists open up their stables or barns – I'm unsure what Ned calls them – but it's like watching an ant farm come to life. People scurrying back and forth across the yard from the conservatory, where I assume the coffee shop is housed, and back to their pitch. I've even spotted that pet duck waddling around the yard; I'm surprised to see it's still here, let alone how much it has grown since the autumn. What I haven't spied is either Ned or his Cinderella, which seems strange, as the hotel staff have bigged up their working ethos of being in attendance at all times.

But I ask you, since when has Ned ever not been on site? He's been present, around the clock, since the day he graduated from

Edinburgh with a first-class degree in History before returning home to the family fold and taking the reins from his father. I've certainly jetted into Shetland more times than he's ever flown out. The poor guy has been tethered to this ancestral home by kith and kin since he was old enough to toddle up the grand staircase under the watchful glare of his forefathers. Personally, I can't bear to raise my eyes while ascending the staircase, but that's because I detest the constant reminder of old blood hanging over my head.

My interest in surveillance was beginning to wane until I spy my number one enemy: Dottie. As spritely as ever, nipping from the rear entrance, with the door that always sticks on the bottom edge, across the cobbled yard to chat with the woman in dungarees who is arranging wrought-iron goods before her stable front. I'm assuming she's the blacksmith; I notice the care with which she handles each piece. Her bright pink hair gives her a sassy look, which I couldn't carry off, but she's on fire and makes light work of heaving her display piece whilst talking to Dottie. Lord knows when that woman will retire. Never, I suppose. I expect she'll be trundling around here with a Zimmer frame, doing her 'bit of light dusting', till her dying day. What Ned will do without her is anyone's guess. Though I've never been fooled by her sweet old lady style. She lulls you into a false sense of security, thinking she's frail, slightly feeble and needs handling with kid gloves. Wrong! She's sharp witted, quick tongued and as crafty as they come. They broke the mould when they made her, that's for sure – and there's few will say it, apart from me, but it's a bloody good job that they did! I'm no fan of hers. Likewise, she's certainly no fan of mine. She only has to lay her watery gaze on me and instinctively her top lip slowly curls in distaste. She can't help it. Mother Nature, I suppose. Protecting Ned is her only aim ... that, and growing more of those sodding tall flowers of hers.

I watch as the two women gleefully talk, their hand gestures increasing to match their smiles. Dottie's got a knack with certain folk; not me, though. I get that she's the nurturing type, the mother hen with an empty nest, but her continual attention verges on intrusive if you're on the receiving end. We clashed heads no end of times over Ned. She thinks she's his stand-in mother since his own passed. It doesn't help matters when Ned respectfully accepts her input without question. But, boy, did it grate on my nerves.

I can admit it now, but there were times when I did things purely to wind her up. Wrong of me, I know, but still. When the older generation meddle in your love life, surely all is fair in love and war! One day, I might apologise for rattling her cage so much; it was mainly silly stuff, which seemed entertaining while she was presiding over the details of life at the manor.

I watch as the pair of women bring their conversation to a close, and each one departs smiling to herself. I can't imagine living the solitary life Dottie has led for so long, alone at home, but for the company of trusted friends. When I'm her age, I want to be surrounded by my own family ... though, given the unexpected turn of events in the last twenty-four hours, I might be further away from that goal than I'd ever imagined.

I jump up from the window seat; my maudlin mood is rapidly bringing me down. It'll do me no good to wallow in self-pity. I push aside the consequences Ned's marriage will inflict on me. At thirty years of age, I need to start again. To secure a family of my own, I now need to build a relationship with a stranger who hasn't even entered my life yet. If we met tomorrow and fell head over heels in love, it could be several years before we were fully settled into a life together. A couple more before commitments are solid and babies are planned. At the earliest, I'd be thirty-five before achieving that goal. Thanks, Ned, a quiet word in advance would have been appreciated.

I hurriedly dress, knowing I need to create a plan of action. There's no use me staying holed up here for evermore, without planning what I will say or do when I confront Ned. Because confronting him is top of my 'To-do' list within the next twenty-four hours. Only days ago, I was busy packing my suitcase to board a flight and give him a lovely surprise. How naïve was I?

Not that Ned's ever wanted such niceties from me; he's always been the generous one. Me, who has been his plus one on many occasions, his Girl Friday any day of the week, and his number one on speed dial when company suited him. And to think, while I was away, honouring my modelling contracts, Ned was negotiating new contracts of his own.

'Housekeeping!' calls the old lady's voice, through the crack of the door, which she's swiftly opened with her service keys. Dottie appears to be coming in without waiting for a reply. She's wrongly assumed the room is vacant.

'No, thank you!' I say, sprinting across the room, arms outstretched, hoping to prevent her from entering my suite.

I can make my own bed, tidy my tea tray and straighten the towels on the bathroom rail, thanks. My heart is in my mouth as my hands connect with the door panelling and push it closed. I can feel the weight of her body on the other side as she moves back more swiftly than I was expecting. Please forgive me if I've bruised her or startled her; I don't wish her any harm.

'OK, thank you, dearie,' calls Dottie. 'I'll come back tomorrow.'

'No, you won't,' I mutter, closing the door and leaning against it while my heart rate slows after that unexpected intrusion. I should have pre-empted such a disturbance by hanging the 'Do not disturb' sign on the handle. I wait for a second, then collect the sign from the dressing table before quietly opening the door to slide the polite notice on to the outside handle. The landing is quiet, so I take an extra step and peer along the corridor . . . and there she is, Dottie in all her glory, with a tiny wheelie trolley laden with cleaning goodies. She totters along with spritely steps in anticipation of her life's purpose: a bit of light dusting.

I dart back inside my suite for fear of being spotted. Bless Ned, regardless of how much pain his life choices are about to cause me, he has a good heart; Dottie will always be cared for while Ned Campbell lives in Lerwick.

Pippa

I slowly manoeuvre Rolly along the manor's driveway. I'm actually on a natural high after completing day one of our designated route. Maybe Jemima knows me better than I know myself; this role could be my rightful place. I have nothing but great feedback to report, suggestions for the coming week, and even a request for a birthday cake for a seven year old for next week, if Isla can quote a reasonable price. If this is the satisfaction which comes with being mobile, then I'm a happy gal. I'll admit it was stressful to begin with, when customers were slow to appear, but as the route continued they appeared thick and fast, eager to browse our goods. I've enjoyed the social interaction, chatting and laughing, and suggesting purchases when people were unsure. My heart was fit to burst when several customers waved goodbye saying, 'See you next week!' I've driven through numerous beautiful villages, and my day's work has been completed without stress or strife.

I glide under the stone arch, avoiding the browsing customers criss-crossing the gallery's cobbled yard, before parking outside The Orangery's glazed entrance. Hardly any bakes remain, so the large trays are virtually empty, which makes unloading easier. I've been so consumed with my own delight that I totally forgot about Callie. But now I spot her, hastily moving back and forth amongst the tables, her silhouette back-lit by the conservatory windows on the far side.

And just like that, my happy bubble is burst.

*   *   *

Sometime later, I climb the grand staircase as nerves jangle in my throat and a nauseous sensation sloshes about my stomach. I'm being ridiculous; all that's required is to reveal the day's takings to Ned and Jemima on the third floor. They've arranged my end-of-day meeting prior to my shift finishing, much like Isla's briefing begins each day. My sales book is tucked beneath my arm, a trick I'm nabbing from Isla and her business course. It means such a lot to me to know they're impressed by my effort, hence my sudden mood change. Could my sales have been much higher? Will the customers return next week? Will they keep and share the printed timetable, or throw it away like junk mail?

I shouldn't feel like this in my cousin's house; you'd think I'd be relaxed. But it's as if Ned's presence twists Jemima's DNA into a different sequence, eliminating our family connection. I appreciate that my employment here is business and not personal. But still, I shouldn't be a bag of nerves going to have a wee chat with my older cousin, boss or no boss.

On reaching the third-floor landing, I gaze up at the skylights overhead. The greying clouds provide little comfort; their rolling appearance suggests something is brewing. Hopefully not an omen for our discussion.

I walk along the landing towards the potted aspidistra, housed in a glazed jardinière, and give the wooden door a hearty rap.

'Come in!' calls Ned's voice.

I take a deep breath before entering.

The duo are seated at the meeting table, Jemima cradling a coffee mug and Ned busily scribbling in his notebook. After a brief greeting, I duly settle in the opposite chair.

'I hope I'm not late,' I say, fearing I might have lost track of time filling Aileen in on the highlights of my first day.

'No worries. How was it?' asks Ned.

Jemima puts her coffee mug down and listens intently.

'I sold everything apart from half a dozen bannocks and a

large rye loaf. I've emptied the Bread Basket and swept it through
and mopped the floor ready for tomorrow. A customer requested
that Isla calls her to discuss an order for a birthday cake.' Both
seem intrigued, so I continue to talk, maintaining the positive
vibe by requesting a chalkboard, plus the suggestion of 'spoils'.
'It might be a good way to offload any bakery mishaps, a bit like
batter bits from the chippy.'

When I finally draw breath, my nerves have vanished and
their interest hasn't diminished. Ned is busily scribbling in his
notebook – I suspect he's never had batter bits – and Jemima is
grinning like a Cheshire cat.

'A very successful day!' says Ned, his face creasing in a broad
smile. 'Well done, Pippa. Are you pleased?'

I'm taken aback that he's asked, let alone cares to hear my
views; I'm liking this. 'I am, actually. I'm quite proud of myself –
it's been a good day at work.'

Jemima's smile grows even wider.

'Can I assume that your indecision about the role has been
put to bed?' asks Ned, glancing at his wife, awaiting my answer.

'It has . . . though I was a little surprised to see the new waitress.' I can't help myself. I'm not entirely comfortable knowing
that my reluctance was probably relayed to him, stoking his frustration that I was going back on my word, so I quickly take the
chance to add, 'I wasn't trying to be difficult . . . more that . . .' My
sentence fades, causing Ned to nod, encouraging me to continue.
'I was disappointed by the vehicle – it wasn't as I'd imagined.'

'I see.' His steady gaze doesn't leave mine.

My jangling nerves, nausea and apprehension have faded, so
if he wants the truth I'll give it to him.

'Honestly, Ned, knowing how you value quality and design, I
imagined you'd buy a brand-new, custom-designed vehicle, built
for the job, not just convert an old ambulance.' There, I've said
it; tough luck if he takes offence.

'You're not a fan of the vehicle?'

'Oh, it runs great. It's roomy and spacious, but there's no fooling anyone what it used to be in a former life, is there?'

'Fair point. Are you aware of how much cheaper the conversion was in comparison to the cost of buying a new vehicle?'

'I've no idea. But I had an image in my head and . . . the Bread Basket didn't live up to my expectations.'

'So why the change of heart now?'

I glance at Jemima. I'll need to choose my words carefully, otherwise I'll be perceived as the family bitch.

'I heard Callie had been for a visit.'

'And that affected your decision?' asks Jemima, exchanging a fleeting look with Ned.

'Yes, and you know why.'

Silence descends. How am I going to back-pedal from this one? It was such a lovely atmosphere a few minutes ago.

'Sorry, you're going to have to bring me up to speed,' says Ned, resting his pen on the notebook.

'Family issues run deep. There's only ever been us three girls and, on too many occasions, Callie has somehow managed to get special treatment over the two of us. She never sticks to what she says – and I, for one, don't wish to work alongside her, family or not!' There, I've said it straight.

'I appreciate your honesty, Pippa. But, since your new role takes you out and about, you won't be around Callie. So can you see there being any chance of issues arising between you?'

'Not if she leaves me alone, there won't be,' I say, before adding, 'but I doubt she will. She has a tendency to steal my thunder, regardless of the occasion or situation.'

Chapter Nine

Autumn

'Mr Drummond, may I have a quick word?' I call across reception as our guest returns to the manor after a day out. I've been on lookout for hours, awaiting his return.

'Good evening, nothing wrong, I hope?' The middle-aged man immediately diverts his route from the grand staircase towards me.

'Not at all. It's about the music lesson you requested for the Shetland gue. I've found a local tutor who is happy to come here, either tomorrow evening or the night after. That's if you still wish to book a lesson.'

His stern features crack into a smile. I've been waiting for this moment all shift.

'Wonderful news! I'm surprised that you've been able to locate someone so quickly.'

'It took a few phone calls, but I was given a contact number of a suitable tutor.'

'That's fabulous. Tomorrow evening suits very well ... and the cost?'

'Twenty pounds for the hour. He'll bring an instrument or two here. I've checked and our library is free from seven thirty onwards'

His smile grows even wider. 'Superb. Can you add the amount to my bill?'

'Certainly. I'll confirm the arrangements with the tutor.' I automatically reach for the telephone to complete the task.

'Thank you and good evening,' says Mr Drummond, turning back towards the staircase. His back is ramrod straight, but I know he's still smiling.

That's the satisfaction of working in hospitality. I have delivered on a guest's request, and that means more to me than receiving praise from the Campbells. I had to Google what the instrument looked like, but I was determined to find someone in the local area who either played or taught.

In my pocket my mobile phone vibrates; I bet it's my sister chasing me to make arrangements for a visit. I make a mental note to call her back on my next coffee break.

'Evening, Autumn, how are you?' calls Hannah, passing through the hallway laden with a large room service tray. She'll be relieving me at the end of my reception shift in a little while.

'I'm good. You?'

'Can't grumble, though room service without the aid of a lift is becoming a drag,' she says, her blonde ponytail swinging as she walks.

'Is that for the Unst Suite?'

'Yep. Third time today, apparently. I don't see the point in booking a holiday and then staying in your hotel suite for the entire duration – you might as well stay at home and save the cost.'

I take in her comment, especially the three deliveries in one day.

'Each to their own, Hannah. The guest might need a break from home and has chosen our establishment to treat herself. A bit of self-care never did anyone any harm, did it?' I glance down at my hands; the mention of self-care has reminded me that I've not used my hand cream to combat the redness caused by my excessive handwashing.

'I suppose not. Anyway, best get going, otherwise Chef will be moaning that other service trays are waiting. See you later.'

My gaze follows Hannah up the staircase until she's out of view. There's nothing wrong with a guest remaining in their suite and requesting room service, but it is unusual. The equivalent of booking a world cruise and enjoying the scenery through your cabin's porthole window. I swiftly pull up the guest's details on the computer: Ms N. Muir. Solo occupant, two-week stay, home address in Edinburgh, plus credit card details.

I specifically remember checking her in; she was the last guest that day, but there was nothing out of the ordinary about her manner. Admittedly, I could tell she was stunning, even behind the large sunglasses and with her cap pulled down low, but I admire women who don't flaunt their assets. I register the fact that I haven't laid eyes on her since. There's a fine line between a guest's right to privacy and flagging up a small concern but, morally, I'm sure we've got a duty of care towards our guests. I make a mental note to mention it in passing to the Campbells, tomorrow morning.

Hannah dashes back down the staircase, minus the wooden tray; I quickly beckon her across to the reception desk.

'Everything OK? Guest well?' I ask quietly.

'Yeah, she's got a face mask on and her hair was twisted into a towel turban – reading magazines, I reckon, given the number spread across the bed.'

'Good to hear. Can you let me know the first time you see her outside her suite?'

Hannah frowns. 'Why?'

'I want to make sure she's OK and enjoying her stay, that's all. Nothing to worry about, just between us.'

'Sure. She's chatty enough when I deliver room service.'

'That's good. I'm not worried,' I lie, fearing I might have inadvertently raised the alarm. 'Just taking care of our guests, that's all.'

Hannah moves away from reception, heading towards the ancient kitchens.

A sudden thought hits me. 'Oh, Hannah.'

'Yeah?' She turns to address me.

'Don't repeat anything amongst the kitchen staff, OK?'

'As if!' says Hannah, disappearing along the corridor. 'I'll relieve you in an hour.'

As if? She must think I was born yesterday. With my experience in hospitality, I'm fully aware of how the more experienced kitchen staff can wheedle information out of the younger staff members about each guest. They feel they're locked out back, kept away from guests, providing the essentials, and no one will ever find out that they ask nosy questions. I've overheard many a pot-washer and chef discussing a guest who they've never met but about whom they know far too much.

I check the hallway clock. Hannah's right, there is only one hour to go until I hand over to her. I've got a good mind to quickly change my clothes after my shift and head out for a trek along the coastal road. I've been inside for much of the day, so it might do me good to have a bit of fresh air.

Natalia

Apart from sticking my nose outside the door to catch a glimpse of Dottie's retreating figure, I haven't left my room. Until now.

I'm dressed to impress as I lock the door of the Unst Suite bang on eight o'clock. I've certainly gone to town, the top-to-toe drill for an evening out, with nails, hair and make-up; I want stylish and classy, not comfort. I've eventually opted for a tight-fitting jumpsuit, knowing the silky fabric will soothe my raw nerves like a comfort blanket calms a newborn baby. My intention isn't to tease or tantalise, but to learn the truth. If I'm to face this situation head on, I'll need armour – and this is my version of protection.

I'm nervous. More so than last night.

I sweep along the first landing, taking the staircase to the third floor. I'm out of breath by the time I reach the final step of the third staircase, which always happened on my previous visits. I used to joke, 'That's my exercise for the day,' which always raised a smile from Ned. I might be fit and young, but the stairs – and possibly undue nerves – have taken their toll. I pause; I need to focus and regain my composure. It won't look good if our conversation crumbles halfway through because I've keeled over, huffing, puffing and demanding an oxygen cylinder. I have a list of questions as long as an Andrex roll, and I intend to ask them.

Deep breath, in and out. Again.

I straighten my jumpsuit, flick my hair back and lift my chin. One thing I've learnt in modelling is always remember to pull your shoulders back and glide like you're wearing an invisible diamond tiara. I reposition my tiara, smile and begin my strut. Actually, this is similar to a modelling assignment in many respects; composure ensures perfect exposure.

Standing before his office door ignites a sense of déjà vu as a montage of memories flood my mind, along with the memory of last night's failed attempt.

On taking a final deep breath, I rap sharply on Ned's office door.

Please let him be alone, I silently pray.

The door opens wide . . .

And there he is. As gorgeous as always; his dark eyes and his temples more salt 'n' peppered than previously, but still the epitome of a silver fox.

'Surprise!' Not the opening line I'd practised but the one I deliver with a faltering smile.

'Natalia!' His blinking eyes and gaping mouth confirm his shock.

'Ned, how the devil are you?' My gaze flits downwards, spying his gold wedding band. Oh crap, it's true. My heart sinks before I've even stepped through the doorway.

'Come in, please,' he says, stepping aside and giving me space, before asking, 'can I get you a drink?'

I glance around the room . . . empty. I'm grateful.

'That would be lovely,' I tell him. 'What are you having?'

'My usual.' He slowly closes the door.

'I'll join you.' Brandy is not my thing, but joining Ned definitely is.

I settle on the couch before the decorative fireplace. I can't help glancing towards the mantelpiece, as if I need further torment, but am surprised to see it is empty. Where's their wedding photo gone?

Ned busies himself at the drinks cabinet which only ever contains brandy and whisky – an old-fashioned accessory at odds with his modern choice of decor and ethos.

'Here,' he says, handing me the crystal glass, the rich amber signalling a double measure. Ned rarely pours doubles. He settles in the opposite armchair, sitting forward, elbows on his knees; his usual spot was beside me on the couch. Boy, how life has changed!

'How are things?' I say, dredging my perky tones from the depths of my sinking heart.

'Why are you here?' he asks, quietly but bluntly.

'I heard you'd opened, so I thought I'd surprise you by booking a little stay . . . so, ta-dah!'

He looks serious. 'Natalia—'

'I think it's amazing what you've achieved,' I interrupt. I don't want to hear him explain the new chapter of his life. Can't I have a few minutes longer without my world crashing down? Don't I deserve such a courtesy? My brain switches to autopilot as I continue to gabble. 'The renovation of the bedrooms, the grand reception area – and so soon after converting the stables into the gallery. You must be delighted with the results, Ned.'

'We got married, Natalia.' He shoehorns his news into the tiniest pause.

I draw a shaky breath. Which then snags in my throat as my stomach swirls uncomfortably. I fall silent and stare. My eyes are pleading with his. Please don't expect me to say 'congratulations'. I should, but I simply can't; my heart will break.

Ned continues to talk, his voice softening. 'You said you had a funny feeling about Jemima. You might have been a little dismissive about the likes of me and the likes of her, but it's worked surprisingly well. It's not what you want to hear, but we were married last October.'

'October?' I can't hide my shock. I take a deep swig of my brandy.

'From the very first moment that I saw her, I knew. Jemima got under my skin, and everything she did simply attracted me more. I won't insult you with an apology, but I'd never felt that way before.'

'Not even with me?' I sound pathetic, but I can't help myself.

Ned doesn't answer; he has breeding.

'I didn't know. I thought it would be a nice idea to visit and . . . well, now I hear this.'

'I'm sorry. I should have done the right thing and called you. I suppose I didn't want to face any fallout that might occur. I've got great memories of us – I selfishly wanted to keep it that way.'

'I see.' A conscious decision, then?

'Do you?'

I shrug, my response had been an instinctive reply.

'It just happened, Natalia. She entered my life, and that was it. I couldn't have predicted such a reaction. Who knows how and why these connections form in an instant?'

I nod. I hear what he's saying. I'm not to blame; I'm simply not her.

'Can I ask you something, Ned?' The words tumble out of my mouth.

'Sure.'

'Did you ever love me?' Bloody hell, Nat – retain some dignity and shut the feck up, woman!

Ned shifts in his seat, chews his lip before speaking in a slow and careful tone. 'It's not as simple as that, Natalia. I thought I knew what I wanted. Thought I knew my type, if that's even a thing. But to find myself wanting to catch the slightest glimpse of her each day, eager to learn the smallest detail . . . I felt giddy knowing she was even near. Yes, I had feelings for you, of course I did over the years, but . . .' he falters.

I lift my palm; I can't bear to hear his final words.

But not as much as her, says my inner voice.

Ned falls silent, takes a sip of his brandy before sitting back in his armchair. His left thumb plays with his wedding ring, circling it around his finger. Obviously thinking of her.

I can feel my tears welling. I need to remain calm. I want to continue in this civilised tone but what the bloody hell is he talking about 'had feelings for you'? We were in love! What else kept us together for so long?

'Did it mean nothing to you that I was flying back and forth whenever I could? Those weekends we spent alone together?' I ask. Has he forgotten those occasions? Or did they mean nothing?

'Our relationship . . .'

I snort rudely. 'I'm glad you're actually calling it a relationship. For a moment there, I thought we'd had some platonic arrangement going on for four years!' My tone snaps. I can't rein it back.

'Natalia.' His voice is barely a whisper.

'Don't Natalia me! I show up, having not heard a bloody thing from you since September, to find you didn't have the common courtesy to tell me you'd moved on! Not even a text message, Ned!'

'When have we ever gone five months without contact? I thought it best to let things lie.'

'Did you now? Well, I've got news for you. We've previously endured much longer spells of silence—'

'Not that I can recollect,' he protests.

'We have! And then you'd snap your bloody fingers and I'd come running. Of course, that suited you back then, but this time . . . well, now I understand why!'

My mind rummages through its internal locked safe, dragging out the piled memory boxes in search of the specific details.

'Every time you needed to focus on estate work, the farming tenants – I waited patiently until you called. There were occasions when months would pass, but did I complain? Oh no! I knew you had to focus on your work and sort any difficulties with the tenant farmers as soon as they came up. Did I ever complain of being neglected, feeling in need of attention? No!'

'Natalia, we were both happy with that arrangement. You had your modelling career and I was busy here – it worked for us.'

'Did it! Did it, really?'

'Yes . . . you know it did.'

'Phuh! What I wouldn't have given to officially be the girl-friend. But oh no, I was obviously the plaything until the real deal turned up!' Defining us out loud sounds totally preposterous. I sound utterly ridiculous.

'That's unfair, Natalia. Neither of us wanted more than we shared.'

Why have I done this? I'd wanted a civilised conversation, yet I've given him exactly what he'd predicted: a drama.

'Couldn't you have at least shown me some respect by letting me know? Instead, I've rocked up to find this!'

'I have no excuse for my behaviour, it was wrong of me. I should have called you.'

'Do you think!' As I spit my words out, the office door opens and in walks Jemima.

Perfect timing, as ever.

'Ned?' Jemima's eyes widen in surprise. She's dressed in a faux fur gilet, faded jeans and walking boots, her glossy hair styled in a messy bun.

'Jemima, Natalia has dropped by for a . . .' He hesitates as she joins us, standing beside his armchair.

'A mini-break.' I jump in.

'Natalia, it's nice to see you again. It seems so long!'

'I hear congratulations are in order,' I say, before adding, 'didn't you do well! A true Cinderella story, from rags to riches, eh?' I could kick myself for the bitchy sarcasm.

'Natalia, enough!' Ned stands up immediately.

I've pushed it too far, I knew I would.

'You're very welcome to stay at the manor, but I won't have you come into our home and insult my wife.'

I want to scream. What an insensitive bastard! That's supposed to be me! Me standing there, offering a reassuring hand on his back to calm the situation. Me wearing a matching gold band. Me! The woman who never moaned or complained but simply stayed loyal, hoping her day would come. The lover who never demanded more than he offered. The woman who my girlfriends said was 'playing it right', by being respectful of his choices, adhering to his wishes and abiding by the rules of a court-ship which she wrongly associated with his social background and upbringing. The same woman who was incredibly strong throughout and who was repeatedly praised by other women for not succumbing to dating stereotypes or deploying underhand tactics to secure the man she loved and wanted.

Where the hell has it got me? Standing, watching, while his wife gently strokes his back, silently reassuring him that everything is fine – and, more importantly, that this 'other woman', this intrusion, the blast from his past, is something they can handle together. Her gold band glints under the ceiling lights, inflicting a physical pain deep within me.

Look at her short stubby fingers in comparison to my svelte, elegant digits, which have featured in hundreds of expensive nail polish adverts worldwide, whilst hers have dug about in the muck and dirt, tending grubby pumpkin seedlings.

'Natalia, I'm very sorry that you've had to find out this way. I can only offer my apologies for not acting as I should have in the circumstances.'

'What do you care? You have her, she has you! You don't care what happens to me!' My tone is shrill and dramatic. My gestures are becoming wilder; it's not an act, more a release of pent-up emotions getting the better of me.

I fall silent, as if the fire has gone out of me. My brandy glass is empty, though I don't remember finishing it, and the newly-weds are simply watching me.

'I hope you'll be very happy together,' I say hollowly, not meaning one word of the sentiment.

'Thank you, Natalia,' says Jemima calmly, whilst blushing as she ought.

Ned gives a small nod. You can't reignite an argument with such a gesture, can you? Or can you?

'I'm staying in the Unst Suite. I'll continue my break as planned ... if there's no objection.' I have no idea what I'm saying or why. I'm simply filling the silence and delaying an outburst of tears.

I want this scene to end. I want to be away from this golden couple with their shiny bright future and doe-eyed expressions. I also wish to remain here, argue it out, underline how unfair he's been, make demands, and for this situation to fall in my favour. But how? He's married – and I look like a prize prat for being blindsided by his choice.

We can't stand here going around in circles, dissecting what is now firmly in the past. I need to leave the room, but that means walking away from this discussion, this moment, and moving on.

Moving on from Ned Campbell is the last thing I want. I arrived here in Shetland intending to embed myself within his world, not erase my own existence from it.

'We'll come to an arrangement regarding your room bill,' says Ned, glancing at Jemima.

'I don't need freebies from you, Ned Campbell.' My words are now purely weapons meant to cause injury. I do the only thing I can: stand, draw myself up to my full height, and stride towards the door. My blood is boiling, my tears collecting along my lashes and my heart dropping faster than Alice down a rabbit hole. I reach the door before my brain thinks of a fresh argument.

I wrench open the door to find a startled Dottie, her head cocked towards the keyhole, standing right outside the door.

'My God, woman, does your cleaning shift ever actually end?'

Dottie immediately straightens up, not wishing to stoop.

I sidestep her fragile body and strut along the third-floor landing towards the staircase. I have no idea if anyone is watching but I do my best runway walk, purely to show what I'm made of, despite my invisible tiara being totally skewed.

Chapter Ten

Friday 4 February

Autumn

'Autumn, has the guest from the Unst Suite been down to breakfast?' asks Jemima, coming through to the back office of reception soon after ten o'clock and sounding a little terse.

'Yes, first thing. I believe she's gone straight back up though.' I look up from my desk to find her nodding. I'm trying to calculate a pile of invoices, which has taken me a lot longer than I'd expected thanks to the numerous interruptions.

'Nothing out of the ordinary?'

I shake my head, but this sounds ominous. 'Actually, I was a little worried about her.' I outline my concerns regarding all the requests for room service.

'I see. Well, the truth is . . . she's a special guest so we, Ned and I, would like her to be looked after in the best way possible,' says Jemima. She seems hesitant and yet fired up at the same time.

'I understand. I thought she was a celebrity when she first checked in, what with her dark glasses and designer swag.'

Jemima smiles briefly. 'If you could let me know when she's out and about, I'd appreciate it.'

'Of course, no problem. Like a mystery shopper type person, is she?'

'Yeah, something like that.'

'I won't mention it to the other staff. I'd prefer you to get a true picture of the hotel's customer service.'

'Thanks, Autumn, I'd appreciate that.' With that she leaves as swiftly as she arrived.

I sit for a few minutes staring at the empty doorway. I hope Hannah hasn't let us down already with mindless chatter during room service delivery. I want this establishment to gain the highest star rating it can. I abandon my calculations and bring the nearest computer screen to life, eager to check which meals our mystery guest has already ordered. I know every plate came back empty, and no complaints received, so that's a good sign for starters.

'Good morning, Lerwick Manor Hotel, Autumn speaking. How may I help you?' I listen to the caller's requirements and hastily tap the computer keyboard, checking our availability for a one-week stay. 'Thank you, we're happy to help and look forward to greeting you.'

I replace the handset and press 'save' on the booking screen with a sense of satisfaction. I'm loving this new role; it's giving me the chance to use my experience and skillset whilst providing scope for new challenges every working day. It makes for an easier life than having to walk miles each shift up and down various decks of a great ocean liner. I might not be getting my fitness steps in every day, but it makes such a difference being back home in Shetland amongst my own. I can enjoy a coffee break with my older sister, or make arrangements to visit her to enjoy a home-cooked meal rather than the rich gourmet food on offer to staff.

'Any sign?' whispers Jemima, appearing from the rear kitchens.

I shake my head. I'm as nervous as a kitten now that I know what I know. I've no doubt it should all be top secret – and I should feel honoured knowing about the Campbells' secret guest. I scratch at my knuckles; my reddening skin itches like crazy

today. I'm disappointed that I've allowed this irritation to raise
its ugly head so quickly in my new role.

'OK.' Jemima sweeps up the grand staircase, no doubt on her
way to perform bedroom inspections, now housekeeping have
finished for the day.

Dottie appears in Jemima's wake, peering around the corner
of the corridor and watching Jemima ascend the stairs. It looks
funny from my position, and even funnier when she scurries over
to my reception desk.

'Morning, Dottie, are you alright?'

'Has she just asked about the blonde woman?' Her watery
blue gaze is brimming with curiosity.

'Sorry?' I'm taken aback as she ignores my question and comes
out with her own.

'Jemima. Has she mentioned the woman in the Unst Suite?'

Now what do I do? And how does she know?

I lick my lips, buying time before answering her. I made a
promise to my employer and that's big in my book. Or is this a test?

'I don't understand what you're asking me. Jemima asked
if I was OK,' I lie, glancing towards the staircase for fear that
Jemima might reappear.

Dottie's gaze shifts back and forth, taking in my stare. She
knows I'm lying. And why am I? If I've been trusted with such
information then surely Dottie has too.

'Phuh!' she says, peering at me some more. Dottie's a lovely
old dear, very bird-like and delicate, but every now and then you
spy a different side to her – like the other morning, when Ned
asked to speak to her about the broken glass. I suppose we each
have our moments. She's definitely got a fire in her belly, despite
her age. I hold her attention, though I wish I didn't have to. The
cogs in my mind spin, as I think up something to say to deflect
her original question.

'Is that all?' That's the best I can muster.

'If you see the lady go out, will you let me know?' asks Dottie, before adding in a softer tone, '*Please.*'

'Sure.'

Dottie turns to leave, before doubling back to reception. 'Natalia's the daughter of an old friend of mine ... I wouldn't want her to get lonely or report back to her nanna that I didn't show any interest during her stay.'

'Of course not.' I watch as Dottie crosses the tiled hallway, opens her cleaning cupboard door under the stairs, has a quick rummage inside whilst glancing up the staircase once or twice, before closing the panelled door and heading back towards the ancient kitchens.

'What was that about?' I mutter, unsure if I should mention the incident to Jemima immediately. No, I'll wait and see how this pans out. I can do without Dottie calling me a snitch. But then the longer I wait, the Campbells might suspect I'm lacking in the loyalty department, and that would never do. I pride myself on maintaining a scrupulous relationship with my employers where trust and respect are paramount to all parties.

Pippa

'Hi there, how can I help you?' I ask the elderly gent waiting by the kerb, whilst opening and securing Rolly's rear doors. I'm delighted that there are six customers awaiting my arrival. I've had an enjoyable drive through the glorious landscape and parishes towards Tingwall. I'd wanted my stop to be beside their picturesque kirk but Ned insisted it be by the houses, which makes sense.

'Archie Kibble awaiting your service. I'm after half a wholemeal loaf, please,' he says, his gnarly fingers playing with a handful of coins.

'Half? I don't usually do halves, Archie.'

'A whole loaf's too much for one person – I end up throwing it away.'

He's got a point.

'My granddad had the same issue after my nanna died.' I swallow, imagining the fragile figure before me morphing into my own flesh and blood. A tired expression, counting every penny of his pension and hating food being wasted. 'What about a small loaf instead?'

He shakes his head, turning his nose up. 'The smaller loaf gives me tiny slices, I like proper-sized sandwiches.'

'OK, here's what'll I'll do, Archie, though don't tell everyone, right?' I grab a wholemeal loaf and gesture a cutting action.

'Right, you are,' mutters Archie, a wry smile dawning. 'Mum's the word. I'll happily make it a regular purchase. And I'll take a bannock too.'

'Excellent, sounds like a deal,' I say, grabbing my bread knife and dividing the large loaf. Fingers crossed, I'll find a taker for the remaining half, otherwise I'll buy it myself.

I travel further along the A971, drawing to a stop beside the post box in Tresta. My routine has quickly established itself. Jump out, smile at the customer queue, open the doors, wash hands, gloves on and welcome.

'But I only want half, lassie,' mutters the elderly lady, clutching a net bag, peering at the nearest loaf tray. 'I can feed the birds, but it's such a waste otherwise.'

'Then I have just the thing for you,' I say cheerfully. I draw out a different wicker tray and select the half-loaf, showing her the size.

'Perfect,' she squeals. 'No one ever agrees to sell me half, not nowadays. It's the waste I object to.'

'Can we agree on a regular order, then?'

'Yes, please. Twice weekly suits me. Nancy Crabtree, that's me, so you can put my name on it. I don't mind a change now and then – be it white, brown or seeded.'

'That'll be perfect, Nancy.'

I quickly wrap her divided wholemeal loaf, securing the bread paper with a gallery sticker, before offering her the neat bundle, which she slips inside her netted bag.

That's the second daily kindness in as many hours. I'd best watch myself; it might appear to others that I'm enjoying myself too much, as if it were a game or I'm not taking my new-found responsibility seriously. The reality is I'm simply loving the freedom of my new role. I feel as if a new and long-awaited chapter of my life has finally begun.

I serve the rest of my customers within no time, but I can't wipe the smile from my face.

'Any more for any more?' I ask boldly, descending the steps to find an empty pavement. 'Nope, thought not!'

I slam the rear doors shut and am making my way towards my driver's seat.

'Excuse me!' comes a faint but shrill voice.

I look up to find a young woman, clutching her pram handles and dashing haphazardly along the road towards me. The pram wheels judder and bounce across the uneven ground, jiggling the bundle inside. Is she calling me? I assume she must be, as there's no one else around. I wait while she hastily crosses the road, without looking either way, and approaches the van.

'Sorry, sorry. I thought I'd missed you. Any chance of a loaf – white or brown, I don't care, anything will do,' she gasps, engaging the brake on the pram. Her red hair is pulled into a tight ponytail and she's wearing fluffy pink slippers.

'Sure. Large or small?' I say, returning to unlock the rear doors.

'Honestly, anything. Whatever you've got. I—' Her words are cut short as the wrapped bundle begins to wail. The noise is ear piercing, causing me to flinch and dart inside Rolly for shelter. The woman sighs heavily and begins jiggling the pram handles in a rather frantic manner, which I wouldn't find soothing, but she must know best.

I put on my serving gloves, pull out a couple of wicker trays and hold up both sizes of loaf to see which she'd prefer.

'Yeah, large then,' she says, momentarily lifting her eyes from the crying babe to indicate which loaf she wants, before returning her attention to the little one. Her brow is creased, her eyes staring, and there's a delicate glow of perspiration appearing on her temples.

'Anything else?' I ask, carefully wrapping the white loaf in bread paper.

'Have you anything sweet?'

'Cake or muffin?'

'Cake.'

The crying gets louder as she begins loudly shushing the baby, now rocking the pram back and forth with some force. Boy, the suspension frame on prams must be pretty sturdy.

'Carrot, lemon or honey?' I ask.

'Honey,' she calls over the sound of the frantic wailing, which I swear is doubling in decibels with every passing second.

I collect my utensils from the countertop, locate the honey cake and begin slicing her a decent-sized piece, bigger than normal but smaller than I've seen Isla secretly deliver to Dottie in The Orangery.

'Did you keep the instruction book?' I ask. The words spill from my lips before I put my brain into gear.

'What?' she says, her tone somewhat agitated.

'I said, did you keep the instruction booklet?'

For a split second, her creased brow softens, her gaze locks on to mine. Sod it, I've spoken out of turn, caused offence, and now I'm in trouble! My humour's not for everyone; my jokes frequently fall flat, even amongst the family.

I attempt to back-pedal quicker than Crispy duck when boisterous children visit the gallery. 'What I mean is, did you leave maternity so quickly that you left your free booklet behind? I know it's about a thousand pages thick, but if you check page 666, there's a returns form which you can fill out to get a replacement. I think this one's faulty, I reckon the volume control is broken!' I fall silent, placing her cake slice into a paper box. She's either going to explode in temper, or laugh.

I dare to peek sideways and witness my bemused customer continuing to frantically jiggle her pram. Phew! Good sign. I quickly continue. Have I lost control of my mouth, much like her baby?

'It's easy, there's loads of faulty options for returning it: cradle cap, sleepless nights, poor feeding, colic or nappy rash. Though you'll need to make sure you fill out the replacement section for what you'd like – you can even change flavour if you want.'

'Change flavour?' There's a definite smile dawning now.

Phew!

'Yeah, pink or blue. You can have a go with another flavour or, if you're brave and this broken volume control hasn't put you off, you can go for a multiple. Try your hand at twins, triplets – or quins, if you want – though I suggest you get a new booklet if you do, as you might need another returns form.'

'And how long do you have before returns are refused?'

'Thirty days, I think. It's a bit like Argos, though without the collection counter and the little pens – a stork delivers it!'

What starts as the tiniest of muffled giggles, slowly and softly develops to escape her in proper, full-blown belly laughs, with her free hand waving away my comments as if swatting flies.

I quickly continue. 'Seriously, I'm not joking. How old is your baby?'

'She's three weeks.'

'You haven't got long then, you'd best get a wiggle on, finding one of those returns forms, otherwise you're lumbered.'

Tears roll down her cheeks, similar to those drying on the little one's face.

'They let you believe it's for eighteen years, but I was still living at home until recently, so I think it's nearer thirty. So best not to miss your chance for swapsies.'

She begins to cough, splutter and pat her own chest whilst trying to speak. 'Is that what you did – swapsies?'

'Me? No. I haven't any children, but there's no fear that I'd have ever left maternity without my returns note. You new mums are too eager, that's the problem. In and out in no time, I hear. I'd have performed a one-woman sit-in whilst demanding my instruction booklet; they've got them out the back – they just don't want to give 'em out. I'd have had a picket line and a burnie bin protest going on, with slogans, placards and marching – the whole lot!'

Finally, I can't keep a straight face any longer. I crease, just like she has. I daren't offer her the goods for fear she'll drop them on the tarmac. Eventually, I take a breath, calm down and point to the pram: it's silent.

'She's stopped crying,' whispers the mother.

'Mmmm, I think she sensed you seemed less ...' I daren't finish my sentence for fear of offending her. 'That'll be three pounds, please.'

She hastily fishes the coins from her pocket and we make our exchange in silence.

'Thank you, that's the first time I've laughed in weeks.'

'You're welcome. I'll see you next week.'

She tucks the goods into the basket between the pram's wheels and slowly crosses the road, this time looking both ways. I step down, slam the rear doors shut and return to my driver's seat, where that bubble of laughter reignites. I sit there belly-laughing, my shoulders juddering as crazily as the pram wheels earlier.

I compose myself, flick the ignition and indicate right. Another wonderful day connecting with my happy customers and thoroughly enjoying the rapport that's developing between us. Though I think I'll keep that last encounter to myself. Lord knows what Ned would have said if I'd returned to The Orangery with a black eye and a thick lip, courtesy of a new mum.

Chapter Eleven

Natalia

It took some effort to pull myself together and go down to breakfast in the hotel's dining room this morning, but now, at four o'clock, having spent the rest of the day in my room, I need fresh air. I remember throwing up the sash windows in this bedroom, causing a gale to zoom round the room, making the lacy voiles dance at the windows like bridal veils caught in March winds. But now the windows no longer open more than a hand's width, letting in a tiny draught of air. Why anyone would choose to fit safety catches to prevent someone jumping from a first-floor window is beyond me.

I descend the staircase in a fake bouncy manner; you can't see who's in the reception area until the very last minute, so I want to be prepared. Fingers crossed neither Ned nor his wife are on front of house duty. I daren't lift my gaze to make eye contact with the generations of family who now stare down from the walls. Their mocking smiles and expressive eyes take on a different meaning after last night.

Autumn is at the front desk; she stops shuffling papers and smiles on seeing me appear.

'Afternoon,' I call, in a bright and breezy tone.

'Afternoon, Ms Muir, it's a fine day.'

'Thank you. I thought I'd take a stroll around the gallery and choose a few gifts for back home,' I lie, not wanting to be curt or sound old-ladyish by mentioning fresh air.

'You'll find loads of gift options, I'm sure. The stables are home to various arts and crafts, plus there's a set of display cabinets inside The Orangery where other small gifts can be found. You'll be spoilt for choice.'

How sweet of her. My plan was to head straight out of the door, regardless of who was present, but maybe not. I tentatively edge nearer the reception desk, almost eager for companionship.

'Any craft stable in particular that I should head for?'

'The blacksmith and glass blower are always popular – it's not overly sooty or dirty in there, so your clothes will be fine. The Yarn Barn is worth a browse and a feel of the soft wool, and there's always delicious cake on offer in The Orangery. The waitresses will add the price to your room bill, if you give them the name of your suite and sign a chit.'

'Sounds lovely. In fact, do you serve afternoon tea here?' I have no idea where that request came from but, true to form, when I'm upset and emotional I reach for food. Hardly the behaviour you'd expect of a figure-conscious model, but we're all human when the unexpected occurs.

'We certainly do. All produce is fresh from our artisan café. It's served in the library or the lounge – whichever you'd prefer.'

'The library, please. Can we say at five o'clock? That'll give me an hour to browse the crafts and get back without rushing.'

'Certainly. For one?'

'Yes, please.' Sadly, just for one! I smile brightly before continuing, 'Thank you, Autumn.' I take a few steps towards the large entrance door, almost lost in my own memories, when her voice brings me back.

'Thank you, Ms Muir.'

I quickly turn. 'You can call me Natalia. I'd prefer that.'

'Sure. Thank you . . . Natalia.'

I give her another warm smile. I like her.

I'm barely down the front steps, pausing to scowl at those

annoying stone-faced lions, when a tiny, bird-like busybody in a tweed skirt catches my eye, fast approaching along the paddock driveway on my right-hand side. Great, here comes Dottie!

'Natalia!'

I don't answer but continue to walk. I'm not up for any trouble or drama today. I've enough on my plate, and my mind is ready to burst with the rerun of last night's confrontation. Though I know I do need to apologise for my condescending remark aimed at her.

'Natalia! Wait!' calls Dottie again.

My feet accelerate, pounding the gravel, before I follow the sweep of the driveway, heading left, towards the stone archway – the entrance to what was once the abandoned stable yard. I'm wrong to ignore Dottie, but if I stop walking she'll catch up and give me a grilling. I should have prepared better for this outing by donning my metaphorical armour, but I honestly thought once I'd passed the reception area I'd be safe, mingling amongst the gallery's customers.

I'm greeted by that pesky pet duck, Crispy, waddling around and pecking at each of the stone cobbles like a frantic litter-picker. He's certainly grown since my last visit; his emerald feathers shimmer navy blue as his erratic movements catch the light. I don't see the attraction myself, but I believe it's *her* beloved pet.

On hearing the rhythmical sound of a hammer pounding metal, I take a sharp right, entering the forge, ignoring any craft signage and without stopping to view the products on display beside the open doorway.

'Hello,' says a chap in a blue checked shirt. He's wearing perspex goggles, sitting at a workbench, switching a globule of molten glass from one gloved hand to the other.

'Hello,' I say, grateful for his immediate attention. I glance around the interior. Autumn's right, it is fairly light and bright in here – even the far end, housing the blacksmith. She ceases hammering and turns, holding an object with a pair of tongs.

She thrusts it into a tub of water before mouthing 'hello' through the rising steam. I could never pull off having my hair dyed pink, but she's rocking the look.

A free-standing, metre-tall twisted blade of metal takes centre stage, occupying most of her floor space. A giant leaf? A human form in abstract? I make a point of moving nearer to her work station, curious to see what she's making; it also has the advantage of hiding me from the sight of anyone who might be giving chase.

'Hi, how's it going?' I ask, glancing at her display of goods. There's everything, from a fire poker to door plates and hanging baskets, arranged neatly on the side counter.

'Good, thanks. You?' she says, inspecting the metal object before shoving it back amongst the hot coals.

'So-so,' I answer, before gesturing to the abstract piece. 'This is interesting.'

'Thank you. It's part of a set of sculptures commissioned for the driveway. That's my interpretation of time – my chosen theme is things we humans waste. It'll stand alongside others I'm making for the unveiling in April.'

'Oh, I get it! That's very clever. It's so delicate. How you managed to stretch the metal so thinly in parts – from certain angles, it's barely visible.'

The blacksmith smiles and shrugs off the compliment before muttering, 'Thanks. That's exactly what I needed to hear.'

'Beauty,' I whisper absent-mindedly.

'Quite.'

I blush; I hadn't realised I'd said it aloud.

'Phew! It's warm at this end,' I say, sweeping my long hair to one side to keep it in order – as if the red-hot glow could singe it from such a distance.

'It sure is,' says the blacksmith with a giggle. 'That's the magic for me . . . a little bit of fire and force creates beauty at this end.'

'Hey, what's that supposed to mean, Nessie?' calls the man from his workbench.

'Just hot air down your end, Isaac!'

I laugh. There's clearly a lot of affection between them; it's a honed routine of banter, like a double act. It's refreshing.

I stand and watch as she places the now glowing metal on the anvil and resumes hammering, her shoulders hunched as she inspects the work in hand.

Then my moment of peace is broken.

'There you are! Can I have a word?' pants the voice I've been avoiding.

'With me?' asks the blacksmith. She ceases hammering and stands tall.

Dottie holds on to the doorjamb and taps her chest, fighting for her words.

'Me?' says Isaac, taking in the elderly lady's agitated state.

Dottie's head shakes whilst she gets her breath back.

'I think she means me,' I pipe up reluctantly, unable to think of any other way around the situation. 'Fair play, Dottie – you've got me trapped.'

Both the blacksmith and glass blower stare open-mouthed as I gesture 'goodbye' with a tiny wave to each and exit the forge. Dottie instantly falls into step behind me, her breath well and truly regained.

'Are you going to follow behind me and nag whilst I browse in every stable?' I ask, as we enter The Yarn Barn.

'How dare you think you can return here and cause havoc by upsetting their happiness.'

'Hi,' calls a smiley lady, sitting in an armchair knitting. 'If you need any help, please shout.'

'Thank you, I will,' I say, before turning towards Dottie and adding, 'such lovely folk around here. It's a pity not everyone can show such perfect manners to hotel guests.'

'And that's because they haven't met the likes of you before, Natalia! I know what you're up to and, believe me, I'm *not* going to let you harm him or her. Do you hear me?' comes her barbed reply.

We lock eyes and glare at each other. I swear Dottie grows three inches in height. Despite our differences, and we have many, Dottie has the most captivating blue eyes I've ever seen. I wouldn't ever tell her that, but she must have been a knockout as a young woman, with more than a few admirers, despite her determined nature with its default setting on 'stubborn'.

When I look away, I notice the smiley lady is eyeing us with caution. I give her a weak smile, signalling all is well.

I wander towards a giant wool display in the shape of a cone and gently spin it, admiring the rainbow of colours.

'He's happy now. You leave him be,' she warns, whispering once more.

'You knew how he was with me . . . and yet you stood by and allowed him to get involved with her?' It sounds like sour grapes, but it is a genuine question.

'She's beautiful, inside and out.'

'And I'm not?' I spit back. She knew that would hurt.

'He fell in love, end of.'

'If she's happy stealing another woman's man, then shame on her!' I retort. The hues of the yarn blur as I absent-mindedly spin the display faster, matching my rising annoyance.

'You need to leave. Go back home and find a man of your own. Don't do this, Natalia.'

'Ned *was* my man!'

'He wasn't. Never truly.' Her voice has softened. 'He'd have acted differently, if he had been. He'd have asked you to stay. He never did, Natalia. I used to watch you both as you'd each go through the motions of laughing, joking around, sipping your brandies before disappearing upstairs, nights on end. But . . .' Her gaze drops from mine.

'But what?' I need to hear her words, however painful they are to accept.

'It doesn't matter.' She shakes her head, as if listening to her inner thoughts.

'It matters to me, Dottie.' No armour could protect me from the force of her words. I can't believe I'm standing with her, as vulnerable as I am, longing for Dottie to finish her sentence and confirm what my heart already knows. Boy, how quickly the tables have turned.

'Lassie, he never saw you from one month to the next. He rarely called, unless he wanted company, and ... urgh ... it reflects so badly on him now, I see that, but I'm not sure he truly missed you when you weren't here. The whole thing was a slightly ridiculous love affair, wasn't it?'

'Don't everyone's intimate relationships sound ridiculous when explained by third parties?' I say, picking a ball of wool from the now motionless display, awaiting Dottie's reaction.

'Not when love is involved, no.'

My gaze meets hers, as she reaches to gently pat my hand.

'Get yourself back home, lovey – it'll be less painful there.'

I butter half a fluffy scone, add a smidgen of strawberry jam and a dollop of clotted cream before setting the china plate aside. I don't really want it. I only want one thing right now; sadly, it isn't appearing on this two-tiered porcelain cake stand.

I press my back into the firm upholstery of the couch and feel the button detailing bite at my spine. How has it come to this? Me, a guest in a home that should have been mine.

The number of times we cosied up on that couch opposite, and kissed on that bench by the window – all these books lining the shelves were witness to our every move. If only these walls could talk ... yet not one syllable is uttered in protest at the injustice of my situation.

It's totally wrong to judge another woman, but I can't help but compare myself with *her*. Beauty is only skin deep – but still, how did I lose? I'm the whole package, the potential trophy wife. I'm nearly six foot – leggy, blonde and a professional model. Whereas Jemima is hardly taller than five foot – and slightly dumpy, for want of a better word. I'm educated, knowledgeable about many topics; from what I saw, she's hardly worldly-wise and hasn't ventured far from her place of birth. I thought *I* was his type. But obviously not, given his recent decision.

I've been blindsided by sticking to the rules and playing the game he wanted me to play. How come we had four years together, albeit interrupted, and then ... it's finished? And finished in a manner that seems so brutally sudden? Did he think I didn't care? That I wasn't interested in building a committed future with him? Did I neglect to tell him how I felt? Did I hold back too much and give off the vibe that I was still searching for 'the one'? My heart answers 'no' to each question, but my head admits 'maybe'. Maybe I was stand-offish. Maybe I was too guarded with my feelings. Maybe. Sodding maybe! *Maybe* I could have been a better person. *Maybe* I could have invested more time in understanding the estate. Maybe comes a close second place to the shoulda-woulda-coulda floating around in my head. Phuh! Second place, just like me in the marriage stakes!

I take a deep breath; I'm exhausted. Is wallowing actually helping me to understand? I don't need to answer my own rhetorical questions; deep down, I know.

I put my head back, stare at the elaborate plaster ceiling of the library, and sigh loudly.

Should I stay or head home on the next flight? Home? That's a good joke – this place, right here, was supposed to be my forever home!

I don't want to admit I've lost him, but it's not as if he's simply dating her. He actually translated thought and feeling into action, and *married* the woman. What's the saying? 'Actions speak louder than words.' Yeah, he did just that – for her.

My chest aches at the very thought. My heart is as heavy as lead at the prospect of him being truly out of my life. Where's that independent, strong woman I have always taken pride in being? She's whittled herself into a simpering mess, sitting alone with a tower of tiny crustless sandwiches, scones and clotted cream in the library.

Chapter Twelve

Saturday 5 February

Autumn

'Good afternoon, Natalia, how may I help?' I say, taking a room service call from the Unst Suite. The words come as naturally as breathing. I never have to think about smiling whilst on the telephone – it just happens as I lift the receiver.

'Is there any chance you could call a local footwear store, order a pair of walking boots in a size six, and have them delivered to the hotel by taxi?' Natalia asks. Her voice is tinged with hesitation, before she continues, 'I could order online but it would take a few days to arrive.'

'Of course. Is there a particular time these are required by?'

'Err, not really, but I'd like to venture out for a trek as soon as possible.'

'Is there a particular style you're looking for? Or a price range I should keep to?'

'Something flat and sturdy, please, but not too hard to break in. Neutral colour – nothing luminous! Under one hundred pounds, please.'

'Nothing designer then?'

'No, though I've limited experience in purchasing hiking boots.'

'OK, leave it with me and I'll give you a call as soon as I've found something suitable, with an estimated delivery time. Thank you.'

'No, thank you, Autumn.'

I await the click from her end.

Yes! I bloody love a guest challenge! It brightens up a work shift and slots in nicely between reading the tourist reviews and totting up the room bills. I grab the nearest piece of paper and jot down the basic details: size six, walking boots, quality not designer. Taxi delivery. No luminous colours. Simple!

Immediately the blood is pumping through my veins. I thought this was going to be a slow afternoon shift when I took over from Hannah, though she left me with a bit of a mess to tidy up. Not to mention a list of guest queries to answer. Honestly, looking at the state in which she left the papers scattered all over the reception desk, you'd have thought she'd been run off her feet with requests and difficult customers, when all she had to deal with was a cushy shift covering breakfast service, a few room service requests for poached eggs, and a handful of easy checkouts. I'll be having a word with her if this continues; we have higher standards than that, here at the Lerwick Manor Hotel.

It takes only three phone calls to locate a decent pair of walking boots in the required size in the local area. I'm a bit disappointed at how easy it was. I like a proper challenge; this one doesn't appear to have stretched my capabilities. Though the taxi driver who delivered the boots certainly tested my patience with his rude remark about it being a 'silly job'. I countered, 'What's the difference? Whether it's a person or a parcel – you're still getting paid the full amount.' He sidled out, cash in hand, looking sheepish at that. I wish it had been Levi who'd delivered them – there'd have been no grumbling then.

I total up the cost of the walking boots, the taxi journey, plus a ten per cent service charge and add it to the bill for the Unst Suite. It's satisfying to complete a task, but I prefer the juicy ones which take hours, lead me down rabbit holes, stretch my research skills and test my patience, before succeeding. Maybe next time. As long as I have sufficient resources to meet any difficulties encountered – otherwise it becomes a nightmare, trying to complete a particularly frustrating quest. Pressing 'save' on the bill entry, I compose myself before making the call to the Unst Suite.

'Afternoon, Natalia, this is Autumn calling from reception. Your requested delivery is being sent up to your room in the next few minutes. The total cost is ninety-eight pounds and thirty pence. I hope you'll be pleased with your purchase.'

'Wow! Thank you, Autumn. That was quicker than I was expecting. Thank you so much!'

'My pleasure. Good afternoon, Natalia.'

I replace the handset, with a satisfying smile adorning my features, as Jemima passes through the hallway from the kitchens.

'Everything OK, Autumn?'

'Fine, thank you. Your guest in the Unst Suite asked if I could source some new walking boots for her, which I've done. They've just arrived, so I'm sending them up to her.'

'She's still up in her room?' asks Jemima, leaning on the reception desk.

'Yes, has been since breakfast. Did you receive my email about yesterday's little tour around the gallery?'

'Yes, followed by afternoon tea. Interesting. Anyway, let me know if you spot anything unusual,' says Jemima, continuing on her way.

'I will do.'

I lift the telephone receiver and press the three digits for the kitchen.

'Yes, hello. Can you send whoever is on room service duty to reception, please? We have a delivery for the Unst Suite. Thank you.'

I return the handset to its cradle and remove the boot box

from the shop's logoed bag, disposing of it beneath the desk for recycling.

A young man appears from the kitchen corridor. He can't be much older than sixteen; obviously a part-time weekend job to earn pocket money and tips.

'Hello, could you take these up to the Unst Suite? The lady staying there is expecting them. There's nothing to bring back, just the delivery,' I say, handing over the cardboard box, hoping they are to her liking.

'OK.'

I watch as he takes the box and dashes up the staircase, two at a time, eager to complete his task. Now, *that's* the kind of young person I find helpful – the energetic and eager ones, not those who leave papers scattered across reception desks for others to clear up!

Natalia

Why have I never walked along this coastal path before when I visited Shetland? The scenery is glorious: dramatic cliff edges, a rolling sea and miles upon miles of ever-changing sky. It's exactly what I need after the shock of recent days. I aim to keep busy and make sure my thoughts are occupied whilst the rawness of my situation wears off, and walking will allow me the solitude I need for a little cry or a good bout of strenuous exercise.

A fresh breeze hangs in the air, so I togged myself up in jeans and a jacket after room service had delivered the goodies. Autumn was at the front desk again as I left. Is the woman another Dottie – permanently on duty? Though she did offer me a smile and a hearty wave. I'm not sure Dottie will ever take delight in seeing me appear.

I could have packed my bags and returned home on the next

flight, but for what? To hide away and lick my wounds. I don't wish to crumble into a wailing mess; I need to have a little dignity and accept the situation, as best I can. I've paid for my stay upfront, so why not make the most of it? My girlfriends and family will be waiting with open arms, willing to listen, whether I return to Edinburgh tomorrow or in ten days, as planned. It could prove therapeutic to have time to myself and say goodbye to what might have been. Consciously allowing the process of healing and letting go to begin, before the discussions and dissection of what went wrong. There'll be time to do that later, with those who truly care about me. Celebrities do it all the time when disaster strikes in their personal or professional lives; they jet off to an exotic location and spend the week on a sun lounger. Being here is what I need.

I need to be surrounded by the beauty of nature, to allow my brain to process my tumbling thoughts. After two hours of walking, it's definitely working. I passed a huge Tesco earlier, which I remember visiting once or twice with Ned, and then walked through the residential area to reach this secluded spot; the last dwelling I encountered was a small cottage surrounded by livestock. And now the only question which keeps invading my thoughts is whether I've crossed the boundary of the Campbell family's estate? Or does he . . . they . . . own all this land too!

I find a flattish rock jutting up from the earth, perch comfortably on it and stare across the sea. I have no idea which sea it is, despite calling myself well travelled. But I can still acknowledge the vast magnificence of the open water, which spreads as far as the eye can see. Its rolling waves crash dramatically on to the black rocks below, before the white surf drains back to repeat the process. Time and time again. My emotions feel somewhat the same: the regret, the guilt, the jealousy repeatedly crashing into my thoughts, flooding my brain, before easing back and repeating. This relentless cycle of emotion, pounding upon the rocks of my being, is exhausting, draining and damaging. I have to acknowledge the truth: I've lost him.

I need to give my future some serious consideration, which can only be achieved if I consciously avoid dredging up painful memories. This surprise visit, which I'd meticulously planned, has been blown apart by confirmation of Ned's marriage. I don't chase married men, nor am I a home wrecker, so there's only one thing I can do and that's focus upon my future. I need to make a decision about my latest modelling contract; signing a new one suddenly seems very appealing.

I jump as the sensation of warmth and wetness felt by my right hand registers with my brain. I flinch at the sight of the dog sitting beside me, licking the back of my hand.

'Urgh!' Instantly, I withdraw my hand from the creature's large lolling tongue, wiping it on the side of my jeans. The dog looks up at me as if offended by my actions. 'Don't give me that look. We haven't been introduced, yet you think you can cosy up to me?'

The dog has a beautiful long coat, a dramatic blend of blue-grey and black swirls, with highlights of white, creating a marbled effect. It has a leather collar, but no name tag.

I glance left and right, searching for any sign of an approaching owner coming over the grassy bank: nothing.

The adult dog inclines its head before gently pawing at my knee.

'I don't know you. In my opinion, you're slightly forward, seeing as we've only just met,' I say aloud, as if it understands me.

The dog gives a whine before resting its chin upon my knee.

'Now, that's taking liberties!'

The long eyebrows twitch as the dog continues to stare up at me. Its dark eyes watch my face as if reading my every thought.

'Can you sense my sadness?' I say, tentatively reaching out to pat its head. 'Hey, you don't know a guy called Ned, do you? You're certainly not one of his dogs. I haven't a clue what breed they are, but they're not as loving as you.' My tentative touch turns into a full-length stroke, from head to tail, and the dog shifts slightly under my hand as if wanting more. I oblige. It feels good to sit and receive comfort whilst making a new friend.

I take a deep breath, drawing the beauty of the bay down into my lungs.

If this is to be my last visit to Shetland, then I need to make the most of it.

'Come on, let's walk and talk,' I announce, standing tall and striding out, with my new buddy following my lead.

Chapter Thirteen

Pippa

I grab the seat furthest away from Ned and Jemima; the last thing I want to do is emulate our work meetings at a family gathering. Instantly, I regret my decision. Callie immediately sits down in the vacant seat on my left, at the other head of the table. Great. Never before has my mother's dining table felt so small.

Despite their change of clothes, I can't forget that I see these faces at work, five days a week. My mum thinks it's strange that I deliver on Sundays, but when many of the local shops still traditionally close all day, Rolly and me are supplying a vital service. My only free days are Saturdays and Mondays, yet here I am! I've spent the day in town catching up with friends. Wow, lucky me, the only work-free banter I'll be having over dinner is with the older generation: my uncle to my right, and my parents opposite me, when my mother eventually sits down.

'How's things going, folks?' asks my uncle, draping his linen napkin across his lap. Our usual paper serviettes have been upgraded in honour of Ned's attendance. My uncle looks expectantly around the table as the younger generation stare blankly at each other. No one answers. This is the downside of us all working for one establishment.

'The gallery is doing well, thank you,' says Ned, taking the lead. 'Our guests are enjoying the facilities and the traditional crafts on offer. Pippa's made a great start with the mobile delivery service, and a steady stream of café customers are keeping Callie busy.'

'Good to hear,' says my uncle, eyeing us three cousins once Ned falls silent. 'And Jemima?'

I want to laugh out loud; he asks the question as if checking she's still pulling her weight.

'Yes, Jemima's doing a stunning job. The compliments from customers, praising the artists and the staff, keep rolling in, don't they?'

Jemima hastily nods; her cheeks are crimson. It was a simple question. Maybe she's embarrassed that Ned forgot to mention her in his round-up? Or that our uncle spoke as if she wasn't here?

'Y-y-yes,' she stutters as my mum places a goat's cheese tartlet in front of her. She swiftly exchanges a glance with Ned before busying herself with the cutlery.

My mum finally sits down, having insisted on acting as head waitress and refusing all offers of help. I tune out as Callie explains how much she loves working for Ned and Jemima, though I suspect she's probably missing her beautician work more than she's letting on. I'm more interested in my food than arse-licking, trying to impress my boss, during my rare down time on a Saturday night. I know everyone else is pretending this is a Sunday lunch, with the full roast and trimmings, but it's not. It's a Saturday night, the most precious night of the week; I'm being unselfish by accepting the invite.

I'm distracted by thoughts tumbling around my mind like ball-bearings slamming around a pinball machine. It's one thing to keep repeating the same phrases about family 'being tight', 'having your back' – and even the proverbial 'blood's thicker than water' – but if actions don't back up those words, then surely it's all an act?

I switch to autopilot as I answer the family, eat, hand over dirty dishes and say 'thank you' as warmed plates arrive, laden with food. Would life be different if our birth order were switched? Would Callie feel overlooked and overshadowed, if she were the baby cousin?

I stare at my family, gathered around the table. I'm present but not truly included. Aren't families supposed to support, offer comfort and provide a safe haven, not ignite dramas, guarantee heartache and instil a deep sense of loneliness in the midst of a family gathering? I see only the hypocrisy of family life: spending time amongst those who supposedly love you, yet fail to see what makes you tick. We've never been like other families; we lack the camaraderie, affection or spirit of togetherness. Yet we'll attempt to convince others that our family is where 'life begins and love never ends'.

The Quinn family tree consists of only five blood relations nowadays, we three cousins, my mum and my uncle. And yet my two cousins couldn't name five things about me or even bother to remember my birthday. I've seen more of my family since the gallery opened than I ever have before. Previously, if it wasn't for my mother and her constant stream of family news, I wouldn't hear from anyone between one funeral and the next.

As was proven when Jemima's mum, my aunty, died. Didn't we dutifully pay our respects on the day of the funeral and all promise to look out for Jemima? The next time I saw her was at Granddad's burial, and then afterwards in the solicitor's office. Hardly the depiction of a loving family, given that there was a seven-month gap between the tragic events.

I couldn't say what she'd done in that time; I had no idea that she'd struggled with anxiety, forcing her to take a sabbatical from the tourist board. I didn't even realise she wasn't there each day as I walked past her office on my way into town. I assumed she was coping and would shout if she needed help. She didn't shout, although she clearly needed to. We failed Jemima, but that'll be brushed under the carpet and forgotten about, not mentioned or dismissed as 'nothing', should Jemima appear disgruntled by our lack of support.

I glance around the table at the happy faces; everyone is busy either eating, chatting or laughing.

What have I actually got in common with them, apart from our DNA? Both my cousins are 'girly' girls, more sociable and amenable than I am. But there's no strength without a struggle; this family has definitely made me stronger. I do my own thing, keep myself to myself and maintain my independence, unlike others I know. I don't ask the family for anything. I don't borrow. I don't lend. I certainly don't seek validation from the endless 'thank yous' the others crave. What I'd like is to be seen, to be heard, and for my efforts to be recognised – without the various family clichés forever attached to my name.

Callie, the eldest, was always Nanna's favourite, Jemima, the next granddaughter, was Granddad's chosen one – and then there's me, the baby of the family, who was forced to tag along with her older cousins, whether she wished to or not. The little one who was bossed about, told what to do and constantly corrected. I resent being the youngest, it feels like I'm chasing their coattails, trying to grab the remnants of attention from whichever direction they fly. Basically, the odd one out, the proverbial cuckoo in the Quinn family nest, the one who doesn't feel like she truly belongs.

'So, Pippa, any news?' asks Mum, clearing my empty dessert dish from which I've inhaled her extra boozy sherry trifle.

I look up, surprised that anyone has addressed me. 'Not really – nothing different from last week.'

Jemima's gaze flits towards Ned. It seems to be her new habit since getting married; everything is silently referred to Ned, as if seeking his approval. Our Mima has never come across as being dependent before; I sense she's lowered her barriers in recent months, or has she other issues to contend with? Maybe she's working too hard, juggling the new ventures, and it's taking its toll. Jemima was never one to share her concerns but there's definitely been a change since they got married; maybe that's the inevitable evolution of things. Solitary and fiercely independent, easing towards a mellow acceptance of a partnership. I'm not sold on the idea, but if it's working for them, who am I to quibble?

'How's your mobile bread bin doing, love?' asks my dad, much to my annoyance, as a bin sounds so derogatory and trashy.

'The Bread *Basket* is doing very well. It's early days, but the customers seem happy with the delivery system I've established. I have a good sense of what they like now and so I've been suggesting something a little new each time, depending on their tastes,' I say proudly. My inner sense of satisfaction blooms at the chance to share this week's success.

'I imagine it's boring tootling around all day,' mutters Callie, scraping her trifle dish.

I whip around in my seat; how dare she! 'Actually, I'll have you know it's very interesting. You might think you get a variety of customers coming into The Orangery but essentially they're all similar – your coffee-shop types. I get a true mixture of customers out on the road: I have my regulars already, but there are always newbies at each stop, some dropping by for an emergency loaf or fresh buns. I even had a birthday cake order on my first day.'

Callie winces. I assume I was a little eager to rectify her error.

'Honestly, Callie, you've no idea. I've even managed to organise a deal for two elderly customers who only want half a loaf each because they live alone. A shop would insist on the sale of two whole loaves. Well, not me. Now I call that innovative. I've worked it in their favour so they're both happy with the arrangement and are going to be regular customers.' I finish speaking, only to find Jemima and Ned looking at me, goggle-eyed, from the other end of the table. 'Sorry, but I'm not having her put me down because I'm not swanning around The Orangery every day.'

'Sounds great!' mutters Callie, pulling a childishly comical expression despite her thirty-three years.

'It is, thanks ... you might want to try it one day!' I want to bite my own tongue off, the second the words spill from my lips. I don't need to look at Ned to know his cogs are whirring. Foolish woman, stop talking!

Autumn

'How are you finding it here?' asks Pippa, pouring herself a large glass of rosé.

We're enjoying a quiet nightcap in the library. I couldn't refuse her tonight when she knocked on my door, just before eleven o'clock; she looked like she needed company, standing there with her wine bottle in hand. I guess she was listening out, awaiting my late return to my room after I finished my afternoon shift. We could have stayed in our rooms, but there are no guests around at this hour, so where's the harm? It's not as if we'll suddenly become raucous – it's just a quiet chat and a tipple.

'It feels like I've been here for ever, which is a credit to the Campbells. I can't complain, the staff seem happy, the facilities are top notch, and my shift rota is reasonable – which is a novelty in this industry. I was dubious at first about living on site. I've had some bad experiences throughout my career, but it was a no-brainer in this case; my accommodation, food and wages came as a package deal. I'd have been a fool to turn it down. I simply need to make it work for me and not slip into old habits.'

'Such as?'

I hesitate, unsure whether to share, but recognising that she seems a pretty frank and open person.

Pippa waits patiently, possibly sensing my discomfort.

'I have a tendency to run myself into the ground at times.

You know the story, you take too much on, say "yes" when it should be a firm "sorry, but no" – and then I run around like a headless chicken, juggling tasks and slowly getting bogged down and eventually stressed out. I left the cruise liners because I burnt myself out, trying to please everyone. Ridiculous really.'

'And that's a lot of people to please, on board those big vessels,' adds Pippa sympathetically.

'Precisely. My "can do, will do" attitude, coupled with striving for perfection, can be my personal strength but also, sadly, my undoing.'

'You'll need to nip that in the bud then, Autumn – especially if you know the triggers and can monitor it in some way.'

'I can and I definitely will. I sometimes don't notice it creeping up on me, but then I'll notice that my fingers and knuckles are becoming cracked and dry from the excessive handwashing; it's one of the things I tend to do.'

'Ouch!'

'Exactly. It looks worse than it is, but it's not a good look when guests see your hands every day. But I'm on it, this time. It's been non-stop since I started, what with a string of late nights, early shifts, first guests arriving . . . I'll sort out a weekly routine for myself, which'll definitely include seeing more of my sister, Sienna, and her family. Which reminds me, I haven't phoned her – and I promised to call her a week ago. Oops!'

'You'd better get a night out sorted, then – though it's good to hear you're enjoying the job.'

'I am. The guests seem very nice, and I've managed to answer a few requests, which brightens up the day.'

'Requests?' Pippa looks astonished at the very mention.

I spend the next few minutes explaining the concept, and how enjoyable I find it when I'm able to successfully deliver and complete a task.

'It takes all sorts; I think of it as a challenge or a game,' I say, before taking a sip of my gin and tonic, which I've brought downstairs from my own private stash. 'Some people like the simple life, with complimentary toiletries ticking their boxes, whilst others want dedicated room service right, left and centre. You can never tell.' I plump up the row of decorative cushions beside me, before eyeing the ones on Pippa's couch opposite. I'll rearrange those before we leave.

'It happens all the time. The more expensive the hotel, the more extravagant the requests – and the more cash that is splashed in an attempt to please the individual guest,' I explain, much to Pippa's horror.

'Urgh! I couldn't do it. I'd be scrambling for cover behind reception, attempting to get away from a ridiculous guest asking for … for … actually, what is the weirdest thing you've been asked for?'

'One woman asked if I could switch the curtains in her room as she hated red tartan,' I say, recalling a previous hotel job. 'Which is strange, as it's almost a given in terms of room decor when you're travelling through Scotland.'

'Jesus wept! Anything personal?'

'Oh, yeah, loads. I don't usually share, as it's a courtesy to keep confidences about such things, but this was years ago now. There was a time when a male guest requested a pair of imitation handcuffs, only for the woman accompanying him to call reception an hour after we delivered them, asking for a hacksaw. That called for a poker face, I can tell you.'

'It gives me the creeps when I hear you talk about people requesting specific items – you don't know if it's for health reasons, cosmetic or fetish stuff,' says Pippa, clearly cringing.

I've only seen her around of an evening, after her delivery shift, so it's been nice to find out a little more about her. I was surprised when she said she'd had a miserable evening earlier, amongst family; Jemima and Ned seemed in high spirits when they returned.

Pippa sits open-mouthed as I entertain her with my funny tales, each one more outlandish than the last.

This is the kind of social connection I've been missing. It's the equivalent of a quiet night in, after a long shift, where friendships are formed and the wine slowly disappears. It feels like chicken broth for the soul after a long day.

'I didn't even know what a Shetland gue actually was until Mr Drummond made a request for a music lesson. I'd have called it a string lyre. Apparently, they look similar but are very different instruments,' I say, explaining my requests from earlier in the week. 'A simpler request was a pair of walking boots for a female guest.'

'And did she use them?'

'Yeah, she came striding down the staircase and was gone for hours after their delivery. So, all's well that ends well,' I say, pausing, unsure whether I should even be mentioning a certain someone. I decide not to elaborate; when I make a promise I keep it.

'What would your hotel request be?' asks Pippa, her eyes sparkling with a devilish gleam.

'Now, there's a question and a half. I might have to get back to you on that one! And yours?'

'Phuh! After tonight's obligatory family dinner . . . some decent company. Ah, look at that, you supplied that too! Well done!' She tilts her glass in my direction as if toasting my presence.

'In that case, I'll raise my glass straight back at you, Pippa. My much-needed request would be for a happy balance between work time and play time, and this tonight –' I gesture around the library – 'was definitely needed and is priceless to me!'

'Cheers and good health to the two of us!' announces Pippa, leaning forward to clink glasses.

We both burst out laughing. I have no idea what her family situation is, or whether the big bosses are included in her remarks, but I vow to phone my sister tomorrow and make plans with my own kith and kin for one night next week.

Chapter Fourteen

Wednesday 9 February

Natalia

It takes four days for me to muster the courage to leave my suite again, escaping the same four walls in search of space and another burst of beauty outdoors. It wasn't that I was avoiding anyone, more that the full force of my sadness bowled me over. I suddenly became aware that not only has Ned gone from my life, but my immediate future as I imagined it has dissolved too: potential offspring, family connections and life's milestones – all squashed and erased, leaving unexpected voids in my world. One day, those events will happen – but with someone else, not Ned. Sadly, that realisation has pushed me into the darkness just a little bit more. I've come down for breakfast in The Orangery each morning, made it to the dining room for a light bite at lunch time, but I've opted for room service come nightfall. I've filled my time reading, sleeping and having a little cry when it suits. I could phone home, but they'd all bombard me with requests to return. I don't want to; I need time to come to terms with what's happened, lick my wounds and allow them to heal a little before going home. I'm used to forcing a smile in front of a camera lens, but I don't think I can fake it with family and friends just yet. With six days remaining of my fortnight's break, I'm determined that today will be a good day.

Midmorning, I sidle around The Orangery, head along the

paved terrace and swiftly navigate the steps leading to the lawned area. My feet pound the grass as I walk along the length of the allotment wall. It forms a boundary line between the estate and the local allotments, though I've never chosen to venture through the gate in the wall that connects the two. Ned would often take that route through, tending to his beehives kept on Dottie's plot.

Underfoot, the springy lawn quickly changes to bark chips and gravel. My inner voice continues to berate me. I should have taken more interest in Ned's world, should have walked the estate alongside him during inspections and visits to the tenant farms, maybe then he'd have viewed me as . . .

The figure sitting beside the fishpond jolts me from my private thoughts. I come to an abrupt halt as my heart rate soars. Instantly, I want to turn back. But I can't; Jemima has clearly seen me. I can't even pretend that I'm heading somewhere else, because apart from the twisted orchard of stunted apple trees there's nothing else for me to be visiting. Could I change direction, take a sharp right turn, and make it look like I'm heading for the interconnecting allotment gate? Sadly not; I'm going to have to brave it out.

Her chin drops, her shoulders stiffen and her gaze flickers nervously in my direction, awaiting my arrival. I'd hoped for some quiet time, reflecting on recent events beside the rippling water, but now, with her seated on the edge of the wall, I'm in an uncomfortable position. I don't wish to ignore the woman, or cause her offence, but the irony of enjoying her hospitality whilst recovering from a broken heart isn't wasted on me. Maybe I was wrong to have stayed, and should have caught the next flight home?

'Hi,' I say, reaching the raised stone wall of the pond.

'Hello, Natalia, how are you?' She glances sideways, attempting to engage, while I focus on the central fountain scattering droplets on to the troubled surface below.

'Fine. And you?' My tone is wooden, as is my manner; I can't help it.

'All good, thank you,' she says, inspecting her fingernails.

Obviously, I'm not the only one feeling the tension. Silence descends.

As I continue to walk, my gaze moves from the fountain to the koi carp dipping and diving beneath the surface. I'm not being surly, simply pretending that she isn't present, so I can enjoy the solitude and the koi carps' ghost-like beauty.

'Dottie mentioned how much you'd enjoyed browsing in the gallery last week,' says Jemima, her voice drifting across the water.

I slowly walk around the pond until I'm on the opposite side, aligned with her back.

'What are you doing?'

'Sorry?' Jemima whips around to face me.

'I said, what are you doing? I realise that this . . . isn't ideal, but you don't have to make small talk for my benefit. I'm happy to enjoy the pond in silence, without your attempt at polite conversation making it awkward between us.'

Jemima inclines her head sharply to one side, looking at me quizzically. 'Natalia, I'm just trying to be friendly, despite what you assume. I don't see why there has to be a war between us. And, given that I was enjoying the peace and quiet of the grounds first, I thought it only polite to acknowledge your arrival. What did you expect me to do – ignore you?'

I don't answer; I'm not buying her speech.

'Is that what you'd prefer?' she asks.

I shrug, hoping to display nonchalance, but suspect I look childish.

'Sorry, but I don't play such games.' Jemima lifts her head and looks squarely at me.

'Phuh!' I scoff. I hear how ridiculous it sounds, but I can't help myself. There's no going back for me; this is the woman who put a stop to my future dreams. The woman who took my place beside Ned. Who moved in on a man I care . . . *cared* for and had every intention of marrying when the time was right.

I look at her staring at me across the rippling pond. This feels like a stalemate situation. Or is it checkmate if the king is taken? I suppose that depends on whether I storm off like last September, leaving her in peace. Why is it always me who makes way for others in every situation? Surely I'm the innocent party in this twisted triangle, and I've paid the price in more ways than one.

Deep down, I want to rant, scream, shout, wail and sob at her for simply existing. For robbing me of my spot amongst the portraits lining the staircase. I want to hate her. I want to empty my anger at her. My guilt, my self-disgust, my self-loathing for losing the only man I have ever truly loved. This woman showed me how much I loved him, and yet she knows nothing of my pain. I want her to admit to being my Nemesis, my lifelong blame puppy who has chewed up all my dreams and spat them out, but I can't. Because the one man I put above all others loves her. Not me. And I can't hate him for that.

'It seems to me that you want all-out war between us, Natalia. Well, I'm not prepared to grant you that. I haven't the time, energy or the inclination to pursue such a toxic relationship. I don't pretend to understand the nature of your relationship with Ned. It's not something we discuss, as I respect my husband's private affairs before he met me, but this . . . this is simply ridiculous.' Jemima stands tall. For a moment I think she's going to march around to my side of the pond but she doesn't, she keeps her distance.

'Ridiculous, is it? You wouldn't think that, if you were the injured party. If you'd planned a trip to surprise Ned, only to find the surprise is on you! I think then you'd definitely be more understanding of the hurt this situation has inflicted on me.'

'You hadn't seen him since last September – and before that it was the previous Christmas! Excuse me for suggesting it, but yours was hardly a regular relationship, was it?'

My jaw drops. The cheeky mare!

'I don't need to justify myself to the likes of you!' I protest.

'Maybe not, but please don't peddle a sob story either. We're both mature women, it's fairly obvious that the connection lacked commitment from one side or the other.'

'You have no idea! If it makes you feel better, then carry on kidding yourself. Ned and I were solid until you showed up, complete with an orphaned duck and a rusty bike, bleating about a sodding pumpkin!' It's official, I've lost control; there's no reining this in. My heart is pumping, my palms are clammy and an untold strength has revived my spirit. 'It's ironic that this is the exact spot where we stood embracing on festival night. You were long gone, after scraping together a handful of sentences in a pitiful attempt to say thank you for hosting the festival. Believe me, it's hardly something you need to praise the local gentry for doing; their heritage dictates that they entertain the locals with annual events!'

'Dictates? Do you seriously not know Ned Campbell? No one dictates anything to him; he's his own man – always has been, always will be!'

'Phuh!' I snort.

'I'm not entirely sure you know him as well as you think, Natalia. For as much as you paint a picture of a harmonious couple, I witnessed what really happened that night.'

'How?' Surely, she's bluffing.

'From over in the copse. I came down here after I left his office, having interrupted your tête-à-tête. I saw Ned sit on the edge of this pond, saw you follow and attempt to engage him in an embrace ... yes, you can look shocked, but I saw it all. He didn't embrace you, Natalia. In fact, quite the opposite. He merely sat there, immobile, whilst you attempted to cajole him into reigniting your affair from the previous Christmas. And then, when he didn't provide the answers you wanted . . . you stormed off, swearing at him.'

I'm speechless. Never in my wildest dreams did I think that she might have been present. How could I have imagined her cowering amongst the twisted branches of the apple orchard? I'm totally lost, I have no comeback.

We stand staring at each other across the expanse of rippling water. The woman I wished to be, staring hard at the woman I've become. I want to cry. The emotion and frustration of that night swiftly return, like a re-enactment that will haunt me for a lifetime. Why had my life taken such a turn at the precise moment when I realised how much I cared for him?

'You can stand and stare all day, Natalia. The reality of the situation is we're never going to be friends, but at least acknowledge that I do have your interests at heart. Whether you like it or not, I'm not the enemy!'

'That's big of you!' I say churlishly.

Jemima shakes her head, conveying her frustration. 'I'm trying here, so give me a break. Do you think I'd have opted for this to happen? The ex-girlfriend turning up and booking into the hotel when we're still virtually newly-weds trying to organise the beginnings of our life together. I'm sure there are a million women out there who would have kicked up a fuss, but I didn't . . . honestly, on hearing the news it was me who suggested you continue your stay. And for what? To be ridiculed like this for showing you some kindness.' Her shoulders sag, her chin lowers.

I've lost the battle; her declaration is bruising in its honesty.

I'm now stuck, rooted to the spot on the opposite side of the pond, staring at a woman who is trying her best in a situation she didn't create. I see her in a new light, maybe a glimmer of what Ned sees.

'I'm going to leave you to enjoy the solitude,' she says. 'I've had more than enough.'

I can't speak as she moves away from the edge of the pond, her slow heavy steps crunching on the gravel.

'Jemima!' I call, demanding her attention.

She stops, turns and waits for me to rant some more.

'Thank you. I realise this can't be easy, but I'm still grieving for what might have been.'

She nods, her gaze fixed on mine.

'I can see that. These past few days, I've tried putting myself in your shoes so many times – and still, I can't imagine how swiftly your life has changed.'

I give a sharp nod; I recognise her sincerity.

'Enjoy your solitude, I'll catch you another time, Natalia.'

With that, she's off. Heading towards her home . . . *their* happy home and future.

Chapter Fifteen

Pippa

Rolly's windscreen wipers can't cope with the torrent of rain which the gales are unleashing on us. The raindrops sound like bullets hitting the bulky metalwork, which started as comforting, but now sounds sinister. It's relentless, like a personal attack on our existence in the barren surroundings of this particular stretch of the A970, heading towards Brae. Any other day, I'm happy driving through such a desolate area; the wide road is banked on either side by emerging bracken, providing a picturesque view through my windscreen, topped with a blue sky, but not in weather such as this.

Today, I peer through a wall of water hammering the screen and bouncing off the bonnet. My knuckles are white from gripping the steering wheel, and my back aches as I lean forward in my seat, my seat belt stretched from the reel, attempting to navigate the next metre of tarmac. My speed is officially a snail's pace, but it makes no difference; the safest thing to do would be to pull over and sit out the passing storm. This ferocity can't last much longer. It'll knock my route times out, but I can't imagine I have a throng of customers queuing in this weather.

I begin scanning the roadside for a safe parking place or a designated layby – not a grassy verge, for fear the soft earth would succumb under the weight of my bulky vehicle, creating an emergency I could do without.

Suddenly, without warning, the steering wheel goes wobbly

in my grasp. The loss of control is instant and what was a difficult drive now feels treacherous, as a deep rumbling noise occurs at the rear end of the van. What the hell! My foot slowly presses the brake pedal; I'm scared stiff of causing Rolly to aquaplane. Do I attempt to turn into a skid or out? The steering wheel wobbles under the pressure of my hands as I slowly draw to the edge of the tarmac and flick the switch for my hazard lights.

I kill the ignition and wait until my heart rate has calmed. I'm guessing at a flat tyre. I have two choices: sit tight until the rain subsides, or risk the elements to view each tyre.

The rain defies gravity and lashes down in a horizontal manner as I stare at the flat rear tyre, and reality dawns. I've waited a full ten minutes before venturing out, but the weather shows no signs of letting up. The rain drenches my flimsy jacket in seconds. There's no point trying to dodge the inevitable, I'm already soaked to the skin. Forked lightning would be the only addition to this dismal scene.

'Flat' is an understatement. This flat tyre redefines the meaning: the metal wheel trim is flush to the tarmac and the black rubber has slumped, creating a thin line that proves how straight the ground truly is. I kick the wheel hub for good measure, as seen in every decent TV drama.

I glance in both directions: not a vehicle in sight. Great! I'm on an open road, with a van full of freshly baked bread, and there's little chance of a passing vehicle. It's mid-morning, mid-week and mid-storm! Crying isn't going to help matters.

Do I wait to flag down a passing motorist, or do I phone Ned pleading for assistance? Phoning the MacDonald trio might be an option; I might get a quicker response from them. This scenario has never been discussed. Despite all the planning, even Jemima didn't envisage this situation occurring, did she?

I'm truly stuck! I've no idea where to locate the spare tyre, and even if I did, I wouldn't know how to change the wheel. I haven't a toolbox or a sturdy jack, and Ned never issued me with the details of a recovery breakdown company, which is a definite oversight on his part. The only bonus is, I won't go hungry if I'm here for hours awaiting rescue.

I open the rear door and climb inside, hoping to locate a surprise stock of spare tyres, a secret team of breakdown specialists or a stash of tools which I've previously overlooked. Nothing, other than bread trays.

I grab a bannock from the nearest wicker tray and begin nibbling – comfort eating – and stare out at the grey day beyond the open doors.

I didn't sign up for this. I used to love the sound of the rain on the glazing of The Orangery, but this is unnerving. How do I defend myself if an axe murderer drops by to offer fake help? I wouldn't stand a chance – not that Shetland has many killers prowling the heather. But it's not as if the police are close at hand. If I call Ned or the MacDonald trio, it'll take at least thirty minutes for them to reach me.

I stare at my half-eaten treat; I could do with some butter – I've never enjoyed bannocks cold and dry.

The low clouds are darkening as the rainfall becomes heavier by the minute. If I were at home, wrapped in a snuggly blanket, I'd feel blessed. But this feels desperate, verging on dangerous, given the isolation.

I can't stand here all day; I need to call Ned, sooner rather than later, if I'm to catch up on my delivery route.

I brush the crumbs from my wet jacket front, pull my mobile from my pocket and locate Ned's number; best get this deed over and done with. He's not going to be happy! And that's another understatement.

'Hello!'

A welcome voice interrupts me as I'm tapping the screen; what perfect timing.

'Hello!' I dash to the open doorway of the van, where I meet a bedraggled Levi peering from beneath a yellow sou'wester hood, his hands clutching the slippery fabric and fighting to hold it in place as the rain teems down before his face. 'Levi – what a godsend!' I've never been so grateful to see him in my life. I direct a silent prayer towards the heavens.

'Are you OK?'

'No,' I say, sounding weak and somewhat feeble. I hastily point towards my predicament – alas, indicating my lack of knowledge.

'Don't worry, the spare will be fixed underneath the van, in a cradle. It's best you climb down from here and stand on the verge. I'll go grab my tools and a jack. OK?'

I'm not about to argue, so I do as he suggests.

I stand against Rolly's nearside, protecting myself from the worst of the rain, but it still soaks me at a constant rate.

'That jack's a bit heavy duty, isn't it?' I say, watching Levi swiftly lift the bodywork.

He's returned from his taxi, armed with equipment. His broad back is bent, his wet hands busily working, his hooded face turned away from me as he shouts over the noise of the weather.

'It certainly is. It's a hefty hydraulic one . . . I can't afford to find myself in trouble whilst taxiing folk around. Could you imagine being en route to an important event, or catching a plane, and your taxi gets a flat. It takes up vital space in my boot, but it's worth it.'

'I'd say.' I fall silent as he cranks each wheel nut with a long-handled gadget.

'It also comes in handy when I spot others in need, like your-self.'

'Thank you, I owe you a favour. Ned and Jemima hadn't considered such an emergency, so I wasn't prepared.'

'Think nothing of it,' mutters the yellow sou'wester.

His words strike a chord; this is a big deal for me. I don't forget an act of kindness, ever. I'm hoping Levi continues to focus on his rescue mission, as my eyes are brimming with tears. Most people don't give me the time of day, as my reputation precedes me, yet he didn't hesitate to stop mid-journey when he saw Rolly parked in a strange place.

Apart from my parents, I can't count on many people to show such kindness. Most people steer clear of me; their opinion is usually jaded, based on hearsay and misgivings rather than anything I've actually done. I guess they've dismissed me, without realising that every child is unique. I'm an individual, not just a clone of my loud-mouthed relatives. If only people knew the truth. I'm as sensitive as they come; everything matters to me. Sadly, my habit of erecting emotional barriers conveys the wrong impression, causing others to believe I'm a hard-nosed cow.

'There . . . all done!' says Levi, releasing the hydraulic jack and lowering the vehicle on to its replacement tyre. 'Are you OK?'

'Me?' I baulk at the question. He's obviously more intuitive than I give him credit for. 'I'm fine.' My usual ballsy tone returns, chasing away my previous wobbly moment. 'I'll be giving Ned and Jemima what for, sending me out in a vehicle with no backup.' I kick the replacement tyre, averting my gaze purely to save face.

Levi nods, giving me a knowing look. There's no fooling him. But still, it was a good try to cover my true appreciation.

'I owe you a drink when I next see you out and about,' I say, eager to get back on schedule.

'No worries. I'll wait for you to drive off first,' he says, collecting his tools together.

I scurry around the side of Rolly and see Levi's empty taxi parked a short distance ahead, hazards blinking.

'Ah, look ... the sun's come out,' he says, gesturing towards a break in the dove-grey clouds.

A shaft of heavenly light streams through.

'When did it stop raining?' I ask, baffled by the sunshine.

'Ages ago. Did you not notice?'

'Nope. I was too busy panicking ...' My words fade as I rein in my honesty.

Levi gives a deep throaty laugh. He's not stupid. I need to watch myself around this one. I'll be showing my softer side before long, and that will never do.

Autumn

I pick at the dry inflamed skin nestled between my fingers. The cracked flaky layers lift and peel, to reveal a tender new, shiny layer as yet undamaged by soap and water. I wince as I tug a strip of old skin connected to the undamaged flesh. I need to stop, otherwise my hands will become increasingly unsightly as the redness spreads to the backs of my hands, clearly visible, for all to see. Hardly appealing to guests who are checking in, or to my colleagues. Twinned with my collection of pocket debris, I can't deny the signs.

That's usually when the questions begin, as others notice the patches on my hands and bombard me with numerous solutions and recommendations for hand creams, lotions and soothing balms. I've tried them all; none work. The solution is to avoid the problem in the first place: stop all the handwashing. Not when necessary for hygiene, of course, but I need to rein in my escalating obsession with perfection. It's over the top, not necessary; I simply can't help myself. In fact, I lie. My routines aren't directly linked to perfection, but they've become a part of my identity. My reputation for neatness, order and timely completion of tasks. What's that old saying – 'If you want something doing, ask a busy person' – that's me, summed up in one line. A busy person, always on the go and ready for duty. I can't describe that sense of achievement I get when I provide what others need, spot the loose thread, spy an anomaly, or correct something that's out of place. The tasks that others don't see, which they walk past for fear of dirtying their hands, I do them, without hesitation – before washing my hands again. A trait which I can keep in check; but if I take my eye off the ball, my hands display the damage within a few days.

I open my desk drawer in the reception's rear office, grab my go-to hand cream and slather my hands until they are saturated in white lotion which refuses to disappear. I sit for a moment, fingers splayed on my knees, close my eyes and breathe deeply. A method of coping I learnt long ago, when I taught yoga in my spare time on the cruise ships, and which I've used ever since. If I empty my mind of all thoughts, focus on the here and now for a few minutes, then the urge to go and wash the lotion from my hands will pass. It will pass. It should pass. It has previously passed. Breathe and exhale. Repeat.

'Autumn!'

My eyes snap open on hearing Jemima's voice.

'Sorry, were you taking a minute?' she asks, clutching a pile of papers to her chest.

'I was. I meditate throughout the day – it helps me to stay focused and motivated,' I say, my usual smile readily appearing.

'Good idea. After the day I've had, I could do with a touch of that myself. Anyway, sorry if I've interrupted you, but Ned wondered if you could file these accounts in the suppliers' cabinet?'

'Sure. Pop them down there and I'll get to it,' I say, rubbing my hands and ensuring the excess lotion has disappeared, forming a protective layer.

'Thank you, I've put them into alphabetical order, which will help,' she adds, plonking the paperwork on to the spare desk.

'That's half the job,' I say cheerfully, mentally slotting the task into my 'To-do' list.

'Do you do that often?' she asks, as I straighten the pile in case it slides.

'Sorry?'

'Your meditating . . . is it often, throughout the day?'

'Yes. A few minutes here and there. Coffee breaks, between phone calls or checkouts – that sort of thing. It doesn't have to include repetitive chanting or sitting crossed-legged, which many people associate with meditation.'

'Mmmm, you'll have to show me, or talk me through it, one of these days. Sounds interesting.'

'Any time,' I say, before adding in a hushed tone, 'I haven't seen much of Ms Muir in recent days; she appears to be staying in her suite.'

'Don't worry, I have,' says Jemima. Her bright features darken, like an eclipse, at the very mention of the woman's name.

Jemima is then gone like a flash from the rear office, leaving me relieved that she is open-minded in accepting my explanation. I can do without people probing into my business and counting how many times I wash my hands every day.

'Hello?' I hear the tinny ding of the reception bell and imme-diately stand up straight, smile in place, to answer.

'Good evening, Mr Drummond, how can I help you?' I ask our guest from the Whalsay Suite.

'Any chance of booking another gue lesson with the same chap from last week?' he asks, drumming his fingers on the reception countertop.

'Certainly. Do you have any particular day in mind?'

'No. Though the sooner the better, as my month's stay will be over in no time.' His stern expression returns, he hasn't worn that look for a few days.

'Of course. I'll telephone straight away.' As Mr Drummond

ascends the staircase, I grab my polishing cloth from under the countertop and wipe away the smeary fingerprints he's left behind.

As I fold the cloth, I can't ignore the itchy dryness creeping between my knuckles. The skin looks red raw.

Chapter Sixteen

Sunday 13 February

Pippa

'There's no reason to get into a strop about it!' mutters Callie, as we traipse through the network of corridors, having come from the third-floor office. 'It makes good business sense.'

'I'm not in a strop. I simply don't understand the point of the task,' I retort, trying not to air my view that it's been organised purely to piss me off.

'Jemima's simply being savvy – and forewarned is forearmed, is it not?'

Have I actually agreed to let Callie ride alongside me for an entire shift? I can't imagine so – I don't even offer her a lift home after a work shift, and that's a short distance. It makes perfect sense, but why couldn't it be Aileen learning the ropes? Seeing as it's Callie, it feels like an encroachment, as always.

I don't answer. As we walk, the events of the last five minutes replay inside my head.

'You never know when an emergency situation is going to arise. Remember, we'd have had no option but to close the café last Christmas Eve, if you hadn't stepped in to cover for Isla,' Jemima had said, looking encouragingly at me along the length of the table.

Ned had remained silent, as if memorising the proceedings for a later discussion with his wife about employing family.

'I'm happy to help out,' Callie had said, her gaze flickering between both bosses.

I'm not, but I doubt that's the answer they were hoping for. I did what I did last Christmas out of necessity, for Isla. The young woman was beside herself, thinking she'd caused a tragedy by arguing with Lachlan, her tosser of an ex-boyfriend. Any decent person would have offered to help out when Jemima called. You can hardly say no in such circumstances.

'Pippa?' Ned's voice had broken into my thoughts.

'Sorry. I don't see the need . . . for this.'

Jemima had exchanged a glance with Ned before she spoke. 'None of us can predict a medical emergency . . . a rumbling appendix, a sudden bout of flu . . . even an upset stomach would mean you shouldn't be serving food to customers, Pippa.'

I'd nodded in agreement, because words failed me.

'Excellent. That's settled then. If you could take Callie out today, show her the basics, explain the route, the storage set-up and how the till works – we'd appreciate it, as it'll cover us for all eventualities in the future,' Jemima had said, holding my gaze.

I don't remember saying goodbye, or standing up, or even replacing my chair beneath the meeting table.

'Pippa!' Callie's curt tone brings me back to reality as we reach the tradesman's entrance leading to the cobbled yard.

'What?'

'We're supposed to be family, surely it won't harm you to be pleasant for one day?'

'Me?'

Callie stares, providing my answer. 'Err, well, I don't mean Jemima, do I?'

'Phuh! You've got a bloody nerve. Being the eldest cousin doesn't make you the boss, you know.'

Callie attempts to yank the door open. I swallow a chuckle

as the bottom edge sticks fast. I knew it would; it always does.

'Bloody thing!' she snipes, covering her embarrassment.

'This is probably the heaviest task of the day,' I say, hauling the portable water tank into the café's sink to fill it. 'I wouldn't fill it higher than this mark, otherwise you might struggle to carry it outside to Rolly.'

'Rolly?'

I ignore the snigger in her voice. 'Given that I work him five days a week, I figured I had a right to name him. We're a team . . . whether others see it like that or not.'

As I watch the water level steadily fill, the weight on my arms increases; I know from experience not to take my eyes off the gushing tap. If the tank fills too much, I'll need to call Isaac from the forge to carry it for me, and that always feels like a fail – not how I want to start the day.

'Up to there . . . right,' I say, hoping she's taking in the details, but knowing Callie won't be needed any day soon. I have no intention of not being present to prep Rolly. I screw the black cap on tightly, giving it an extra turn, ensuring I don't slop cold water down my front when I move the tank.

'And this is for what?' asks Callie.

'Washing your hands throughout the day, wiping down the countertop, and general cleaning when it's quiet.'

'You clean?'

I heave the water canister from the stainless-steel sink. 'Do you think Ned arranges for Dottie, housekeeping or the Monday cleaning team to pick up after me?'

'No, but . . .'

I raise an eyebrow at her; I get it. I assume I'm in for a day of subtle digs and pointed remarks with undefined meanings.

'Anyway, apart from the wicker bread trays, this is the only thing you'll need to install before setting off. I usually do this first, so you don't forget, or else you'll risk running out of water during the shift. It puts the customers off, seeing breadcrumbs scattered on the countertop or floor. This way.' I don't wait for a reply, or for her to question me further. I steady the heavy canister on my thighs and begin the slow walk towards Rolly.

Today, I don't struggle with The Orangery door, as my assistant happily holds it wide, which I admit is easier. I cross the cobbled stones, open and pin back Rolly's rear doors, before walking the canister up each step and sliding it along the floor.

'I'm not expecting you to follow what I do, I've found my own prep routine, but Jemima wants you to see the basic checks I carry out each day. I tend to grab the wicker bread trays once the canister is secured under the counter unit.' I swiftly open the custom-built unit, slide and connect the canister, much like a magician's assistant does, making exaggerated hand movements at all times, giving Callie a clear view of my actions. I'm not acting up that much – well actually, maybe a little. I don't expect Callie to grab a notebook and take details, but if I'm required to spend my valuable time on an extensive 'show and tell' she'd best be watching. I won't be repeating today's exercise; a work experience apprentice was never my intention.

Who knew that explaining your every move added so much time to each task? I'm relieved it's a Sunday; leaving the gallery ten minutes late won't be such an issue.

'Strap yourself in, please,' I say, gesturing to the seat belt as Callie climbs into the passenger seat. 'The radio doesn't work, so if you want music you'll need to make sure your mobile is fully charged,' I say, pre-empting the icy silence which I'm not prepared to fill by ad-libbing with glib remarks and polite chat.

We trundle along the A970 – I seem to spend my life on this road or the A971 nowadays – but I'm happy to focus on the road ahead, knowing we've got many stops before reaching Heylor and parking outside the tropical fish store.

'Are you still angry about Gran's engagement ring?' asks Callie, breaking our permafrost silence.

'Nope.'

'Still annoyed that Jemima inherited a legacy from Granddad, and we didn't?'

'Nah.'

'Miffed that I stole Jimmy McArthur from you?' she asks, knowing that might still sting – he was my first love, after all.

'You didn't steal him! I dumped him good and proper. You got him on the rebound!'

'Yeah, right. Like that's what happened. You got dumped in preference for me, and it's narked you ever since.'

'I deal in facts, actually. Another fact regarding that incident is that you were pathetic enough to date a sixth former younger than you, because the lads of your own age weren't interested.'

'That's a lie!'

'Is it, Callie?'

'Yeah, and you know it.'

I shrug. Grateful for the swift return of silence.

'Is your mum alright?' she asks, filling the void.

'Yeah. Your dad?'

'Yeah.'

Silence. This is going to be the longest shift in human history if we continue in this manner.

'Look. I wish I didn't have to complete today, but I have no choice. So, let's make it as simple and as easy as possible. I'm not interested in getting pally with you, Callie. I'm not interested in small talk either. I'll stick to explaining the route, chatting about the weather, and talking you through the regular customers. Anything else doesn't interest me. OK?'

'Same here. We might be blood, but it's not as if we three

cousins are tight knit. I only ever see the rest of yee at weddings, christenings and funerals – it's no skin off my nose.'

'Good. I'm glad that's sorted. Now, can we get on with the rest of our day?' I haven't taken my eyes off the road ahead throughout that little speech, but I sense her acceptance; her frame has relaxed into the passenger seat rather than the rigid stance of a few minutes ago. 'There's no pretending: blood might be thicker than water, but that doesn't mean we get along, or even like one another.'

'I like you,' says Callie.

'Yeah, right.'

'Pippa?'

'You don't need to pretend. I get it.'

'Don't you like me then?'

'Not really. I've always found you bossy and overbearing, to be fair.'

'And Jemima?'

'Now there's a question. As my boss, she's been fair – I can't complain. As my cousin, I've always found her difficult to get along with, and somewhat tiresome.'

'Tiresome?'

'Yeah! Like you're going to argue her corner whilst we're alone, are you?'

'No, but I wouldn't say tiresome, more . . . insular and difficult to get to know.'

'My mum says it dates back to her parents' divorce.'

'Yeah, my dad says the same.'

We both fall silent.

Have we actually agreed on something?

Our arrival back at the gallery can't come soon enough, but the experience hasn't been half as tragic as I'd imagined when we left this morning. I slowly draw Rolly into the cobbled yard at a snail's pace, anticipating that a small child might dash out from one of the stables at any moment.

'So that's that,' I say, pulling on the handbrake. 'A quick ten minutes of unloading the empty wicker trays, and then we'll be off home.'

'Cheers. The time has flown; it seems like only a few hours since we were prepping.'

'It does. I suppose I could have given you a quick road test . . . it only takes fifteen minutes to get used to handling him around the lanes.'

'Thanks.'

'No worries.'

I undo my seat belt, busying myself; this scenario feels as awkward as the goodbye on a first date.

'Pippa?'

'Yep.'

'Sorry.'

I look up, to find her staring directly at me, her gaze fixed on mine.

'Everyone expects cousins to get along, but I don't really know you, to be fair. As a teenager, I was always first in line for babysitting duties, but since then . . . well, I rarely see you. I've heard stuff on the family grapevine . . . a mention of pumpkins and loose change on the allotments . . . but you never know what's true, hearing titbits from third parties. Today's been nice, in a strange kind of way.'

'Th-thank y-you,' I stutter, unsure if she expects me to repeat the sentiment. I can't, so I won't.

She should be grateful that we survived the day without killing each other.

Natalia

I have no idea where my sudden burst of energy came from, but this morning I woke up feeling alive. Not the drained specimen that I've felt on previous days, but the all-singing, all-dancing version of me that you experience on summer days when the warmth kisses your skin and you feel you'll live for ever.

With only a few days remaining, I don't want to waste my day over-analysing the whys and wherefores. After breakfasting in the dining room, I decide to take immediate action, to explore and have fun with a night out. I drop by reception before I can change my mind and return to my suite, banishing the thought of slumping back into comfy pjs, bare-faced and with unkempt hair.

I have no idea where I'll be heading; it's not as if we ever frequented the bars and pubs in the town centre. Ned always opted for nights in or fancy restaurants, but tonight I'm willing to mingle with the good folk of Lerwick and hope someone points me in the right direction for a girl to enjoy a cocktail or two.

I'm pleased to find Autumn at the desk, as smiley as ever; so efficient in every aspect of service, such a doll.

'Hi, Autumn, could I order a taxi to take me into town at eight p.m.? Levi is a name I remember from days gone by.'

'Of course. Would you like a call to your room when the taxi arrives?'

'No, I'll be down here bang on eight o'clock. Could you request the same driver for a return journey at say eleven o'clock? I'll arrange a pick-up point with him during our journey into town.'

'Absolutely. Anything else?'

'Any suggestions of where to go for a decent cocktail?'

'Personally, I'd choose The Dowry – the food is to die for, and the bar is bright and cheerful.'

'I'm not really after food, I'll be eating here beforehand.'

'OK. The Thule bar is a friendly place, very down to earth, with decent prices for cocktails and a huge selection of flavoured gins.'

'Thank you, would you mind jotting those names down, please?' I ask, before adding, 'One last thing. Could I arrange a late checkout for Tuesday as my flight doesn't leave until early evening?'

By the time eight o'clock arrives, I'm giddy at the prospect of a couple of espresso martinis, a friendly chat with bar staff or the locals, before returning to my suite. It might be Sunday night, but surely a Sunday night can be the new Saturday night, if I wish.

I've spent a leisurely day pampering myself from top to toe, with a delightful bubble bath, styling my hair and taking plenty of time to apply my make-up – as if it were a professional photo shoot and modelling assignment. And now, I feel good; there's a distinct resemblance to the true me, the woman who arrived here unexpectedly, nearly two weeks ago, full of hope and vitality.

I've opted for a classy wrap-over dress, nothing too glamorous, as I'd prefer to mingle rather than stand out and attract attention. Attention is the last thing I am after; genuine chat, a decent drink and a few hours away from my suite are what this girl needs.

As I descend the staircase, I find a new face on duty at reception. I'm delighted to think that Autumn has a life outside her job. A career isn't the be-all and end-all in life, as recent events have proven. Which reminds me: I need to contact my modelling agency first thing tomorrow to discuss signing my new contract. A decision that's been made far easier thanks to recent revelations.

'Good evening, your taxi is waiting beside the entrance steps,' says the young woman, as I cross the tiled hallway. I love the way the crystal chandelier sparkles at this time of night.

'Thank you, I appreciate that. Do I need a key to access the front door after hours?'

'Your room fob has the necessary key – the gold one.'

'Thank you.' I quickly check my key fob. She's correct. A small gold door key, which I haven't used.

'Enjoy your evening, Ms Muir,' calls the receptionist as I exit the hotel.

The cool night air surprises me after the warmth of the hotel foyer, and I'm glad I won't be walking too far. As promised, there is my taxi.

'Good evening!' calls the man, getting out of the driver's seat to open the rear door as I approach.

'Evening. Levi, isn't it?'

'Yes.' I hear the surprise in his voice, as I slip into the taxi and he closes the door.

He returns to the driver's seat and settles himself, before pulling his seat belt across his torso.

'Have we met before?' he asks, glancing into the rear-view mirror, his piercing blue eyes demanding my attention.

'No, not previously. I've heard others praise you in the past and remembered the name, it's unusual.'

His gaze flickers and he blinks at me in the slender mirror. Ah bless, not used to compliments. I settle back in my seat as he starts the ignition.

'An espresso martini, please,' I say to the barman, who instantly pays me attention, ignoring the two men who are waiting to be served. I send a silent apology their way, knowing how frustrating that can be. Each one smiles and returns an accepting nod. I take in my surroundings in the meantime, there's a fair-sized crowd filling The Thule; many are in groups, but a handful of singletons stand around, watching the scene before them. Do I remain at the bar? I'd prefer a quiet table.

Other women tell me they hate going out alone; they feel self-conscious at being judged, or worse. I've never had an issue. Maybe because I've jetted around the world, spending time alone in numerous hotels. I've generally received the best service in restaurants and bars by going solo; serving staff always ensure you are well looked after. And I show my gratitude by tipping generously.

I spot an empty table a short distance away.

'Excuse me, could I possibly ask you to bring it over?' I say, gesturing towards the vacant spot.

'Sure.'

I smile. I love people who are obliging, they make the world a nicer place.

I cross the floor, settle myself on the padded seat and grab my mobile from my handbag, purely as a distraction until my drink arrives. I collect a fiver from my purse ready for the barman's tip.

Chapter Seventeen

Autumn

'Pass me your glass,' I say, gesturing towards Pippa's empty tumbler clasped to her chest.

She leans awkwardly across the bed, holding her glass at an angle as I pour a generous helping, careful not to slosh it on my clean duvet. Leaning against the wall like a couple of teenagers, we've turned my bed into a makeshift couch for our late-night tipple. There were hotel guests quietly reading in the library this evening, so we reluctantly accepted it as out of bounds.

'Anyway, everyone assumes we must be the best of friends, almost like sisters, given there's only us three cousins . . . "and so close in age" – folk always mention that. Phuh! If only they knew.'

I empty the remains of the wine bottle into my own tumbler, grateful for a steady hand and a decent measure. It has been a trying day, my feet ache with the constant demands of guests and bosses, but now I can finally chill out.

'Like that, is it?'

'You bet. Callie's never been interested in getting to know me before now. I tend to shy away from her, if I'm honest. She acts all bolshie and superior, yet she's come down to the earth with a sodding bump in recent months. Boy, how the mighty have fallen. I don't like to pry but she's gone from working in a posh beauty salon, which I believe she partly owned, to asking our Jemima for a job.'

'She replaced you, didn't she?' I ask, unsure if my knowledge is accurate.

'She did; I'd been waitressing in the coffee shop since opening day, until Rolly arrived. Though between me and you, I didn't much like The Orangery, which is why I'm surprised that Callie has managed to stick it for this long. I doubt she'll last much longer.'

'What didn't you like?' I ask, settling at one end of my bed and using the wall as a back rest, matching Pippa's relaxed posture at the far end.

'It's not exactly a taxing job, is it? And hardly the dream job of any child I know. It's mind-numbing clearing dirty crockery, wiping tables and repeating the same three phrases every hour with a smile: "yes, all baked fresh today", "we close at half five" and "you'll find cutlery on the side counter by the till". Seriously, I wanted to pull my hair out, some days! And don't get me started on the constant rudeness, the mess some folks create eating cake – and all for what? A measly basic wage. I shouldn't complain, I was grateful when Jemima offered me the position, as I hated my previous admin job.'

I nod along as she speaks. I get where she's coming from: working in hospitality means we bear the brunt of everyone else's bad day when it suits them. Thankfully, I can look beyond the negative clutter which litters my day.

'Surely there were some highlights to a waitressing shift?'

Pippa grimaces, takes another swig of her wine, before answering. 'Isla's pretty generous with the leftover odds and sods from the cake displays. She'll let you take a couple of pieces home if the remaining portions aren't up to scratch at the end of a shift. She's not mean in that way, which was always a bonus. There's rarely any bread left over; she's got that down to a fine art, which saves on wastage.'

'Maybe it's Isla's management that Callie's enjoying. She might be used to stricter bosses or unpleasant colleagues – it all takes its toll, when you have to grit your teeth to get through eight hours a day alongside them. A basic routine, secure employment within a family business and a few perks might be all she wants.'

'It's possible, I suppose ... though she's a crafty one, is our Callie. You know when people behave one way in public, purely for show and to suck up to others, only to do and say the complete opposite in private?'

I give a nod. I know that sort. My gaze is snagged by the pile of debris from my pockets, sitting on the dressing table; I was heading towards the bin when Pippa knocked on the door. Admittedly, the pile probably doesn't seem huge to anyone else, but the collection represents today's obsessional wanderings: a duck feather, a tiny coal chipping, plenty of grey fluff and loose threads, mingled and rolled into a ball, courtesy of my pocket lining.

'Yeah, that's her. When our granddad died last year, I saw another side to her. She was so materialistic when we sorted through his possessions. "I want *this* ... I want *that* ..." She bagsied our nanna's engagement ring before she even got inside Granddad's apartment.' Pippa halts, checks herself before muttering, 'It doesn't matter. Let's just say she shocked me that day, and I'm not going to forget about it or brush it under the carpet.' She shakes her head before changing tack. 'And you, are you liking it here?'

'I'm loving it. I get a real buzz from seeing the guests enjoying themselves, and sorting out their issues or requests.'

'Any more unusual requests?'

'Not today. Though one woman ordered a taxi to head out into Lerwick, alone.' I raise my eyebrows. 'Now, who does that around these parts, and on a Sunday night?'

'No one,' mutters Pippa.

I mentioned it to Jemima in passing; her reaction had been exactly the same.

'I was surprised, but each to their own. I suggested a couple of bars where she can enjoy a cocktail or two. Though she'll be in safe hands as she specifically requested Levi – don't know how she knows him, but it was hardly a difficult request.'

'She asked for Levi?'

'Yeah, taxi control confirmed he was working the night shift, so they gave him the booking.'

Pippa falls silent, before knocking back her wine.

'Are you OK?' I ask, knowing that's all the wine I had . . . gone.

'Yep, fine.'

She doesn't look it, but I continue. 'Anyway, Hannah took over reception from me before his arrival time, so I didn't see what outfit she was wearing when she went out, but I bet she looked drop-dead gorgeous.'

'No doubt. Though I doubt she'll be as stunning as Ned's ex-girlfriend – now she was a proper model type. A thick mane of blonde hair, which gave her the appearance of a goddess, and legs up to here.' Pippa gestures towards her armpits.

'What was her name?'

'Don't know. I only saw her once, at last year's annual allot-ment festival. She came swanning in like a celebrity sort – I thought she was here to open the fête, she looked that glam, even in casuals.'

Interesting.

'And you don't remember her name?'

'I never actually spoke to her. I'd had a few cross words with Dottie earlier in the day, so I was spitting feathers over an accu-sation she'd made about me. When I went back for round two with Dottie, I spied the pair of them chatting. A bloke in the beer tent – a tenant farmer on the estate, I think – explained who the blonde woman was.'

'She must have been pretty miffed with Ned marrying so quickly afterwards – October, wasn't it?'

'Yeah, Halloween.'

Pippa seems distracted. She was bright and eager to chat, but now she's content playing with the rim of her empty tumbler. Is it something I said?

'Are you enjoying your new role?' I ask, returning to a safer subject.

'Absolutely. I miss working alongside Isla, but now I get to stamp my own personality and flair on the service I provide. Sometimes the customer queue disappears in seconds, other times people linger for a little chat after being served. I suspect they don't get out much or have many opportunities to socialise with others. I make an effort to spend an extra few minutes chatting about their dog's appointment with the vet, last night's TV, or their grandchild's wobbly tooth. It's great, every day is different. And you?'

'So-so, you know how it is. Some days are easier than others, but it's my own fault; I promise too much and attempt to deliver perfection,' I say, sliding my one hand from view, knowing that my cracked knuckles will give the game away.

'You said previously you'd try to get a better balance,' she says sympathetically, before gesturing towards the end of the bed. 'Could you pass me my bag? I brought a bottle with me, in case you only had gin.'

I pass it over and she pulls out a brand-new bottle of wine, unscrews the top and fills her tumbler before waving the bottle towards my glass. I shake my head; I'm only halfway through. She rests the open bottle on my nightstand, before indicating that she's still awaiting my answer.

'I know. I am trying, but it's difficult when it's your nature to please. You say yes to a small task, then yes to another unexpected job, and before you know it your "To-do" list is growing rather than shrinking. It doesn't help when Hannah doesn't pull her weight properly, but then I instantly make excuses for her because she is quite young, isn't she?'

'She is, but she needs correcting if her behaviour impacts on you. Have you seen your sister this week?'

I shake my head, pulling a glum expression. I feel bad each time I'm reminded that I keep reneging on my promises.

'I've had six missed calls, though – does that count?'

'No, but I'm the same. My parents don't live too far away, yet I jumped at the opportunity when Jemima suggested living in. It gives me a chance to move out and have some independence. Though it would be better if there were more of us living up here.'

'Sure, though I can't see others being invited at present. Unless your Callie joins us,' I say, knowing that suggestion will reawaken her objections.

'I sodding hope not!' Pippa splutters and then frantically dabs at the wine on her front. 'Seriously, I can do without the likes of her around me twenty-four/seven.'

'Wow, there's no love lost between the cousins, is there?'

Pippa shakes her head dramatically. 'Nope, and I can't see the situation improving any day soon,' she mumbles, eyeing me while circling the rim of her glass with her fingers.

Natalia

My evening flies by in a blur of laughter, cocktails and good company – exactly what I needed. Life is for living, and tonight I'm definitely living dangerously. I've met and spoken to more locals in one night than I ever have on previous visits to Shetland. But now I'm ready for home – I give a little giggle as we stumble from the bar, hand in hand, at my allotted time to meet my prearranged taxi on the Esplanade.

'Good man,' I mutter, on spying my taxi ready and waiting. 'Come on!'

I notice Levi's blond head turn towards me, and he performs

a double take as I get nearer; this time, he doesn't jump out to assist with the rear door.

'Evening!' I say, settling in and scooting along the back seat, making room for my new friend.

'Back to the Lerwick Manor Hotel?' asks Levi, glancing into the rear-view mirror.

'Please,' I say, giggling as my friend wraps his arm around my shoulder and pulls me close. As I twist to nuzzle into his neck, the tribal tattoo poking above his shirt collar looks intriguing.

Chapter Eighteen

Tuesday 15 February

Autumn

I'm gasping for breath by the time I reach the Sumburgh Suite. Not surprising, as I've just raced up a flight of stairs from reception, unable to comprehend Dottie's garbled telephone message.

On my arrival, she's waiting in the open doorway, dressed in her cleaning pinny, duster in hand. I don't wait for her to speak; I can tell she's annoyed by the expression on her face. I sweep past her to see for myself. The Sumburgh Suite is in total disarray, as if trashed by a rock band passing through for one night on tour. The four-poster bed is a mess, with a sizeable mountain of pillows, duvet and tangled sheets billowing from the canopy.

'Who the hell has used this suite?' I demand, shocked by the sight before me. 'It isn't assigned to a guest.'

'Nobody. I only came in to dust as a matter of routine.'

'Well, someone has!' I say, pointing out the obvious to the startled Dottie.

'I don't remember doing it last week, though I did the week before,' she says, wringing her yellow duster between her hands.

'Surely this hasn't lain undiscovered for that length of time!' I walk around the bed to view the decorative ornaments knocked from the dressing table and bedside cabinets, now lying smashed on the floor. The curtains are erratically half drawn across the three bay windows, the rug is rumpled on the plush carpet and every picture is skewed upon its hook. 'Does Jemima know?'

'Good Lord, no. I phoned you straight away. She and Ned can do without an upset such as this – his dear mother loved this bedroom.'

'Was the door locked?' I ask, moving around the room to survey the full extent of the damage.

'Secured, as expected,' says Dottie, pulling her keys from her pocket.

'And the bathroom?' I say, moving towards the adjoining en-suite.

'Same.'

'If not worse,' I observe, on seeing the contents of the luxury hamper smeared and squirted all over the ceramic tiles, vanity unit and porcelain claw-footed bathtub.

Dottie follows me, to stand staring in horror at the scene before us.

I continue my questions, trying to get a handle on the situation. 'Is the room key still at reception?'

Dottie shrugs. 'I'll go and check.'

I couldn't possibly ask her to go on such an errand, so I hastily retrace my steps: along the corridor, down the stairs and across the tiled hallway. My heart is pounding as I nip behind the reception counter and view the key hooks. The Sumburgh Suite key is present and correct – shiny and hanging on its allotted hook. Who the hell has borrowed it? Plus had the chance to replace it afterwards? I reach for my mobile, take a photograph as proof and head back upstairs to inform Dottie. My mind is racing with every conceivable explanation. Is it a prank? Are the Campbells consciously testing housekeeping? Has any member of staff been skiving for a few hours of each day? But why would anyone do this?

I remain flummoxed on returning to the dishevelled suite. I find Dottie standing before a window, staring out across the grounds below. She turns as I cross the room and say, 'The key's hanging up.'

'Well, I'll be damned! I didn't expect this!' she mutters, clearly upset by her discovery. 'The shower has been used, the toilet too, and I reckon those sheets are soiled as well. This won't be a prank pulled to raise a giggle. Someone has stayed overnight in this room. Don't the Monday cleaning team do their job properly by checking vacant rooms?'

Did I hear her correctly? Does Dottie know about the other cleaning team doing a weekly flit? Monday's her day off, so Ned discreetly employs another team of cleaners to lighten her load.

'We've no choice but to lock the door and view the CCTV,' I say, unsettled by the prospect.

'You've got CCTV in here?'

'Not in the suites, but there are cameras covering the public areas from reception, up the staircase and along each landing.'

'No one told me!' Dottie's horrified expression says it all.

I don't answer; I can't imagine why they would feel the need to mention it.

'The modern age of technology is beyond me, you're filmed everywhere you go nowadays,' she splutters indignantly.

'That's because some folks don't behave in a manner appropriate, as proven,' I remark, briskly ushering her from the room. 'Let's lock this door and head back to reception. Though I've no idea which day or night we should be focusing on.'

'It was Valentine's Day yesterday, so I'd work backwards and pray we find it sooner rather than later,' says Dottie, watching as I turn the key and secure the suite.

'My God, the woman has no shame!' scowls Dottie, her nose inches from the screen, peering at the CCTV footage for the umpteenth time. 'I'd be having serious words if she were my daughter!'

I'm lost for words too after witnessing the footage, but I'm taken back by Dottie's outspoken attitude. I always expect elderly folk to refrain from passing judgement, but there's no holding back with this old dear.

'Will you mention it to your friend?'

Dottie scowls at me, as if confused by my question.

'In our day, we showed more respect for other folk's possessions, but nowadays it's grab all you can, when you can, and bugger everyone else – regardless of the consequences,' says Mungo from behind us, making me jump. I turn to see that he's sidled in on the quiet. Dottie doesn't seem surprised by his presence. When did he join the viewing? Does he recognise the woman in question as Dottie's friend's daughter?

'Bugger-all respect nowadays, Mungo – that's simply how it is,' adds Dottie, unperturbed by his choice of words.

'Excuse me, us ladies have as much right to our jollies as the men, Dottie,' I say, doubting the older generation will agree with me.

'The footage clearly shows what happened. They came in together, collected the key from reception, then went upstairs for . . . a bit of how's-your-father. She leaves the suite in the early hours, leaving him alone for two more hours. After which he sneaks down the staircase, returns the key and leaves.' I appreciate Mungo's commentary rerun, though I doubt I'll forget the sequence of events.

'The question is . . . what do I do now?' I ask, glancing between the pair. 'She's supposed to check out later today.'

'You can clearly see who it is, and when it was,' says Dottie, drawing back from the screen. 'The question being . . . who's the chappy?'

'A guest?' asks Mungo.

'Why leave then? He'd have returned to his room, surely.' I'm confused, my head is spinning with names and faces.

'The bloke in the Whalsay Suite?' asks Dottie, before adding, 'He looks pretty similar in build.'

'That's not Mr Drummond ... the guy in the footage is younger. Much younger.'

'A scallywag, from what I can see,' adds Mungo, stroking his grey beard. 'Probably dragged up, without being taught any manners.'

'I have no idea, but you're both ahead of me. Doesn't the next step lie with Ned or Jemima?'

'Ned,' bleats Dottie.

'Just Ned,' repeats Mungo, talking over Dottie's response.

'Are you sure, given the circumstances?' There's much eyeballing occurring between the pair. This is followed by a unanimous nodding of heads, confirming my next step.

Pippa

'That's not fair, you're as bad as they are,' I snap, turning away to stare from my driver's window at the surrounding bracken-covered landscape, taking in the signs of fresh growth and budding.

'You can't deny it – you've got form, Pippa. Some of us remember last autumn when you were rude to Dottie about the allotment keys. You were spiteful to Jemima about her prize-winning pumpkin, and you never pass up a chance to have a snipe at Callie.'

No one ever trusts me; everyone assumes I'm always up to no good. If only Levi knew that earlier today I've bought and delivered a bottle of milk and six eggs to an elderly lady who I heard was housebound. Plus I gave a young child the loaf his mum had asked for, despite him not quite having the right amount of money.

I turn around to speak but think twice on seeing his calm

expression. I won't win this one by getting agitated; there's no point arguing with Levi. I decide not to tell him about my acts of kindness to strangers whilst I've been driving Rolly.

'You can act all innocent with me, but I've seen both sides of you, Pippa. Isla was grateful when you opened up on Christmas Eve, when she needed to go to the police station. And Verity said she was taken aback by the sympathy you showed that morning whilst serving the artists their morning drinks. See – I don't forget things like that either, so please don't tell me I'm just like the rest. I'm not!'

He's got a point. It was my go-to defence – said to the wrong person, this time.

'Sorry, you're right. You're not!'

'Ha, ha . . . come again?' he jests, elbowing my folded arms.

'Meh! You heard.'

'Sorry, I didn't catch that. You were saying . . .?'

'I'm not repeating it. Next time, listen up when I'm chatting.' I continue to stare from my driver's window, sensing he's grinning from ear to ear. He's kind of cute, in an annoying way.

'Don't worry, your secret is safe with me,' he jibes, pushing my buttons a little further.

'What are you even doing here, anyway?' I say, narked that I've talked myself into a corner.

'Having my lunch break and annoying the hell out of you – though I suspect that wasn't the reason you invited me to join you for an early lunch in a layby off the A971. Though it beats sitting outside the taxi rank and eating my sandwich on my tod. Plus you've got fresh bread, if I need another butty.'

'And?' I throw him a suspicious glance, wondering at his intentions. I've noticed that our friendly waves and headlight flashing, like true roadies, has increased with each delivery day.

'And nothing . . . that's all. Boy, are you a snap dragon when someone's trying to be nice.' He takes a bite from his cheese butty.

'Mumph! It doesn't happen very often, that's why.' My sand-wich box remains unopened in my lap.

'Which comes first – the chicken or the egg?' he says, whilst chewing.

'Ha, ha, you know there's an answer to that question, don't you?'

'Likewise, there's an answer to your predicament too.'

'Don't pretend you know it all, because you have no idea what I've encountered growing up!'

'We can all blame everything on our past, but there comes a day when you have to leave your childhood behind and focus on the here and now, regardless of the scars.'

I pout – not attractive at my age – but Levi's yapping like the older brother I never had. Can't he sense that I've got my guard up, that my boundaries extend way beyond my actual height? I'm a long way off from being where I wish to be in life – where I can be open, totally honest and true to myself, without being ridiculed or overshadowed – but I'm also a country mile away from admitting this guy's right. My issues and insecurities could give the San Andreas Fault a run for its money; Levi has no idea of their depth and potential damage.

'Just be yourself and do you,' he whispers conspiratorially.

'Easier said than done.'

'Not really; I've done it for long enough. There's a knack to it, which soon becomes a habit.'

He's possibly right.

'And who do I fall back on, if the shit hits the fan?' I ask defensively.

'You'll find your safety net.'

'What, like you and Mungo?'

'Exactly. He might be many years older than me, but he's got my back. He and Dottie would act as my safety net, should I ever need them.'

I'm not sure if that's slightly sad, or endearing. The psychology is easy: a couple without children providing a lifeline to the son they never had. Or a fit healthy guy relying on two old codgers to prop up his world if disaster ever strikes?

'You are more like father and son than best friends,' I add, hedging my bets.

'I've still got my own parents, but I've a different relationship with them. Mungo and Dottie know me as a real person rather than the imaginary son my parents expect me to be.'

'That's exactly it! My family expect me to fit into the box they've constructed and labelled for me, always following in my cousins' footsteps . . . and sadly, I don't fit inside it, because I'm me! I've tried to make myself fit – but they can't get the lid to close.'

'My parents are the same. They don't see the real me, just the illusion they've created in their heads, which I'm supposed to live up to. But I can't match the weird imaginary twin they've created. Mungo and Dottie totally accept me for who I am, nothing more.'

And that's my issue.

'Everyone tells you to be yourself, but family soon complain if you actually are.'

'Precisely,' says Levi, giving a knowing nod. 'Be you, do you and enjoy yourself.'

I rip the lid from my sandwich box and tuck in. Maybe issuing a lunch invite to Levi wasn't such a bad idea, after all.

Chapter Nineteen

Autumn

'Come and have a look … seriously, they're beautiful,' says Dottie, her watery eyes twinkling with excitement across the reception desk.

It's just gone midday. Has she forgotten about the drama unfolding in the Sumburgh Suite this morning?

'I'm busy holding the fort,' I say, unsure if others take their role as diligently as I do. I get that they see a lot of me swanning around, titivating rooms as I pass through, but I'm on a tight schedule as much as the next person. And today I need to urgently speak to the boss about a difficult situation.

'It'll only take a minute. What harm can it do?' she says, making me feel guilty for being a stick in the mud.

Can I deny that dear little face? She beams as excitedly as a child, yet has the wisdom of more than eight decades. I hope I'm half as enthused by the novelties of life when I am her age.

'Come on then, Dottie, there'll be no peace otherwise.'

'This way, it'll be quicker,' says Dottie, scurrying towards the main entrance doors. It's not a route she usually takes, but her excitement has definitely got the better of her. 'Quick now!' she urges me.

I am being quick, but I have to make sure reception is left in a suitable manner. I glance at the switchboard panel: no incoming phone calls, no room service calls awaiting attention. I grab my keys and sidle from behind the polished desk, bringing the hinged countertop down behind me as if signalling 'closed shop'. I'll be all of ten minutes, nothing more. I scribble a quick note, making sure my handwriting is neat and legible, and prop it against the reception bell.

I hasten to catch up with the elderly lady who has convinced me to abandon my post in order to see the new arrivals. I'm half expecting it to be a waste of my time; I'm underwhelmed by the prospect of a livestock delivery, wondering why Ned and Jemima have been on tenterhooks about it all week. Personally, I can't see the fascination in sheep; they do very little, apart from stand, stare and chew. Though being part of the Campbells' great venture, and showing willing when it's necessary, is part of my personality; if I can encourage others, then I always do.

As I descend the stone steps under the watchful gaze of the ornate lions, Dottie is long gone. She must have scurried off, forgetting she'd invited me to tag along. I bend to retrieve an elastic band lying on the gravel, shoving it into my pocket. Should I return to my duties, or follow Dottie like I promised? Poor dear, she probably has little else in her daily life.

I turn right, following the sweep of the gravel driveway and heading towards the private side of Lerwick Manor. I rarely venture this far; I always regard it as the Campbells' personal estate. I've seen the vast open pastures beyond and, in recent days, I've watched a section being measured, fenced off, and a large barn erected. But I haven't explored any further, until now. Now, I can see the empty livestock wagon parked by the manor's boundary wall. There is a small gathering of artists from the gallery, standing alongside the Campbells, with Dottie now centre stage. Beyond them, the sectioned field is no longer empty but . . . I stop in my tracks and stare open-mouthed. In the field, gracefully grazing on tufted grass, isn't the herd of Shetland sheep I was imagining – all picture-book plump and frolicking – but six alpacas. Two fawn, two russet, one brown and a black alpaca, all peacefully grazing in a huddled group at the far end of the field.

'They're not sheep!' seems a stupid remark to make as I approach the admiring group, who are all clearly enraptured by the new arrivals.

'Aren't they beautiful?' says Dottie, her face radiant with sheer pleasure.

I glance at the silent gathering; even the two herdsmen seem bewitched by the sight.

'Does Verity know?' I whisper to Nessie, who stands alongside the wooden fencing enjoying a well-earned break.

'Nope, and I'll not be breaking the news to her. She's expecting twenty sheep from which to gather a supply of Lerwick wool. Our Magnus will have his work cut out shearing these beauties.'

'I can't see him manhandling these boys in the same manner as he does those sheep of his,' adds Isaac, leaning over her shoulder. 'Though it'll be worth seeing Floss' reaction to her new herd.'

'That dog has never baulked when faced with any animal, and it's my guess she won't be starting now. Look how she responds to Crispy duck! Not many dogs could resist giving chase to fowl when they have the chance,' says Nessie.

She's right, on all counts. Only yesterday, Verity mentioned how she's spent the entire winter attempting to spin fleece. I'm not sure if alpaca fleece needs spinning. And as for Magnus and Floss, at least one of them is certainly abreast of the Campbells' plans; the other simply complies.

We fall silent and contemplate the various conversations which are probably happening right now in several quarters, when Ned wanders over.

'What do you all think?' he says, gesturing towards the herd.

The alpacas are looking lively and showing their appreciation of their new home by galloping around in a giraffe-like manner, all gangly legs and lolloping necks.

'Quite amazing. I never imagined seeing alpacas in Shetland,' I confess, unsure if Ned is aware of the surprise most of the staff have had.

'They're perfect for the environment. Tough little creatures, with protective coats which'll give plenty of fleece – and they can withstand pretty harsh conditions. Though we won't be leaving this herd outside to face the elements, as we probably would have done with sheep.'

'You're stabling them?' asks Isaac, pointing to the newly erected barn which appears extremely generous as overnight accommodation for only six animals.

'We are, but in the end stable for now ... the one Mungo used as Santa's grotto. It's perfectly situated, with fresh water, and a solid shelter. A slight variance from our original plan, but apparently alpaca wool is growing in popularity and demand. So we thought, why not introduce them to Shetland? It'll save competing with the traditional wool trade here.'

'Makes sense,' adds Nessie, before adding, 'is our Magnus on board with this new herd?'

'Of course. It was his idea, actually. Once Jemima got wind of his suggestion, she started honing her knowledge, and she's become quite an expert.'

'She'll be expanding the herd in no time. I bet you're expecting a delivery of females to roll up, aren't you?' jests Isaac, with a coy smile.

'I wouldn't be surprised by anything my wife conjures up. This entire venture has grown out of her ideas whilst weeding an allotment, so I can't knock it. Though we'll need other males; these have all been castrated to ensure they're nice and calm, shall we say,' adds Ned, pulling a comical expression.

'In that case, Jemima will be organising and advertising alpaca walks around the estate before you can blink,' I add, unsure if I should be interrupting the big boss.

Ned looks at me, bemused and slightly confused. 'Alpaca walks?'

'Yes, they're a big thing back on the mainland,' I say, taking in his look of surprise. 'Like dog walking but with . . .' I gesture towards the new herd. 'Guests happily pay to walk a mile, learn about the species, and then settle down for a cosy afternoon tea – that's a whole new venture in itself.'

'Autumn, you've done it now!' jests Nessie, glancing between Ned's shocked expression and my gleeful one. 'You'll be taking bookings for bed, breakfast and birthday treats!'

'A herd that earns its daily keep whilst growing your harvest of fleece sounds perfect to me,' says Isaac, with a joyful belly laugh.

'I'm amazed. Is that actually a thing?' asks Ned, glancing between us for confirmation. We eagerly nod in unison. 'Well I never. Nothing surprises me nowadays, honestly. If there's a market for such events, I'd best get Jemima investigating the possibilities.'

Isaac guffaws again. 'I doubt she needs your prompting, Ned. She's never one to be behind on the info front, is she?'

'You've a point there,' agrees Ned, sidestepping us to go and rejoin Jemima – and no doubt query her insight regarding alpaca walking.

'I'd best be going too,' I say, aware that my quick peek has been longer than I anticipated. 'Catch you later, folks.'

I hotfoot it back towards the hotel reception; not that I wish to return just yet, but needs must. It takes me all of two minutes to reinstate myself behind the well-organised reception counter. Instantly, I spot the insistent flashing light on the switchboard console: five unanswered calls from our guest in the Unst Suite. Now what am I supposed to do and say to her? Or is it better to somehow divert the situation until I've spoken to Ned? I'm overthinking this, it might simply be a request to pre-book her taxi for Sumburgh airport. Though if she's an irate guest thinking she's been ignored, I might need my wits about me to avoid having a worsening situation on my hands.

I swiftly retrieve the handset and immediately try to return the call: engaged.

Chapter Twenty

Natalia

I've a pounding headache. My left arm feels as weak as a kitten – not the pins and needles, sausage fingers kind of sensation, but more a dead weight. I look at the long pale limb, with my bracelet encircling the wrist and my choice of nail colour decorating each nail, but it's not reacting or responding as it has every day of my life. *Up! Lift! Rise!* Nothing.

I'm checking out today, so I can't just lie here enduring the pain, but force myself to get up and find some tablets for relief. I've got plenty in my toiletries bag. I attempt to raise my body from the bed but nothing happens.

I'm awake, definitely awake. I wiggle my feet, bend my knees and raise my right arm, but my left arm doesn't appear to belong to me. I twist my torso towards the bedside cabinet, my right hand reaching to lift the telephone's handset. My left arm is dragged from its position, forced to follow, limp and useless. My index finger presses the 'zero' button before raising the clasped handset to my ear.

It simply rings off the hook. I'm expecting a cheery 'Good afternoon, Natalia – how may I help you?' but nothing, despite numerous attempts.

I awkwardly replace the handset, unsure what to do.

It's very late to be waking up, but my body must have needed it after the other night – when I was awake all night and living dangerously. I didn't sleep much yesterday but chose to bathe in the afterglow of my night of passion, lounging around my suite and ordering room service, rather than endure the walk of shame whilst descending the grand staircase.

Despite spending the entire day alone, I kept giggling at my most inappropriate behaviour – but a girl's got needs. I couldn't help chuckling at the memory of my hand clasped in his as I hastily led the way towards a night filled with lust and wild abandon.

We'd sneaked behind the reception area to retrieve a room key; it was hardly a lucky dip. I knew which key fob I was choosing from the board: the Sumburgh Suite – the equivalent to any bridal suite.

The attraction between us had smouldered all evening, only to intensify as closing time neared, concluding in a display of desire and lust once the taxi dropped us back at the hotel.

'I can't believe we're doing this. It is so wrong ... it's off the scale of unacceptable behaviour, but right now I'm past caring,' I'd said, as we scampered up the staircase beneath the swathes of Black Watch tartan and burgundy velvet encircling the crystal chandelier, heading drunkenly towards the first landing. I wasn't thinking about the consequences, just of myself and the urgency of my desire. Call me selfish, but I was living in the present, forgetting my painful past and my cancelled future.

'This way,' I'd whispered as we tiptoed in the dark.

He didn't complain or protest as we fumbled with the key in the lock, falling into the suite, our stumbling feet sinking into the luxury carpet, before snapping on the lights. Behind the closed door, our limbs locked. Our lips were working the heat of the other's mouth as our clothing was hastily removed without questions. Our drunken 'shhhhhhh' at each other was lost amidst our giggles; I knew there was no going back.

I took my chance to live in the moment. We played it safe with condoms, so where's the harm between two consenting adults? Not that he was my usual type, but doesn't every girl deserve a Lachlan now and then – if that was indeed his real name. I doubt very much if twenty-five was his true age! People lie about everything nowadays to get their way. As a local bloke, I'm unlikely to see him again, but he knew whose home he'd entered. If he had no regrets, why should I?

The phone rings loudly, making me jump. I snatch at the handset with my able right hand.

I go to speak as the connection is made, but my lips flutter without forming a single word. Nothing but air comes out. Is the disconnection with the phone or me?

Am I actually awake? I extend a finger from holding the handset to touch my lips – they are there, but no longer working.

'Hello, Natalia, how may I help you?'

I hear the female voice, polite and perky as always. I can't answer her. I try again, but still nothing.

The line goes dead. Without bidding me goodbye she is gone.

My arm. My lips. My voice. My pounding head. What the hell is happening to me? Something is wrong, very wrong!

I must call reception again. It sounded like Autumn, it has to be Autumn – the other receptionist isn't as efficient.

I press the key pad button, again.

'Hello, Natalia, how may I help you?'

We start the process again. She asking politely, me fluffing breath into the handset in an attempt to answer her, but failing miserably. Within seconds, a gentle click ends our call, conveying nothing but her polite and pleasant nature.

How do I call for help if I can't call for help?

I lie staring at the ceiling, willing Autumn to respond as her nature dictates. Eventually, after a five-minute wait, there's a light rapping on my suite door. I can't call out. How I wish I could request her to enter!

I can do nothing but wait until she ventures into my suite to investigate . . . and then she'll see. She'll see that her instinct was right and that she shouldn't have wasted a moment doubting her gut reaction before rushing up to my suite.

I hear her key in the lock. My face is turned towards the door, waiting.

'Hello? Ms Muir? Natalia, are you . . .?' She begins to apologise the moment the door is open by a fraction.

My wide eyes are staring hard in her direction, prepared to communicate in an instant what my muted lips can't convey. She tentatively enters the room, her attitude professional and her attire neat, surveys the bed and meets my stricken gaze. My eyes are silently pleading.

'Oh dear, are you OK?'

I shut my eyes tight and give a small shake of the head, before opening my eyes to view her reaction.

'Oh . . . I see, I thought for one moment that . . .' She nears the bed, taking in my skewed position: lying on my side with my left arm dangling limply. 'Natalia . . . do you need an ambulance?'

I give a curt nod.

Her expression instantly changes as the emergency registers. She swiftly takes action, snatches up the phone's handset and repeatedly dials a single digit.

'Hello, yes, ambulance, please. The Lerwick Manor Hotel . . . to the reception area. We've a guest who doesn't appear able to move properly or speak.' She sends a weak smile in my direction by means of an apology for talking about me whilst I'm present. Within seconds, she's replaced the handset and unhooks her staff radio from her belt, depressing the button before speaking. 'Hello, Mungo, are you receiving me?'

'Sure. Go ahead,' comes Mungo's gruff response.

I don't want to hear this part, but I have little choice.

'Mungo, we're expecting an ambulance to attend the hotel. Could you greet the crew at the front entrance please and bring them upstairs to the Unst Suite?' Her finger releases the button, her gaze looks out across the manicured lawn towards the entrance drive.

'An ambulance did you say?'

'That's correct.'

'The Unst Suite?'

'Correct, Mungo.'

'Right you are . . . for Ned's ex-girlfriend, is it?'

The radio falls silent. Autumn does a double take, glancing at her handset, but is professional enough to maintain her composure.

'To the Unst Suite, please, Mungo,' is all she says, before reattaching the radio to her belt.

'Now, shall we try to make you a little more comfortable whilst we wait?'

I give a tiny nod. I might survive the indignity of being helpless in the hands of strangers if they all convey such humility. Autumn slips her arms beneath mine, wraps them around my back and hoists me up against the bed pillows. The movement straightens my left arm purely by association. I look down at the useless limb and notice that her gaze follows mine.

'I'm sure they won't be long, the local service are pretty swift to respond. Mungo will be waiting, so we won't lose a minute. Now, there's nothing for you to worry about. I'll make sure that your room is securely locked whilst you're at the hospital. Before the crew arrive, would you like me to pack a few overnight things into your vanity case?' She pauses to observe my nodding response.

'No worries, I'll pack the basics: toothbrush, soap and fresh underwear. I'm sure you won't be needing much else for the time being. I'll speak to the proprietor later; they're very understanding, and we'll make arrangements on your behalf when you let us know how things are. OK?'

I agree with her plan. There's nothing much for her to say, but

Autumn keeps talking, for which I'm grateful. She tells me what the weather is doing. She describes the new alpaca herd and a fleeting mention of Crispy duck's litter-picking antics around the cobblestoned yard.

Eventually the wail of a siren rudely interrupts her efforts to distract her patient; as the noise gets louder we exchange a relieved glance. I instinctively knew I liked her, from the moment we met; I now understand why.

I don't remember the arrival of the ambulance crew at my bedside, or my removal on a stretcher from the Unst Suite. The journey to hospital took as long as it took, accompanied by a wailing two-tone siren and the delicate blue hues colouring the interior walls. Eyes open or tightly closed, all I can see is Dottie's shocked expression and her frozen stance as our paths crossed on the grand staircase. Those watery blue eyes fixed, staring and glistening more brightly than ever. Gone was the hardened glare that I've received on so many occasions, replaced by a sympathetic expression, conveying kindness and deep concern for my welfare. For a fleeting moment, I believe I glimpsed the true Dottie Nesbit who Ned respects and loves so dearly.

On arrival at A&E, I'm speedily manoeuvred through corridors; the ceiling strip lights speed past at a rate of knots, before I'm wheeled into a curtained cubicle where the questions come thick and fast. All of which I answer in my head, but not a sound do I utter.

The ambulance crew continue their running commentary as if all is normal, but this is far from my usual existence. My vanity case, which Autumn speedily packed, is transferred from the ambulance stretcher to the foot of my hospital trolley.

A new face appears, staring down at mine. 'My name is Anil, I'm a consultant here at Gilbert Bain hospital. We're going to move you across on to the bed – you'll be more comfortable.'

I'm mute and cocooned from interacting or communicating with anyone; all I can do is watch their actions, movements and mannerisms. I am listening intently for possible clues or snippets of medical information that I don't already know. I hand my body over to the experts and watch as they perform their roles, completing each task with as much care and attention as is humanly possible.

I run through the foods and drink I consumed in the last twenty-four hours. Nothing unusual. I've never had an allergic reaction in my life, so what has brought this on? Stress?

Within thirty minutes, I'm alone, lying perfectly still on a wipe-able blue mattress with a paper sheet for comfort. In a brightly lit room, with a small hand basin, a redundant drip stand in the corner, and the daunting realisation that I can't smile. They asked. I tried and failed, miserably.

Autumn

'Autumn, are you OK?' asks Ned, entering the third-floor meeting room to join Jemima and myself at the table.

Jemima found me lingering on the stone steps beside the ornate lions, feeling helpless as the ambulance crew carefully manoeuvred their stretcher trolley and closed the rear doors. We stood watching the ambulance trundle along the driveway; I was urging it to hurry, move faster, but it didn't seem to pick up speed, despite the flashing blue lights. I'm no medic, but having watched numerous hospital programmes over the years, I presume she's had a stroke.

'I'm a bit wobbly,' I say now, not wishing to let my guard down, before adding, 'I didn't know someone so young could have a stroke!'

'It'll be life changing, whatever it was,' replies Jemima, gently rubbing my forearm and offering comfort. 'I understand from Ned that an earlier incident today may need to wait to be resolved. Now isn't the time.'

'I came back from seeing the alpacas to find the switchboard light flashing – I tried calling but there was no answer, so I flew up the staircase, knocked on the door ... only to find ...' My words fade, as my voice cracks with emotion. I try to continue; they need the details. 'Her one arm wasn't right and her face had that lopsided expression.'

Ned walks a short distance to his desk and turns, as if preparing to speak, before changing his mind and walking distractedly around the room. He rakes his hand through his hair, a look of anguish etched on his features. Jemima is glancing from me to him, then back to me, nervously repeating the action.

'Shall I go up and tidy her room ... curtains, bedding, that sort of thing?' I ask, more to Jemima than Ned.

'Would you mind?' asks Ned, sheepishly standing in the centre of the floor before the mantelpiece, as if lost.

'Sure. Until we hear from the hospital, we need to assume that she'll be ... returning.' The final word snags in my throat. I meant it kindly, but it sounded blunt.

'Exactly. No news will be good news until then,' offers Jemima.

Ned turns, stares at us before directing his gaze towards the empty mantel, shifting his stance; he is like a fish out of water. He's aged twenty years in the last hour.

'Wouldn't you prefer housekeeping to straighten the room?' asks Ned, keeping his back to us.

'I need to keep busy, plus I think Natalia would prefer that too.' I immediately pull my keys from my pocket, standing up from the table. 'I'll report back once I've finished.'

I stride from the room, to their grateful chorus of, 'Thank you, Autumn.'

*   *   *

I'm a stranger to Natalia but I still feel obliged to tidy her belongings. It wouldn't be right for housekeeping to complete the job; it would seem impersonal, given the tragic circumstances.

I discovered her, stayed alongside her, and I will ensure her possessions are safe and sound. I have no idea if she'll be returning to us but, if my actions can give her any peace of mind in the meantime, that'll be something.

I hesitate at the door of the Unst Suite. Was it just an hour ago that I came up simply to enquire if she needed anything? To apologise for not answering her initial call? To think, as I approached earlier, pausing to regain my breath and compose myself before knocking, that she'd been lying on the other side of the locked door. God knows what she must have been going through! Poor woman. The world must have seemed a very lonely place at that precise moment. Bless her, she must have been frightened. I wonder how long she'd been awake before attempting to call reception for help. I hadn't realised that she'd missed breakfast.

I hastily unlock the door, putting my own emotions aside, and enter; brisk efficiency needs to be the name of the game. The darkened room looks much the same, apart from the empty bed. I draw back each curtain with a hearty swish, allowing the bright sunshine to stream in. I can't feel sombre when the room is bathed in glorious sunlight. Without thinking, just doing, I turn my attention to the dishevelled bed linen; a twisted mass of covers and duvet which I originally plan to straighten but then decide it doesn't deserve remaking. So, with an almighty yank, I disrobe the mattress in one move. Fresh sheets, straight lines and hospital corners will be more inviting for her return. Her return. Yes, that's more like it. Positive vibes equal a positive outcome. Bearing that in mind, I might find myself a quiet corner and meditate before I return to reception; I need to take good care of myself if I'm to finish this shift emotionally intact.

I busy myself as if Natalia were returning in thirty minutes. I roll the removed linen into a bundle and deposit it by the door, straighten her possessions and adjust the telephone on the bedside cabinet, then quickly rearrange the furniture in its original position.

Every item exudes quality. Every bottle, tube or product is high-end; Natalia obviously doesn't do cheap. 'High maintenance' springs to mind and yet I can't summon my usual attitude towards such extravagance, knowing she's facing an uncertain future. Ill health and sickness are game changers, levellers in life, bringing us mere mortals down from our high horses to face reality. All the money in the world can't erase what she's experienced this morning. Alone. Helpless and distressed in a hotel bedroom, miles from friends and family, with only strangers to assist in her hour of need. How frantically had those blue eyes signalled their plea. The only gift I could offer her was kindness.

My melancholy mood lifts as my busy hands continue each activity, their redness signalling my own inner turmoil whilst I straighten Natalia's belongings. Within minutes, I've folded the clothes strewn across the nearest chair, replaced them in her suitcase, closed the lid and carefully returned her make-up products to a smaller vanity case. A quick tidy of the bathroom shelving, the shower cubicle and towel rail ensures that her possessions are neatly lined up, waiting for the return of their mistress. I instantly push aside that word. Surely Mungo hadn't meant to say, 'Ned's ex-girlfriend'?

On giving the suite a final inspection, I exhale and feel my shoulders relax. When I came in, I thought my emotions were going to spill over, getting the better of me, but now that all is spick and span, all will be well with the room. And Natalia.

Chapter Twenty-One

Thursday 17 February

Dottie's diary
I'm shocked! That poor lassie's face said it all! I sent up a prayer as they carried her down the grand staircase. I wouldn't wish that on anyone, certainly not one so bonnie.

Pippa

'Ned's ex-girlfriend, apparently. Can you believe it?' I ask, leaning on the countertop in The Orangery and chatting to Isla as she expertly cuts today's selection of gorgeous cakes – lemon, carrot, honey, raspberry and white chocolate – before displaying each under a glass cloche.

'Not really, but we shouldn't speculate,' warns Isla.

'It could be a Chinese whisper which has drifted across from the hotel, though it was Mungo who mentioned it to me.' I absent-mindedly play with the dried flowers and ornamental grass arranged in a large ceramic vase which stands beside the counter. 'And who knows more than Mungo and Dottie? No one, that's who!' I say, knowing that fact alone confirms everything I've heard. 'A stroke, he said. I didn't expect that, she's only in her thirties.'

'Nor me. Can you imagine lying there waiting to be found? Not able to form your words properly, like a newborn baby, awaiting attention?' Isla visibly shudders at the thought. 'I feel for her, I really do.'

'I do too. Worse still for it to happen in your ex's home.'

Isla eyes me before speaking. 'I saw her arguing with Dottie last September.'

I lean in closer, ready to hear any details.

'I didn't click when I saw her browsing the gallery earlier in the week, but yeah, there's no love lost there.'

'I always suspected that Dottie pushed our Jemima towards Ned, encouraging him to open his eyes, if you get my drift.'

Isla gives a tiny nod. 'Apparently, Jemima wants to organise a fund-raising event on Natalia's behalf, but Ned said she needs to wait . . . wait and see.' Isla raises her brows, driving home the serious nature of the ex-girlfriend's condition.

A gust of cold air hits my legs, signalling that the glazed door has been opened. I turn to find Levi and Mungo entering for their usual morning cuppa. I immediately cease slouching on the countertop and stand up straight.

'Morning, ladies, anything nice?' asks Mungo, peering at the cake cloches.

'There's always something nice in here,' retorts Isla, shaking her head. Her auburn hair is secured under a hairnet, but unruly wisps escape, much like Mungo's grey beard.

My gaze flickers to meet Levi's. He smiles. Instantly, we both look away, but not before I spot the flush appearing on his pale cheeks.

'What can I get you, fellas?' asks Isla, wiping her hands and preparing to serve.

'The usual,' says Mungo, which means two coffees: a flat white and a latte.

I can't think of a damn thing to say. I'd like to come out with something witty, maybe intelligent or even inviting, but my mind is blank. Great! I bet I'll think of a hundred interesting things when I'm driving towards Gulberwick. Levi bounces from foot to foot and Mungo jiggles his change in his palm, while I count the heartbeats thumping in my chest.

How ridiculous is this? I've known this guy for months and yet suddenly I'm like a gawky teenager at a school dance in his presence. It's Levi, for heaven's sake. Levi the taxi driver. Levi the allotment holder. Levi the local fourth emergency service around Lerwick. The down-to-earth, good guy who never falters but is always stepping forward to help, honour or humour each one of us. Sodding hell, the one I've apparently got 'feels' for, which have appeared from nowhere, thanks to his kindness. The Levi who senses there's a softer side to my nature, despite the protective boundaries I hide behind and the hard exterior I display to the outside world.

The door opens again, emitting another chilly breeze, causing the dried flower heads and ornamental grass to dance within their vase. We all turn to view the newcomer: Callie.

'Are you still here?' she says in an icy tone. I assume the question is directed at me. Typical Callie, being as bolshie as ever and showing her true colours – you wouldn't have thought we'd shared a pleasant day together just four days ago.

'I believe I am!' I say, comically gesturing down the length of my frame, top to toe, like a magician's assistant. 'Rolly is loaded up with bread, ready and waiting to go in the next few minutes, actually.'

Isla sighs, Mungo stares and Levi frowns.

Stop it, Pippa. Just stop! Regardless of the beef between cousins, Levi is present and possibly noting my attitude.

'What I wouldn't give to have an easy job, sauntering around all day, when we're rushed off our feet in here, unable to clear dirty crockery and tables quickly enough for customers' liking. And then there's you swanning around the villages.'

'I don't swan . . .' I cease talking, on receiving a fleeting glance from Levi.

'Yeah, right!' says Callie, sidling past us and heading for the rear stockroom where she'll hang her coat.

Silence descends as we all watch Isla put the finishing touches to the coffee order.

'Right, I'd best be off,' I announce reluctantly, not wishing to leave and attend to my duties.

'Catch you later,' says Isla, handing over their drinks.

Mungo takes the two mugs and heads towards their usual boys' spot near the log burner.

'See you, Pippa,' says Levi. A tiny smile curls at the corner of his lip; there's a definite warmth growing between us.

'Bye,' I mouth, attempting to suppress a coy smile, as Isla's gaze suspiciously flicks between the two of us.

Natalia

Having spent the last three days on a hospital ward in the company of five elderly women who have been repeatedly rude and snappy towards the on-duty nurses, the last thing I need to see is another elderly lady, heaving her bulging shopping bag, tottering along my ward. Especially this particular one!

If I were able to move faster than lightning and dash from my bed, I would. Right now! Damn this sodding limp arm for dragging me down and holding me back.

'Hello, lassie, how are we doing?' asks Dottie, her watery blue gaze holding mine, awaiting my silent answer.

I've given up trying to control these fluttering mute lips. I attempt to smile sweetly, acknowledging her question, whilst inside my head my voice screams 'Bugger off! We're not friends, so don't pretend otherwise because of my misfortune.' I'm convinced Dottie doesn't hear my inner voice. She draws my visitor chair a little closer and plonks herself and her bag down. Instantly, I remember our silent exchange on the grand staircase, as the ambulance crew carried me down on that fateful morning, and feel guilty for being unkind.

'Eyyy, these corridors are a bugger to walk, aren't they?'

I take it you're stopping, then – let's hope it's a brief visit and not the full three hours.

'Now, let's see,' she says, rummaging in her hessian bag and drawing out a mini whiteboard and felt pens. 'Melissa sent these. I don't think you know her, nice lady ... an art teacher who makes wonderful things in ceramics. She's borrowed them from the college supplies; she reckons it'll help you communicate with folk if you can write words down. There's a little sponge somewhere in here too.' Dottie passes me the sheet of flimsy white plastic and two felt pens, before delving back into her bag. 'Where's that gone?'

I try to put aside my previous reactions towards her; Ned always said she means well.

'Here it is,' exclaims Dottie, finally emerging triumphant from her search. 'Now, Ned and Jemima asked me to ask you if there's anything you need?' She waits, glancing from my face to the whiteboard.

I shake my head.

'Really? Not some toiletries, nice treats or reading books?'

I shake my head again. I see the disappointment in her eyes. I'm not sure if that's because I'm not using the whiteboard or because she's had a wasted journey if every answer is a shake of the head.

'So, nothing needed?'

I nod.

'In that case then, Kaspar from the allotments – you don't know him either – sent these,' says Dottie, offering me a pretty food tin from her bag. 'They're gorgeous, but very moreish, so go easy. He thought they might fill a gap between meals if you get a bit peckish.'

Who? From where? What?

Dottie reads my furrowed brow. 'Kaspar, he's a dear friend

of mine. He always shares his condensed milk cookies with me in The Cabbage Patch at gin o'clock on Fridays. You never attended . . . anyway, he's a very nice man from Estonia.'

Dottie sits back in her chair, viewing her surroundings and the other occupants of my ward, while I awkwardly prise the lid off the tin with my good hand, to find diamond-shaped cookies inside. I nod a thank you; the kindness of strangers is overwhelming.

'Lassie, fancy putting you in amongst elderly ladies – you won't get a minute's rest, day or night.'

I nearly choke on my next breath.

'Seriously, you won't,' she continues, before frantically waving at the lady in the opposite bed. 'Hi, Nora, fancy seeing you here!'

I watch the two converse as if they're attending a local senior social for a cuppa and a biscuit. They enjoy a pleasant natter for a few minutes before Dottie turns back to me, her head cocked, and whispers, 'She comes from a damned awful family, but she straightened herself out when she married the butcher's apprentice. Nice lad he was, with decent manners.'

Is she serious?

I snatch up my pen, I can't resist asking. I swiftly write, *In what year was that?*

Dottie leans forward, peering at my handwriting, before I tilt the board towards her to view.

'Oooo, let me see . . . it was definitely the year that . . .'

I don't focus on her explanation. I simply watch as she chunters on about the thunderous gales in the autumn of 1961. I can't help myself, it sounds unkind, but watching this elderly lady zip through the library of her mind, recalling the exact details of a particular wedding night ruined by hurricane Debbie, puts my current recall to shame. She can't be a day under eighty, her skin is almost transparent, her gaze cloudy and watery, yet as quick as a flash she's got all the details to hand from decades ago.

Why don't you like me? I'm as surprised as she is to read the words on the whiteboard.

'Well, I wasn't expecting that,' splutters Dottie, shifting in her seat and sitting a little taller.

Neither was I. My right hand is now still; I'm not about to lose face by retracting the question. I refrain from wiping the slate clean, so to speak.

'Now don't take this personally, but you and I are not cut from the same cloth, are we? You have your ways and I have mine.'

Very tactful, Dottie.

Sadly, she continues, 'It's not that I don't like you, it's more that my judgement was influenced by the things I saw and heard when you spent time with Ned. I didn't appreciate watching how you gave so little to the relationship, but frequently took what you could in many ways. If you get my drift?'

My jaw would drop open, if I had control of my facial muscles. I can't help myself, much like my left arm.

Dottie rubs my forearm. 'Don't be offended, you asked, so I'll answer. I wanted what was best for him in the circumstances. You're a smashing young woman, but not for our Ned, that's how I saw it.'

What was wrong in the way I acted? I write.

'Now surely . . .?'

Go on, I quickly add.

'You with your high and fancy ways, your expensive taste, plus all your wants and needs – it all became a bit much after a while, lassie. I was waiting to see the emotional connection develop, but I never saw that side of you.'

I swiftly wipe the board clean, eager to write more.

Didn't you see strength in our relationship? I scribble.

Dottie pouts before answering, 'Not really. As the Campbells say, "When you know, you know." I figured Ned simply didn't know until, well . . . he did.'

Boom! Tell it to me straight, Dottie! I leave the felt pen alone while I digest her words, as if giving her the silent treatment.

Dottie waits for a response. I can't pretend it doesn't hurt, because it does. I can't pretend that I'm not distraught at discovering the truth, but still she stares at me. Waiting. I shake my head.

'It's hard facing the truth, but he wasn't the right beau for yee, lassie,' she says in a soothing tone. 'You haven't met that one yet.'

I crumple my brow, wanting her to stop. In recent days, I've endured CT scans, prodding and poking by many medics, endless sleepless nights worrying about my career prospects, and difficult one-sided conversations with specialists about the bleed on my brain, yet this examination by Dottie is the most painful.

'Yee canna have, lassie … otherwise you'd have known it. Look at me and Mungo – for years I talked myself out of there being anything between us. We're just friends, we're just old school mates, we're … anything, apart from facing the truth. Which is that me and the old bugger go back decades in our admiration for each other. And what was the point? We've spent a lifetime wasting time, when things could have been different. And the same with you. Four years of chasing Ned, when the reality was you should have been focusing your sights on other guys, who shared your glamorous lifestyle.'

Jemima doesn't share Ned's lifestyle, I write, hastily correcting her.

'Ach, that's where you're wrong. She does. He's a simple soul at heart, is our Ned. He focuses on his work, he enjoys the traditions of life, but he likes his down time to be spent on practical matters. Jemima offers him just that. She's got a savvy head for business, she embraces his traditional values, and she'll happily toil all day getting her hands dirty with the practical side of managing the estate. She's not scared of a hard day's work, that's for sure. Whereas you never wanted to ruin your manicure, never showed much interest in the estate or suggested ways to secure his legacy. You must have seen how stressed he was about shouldering the workload and the burden of worry. He couldn't see the wood for the trees … thought his only way out was to sign the estate over to a tourist trust to maintain. You see, lovey, everything happens for a reason. Jemima showed up when he needed her – and believe me, that'll happen for you too.'

If I could scream – loud, proud and frustratingly ear piercing – I would. Right now, in front of these other five patients and their visitors. I stare agitatedly at Dottie's mild, mellow features. She's got some nerve. I don't think she has any idea what she's just said straight to my lopsided face. Or its impact on my world.

I've had a stroke, for Christ's sake. Right now, I feel I'm trapped and silenced within a body which has always done what I wanted it to; it's carried me through my daily life and supported a fabulous career. Now what am I to do? Opt for a life I didn't choose? Submit to my limitations, depending on my progress in the coming days and weeks? I'm supposed to sign a new contract with the agency – how's that ever going to work if I can't smile or move my left arm?

'Now, before I go. I appreciate there was a delay with the hospital informing your parents, but I made a little phone call last night and they're going to catch a flight later tonight. Don't be annoyed, but Ned gave me their landline number and offered them a suite for the duration of their stay. As you can imagine, they refused once they received an update on recent circumstances. Anyway, your loved ones will be here soon, lovey,' says Dottie. She glances at my face, no doubt registering my stunned but skewed expression, and then at the blank whiteboard, awaiting my response.

Chapter Twenty-Two

Tuesday 22 February

Autumn

I smile politely as Mr Drummond from the Whalsay Suite leaves reception and ascends the staircase after making his request. I daren't allow my smile to falter, as Jemima is standing two steps behind me, having overheard, and is probably awaiting my reaction. I'm not saying anything until the guest is out of sight and earshot.

She sidles up beside me and whispers, 'Sorry, what did he ask for?'

I suck in my cheeks, attempting to maintain my smile, and answer her honestly. 'He asked if there was any chance of having his bath filled with alpaca milk.' I can't meet her gaze, so I stare at the bridge of her nose, anticipating her reaction.

She blinks rapidly, looks across the counter as if to make sure the man has gone, before returning her troubled gaze to me.

'Is the hot water not good enough?'

I shrug. I want to crack a smile. I curl my toes instead, helping me to focus on the moment and not the hilarity of his request. Plus Jemima's startled expression.

'Well I never! I was about to mention that Ms Muir will be returning in a day or so. Could you have her suite freshened up? Not in a month of Sundays would I ever have imagined such a request being made by such a . . . a . . . regular-looking chap. Is this some sort of new trend?'

Again I shrug. I've learnt that you can never be too careful when passing comments in front of a boss, or jumping to the wrong conclusion about a guest's behaviour. Either way, you'll come unstuck sooner rather than later.

'Autumn, is that kind of request usual?' Jemima persists.

'Mmmm,' I say, pursing my lips, choosing my words carefully. 'Reception is usually the first port of call, we're often expected to source and organise personal requests ... ensuring the pleasure of our guests.'

Jemima's brow furrows deeply. 'And he's expecting you to source a bathful of alpaca milk to be delivered to his suite?'

'Yep, I'll find the details first, then phone his suite with the price ... and take it from there. If he wishes to pursue the idea and pay the price, I'll arrange delivery and add the cost to his bill.' I make it all sound so simple.

Jemima's expression is relaxing with each word. 'Never in my life have I heard of such things,' she repeats, with a baffled shake of the head. 'I thought the most you'd be asked for is a spare shower cap, a replacement toothbrush or an extra blanket, but this ... this seems totally absurd.'

'I've had worse,' I say, as Ned appears through the front entrance.

Jemima frantically beckons him to join us. Her shocked expression is enough to gain his attention. I stand poker-faced while she explains the situation in hushed but hurried tones. Ned's eyebrows rise as his wife delivers the final fact: single occupancy.

'Is this his first request?' asks Ned, turning his attention to me.

'No. He's booked music lessons prior to this. Alpaca milk might sound outlandish but, believe me, that's pretty tame.'

The Campbells both stare, waiting for me to elaborate further.

'I've had various requests over the years: an adult-sized Robin Hood outfit, five hundred helium balloon in pink heart shapes, a deep-fried Snickers bar delivered at two in the morning, an empty rabbit hutch and a candlewick bedspread.'

Both mouth 'rabbit hutch' on completion of my list.

I nod, confirming they heard me correctly.

'He's obviously spied the herd and imagines that we can supply his needs,' suggests Ned, as if partly satisfied with this reasoning.

'In time,' agrees Jemima. 'But even with nursing mothers, I doubt we'd have that amount spare to accommodate such a request. They're hardly bred for milking, are they?' She hesitates, before adding, 'It seems a strange request for an adult male.'

'Cleopatra bathed in ass' milk,' I say.

Ned sighs before addressing me. 'Autumn, I'm not sure this is a feasible request.'

'Some guests cancel a request when they hear the cost implications,' I quickly add.

'Let's hope so,' mutters Jemima. 'The logistics of delivering it to his room will be a nightmare. I suppose Levi or Isaac might help out.'

'It isn't simply the logistics – remember, we don't have a lift – but being realistic, we're a hotel offering accommodation not . . . well, I'm not sure how to term it,' says Ned, glancing between us for assistance.

'Catering for requests of a more personal nature?' I say.

'Sorry, but we shouldn't be encouraging such requests. Surely the time taken sourcing such items diverts staff away from other hotel business.'

'Do you want us to refuse him?' asks Jemima.

'I think that'd be wise, don't you?' Ned looks at his wife for confirmation.

Jemima nods, siding with her husband. 'You're right, Ned – potentially it could get out of hand and take up Autumn's entire shift.'

My heart sinks. I understand where they're coming from – after all, it's their establishment – but I'm instantly disappointed that I can't deliver what's been asked of me.

'If he chooses to complain, then I'll step in,' says Ned to Jemima, before speaking to me. 'Autumn, could you please call his room and explain our decision?'

'Certainly.' I quickly scribble a note to myself on my 'To-do' list.

'Keep me in the loop.' Ned gently pats his wife's shoulder before departing. He strides halfway across the hallway before turning around to add, 'Though please let us know if he requests any "additional services".' He wiggles his eyebrows suggestively. I'd usually giggle at such humour, but my disappointment at the cancelled request prevents me from seeing the funny side.

'Ned, please. Don't even go there!' gasps Jemima, her hands fluttering to her chest.

'You never know, ladies,' he says, walking backwards and watching our response. 'Call if you need me to have a word.'

I give a smile in acknowledgement, while Jemima continues to gasp.

'Surely not?' she says, once Ned has disappeared.

'I've never received such a request myself, but I've heard from numerous colleagues about guests who have requested company . . . be it in house or otherwise.'

'Well, not here, they won't be. I can assure you of that!'

'You really are new to this business, aren't you?'

'I certainly am. I used to work for the tourist board, but this – well, I'm seeing a whole new side to human nature with this venture,' explains Jemima, shaking her head in a bemused fashion. 'Let me know how you get on.' With that, Jemima leaves the reception area, still shaking her head as she disappears towards the kitchens.

I want to call after her, but I know it would be futile to attempt to talk her round.

Their decision is final. No guest requests.

'Dare I ask how our guest took your call regarding his milk request?' asks Ned, coming into reception just after four o'clock.

I look up from my computer; I've been settled in front of the screen for hours.

'He was fine about it, he fully understood.' Instantly, I feel guilty. I opt to remain quiet, there's no point embellishing the actual details.

'Ahh, that was simple enough. I was half expecting he'd show more resistance, and a chat would be necessary. Just shows you how whimsical his request was in the first place. I'm glad we didn't honour it. Well done,' he says, collecting a pile of mail from the desk and heading straight back out.

I'd had little joy in my attempts to source alpaca milk. I discovered that they aren't bred for milking. The websites cater mainly for breeders who need to hand-feed a cria – apparently, the name for a baby alpaca – so the prices offered relate to colostrum substitutes rather than actual bottled alpaca milk. I researched a substitute, camel milk, because you should always offer alternatives when a guest's needs can't be met. I'd even completed the calculation, based on the volume of the bath and the size of a carton of camel milk. Not quite as the Campbells instructed, but kind of.

Anyway, I'd called Mr Drummond's suite to relay the details. Which was wrong of me, but I know from experience that if you deny a guest a request they only kick up a fuss. Far better for the guest to decline your offer than be forced to accept a refusal. 'Frozen camel milk costs £11.99 per half a litre,' I told him. 'You'd need a hundred and fifty litres for half a bathtub, and three hundred litres for a full tub. Making a total of £3,597 or £7,194, depending on which option you choose. Delivery is two days and potentially another day for defrosting prior to use.' I'd completed my explanation and awaited the expected 'thanks, but no thanks' given the extortionate price.

'Thank you for the details. Who knew it was so costly? In which case, is there a chance of changing it to goat's milk instead?' asked Mr Drummond, before ending the call abruptly.

I wasn't expecting that! I felt a little sick as I replaced the handset on the reception's main switchboard. I need to do this. It won't take long to source a bathful of goat's milk.

I'd returned to my desk in the rear office, angled the computer screen a little, preventing anyone entering the office from seeing what's displayed, and began a new online search.

Pippa

'Can I ask why you were mean to her?'

'Who? Jemima?'

Levi nods. His mouth does a weird twitch, as if he's holding back more questions.

I knew this would be brought up, so I might as well give my side of the story. I stare out of my driver's window as I attempt to explain.

'You're right, it was mean, especially the honesty boxes. But you need to put yourself in my shoes. Our Granddad Tommy had just died. When we visited the solicitor's office, we discovered there was a provision in his will for money to pass to any grandchildren if one of his own children had died. Jemima's mum had passed, so she inherited her mother's share.' I glance at Levi, not sure if he knew that information.

His gaze is fixed squarely on me, despite him eating his

sandwiches. This doesn't help, if I'm totally honest. I blush. This is going to make me look bad, however I explain it.

I take a deep breath. 'Anyway, that means that my mum, my uncle and Jemima received the same amount as a legacy. Now, I get that it was pure chance, it could have been me, but . . .' I lift my hand, preventing him from interrupting me. I need to say it aloud to clear my conscience. 'I felt snubbed; it was out of order for Granddad to overlook Callie and me. Jemima's no better than me . . . us. In a family, you're supposed to be equal, but here she was getting the same reward, if you want to call it that, as my mum and uncle, his own children. Callie and I sat there like two stuffed turkeys and didn't even get a mention. That makes me sound utterly selfish . . . so jealous, I'll admit, but it was the injustice of the situation. It made me feel as if my granddad didn't care about me; I'd been overshadowed, yet again.'

Levi clicks his tongue on hearing my words.

I continue for fear of stalling, 'And deep down, I know that isn't true. Granddad loved us three girls all the same, it was purely Jemima's tragic circumstances that went in her favour. He wasn't ill before he died, he didn't know he'd pass in his sleep, so he didn't change the will he made after our nanna died. But that hurt me, it really did.'

'But still, it wasn't Jemima who wrote the will, so why take it out on her?'

'That's where it went wrong. Levi, I haven't told anyone else this. I lashed out. I've apologised to Jemima . . . properly, but still, I should never have damaged her prize pumpkin. Though I think Mungo was more upset about it than she was.' I stifle a giggle at recalling his outburst of temper.

'I hear he nearly had a heart attack when he saw it,' adds Levi, pursing his lips.

'And I shouldn't have taken the money, but I can explain. Please let me, because it looks much worse than it was.'

Levi raises an eyebrow, as if questioning how.

'Hear me out, please. I'm not making excuses for what I did, but it went wrong, my intention was never to steal the change from the honesty boxes on the allotments.' I take another deep breath before continuing. I need to confess. Levi will just have to make of it what he will.

'It was a prank that went wrong. I went to the allotments purely to talk to Jemima, but she wasn't there when I reached her plot. I popped over to The Veggie Rack instead, as I knew she'd been spending a lot of time there setting it up, but I found it unmanned. My frustration simply got the better of me. I felt that, yet again, I was being snubbed. Please believe me when I tell you there was a total of £19.24 in six of the trays. And before you ask, no I wasn't going to keep it. I was going to put it back.'

'When?'

'Once Jemima had realised the money was missing and panicked. I just wanted to stir things up a bit . . . disrupt her perfect life. Call it a moment of madness, whatever you will . . . there is no excuse for my behaviour.'

'So why didn't you put it back?'

'Because she didn't turn up. Mungo did – and, of course, intervened.'

Levi gives a puzzled frown. 'How do you even know that?'

'I stood by The Cabbage Patch social shack watching, I expected Jemima to show up, realise the cash had gone and then seek help from you or another allotment holder, in which time I'd have replaced the money. It's still mean, but more of a prank than it now appears.'

'I assume you took off when Mungo returned with Jemima?'

I nod, my chin lowered in sheer embarrassment at my admission.

'And the money, what did you do with it?'

I can't raise my head, so I talk into my chest. 'The next day,

I hoped to see Jemima to apologise, return the cash and explain how stupid I'd been. But I panicked, knowing just how bad it looked. I went to the corner shop and put all the money into their charity box for donations to the Samaritans based in Lerwick.' I dare to glance up and witness Levi's expression. 'I added a donation from myself, as well – not that it absolves my mean actions.'

'Does Jemima know that?'

'No, nobody does, except, well . . . you.'

'It doesn't paint a great picture, does it? Though the full details make it a little more bearable, I suppose. What a ridiculous feud to have within a family, snipping and sniping at every possible opportunity.'

I don't usually care what others think, but right now it matters that Levi understands my viewpoint. He's close friends with Jemima from their allotment days, but still his opinion carries weight with me. I don't expect him to ignore my actions, but knowing where they sprang from matters more than it should, or once did.

'And what do you think, now you know the full story?' I ask him.

'It was uncalled for. I hardly knew you then, and I saw you in a different light when Dottie tackled you at the festival, but I haven't been in that situation yet. My grandparents died when I was a nipper, so I can't say how I'd react. As you said, you were hurt.'

'I would never stoop to doing anything like that again, if that's what you're thinking,' I say, as the silence lingers between us.

'I don't doubt it. You seem to have made peace with Jemima and Dottie since working in The Orangery.'

I shrug. Have I? Haven't I?

'Not really, more a case of needing to get along. I was desperate to leave my admin job, and they needed a waitress . . . I suppose I had little choice. I can hardly accept their wages and be all moody behind their backs, now can I?'

'I suppose not,' he says, laughing.

'Though it's made my life difficult. Isla's now admitted she thought I stole her gran's recipe book, which she totally relied on, as a way of undermining her position. She thought I was deliberately thwarting her efforts – as if I felt entitled to a promotion because of my family ties.'

Levi gives a belly laugh.

'Seriously, she told me it was eventually retrieved from that Lachlan guy. I was mortified by her suspicions. As if I'd do such a thing!'

'As if? Are you serious? If you can sabotage your cousin's pumpkin in the middle of the night then surely you're capable of doing most things.'

'Do you think?'

'There's not much I wouldn't put past you. You're like a set of twins. You never know which one you're going to get – the good twin or the mischievous one!'

'Thanks a bunch!' I act as if I'm put out, but I get where he's coming from. Once I've got a bee in my bonnet about something, there's no stopping me – whatever the consequences.

'What I'm learning about you is to expect the unexpected!'

'Mmmm, the question is . . . what am I learning about you, Levi?' There's a coyness in my tone. It wasn't intentional, or meant to be flirty, yet his eyes sparkle in response. What am I doing? He's one of my cousin's closest friends. Am I mixing business with pleasure?

'Now there's a question,' he says, tucking into a cold buttered bannock.

Autumn

'I'm waiting!' calls an impatient voice from reception.

I jump up from my chair, instantly guilty that I've been caught at my computer when I should be elsewhere – performing a spot check on housekeeping, or planning a charity event Jemima wishes to hold.

'I'm sorry, madam. How may I help you?' I switch into service mode, smile in place, and stride from the rear office, to be confronted by an attractive woman, late forties, subtle make-up defining her to-die-for cheekbones. My older sister, Sienna.

'Well, it's about bloody time I had some service around here,' she jokes, repeatedly tapping the counter bell. *Ding! Ding! Ding!*

'Stop it, you fool!' I dash around the counter to give her a huge embrace. 'How are you?'

'I'm very well. Since you've stood me up so many times in recent weeks, I thought I'd ambush you at work,' she quips, pulling a comical face as I retract from our hug. This is her way of telling me off for cancelling her. 'And ignoring my calls!'

'Sorry, sorry. You still love me though.'

'Are you due a coffee break anytime soon?' asks Sienna, looking around the manor's impressive hallway.

'Too right, it's three o'clock and I'm yet to eat my lunch.'

'Is the coffee shop open on Tuesdays?'

'It is, despite the gallery being officially closed on Mondays and Tuesdays. Isla's changed her working hours to supply the bakes for the hotel, so she might as well be open and serve the odd customer who drops by.'

'I'll go and order then, shall I?'

'Sounds great. Can you order me a large latte and a bowl of soup, with a crusty roll?'

'Are you sure? You're not going to go AWOL if I head over to the coffee shop and order for us?'

'I'm sure. I'll be over in two seconds, I just need to radio the kitchen so my replacement can cover the main desk, and then I'll be with you.'

'Two minutes . . . promise?' With that, Sienna exits the hotel

and I imagine her striding through the stone archway towards
The Orangery.

I'm grateful to see her but irked that it's come to this. My sister
shouldn't have to stage an ambush to see me when I'm living and
working pretty much on her doorstep. It's another reminder that I'm
letting things slip, my initial promises are flying out of the window.
I glance at my hands; my flaky knuckles aren't too bad today, she
might not notice. Though, on second thoughts, it's Sienna.

'Yay! You've arrived. For a minute there, I wondered if you'd
got lost crossing an empty yard,' says Sienna.

I hurry towards her table; she's chosen one beside the burning
log fire. The drinks are waiting, and my bowl of soup is cooling.
Sienna sips her tea whilst pulling a pastry apart.

'Honestly, you can never find folk when you need them. My
cover, Hannah, had disappeared on an errand for the chef. Never
mind, I'm here now.' I sit down with a hefty sigh.

'Like that, is it?'

'Some days, though the majority run perfectly smooth. Anyway,
less about me. Are the lads at school?' I ask, picking up my spoon
and tucking into my carrot soup.

'Yes, though Josh didn't want to go today; he's trying to avoid
sitting a maths paper as prep for his summer exams. Jake's fine,
plodding along nicely without any complaints.'

I eat while Sienna speaks; it's so lovely to hear about her
family, *my* family. This is what I came home for.

'They're like chalk and bloody cheese, as always,' Sienna
complains.

'Just how we were,' I remark, my smile indicating it wasn't
a bad thing.

'Yep, we still are. And you? How are you coping with the
switch from the cruise liners to hotel management?' she asks,
glancing at my hands as I spoon my soup.

'So-so. Ah, you've noticed . . .' I gesture towards my hands.

'Couldn't miss them really, could I?'

'I suppose not. Though I'm trying not to fall into old habits. But it's hard, when it's in your nature to offer assistance . . . I know I bring it on myself.'

'You act like a bloody mug by doing too much! Others will put on you if they can, you know. You'll end up paying the price for it.'

I laugh; I play it down and pretend it doesn't matter, but Sienna says it how it is.

'So tell me, what are you juggling?' she asks.

I grimace but am relieved, knowing I need to share. I spend the next few minutes explaining about the request for alpaca milk, camel milk and, eventually, goat's milk, admitting I've allowed the situation to run away with me.

'If the Campbells find out, I'll be so embarrassed. How do I put a stop to the request now, when I was instructed to do so earlier! It's ridiculous.'

'Why does he want it?'

'I haven't asked!' I cringe at the very thought of what he might be doing in his bathtub. 'You don't ask why, you simply deliver, Sienna.'

'You do ask why when there might be an alternative or an easier option available. Otherwise, you spend days searching for suppliers of cheap goat's milk – and all for a mysterious reason, behind the bosses' backs!'

'One pound eighty is the cheapest price for a litre, but I suspect that's reflected in the quality, plus it didn't state organic . . . which is still pricy for an entire bathful.'

'Congratulations, you're now an expert!' Sienna offers me a round of applause.

'Stop it, it's my job.'

'No, it's not! Your job is to organise and run a hotel under the watchful eye of your bosses, not this nonsense. I'm with them, I'd have cancelled his request. I say buy a load of cow's milk and be done, he'll never know the difference. Let him play out his kink – job done, then you can focus on what's important. Though get housekeeping to thoroughly scrub that bathtub!'

'You are rotten,' I say, giggling at her laid-back attitude.

I feel refreshed when I return to work after seeing Sienna. I've promised to address my workload, and agreed to accompany her to the local theatre on Sunday evening.

My first task is to call Mr Drummond to ask the big question. His room rate is being paid on a company account, but even so, hundreds of pounds for one bath does seem ludicrous. I locate his checking-in details on the office computer and call his mobile, knowing he left early, straight after breakfast.

'Good afternoon, Mr Drummond ... Autumn here, the general manager at Lerwick Manor Hotel. I have a question regarding your request for goat's milk ... could I ask if there's a reason, be it health or well-being related, that you're specifically attempting to address? I've had a supplier ask whilst making my enquiries.'

'Afternoon, Autumn, primarily it's to help with my eczema, which has flared up quite unexpectedly. The outbreak is probably connected with my job relocation, but a new colleague noticed and mentioned the benefit of various milks, which is something I've never tried. I didn't realise they would be so expensive.'

'I see, well, thank you for explaining, I have similar issues with my skin, so I know how uncomfortable it actually is. Could I suggest a cheaper alternative might be to drink the milk, rather than bathe in it, which is something I could easily arrange. If you wish, I could ask housekeeping to replace the milk cartons in your room and also to provide goat's milk for the breakfast service. In addition, I do have an idea which might ease some of your discomfort – something created by one of our gallery artists.'

'I'd appreciate that, Autumn. Thank you.'

'Have a good afternoon, Mr Drummond.' I quickly end the call, just as Ned descends the grand staircase.

'Everything OK?' he says, passing through.

'Yes, thank you,' I say, busily tidying leaflets and trying not to look furtive.

I reach for my staff radio and depress the button. One final step and this request might be completed.

'Autumn here, a message for Hannah, please.'

'Hannah here.'

'Could you cover reception for about ten minutes, please? I need to visit the gallery.'

'I'll be there in two minutes,' comes the instant reply.

Her words soothe my fraught mind, knowing Mr Drummond's quest is nearly at an end.

Chapter Twenty-Three

Friday 25 February

Natalia

'Thank you, but that's not necessary, Dottie,' I say slowly, given the vast improvement in my speech since leaving hospital and returning to Lerwick Manor Hotel. I gesture towards the wooden sun lounger and the accompanying tartan blanket awaiting my arrival on the paved terrace, as I bring my coffee outside to drink. 'I'm happy ... standing.'

There's a heavy slur to each of my words, and I hate it. I appreciate that anything is better than the fluttering-lipped silence I originally experienced. The specialists are delighted with my progress. Sadly, it's not happening fast enough for me. My left arm remains unchanged, my expression is slightly improved but still droops, and my magic whiteboard has been returned to Melissa. I've got a long way to go, but the Campbells have been gracious in allowing me to remain here for as long as I need or wish. It's provided peace of mind for my family, knowing I'll be near my original medical team without switching my care to another hospital. My parents stayed for a matter of days, until I convinced them to return to Edinburgh. After all, I'm in the best possible place and under the most stringent of carers: Dottie Nesbit.

'Now do as you're told, lassie. Relaxation and recuperation seem to have gone amiss in the modern world amidst the

hurly-burly of getting better as fast as yee can. Good old-fashioned peace and quiet will do wonders for your mind and your
nerves, letting that body of yours heal as nature intended. Now,
no more of your squawking . . . my coffee's getting cold.' Dottie's
cup of coffee waits on the nearest terrace table. She's proved as
faithful as a dog; I have to admit, I'm not good at being cared for.

Her sharp tone warns me that protesting is futile. I sense I
could stand here for ten minutes arguing my point, and still
lose. I walk slowly towards the reclining lounger, coffee mug in
my good hand and, with help, settle myself. Dottie immediately
drapes the blanket across my lower body, tucking it briskly
beneath my feet as if I were a child in a pushchair. I can't help
but smile; she means well, but her mannerisms come across as
harsh and slightly too matron-like.

'That's better. You can enjoy the fresh air without getting a
chill,' she says, standing back to admire her handiwork.

I sip my coffee, conscious that our history of sniping is rapidly fading. I've always suspected that she has a softer side – in
essence, something of a mother hen – but never have I been on
the receiving end. Until now. She visited every day when I was
in hospital, bringing me tissues, fresh mints and sweet nibbles
to tempt my appetite.

'Is there anything I can fetch for you?' she says, straightening
up.

'No, thanks.'

'A magazine? A book? Your phone?'

I shake my head at each suggestion. I'm not trying to be difficult but I just want to be left in peace to drink my coffee outdoors
and enjoy the morning view across the manicured lawns. This
was my routine on many mornings when I used to visit Ned,
when we'd enjoy a lazy breakfast and chat about our busy lives.

After being confined to a hospital ward for more than a
week, I need to feel the sun on my face. My mind remains busy

contemplating whether my previous lifestyle has resulted in this medical emergency: the constant stress, some sort of predisposition, or a lack of healthy choices around diet and exercise. Could I have prevented this happening or has it been silently stalking me, waiting for that fateful day?

Dottie grabs her coffee cup and takes a fleeting sip. She seems pent up and slightly hyper, like a neurotic nursemaid. Where she's obtained her blood pressure machine from is anyone's guess, but my readings have become her new obsession! She follows my gaze, staring out across the paved terrace and the balustrade, towards the unseen orchard way beyond our vision. A sea of green swathes the garden; every border, shrub and ornamental urn appears healthy and very much alive. There's nothing limp, broken or decaying in sight. Apart from me.

'Beautiful, isn't it?' I say, holding my drink with my right hand.

'It is. I remember a time before the copse was planted, when the lawn sloped away into the distance as far as the eye could see. The nearest interruption to the landscape was a field of sheep who frequently escaped and ran amok, spraying their pellets here, there and everywhere.' She falls silent.

I glance up, expecting her to continue, but there's a certain cast to her expression. Her cheeks soften, her brow too, as the years fall away. It's mesmerising to watch her reminisce about yesteryear. I can imagine the cinema footage replaying inside her head as she recalls her youth. Has she finished, or will I hear more?

'How old were you?' I ask, unsure if I should pry or leave her be.

'Fifteen years old, which seems a lifetime ago and yet it was only yesterday.'

'Why plant an orchard?'

She visibly shakes herself from her trance. 'Ned's great-daa had some bright idea about harvesting apples and turning his hand to cider-making, but the trees are all twisted and gnarly; such stunted specimens never had a chance against these winds.'

'And did he make lots of cider?'

'Did he heck! My mother used to make him a couple of decent-sized apple pies each year, nothing more and nothing since. Ned leaves the windfalls for the birds and other wildlife.'

'Leftovers scattered,' I mutter to myself.

Slowly she turns to face me. 'He's done you a favour. It might not appear that way right now, but in time it will.'

I glance up to meet her watery gaze. I don't answer. Not that I don't agree; I simply don't wish to hear her justification or receive her pity.

'You wouldn't have been happy here long-term, lassie. I've no doubt it would have suited you for a couple of years, but Shetland life isn't truly for you, Natalia. Your heart lies elsewhere, living a different life to the one offered here.'

'A different life . . . elsewhere!'

Dottie inclines her head before answering. 'Yes, elsewhere . . . but not here, lassie.'

I nod, confirming my attempt to accept the new future unfurling before me. I'd arrived in Shetland knowing what I wanted, but now all the jigsaw pieces have shifted. Even the previous pieces of my life are still out of place. I still haven't signed my new contract; my agency have sent a message, underlining their 'best wishes', but nothing more. If I'd signed beforehand, would they have reneged on the contract? I'm unsure how things would have panned out – it's not as if I know other models in my situation! The question being, is the industry ready to accept the new me . . . whenever that may be, when I'm fit and strong enough to work?

For now, I'll continue to do as I'm told by the Stroke Outreach Team. And, of course, Dottie.

Autumn

I'm still awaiting Mr Drummond's feedback from three days ago. It's not that I'm seeking praise, I just want to know that he's satisfied; until then, the request looms over me. I want it gone, mentally ticked off my 'To-do' list. I thought my solution was pretty ingenious: switch his milk consumption and send a couple of bars of goat's milk and coconut oil soap up to his suite. Thankfully, when I asked Tabitha, our resident artist who runs the soapery, she happily provided a few complimentary bars. Given her range of glorious fragrances and botanical ingredients, I was tempted to mention my own hands, but I didn't want to draw attention to myself. My biggest fear is that if Mr Drummond isn't happy with the complimentary soaps and substitute milk cartons, he might complain to my bosses, which will drop me right in the mire.

In the meantime, I've begun organising the charity Scarecrow Parade, as instructed by Jemima. I've typed up a list of names, provided by Jemima, each one associated with the neighbouring allotments, The Stables gallery or Lerwick Manor Hotel. I run my index finger down the printed list of names, checking I haven't missed anyone; there's sure to be trouble if I have. Jemima has envisaged a scarecrow parade on the allotments, to be created in the same manner as a festive Secret Santa draw. Fingers crossed, those taking part will know the person whose likeness and style they're meant to imitate; I'm not entirely sure who everyone is. I've created a project folder labelled 'Charity Event', not that anyone but me will be referring to it. I'm excluding myself from the frivolity; instead, I'll do the organising and provide an unbiased opinion on each scarecrow, if needed.

I head into the rear office to make a start on the many weekly tasks my role demands: organising the staff rotas, checking local

B&B promotions and computing our occupancy rate figures – all necessary information, ready for my regular meetings with the Campbells. I'm yet to see them displeased with my reported data. I settle myself before the computer, swiftly tapping the keys and watching the screen change as it requests my password.

'Morning, Autumn!'

I hear a male voice call my name. It's par for the course with this role: the minute you settle in a chair, someone arrives at reception.

'Good morning, Mungo. How are you today?'

'Good, good. I wondered if that secret lucky dip thing is ready ... the likes of me needs to make sure I get someone I know.' His grey beard dances as he speaks. 'I don't know half of these newcomers in the gallery, or the Far Siders on the allotment, so there's no point lumbering myself with an impossible task. I might as well not bother.'

'I'm sure your contribution will be wonderful.'

'Not if I get a stranger. It'll be an utter waste of my time and energy – and I haven't got an endless source of either, young lady.' His usual gruffness reappears in an instant.

I grab my prepared folder from beneath the countertop, but before I have a chance to open it and retrieve my printed list of names, he issues his demand.

'I want our Dottie.'

'That's not how it works, Mungo. It's supposed to be a surprise. You put your hand in the bag and select a paper slip. You'll be creating the scarecrow to represent that person, and no one else.' I was delighted when Jemima hadn't wasted any time confirming a charity event after Ms Muir's return from hospital. It was vital that someone other than the Campbells took a leading role, so I volunteered.

'Phuh! I bloody knew it. A complete waste of my time.'

'A charity event is never a waste of time, Mungo. Especially when it's for such a good cause. None of us know when we might need such services and treatment ourselves.'

I hold a cloth money bag aloft, containing the names of everyone who has agreed to take part, and give it a gentle shake. Offering Mungo the bag, I am careful to hold it high above the countertop, so that neither of us can peer inside.

'It's hardly the Secret Service,' he mutters, plunging his hand in and swirling it around.

'It's not the World Cup draw either,' I retort, in response to his feverish hand actions.

Mungo continues to swirl his hand inside the cloth bag. 'I don't understand the concept, stuff like this wasn't around in my day.'

'We've copied the concept of Secret Santa, but instead of buying a Christmas gift, each person taking part creates a scarecrow. I'm sure you'll have a lot of fun depicting the personality of your chosen participant.'

'I don't see what's wrong with keeping it simple and allowing folks to donate to charities, without all this palaver.' His hand is still churning the slips of paper in the money bag, like the paddle in an ice cream maker.

'Mungo, have you quite finished?'

His brow furrows and he glares at me. 'I want Dottie . . . I'm not joining in otherwise.'

I keep hold of the cloth bag, the fabric rubbing against my reddened sore fingers. With my free hand I grab his wrist and hold tight.

'That ruins the game for everyone. The whole concept of the scarecrow parade relies on everyone playing their part. Now, you'll comply with the rules and have whichever name you pick out. OK?'

Mungo's steely gaze avoids mine.

'Mungo?'

'I suppose . . . these new-fangled schemes aren't to my liking.'

'Are you in or out?' I demand, still holding his wrist. He obviously hasn't finished twirling and swirling the names.

'In,' comes his barely audible reply.

I release his wrist, giving him a hearty smile.

Mungo rotates his hand one last time, showing his stubborn spirit, and then retrieves a single slip.

'Let me look,' I say, eager to note on my list who he's selected. *Dottie Nesbit*. The black font mocks me as Mungo lays the slip of paper on to the countertop.

'Don't look so smug, it was pure chance,' I snipe, narked that he's got exactly what he wanted.

'Don't you be so sure, lassie,' he says, tapping his nose in an annoying manner.

I scribble his name alongside Dottie's on the register and quickly close my file.

'It's a secret now, you're not to hint or mention it to her, so it'll be a surprise on the day!' I instruct, for fear he'll ruin it.

'You must think I'm a fool,' he snorts, shaking his head and striding across the hallway towards the entrance doors.

I collect the slip of paper bearing Dottie's name from the countertop and secure it beneath a paperclip at the back of the file, before returning everything to its place.

One down, another thirty-four to go.

Ding, ding! The reception bell is rung abruptly.

I jump up, my smile instantly in place, ready to answer the summons. I head through to the front of house to find Levi leaning over the countertop as if searching for something.

'Hello, Autumn!'

'Hello, lost something?'

'No. Mungo told me the scarecrow name draw is up and running, so I'm here to choose before the name I want goes to someone else.'

'It doesn't work like that, Levi,' I say, about to launch into my spiel about Secret Santa draws and random probability.

'Ha, ha, but you see it might, because Mungo picked Dottie.'

My mouth drops wide.

'What's the matter?' asks Levi.

'He's not supposed to tell people.'

'Ackkk, be away with you, as if I'd tell a soul.'

For the second time, I grab my file and cloth bag to begin the selection. If every participant who comes in follows this school of thought, I'll regret volunteering for this event – which is hardly a charitable attitude to have.

Chapter Twenty-Four

Pippa

I'm fairly chuffed with my sales for today. A few new customers have shown an interest in the Bread Basket, I've had a decent laugh with the new mum and her baby, and now I'm having a lovely chat whilst serving Nancy Crabtree her regular half-loaf in Tresta.

'Morning, Nancy, your usual?' I say, when she appears with her netted bag.

'Yes, please. I look forward to my fresh loaf.'

Bless her, you'd think it was the highlight of her week.

'There you go,' I say, offering her the wrapped loaf. 'Archie will be pleased to know it wasn't wasted.'

'Archie?'

'Yes, an elderly gent from Tingwall. It's like a bookend loaf, each half sold an hour apart,' I say, wrapping her purchase.

'My goodness, is Archie Kibble still alive and kicking? I haven't seen him for years.' Nancy leans in closer, before continuing, 'We had a summer fling in our younger days, did me and Archie.'

I watch as Nancy blushes, chuckling to herself.

At the end of the day, with the open road ahead of me and the sun shining, I feel blessed. I'm returning to the gallery with empty wicker baskets, having sold out of all my bakes. It's a first for me, as I usually have the odd bannock or two remaining.

It's hard to believe that I contemplated staying in The Orangery, wiping endless tables, when I could be driving around, with no bosses breathing down my neck and actually enjoying my day's work. Unlike Callie.

My mind's about to wander along that well-trodden path when I spy a dark object lying at the side of the kerb, about a mile from the gallery. The misshapen outline looks like a discarded sofa cushion at first glance. Why people do their fly tipping, spoiling such beautiful scenery, is beyond me. As I draw near, the undistinguished blob takes on a clearer form. It looks like a dog lying on its side. The blue merle coat is instantly recognisable. Floss.

I'm parked and dashing from my driver's seat in seconds. There's no other traffic, the road is empty, but I can't believe that others haven't driven past recently.

'Floss! Floss!' I call as I get nearer, unsure what I'm about to find.

The dog doesn't move, her back legs are twisted, and there's a dark pool of blood beneath the long-haired blue coat. She doesn't react to her name. I hesitate, unsure if I can stomach what I'm about to see. What Magnus will do when he finds out what has happened to his beloved dog, Lord only knows.

I kneel down alongside her. Her head doesn't move but those dark doleful eyes sweep sideways, greeting my face. Her eyebrows twitch in recognition – not of me, but a welcome human presence.

'It's OK, old girl. I'm not going to hurt you,' I whisper as my hand gently strokes her muzzle.

I crash through the doors of Lerwick's veterinary surgery, struggling under the hefty weight of a limp dog. The reception lady jumps up from behind her desk and scurries forward in a stumbling attempt to assist me.

'She's been knocked over. I found her on the road just off the

A970 into Lerwick. I assume she's been out and about on one of her solo walks and some sad bastard has ploughed into her and then buggered off.'

'This way, please,' instructs the lady who, having grabbed the door handle, is now gesturing towards the corridor, which I know from previous experience with childhood hamsters and guinea pigs leads to the consulting rooms. 'Knock the door and go straight in.'

Thankfully, the consultation room door is ajar, so I don't need a free hand. I push it open to find Vet MacKay scrubbing his table after finishing with the previous appointment.

'Hi, the lady said to come straight through . . . I found her . . . she's been knocked over.'

I gently lay the limp dog down on the rubberised surface and willingly step backwards from the examination table. I feel my mission is accomplished; I got her here alive.

'Floss, isn't it?' says MacKay.

'Magnus Sinclair's dog – out on one of her usual jaunts, I imagine.' I fall silent as he grabs his stethoscope and pops it into his ears.

The reception lady appears in the doorway. 'I'll give Magnus a quick call,' she says, peering at the dog before disappearing from view.

It's comforting to know that the surgery recognises their clients, though I don't suppose many folk around Lerwick could fail to identify Floss. Magnus will be gutted if anything happens to her. My stomach lurches at the very thought.

Vet MacKay listens to the dog's chest before slowly feeling along her body, pressing and prodding as he goes. I can't make out what he's muttering, but it seems to appease the animal, which is the most important thing.

I look down to find my tabard is displaying an unsightly dark blob, which I assume is her blood.

'There was a pool of blood on the roadside,' I say, once he removes the stethoscope from his ears.

'She's not in a good way, poor lassie. I can do the basics and make her comfortable in the absence of Magnus, but I'll be needing a serious chat before we decide on anything else.'

I feel sick. What would have happened if I hadn't driven past when I did? Would another car have stopped to help her, or would they have knocked her over for a second time, not realising it was a dog? I wince at the very thought. The poor mite looks pretty pathetic sprawled on the consulting table, her dark eyes switching between us as we speak. It's as if she knows how serious the situation is.

The reception lady reappears at the door. 'Magnus is on his way. He said to give her anything she needs in the meantime.'

'Thank you, I was expecting that,' says Vet MacKay, reaching into an overhead cupboard to retrieve a syringe and small vials. The door to the consulting room closes, and his hands swiftly draw up the liquid before gently taking hold of the dog's scruff and injecting her. 'You'll feel some relief after this, Floss, though we'll need X-rays to understand the full extent of this afternoon's adventures.'

His words calm me, if not the dog. I don't know what to say or do, so I do the only feasible thing and hold the dog's paw. I'm sure deep down she appreciates it. I certainly do; my adrenalin is kicking in now the dog is in good hands. My legs are quivering and my hands feel jittery too. Local folk think I'm the stray sheep of the family flock, who's always up to no good, yet here I am morphing into a quivering wreck. As tough as Magnus appears – physically, mentally and no doubt emotionally – I have no idea how he'll react when he sees Floss in this state.

'Maybe it's best I leave now, let you get on?' I say, questioning the vet as he checks the previous notes on his computer.

'The choice is yours. I'm sure Magnus will wish to thank you for bringing her in.'

He's got a point. But when do I make my excuses to leave, once that task is complete? The man might break down in tears, yelp like a puppy and not wish for his reaction to be witnessed by someone he sees on a regular basis. Some men are funny like that; so conscious of appearing human when the rest of the time they act like they're almost superhuman.

'I think I'll go now. I've done all I can for her . . . it's best I get going. I'll catch up with Magnus another time.'

Bang on cue, the surgery door opens wide and Magnus fills the door frame.

'I might have known . . . speeding again, were we?' His gruff tone hits me first, before his words register.

My mouth drops open, my eyes widen in shock and I burst into tears. I dash past him, squeezing through the tiny gap remaining in the doorway, as quick as my legs can carry me. Magnus believes me capable of this! He thinks *I* hit his dog! He assumes that it's my guilty conscience which has forced me to do the right thing in bringing her here.

Why couldn't I answer him? Blurting out an objection to his insinuation is beyond me; I'm simply too emotional and shocked to speak.

The fresh air does little to dry my angry tears as I march across to the Bread Basket. I've left the van erratically parked across two white lines of the car park. The angry voice in my head begins to rant as I clamber into the driver's seat. My knee knocks the keys, still dangling from the ignition where I left them.

'My God, I didn't even bother to remove them! Ned would have had a fit if I'd called to say Rolly had been nicked,' I mutter, relieved that the van is still here. But it's not enough of a silver lining to obliterate Magnus' accusation.

Tears continue to flow. I can't see clearly to reverse, so I slump down in the driver's seat, knowing this tsunami of anger and emotion will subside in a matter of minutes.

There's a sudden rap on my driver's window, which causes me to jump.

'What now?' I say, not even bothering to wipe my tears away.

My driver's door is wrenched wide open and Levi stands there, eyes agog at the messy scene before him.

'Whatever is wrong, Pippa?'

I go to answer, but the knot in my throat, the angry voices in my head and the sheer wash of tears, all mute my voice. I simply reach out both arms and sink into his outstretched arms. I must look a complete fright, but I've nothing and no one else ... only Levi ... right here, right now.

'OK, OK. It'll pass, whatever's happened, simply let it go. A few deep breaths will calm you down and then you can explain.'

I feel him rocking me from side to side as he gently speaks, my tears drenching his lumberjack shirt, which has a comforting smell of fabric softener. A surprisingly nice touch for a man.

It seems like an age, but still not long enough to dry the continual flow of my tears, before I begin to speak in a staccato fashion. My voice snags on every syllable, making me sound nasal and blocked.

'Floss ... hit and run ... I brought her in ... but Magnus accused me of s-speeding ... and now, he's in there ... and I'm out h-here ... and I didn't say a b-bloody thing ... I ran,' I stammer.

'Did he now?' Levi's tone has an edge to it. 'I've a good mind to go in there and—'

'No, don't! His dog's about to die or be put to sleep or something as drastic ... you can't, Levi.'

'He'd best apologise for his misunderstanding when he's calmed down,' says Levi, holding me at arm's length and scrutinising my face. 'I was on my way back to the taxi rank and only dropped by when I spotted your erratic parking. It's a bloody good job that I did, just look at the state of yee.'

I give a loud sniff, totally unattractive for a damsel in distress, but essential if his shirt is to remain snot free.

'Look at ya, snot and tears everywhere,' he says, gently lifting my wet fringe from my red and puffy eyes. 'And all for what . . . trying to help out and save his bloody dog from dying on the side of the road. Hey up, talk of the devil!'

I turn and peer sideways over Levi's bulky arms, to witness Magnus striding towards us, his hand vigorously wiping his features as if tired after a hard day's graft. Both men give a silent blokeish nod of acknowledgement before Magnus speaks directly to me.

'Can I have a word?'

'Sure.' My tone is curt, I can't help myself. I've been here a million times, with folk jumping to conclusions just because it's me.

'I just heard that you didn't . . . you know, and that I was wrong to say . . .' Magnus thumbs a gesture over his shoulder towards the veterinary surgery. 'Look, what I'm struggling to say is . . . I was totally out of order saying what I did about speeding. Vet MacKay said that Floss has a chance thanks to you and the speed with which you brought her straight in. She's in a pretty bad way and, well, it's not looking too good for one of her back legs, but . . . Pippa, I'm sorry for suggesting it was you who hit her. Obviously it wasn't.'

I sit and stare. I don't attempt to ease his discomfort by inter-rupting with a casual 'it's fine', 'it's OK' or even a 'don't worry about it', because it isn't . . . not in my rule book.

Magnus waits, roughly rubbing his mouth with his thumb, as if unsure that his apology is sufficient in the circumstances. Levi glances between us.

'Thank you,' I mumble. 'I appreciate you saying that. It's the usual tale, though, isn't it? Everyone jumps to the same conclu-sion, simply because I'm involved with the situation. I've made mistakes in my time, and I get that folk have long memories, but if they'd only give me a chance, they'd see I'm not all bad; I've got a big heart when treated fairly.' My voice is steely, but it cracks as I finish the sentence.

Magnus flinches and looks away, as if viewing the traffic, before refocusing on me. 'Yep, you're right. I'll admit it. As soon as I saw your van, your dire parking, and then you alongside Floss, I jumped to the wrong conclusion. I'm admitting it; I'm grateful for the attention you've paid her and, fingers crossed, she'll pull through as a result.' It's now his voice which cracks with emotion. 'Cheers, Pippa. I owe you.'

Levi looks at me, raises his eyebrows, silently asking the question, 'Is there any more for the guy to say, given he's clearly upset and shaken?'

'Thanks, Magnus.' It's easy enough to say when you're in the right. Despite having been wronged, and judged so swiftly, I'll be the bigger person and end this episode.

'So, we're all good?' asks Levi, glancing between us again.

I'm not sure if it's meant to put us all on an equal footing, or more likely it's his blokey way of calming the tension.

I nod. 'All good,' I mouth, purely for effect.

'Cheers, pet,' mutters Magnus, before adding, 'I'd best get back inside as they're preparing to X-ray her.'

'All the best, mate. Shout if you need anything,' says Levi, receiving a slap on the back from Magnus before he swiftly departs.

Levi licks his lips and sighs before eyeballing me.

'What?' I ask belligerently.

'Bloody hell, for a minute there I thought you were going to lamp him one.'

'Mmmm.'

'Seriously, woman. You are a sassy mare.'

A smile cracks my tear-stained features. 'I can't help it.' A titter of laughter escapes as I recall my edgy tone and Magnus' crumpled appearance.

'The man's nearly lost his dog and still you're up for a fight,' says Levi, shaking his head in disbelief. 'You've certainly got some fire in your belly.'

Chapter Twenty-Five

Sunday 27 February

Natalia

There's a definite nip in the morning air as I stand back, watching Mungo lead the alpaca herd from their overnight stable to open pasture. Jemima follows the herd, sending a wry smile in my direction. I'm not wholly sure if it's edged with embarrassment at my presence, or pity. I can do without either. I return the gesture as best I can, though no doubt my smile resembles a grimace.

I keep my distance, imagining them to be nervous creatures, easily spooked by my presence. I don't wish to be blamed for them racing off along the gravelled driveway; they'll be halfway to Lerwick town centre in no time. They're an amusing sight as they walk in a huddle, bumping and nudging each other out of the way, tethered by reins which entwine and come together in Mungo's secure grasp.

Safely delivered through their paddock gate, he releases the herd to gallop in a giraffe-like manner across the grassy pasture, celebrating their freedom. I remember how good that feels. To move unencumbered within an open space, doing as you please, showing joy, burning energy, displaying vitality and health, seems a distant memory to me as I slowly cross the paved area and rest my arms along the wooden fencing to admire these beautiful creatures for a little longer.

I'd promised Dottie that my first task each day would be a

gentle walk in the fresh air; I can now tick that off my daily list. It hasn't escaped my notice that this one item ticks numerous boxes on her nursing checklist. Despite my struggles, I'm out of bed, washed and dressed; she knows I'd never venture out in my night clothes, without my hair and make-up done. Not that she admits to nursing me, but that's my take on her behaviour. It dates back to that simple exchange when we crossed on the staircase as the ambulance crew carried me out. One glance, and a million unsaid apologies flowed between us.

Jemima and Mungo exit the paddock, securing the gate and gesturing a farewell, which I acknowledge with a nod. I can't keep grimacing at folk, though repeated muscle use may support my recovery somewhat. I simply wish to be alone, to watch the alpacas and gather my thoughts for the day ahead. When others are present I'm hyper aware of my physical being, as if my skin is vibrating like an electric fence; a warning sign alerting others to unspoken dangers, should they venture near enough to be exposed to the realities of my condition. Not just the realities of my physical restrictions but also my mood, emotions and frustrations, which I'm juggling with every hour of every day. People have tried to show compassion, but nine times out of ten it comes across as pity, embarrassment or awkwardness at the realisation that I'm not the person I once was. But I *am*, on the inside, which is where I was always told it mattered. Obviously another of life's lies.

I glance over my shoulder, making sure the pair have returned to the gallery yard. I'm seeking solitude without fear of interruption. Never before have I craved such a state. Everyone's trying their best with me, doing all they can and offering their time in a selfless fashion, but I desire inner peace which only appears when I'm truly alone.

I rest my chin on my folded arms and gaze at the alpacas. Will I ever run again as they do? Will my movements ever be as fluid as theirs? Who am I kidding, says a quiet voice inside my head.

I have to be honest with myself and acknowledge all that has happened to me. Hold my head up, challenge people's ideas of who I am, and work out what I want for my future.

'Hello.'

My skin prickles at the interruption. More so, when I turn to view Ned approaching with an air of caution. Every fibre of my being wishes to run, dart past him back to my suite and pretend I didn't see him, but my body won't cooperate. In any case, I can't show such rudeness – not when my feelings towards him and memories of our time together remain so vivid. I am who I am – I need to show some self-respect and maintain my dignity, not run and hide.

'Hi,' I reply, standing tall and selecting an upbeat mode from my dial of choices. I hear the heavy slur on my speech and cringe. I want him to walk on by, I don't need him to stop and chat politely or concern himself with my well-being. They've done enough by allowing me to stay on here, in the same suite, without charge.

'How's it going?' he says, arriving to stand alongside me.

'I'm fine, just admiring the herd.' To whom I silently apologise for using them as an excuse to avert my gaze from his.

'No. How are you really?'

Damn!

I turn my face slightly, enabling him to view my profile whilst my hands clutch the top bar of the fencing, guaranteeing stability.

'Ned, I'm not lying. I promised Dottie I'd get fresh air, and as you can see, here I am.'

There's a tension between us, as if my invisible electric fence is buzzing and he's ignoring the warnings.

'I can see that but . . .'

I don't want this conversation. It sounds selfish that I am

prepared to stay on his property, accepting his offer of accommodation, but I wish he'd simply let me be.

'Ned, please. I don't need to hear it. I think I've been through enough, these past few weeks, and I'm still making sense of my world.'

His shoulders drop. 'I get that, but it doesn't stop me worrying about how you are. I realise that Dottie and Autumn are doing all they can, providing everything you need. Natalia, we were together long enough for me to know . . . that this isn't you.'

'Together?' I repeat, without thinking. I turn my head, forcing his eyes to meet mine.

His gaze flickers, a deep crease forms above his brow.

'Is that what you call it? Because I don't, not now. We weren't together as in a serious commitment, or a true couple as such . . . looking back, I don't even think I could claim we were in a long-distance relationship. Hell no, can you even class us as together when we were always apart?'

'Natalia?' His stance shifts as he squares his shoulders. 'I was with you for longer than any other relationship in my life.'

'I didn't count for much, given the speed with which you moved on.' I hear my own accusation and wince; emotions always surface when you least expect them. I don't want to argue but I can't ignore the pennies which have dropped in recent weeks.

His face falls as my words land.

'Look, I can't explain how it was. I cared for you, was happy to see you each time you visited, and yet there was something . . .'

'Missing? Yeah, so I keep being told.'

His shoulders twitch in reply.

'I wasn't enough and she was – that's the reality of the situation, Ned. And sorry for sounding so damned shallow, but you moved heaven and earth to ensure the path was clear for you to get to know her.'

'It simply happened, Natalia. I didn't plan for it. Jemima appeared and I fell in love.'

His final word hangs between us like dynamite.

'Sorry, that was too honest,' he says, looking down.

'No, don't apologise. She walked in and you were smitten. It's how it should be . . . it's what I wanted.'

I want to kick myself for being so trusting. Or gag myself before another word spills from my slurring lips. I didn't intend for it to sound like begging, pleading or pity talk.

I return my gaze to the herd. The alpacas are now gleefully frolicking, without a care in the world.

'I fell into the trap of thinking you'd missed me, wanted me, and even needed me in your life. I would fly in like a love-sick puppy when the reality was probably sheer loneliness.' I hear Ned sigh, but I continue, 'And that's where I went wrong. I was fearful of raising certain topics, appearing needy or demanding, yet your silence fed my hopes.'

He looks at me, clearly uncomfortable, but my own self-respect doesn't wish to relieve him of his embarrassment. But still, it isn't nice to watch. My voice doesn't sound how it used to, my facial features, my stance and my outlook on life have all changed – it must feel strange for him to stand before me, not seeing the woman he once knew so intimately.

'We never had "the talk", did we?' he says.

'Nope. Never. So I drifted along, expecting and assuming.'

His expression is doleful. 'Sorry, you seemed happy sharing our time together.'

'I probably did, but I realise now I was hurting inside.'

Silence descends.

'I never meant to cause you hurt or harm. I did care for you.'

'Care? Didn't you ever . . .?' My slurring lips falter on the 'L' word.

He gently shakes his head.

'But you knew instantly when you saw her?'

His smile says it all.

'Ackk right, I see, it's that ... that, right there. The magic.' I want to laugh. For here lies the jigsaw piece that we were missing; this is possibly the most truthful conversation we've ever had. My mind swims with further questions but, thankfully, my pride refuses to relinquish its crown.

'Natalia, if you need anything, please tell me,' he says, signalling a close to our conversation.

'I will.'

Ned gently taps my forearm, which I interpret as a farewell gesture, before striding away. I urge myself to stay schtum, with my pride somewhat intact; I need to let him go, there's no more to say. I watch him retreat towards the manor, returning to his livelihood and his wife. I swallow the emotional knot clogging my throat.

I linger for a little longer, before returning to my suite feeling melancholy and in need of isolation. I can't handle such conversations. I slump on to my bed and have a good cry; it seems the only sensible thing to do.

Autumn

It's been a long, tiring day in which I've dealt with queries from departing guests, located a missing suitcase at Sumburgh Airport and settled an argument between two disgruntled chefs. I gladly tidy the reception desk, preparing to finish my shift. It's simply a matter of routine for me, given my nature, but I know others struggle with such basic tasks, thinking they're beneath them. Many a time I've had to scoot around at the beginning of a shift to restore order and locate what I need for the job. Tidiness is second nature to me; everything has a place and should live there until required. Sadly not a mantra that everyone has adopted in life. It infuriates me watching others spend an entire day retracing their steps in search of an item, only to lose it again thirty seconds later amongst a tsunami of papers.

'Evening, Autumn,' calls Mungo, entering reception clutching two bowls of dusky-blue hyacinths. 'Dottie sent these as per Jemima's request. She said they're to be displayed somewhere in the hallway, but not where they'll get in the way.'

'Right you are, thank you,' I say, taking the offering from his grasp.

'And mind you turn the bowls each day, otherwise they'll lean towards the light and never last,' he adds.

'Thanks for pointing out the obvious, Mungo – you're a life saver.' I give a wry smile, which obviously confuses him when twinned with my sarcastic comment.

He twitches his brow. 'You'll soon be off then?' he asks, lingering at the counter, having performed his duty.

'As soon as Hannah arrives.'

'Peerie gal, blonde hair?' He gestures with his hand halfway down his chest.

'That'll be her.'

'She won't be coming. She's off out, I just passed her on Charlotte Street amongst a crowd of women.'

I don't know if he's pulling my leg or not. He looks serious enough.

'Away with you, she's on the rota for the late shift.'

Mungo gestures over his shoulder, as if Charlotte Street were right outside the hotel's doors.

'No, you don't fool me. You and Levi think it's funny to play tricks on me, but I won't be falling for that one any day soon. I am off duty with a free night to myself and I'll be enjoying a leisurely evening at . . .' I don't finish my sentence, as his expression changes.

'You might not think much of my manner, young lady, but I'll tell you something for nowt, Mungo Tulloch doesn't joke where work is concerned. Do you hear me? And I can vouch for Levi too – he's a grafter is that lad, and as good as his word.'

I wasn't expecting him to take it to heart. But likewise, if he is genuine about Hannah not attending her shift, who is going to man the reception desk?

'I've known that young lassie since she was a bairn, and I tell you I've just seen her going out. I suggest you call Jemima if you're concerned about your working hours.'

'Excuse me, I'm not concerned about my working hours. It's just that I'm supposed to be clocking off for an evening at The Garrison theatre, but now it seems that might not be happening.' I'm not sure which saddens me more: the prospect of another cover shift or phoning my sister to cancel our arrangement.

'In my day, we stopped working when the bosses told us to, we weren't inclined to decide for ourselves.'

'Inclined? We work to a rota system, Mungo. I'm sure that concept was freely available back in your day.' I'm fuming. If it's an honest mistake by Hannah, then that can't be helped. But if she's gone out on the razz, leaving me in the lurch on purpose, then that opens a whole new can of worms.

'Anyway, I'll be seeing you,' says Mungo, raising his cap as he backs away from reception.

I've definitely offended him, but there's a spring to his step which suggests he's scared in case I ask him for a favour. I'd laugh if I wasn't so sodding miffed in case he proves to be correct. I glance at the clock: quarter to six. I'll know soon enough.

Chapter Twenty-Six

Pippa

'What are you even doing here?' I say, knowing which nerve to twang.

I'm late arriving back at the gallery for a Sunday, but still, I don't expect to encounter animosity from Callie. We've spent the last twenty minutes in silence, with me walking back and forth emptying Rolly of wicker baskets and dirty utensils, while she performs the closing routine for The Orangery by wiping the tables.

Callie's mouth drops wide open, her stance is feisty, similar to mine, as we face each other across the empty space.

'I won't even grace that with a response . . . it's you who needs to shape up or ship out, Pippa. Not me!'

'Ship out? Pah!' I thrust my chin forward as I ready myself for the spat that's been brewing for the past few weeks. I grab a box of paper serviettes and begin filling my dispenser ready for Rolly's next outing.

'Pah yourself!' she retorts. 'Jemima said you'd be a handful to contend with, and she was right. Stomping back and forth like you're hard done by for completing a day's work. You take the bloody biscuit, you do, yet you act like you're the victim at every possible opportunity.'

'Me? Stomping? You must be joking. I've emptied the Bread Basket like I do every day. And now I want to go home.'

'You've done it all your life, Pippa. You'd best get over yourself, because others won't give in like they did when you were a child. Your sulky tantrums need to disappear ... start acting like a grown-up not a spoilt little girl.'

She's wrong on so many levels that my brain struggles to correctly order the sequence in which I had best answer her statement.

'You've got some nerve, Callie. Just because you're the eldest you think you're entitled to say what you wish and have first dibs on everything, before me and Jemima even get a look-in.'

'Ah, here we go ... the same old record. Let's hear it, Pippa.'

'Ah, here we go ...' I mimic, which is a pathetic response, but I can't help myself.

'Very mature.'

'You'd think you were the only one entitled to Nanna's sapphire engagement ring ... it didn't enter your head to ask if I wanted it, did it?'

Callie pulls a face, throwing a disgusted look in my direction. Bingo, no answer, because I'm right!

I swiftly continue, before she can answer. 'You don't even wear it!'

'It's hardly an everyday object, is it?'

'Nanna wore it every day of her married life till her dying day.' I pride myself on the quick answers; Callie's cornered and she knows it.

'Are you still harping on about that bloody ring?'

'Harping on? You were calculated in the way you asked for it, "Please, Daddy, Nanna would want me to have it, being the eldest granddaughter, please, Daddy." That was sodding embarrassing!'

'You were there ... you could have spoken up, or did the cat nab your tongue?'

'I didn't stand a chance against you and your calculated ways ... Jemima wasn't even invited, so you can't say she had the opportunity to speak up.'

'Mmmph, I think she got enough, don't you?'

'I did at the time, but I've realised a lot since then.'

'Such as?'

'Granddad drew up a new will after Nanna died, so the provision regarding the death of a child was there before Jemima's mum died. It could have been any one of us that benefited from that clause. Plus, she did a lot for Granddad – her weekly visits to the sheltered housing complex, paying for his annual allotment subs as a birthday gift – so it makes sense.'

'Makes sense? Blimey, she's clearly got you under her wing.'

I'm not being biased, simply honest. 'Not at all. I've seen a lot more of Jemima since I've been working here. I didn't truly know her until then – I'll admit my initial reaction after the funeral was wrong, and I injured her further out of spite, but now . . .'

'My God, don't you dare say it, Pippa.'

'If you got to know her a bit more, you'd probably feel the same. Jemima's alright, she's got a heart of gold.'

'I've heard it all now.' Callie throws down her cleaning cloth and stares me out. 'Are you feeling OK?'

'Fine, thanks.' I continue to stuff the serviettes into the metal holder, knowing she's dumbstruck by my change of attitude.

I get it. I'd be surprised too, knowing how much I've disliked Jemima in the past, but now, well, now things are different. I've spent time around her, seen how hard she works, and actually admire the woman she's become. And deep down, I'm proud of myself for airing such an honest view.

'I sold it.'

I hear her words but they don't register or make sense in relation to our conversation.

'Sorry, I don't understand . . .' I mutter, turning to face her.

'I said, I sold it – Nanna's ring, I mean.'

I'm speechless. It's not that I wanted it, it's not that I ever truly admired it when Nanna wore it, but to think that Callie made a play for the one item that Nanna treasured throughout her life . . . and now she confesses this.

'You're joking me, right?'

Callie bites her lip before shaking her head.

Who'd have thought goody-goody Callie would indulge in such antics! Words fail me. My gut reaction is to rant and shout at her, but what's the point? She's a grown woman who can do what she wishes.

'How much did you get?'

'A grand.' She has the decency to blush and mumble. 'Actually, eight hundred. I wanted a grand but the jeweller refused.'

'You could have asked if you were a bit short, rather than flog it.'

She shrugs. It's not a nonchalant gesture but a heavy-hearted admission that she has no answer to give.

'Who to?'

'The local antiques guy.'

'Right. And was that necessary?'

'I was never going to wear it so I thought I might as well treat myself. Why have it sitting in my jewellery box for eternity. Would you have bought it?'

'I'd have preferred to, rather than see it leave the family.'

'You're going to tell Jemima, aren't you?'

'No.'

'You're not?'

'That would be opening a can of worms, because there's absolutely no way she would have refused you the money. She'd have insisted, even I know that.'

'I feel awful now.' Callie collects her damp cloth and begins to wipe the nearest table.

I watch as she works at a stubborn mark before wringing out her cloth. She looks utterly dejected. Deep inside I feel numb; our grandparents would be devastated if they knew.

Autumn

'My God, you look whacked!' says Pippa, stepping out of her room as I unlock my door.

'Do you think?' My voice is heavy, matching my mood.

'Are you OK?'

I give the key a twist, and sigh. It's one of those moments when, if anyone is nice to me, there's a chance I'll cry. I need to hold it together for a few more minutes until I'm alone. In a hot bath, behind a locked door or tucked up in bed – then I can let go. I can cry over the injustice of a double shift, the annoyance of missing a night out, the anger of continually smiling to portray the image of a happy worker, when I've spent the last four hours cursing Hannah with every breath for denying me the chance to have a life outside of work. The only silver lining to my evening was Mr Drummond's brief attendance at reception to ask for details of where he could purchase additional goat's milk soap. I was grateful to officially complete his task, ticking it off my list, with no likelihood of him mentioning it to the Campbells.

My sister will forgive me for cancelling on her, we can arrange another night, but that's not the point. I'd waited all day, looked forward to some quality time outside work, only to have it dashed by someone else's lack of consideration.

'Autumn, can I get you anything?' asks Pippa carefully. Her voice is barely a whisper as she reads my distress.

I shake my head, bite my lip to prevent myself from speaking, because I know deep down I'll be totally unprofessional and say more than I should. I've done all that is required of me, plus more, and still I don't get to enjoy myself.

'Let me go and fetch you a hot drink.'

'Thanks, but no thanks. I simply want a hot bath and bed.' I offer a weak smile but there's no disguising my anguish; I'm on the verge of tears. I push the door a little way, indicating that now is the moment to let me go, cease talking and let me slip into my own private abyss, allow me to unwind towards sleep.

Pippa doesn't take the hint. She gives it one last push, trying to be helpful, as most people do when others appear to be in need.

'It wouldn't be any trouble, honest. I'll gladly fetch . . .'

Too much. My tears well up, spilling over my lashes quicker than my next heartbeat. I know she's trying to be helpful, but why do others not listen? Why couldn't she accept my first refusal? But no. And now here I am, in tears, when I could have been safely in my bathroom, running a soothing bubble bath. Why should I fight for everything that I need? Given the effort and hard work I invest in my daily routine, why is my path always so difficult?

'Autumn, come here.' Pippa springs forward, wrapping a comforting arm about my shoulders.

But I'm now angry, not only for working myself into this state but for acting like a cry baby too. I want to shrug her off, escape into my room, but that'll offend her and cause more damage to our newly formed friendship, so I stand and tolerate an embrace I don't need and wouldn't have required if she'd just allowed me to retreat into my room.

'Listen, it's not that bad. Everything will look better in the morning,' Pippa attempts to reassure me. 'You need a decent night's sleep and you'll feel as right as rain.'

'I know.' And I do know. I'm not just saying it to appease her. I know exactly what I need, yet when I try to do what is best for me, my plans are always scuppered. 'Thank you, good night, Pippa.' I gently wriggle from her warm embrace, offering a grateful smile, before disappearing into my room.

Chapter Twenty-Seven

Tuesday 1 March

Dottie's diary
The layer of dust on the Black Watch tartan and crystal chandelier is making me
crabbit. I've reported my concerns to Ned; housekeeping need speaking to.
That poor lassie's speech seems to be a permanent slur. Life's so cruel – Mungo agrees.

Natalia

Having entered through the adjoining gate, I wander along the allotment pathway, which appears to be leading me in a figure-of-eight shape. I've never visited before, so I surprised myself by turning the gate's ancient iron ring and lifting the latch. I was getting a sense of Groundhog Day during my daily walk around the courtyard; there are only so many times I can enquire about how the blacksmith's sculptures are progressing.

I'm embarrassed that this is my first visit. Ned always spent an hour or two of our weekends together down here tending his bees. I frequently grumbled about such visits during my short breaks. I always wanted to be the centre of his attention, with no other distractions stealing our time. Maybe I could have enjoyed more of his time if I'd taken an interest in this green-fingered enterprise. Like now, I could have amused myself wandering around looking at the ramshackle sheds, spiked mannequin heads and a multitude of white plastic chairs. I'm surprised by the amount of junk stashed on some plots; I thought their sole purpose was supposed to be growing produce.

I follow one loop of the twisting pathway at the halfway section, to discover two larger sheds: The Cabbage Patch and The Veggie Rack, as the signage announces. This is what Dottie frequently refers to as gin o'clock and her Friday afternoon socials. I eye each shed warily. They're sturdy enough, clean and tidy from the outside, but I can't imagine that two glorified sheds equate to the 'hot spot' in town – unless they're sniffing the fertiliser mix.

The door to The Veggie Rack is pinned wide open, so I pop my head inside to view the interior; it's decked with wooden shelving on which fresh produce and bottled goods are displayed alongside plastic tubs. An elderly guy sleeps in a low-slung deck chair. His distinctive greying beard curls down the front of his knitted jumper, and his gentle snores are filling the silence. I've seen him around before, one of Dottie's friends, I imagine. I leave without waking him; I've no intention of purchasing goods or embarking on the pleasantries of a mid-morning chat.

I continue along the intersection, crossing from one row of allotments to the other. As I round the corner, taking a left turn, I spy a blue, black and white flag flying high. Hardly from around these parts; I recognise every other flag fluttering on the breeze, but not this one.

My gaze drops from the large flag to its makeshift flagpole, then to the owner's plot. I'm open-mouthed and a snort escapes me. There in full view, as if in pride of place in the centre, sits an entire bathroom suite: bathtub, toilet, hand basin and what looks like a urinal trough, all planted with colourful blooms. Who in their right mind uses such items for gardening? I'm intrigued, though slightly baffled.

'They are good? No?' comes a deep voice.

I jump at his question and turn to see a man in yellow waders, crouching down while peering up at me through the fence a short distance away, his hand trowel suspended in his grasp.

'Sorry, I've never seen . . .' I wave my good hand, gesturing to his bathroom display. 'It looks quite . . .' Words fail me.

'I use anything I can find. The curves they are beautiful, are they not?'

'They are.' I'm suddenly conscious of my slurring tones.

'And they are sturdy and strong, so why dispose of something when its primary function is no more. I see a thing of beauty which can have a second life and be just as beautiful in another way. You agree?'

Is he talking about the Armitage Shanks or me? I stare at him intently, not sure how to respond.

'You look confused?' he asks, standing tall.

'No. I was thinking . . . you mean the bathroom equipment, right?'

'Well, yes, but I mean anything that can have a new life after its old life has expired. Why discard everything like rubbish . . . not everything need be thrown away as worthless. Yes?'

'Yes,' I mumble. A lump forms in my throat, which stubbornly defies several deep gulps.

'In Estonia, where I come from, we keep things for a lifetime – we know how precious they are – and then, if still good after our death, we pass them on to be loved and enjoyed some more. Here, everything has to be perfect, otherwise it is scowled at or frowned upon. You agree?'

'Sadly, yes.' I'm reminded of the Japanese tradition of kintsugi, whereby broken pottery is enhanced and made whole again using molten gold. I glance down at my left arm, weighty and still. My hand is masterfully placed into my jeans pocket for effect and purpose. Is this my thread of gold? Why can't we appreciate our inner beauty by enhancing and embracing our natural flaws? The man is watching me intently. 'I'm Natalia,' I say, as if that explains my presence at his allotment fencing.

'Ah, Natalia, guest from the Lerwick Manor Hotel? I sent you some cookies; Dottie asked if I would make my special home recipe – I put them in her pretty tin. Did you enjoy?'

'That was you? Kaspar? Yes, Dottie delivered the cookies. Thank you, they were lovely. I was craving sweet foods.'

'You are most welcome. Dottie enjoys my treats whilst sipping her gin o'clock,' he says, with pride. 'Sharing food reminds me of home.'

'I'm sure the condensed milk helped to boost my recovery.'

'There's nothing better. Like mother's milk in my country,' says Kaspar, nearing the wire fencing. He's not as tall as me but he's broad in stature, definitely solid and sturdy, compared to my willowy frame. 'And you are feeling much better?'

My smile instantly fades. I can't pretend when asked. I should be channelling brightness and light, grateful for my steady progress, but I'm not. I want the old me back.

'Not really. My arm doesn't function properly, it feels heavy and lifeless, but at least my speech has returned to a degree.' I'm trying to look on the bright side; maybe I need to view myself as an example of kintsugi, and embrace my additional gold thread.

'Exercise and patience will help.'

'Who knows?' My shrug is dominated by my right side, though my left arm awkwardly jerks. I'm now as glum as I was on leaving the hotel's front steps. Is this the new me? A roller coaster of emotion, rattled by the focus of any conversation.

'Always the case. Exercise make muscles good and strong again, give ease to movement and help the mind.'

Bless him, bolstering a positive attitude on my behalf.

'You do not believe me?'

'I do. I've never been into running or gym sessions, though I used to go to yoga classes whenever I could. I'm not sure I could manage half the poses now.'

'No, no, you misunderstand, I mean here . . . exercise,' he gestures to his allotment. 'Gentle work, active work that exercises

the body and mind, not a hard slog, pounding in gym, no, no.
You want to help?'

I glance around the plot. It is pristine. Surely there isn't much
work to be done, especially when you compare it to some of the
other ones I've viewed.

'Ten minutes?' He passes me the trowel. His dark eyes look
expectantly into mine.

I haven't anything else to do.

'Why not . . . for a little while.' I take the offered tool.

Kaspar returns to his kneeling position in the soil and I tentatively join him. I doubt my current manicure is worth a second
thought.

I hadn't expected to enjoy trowelling a small patch of earth.
The weeds which Kaspar asked me to remove were minuscule,
cress-like in size and formation. It took more patience than I
care to admit to pinch out the tiny specimens but the dexterity
in my left hand managed it, slowly. I won't be winning any
prizes for speed, but Kaspar seemed chuffed by the patch of
brown, bare earth.

'I'll be heading back to the hotel,' I say, grappling to heave
myself upright from my crouched position.

'You are welcome to visit anytime,' says Kaspar, as he fills a
watering can from the nearest water butt. 'Would you like a key?'
His generosity takes me back.

'It's OK, you don't have to do that,' I say, trampling over his
kind gesture in embarrassment. I can do without others making
allowances purely to accommodate me.

'I would like to help. Here.' He digs into a pocket on his yellow
waders and produces a tiny key. 'You won't need an entrance
key – you can gain access through the walled gate?'

'That's what I did today, yes.' I'm hesitant. Does it look
grasping? It'll make a change, spending an hour on Kaspar's

allotment on a nice day, instead of the alpaca paddock. 'Thank you, I appreciate your kindness.'

'And I appreciate your handiwork,' he says, smiling.

It takes all of ten minutes to walk the length of the remaining allotment plots before returning to the car park and walled gate, with its iron ring and aged wood. I feel like Alice returning from her adventures; I didn't need to drink, eat or follow instructions, yet I feel renewed as I re-enter the private estate. My short absence has taken an unexpected turn, based on curiosity about what lay beyond the wall, unseen. The tiny weeds discarded before they develop, the kintsugi pottery laden with precious faults, and the kindness of a stranger have all mingled to reignite my spirit.

Instantly, I avert my gaze from the copse, wishing to retain my newfound energy rather than viewing Ned's ornate carp pond and revisiting that fateful September night. There's no point torturing myself.

Autumn

'Are you sitting comfortably?' I ask, settled in my office seat, with Jemima opting for a chair nearby. 'You won't need anything else. Place your open hands into your lap – you can touch your index finger and thumb, if you wish. Close your eyes and focus on the route of each breath. Imagine it entering your nose, travelling along the nasal passages deep into your body, separating into the bronchi, travelling deep into the capillaries and alveoli, delivering rich oxygen into your bloodstream.' I fall silent, allowing Jemima to follow my lead. 'Now make each breath a little deeper than the previous one, and control each exhalation a little longer before inhaling again. Chase away any stray thoughts which flit into your mind, simply focus on the here and now through each breath.'

I half open one eye, checking she's following my instructions.

Her dark brows have softened, her taut cheeks relaxed, as her diaphragm gently lifts and lowers at a controlled pace. Her hands rest loosely in her lap, fingers softly curled and barely touching to create an 'O' between thumb and finger. It seems strange, this reversal of roles, but invigorating that she should have asked for a demonstration. Meditation is hardly something you perform to an audience; far better to experience it for yourself.

I close my eyes again, take a deep breath and slowly exhale; it's been a busy morning.

'Are you both OK, ladies?' Ned's voice makes us both jump.

My eyes snap open to find him glancing between the pair of us. We're both blinking frantically, having been brought back from our quiet place in the harshest manner.

'Ned, you scared the life out of me,' chides Jemima, clutching at her heart. 'I was well away then.'

'And me.'

'What are you doing?' The man looks baffled.

'Meditating. Autumn uses it every day to help her remain calm and focused. I thought I'd give it a try.'

Ned shakes his head with a wry smile. 'Seriously, I wondered what you were both doing when I walked in, eyes closed, deep breathing . . . I thought we might need an ambulance!'

'Ridiculous idea,' giggles Jemima. 'You could do with a session or two yourself, given the workload you're juggling at present.'

'Phuh! I haven't the time to sit around, my darling.'

'You can spare five minutes,' replies Jemima, inclining her head to reinforce her point.

'That's all it takes,' I add, unsure why everyone assumes a free hour is necessary. 'A few minutes, here and there, throughout each day. It works wonders, though I don't always close my eyes if I'm in public places or queuing for petrol.'

'Another time, ladies, another time,' says Ned, passing an A4 file to Jemima. 'I wondered if you'd take a look – it's what we discussed earlier. And did you know that Verity has the injured dog staying with her in The Yarn Barn each day?'

'Sure,' she says, taking the offered file. 'Yes, Verity asked me. Floss is such a well-trained dog, she's hardly going to cause mayhem, especially given her horrific injuries. Magnus can't keep an eye on her throughout the day, whereas Verity can. I believe Vet MacKay prescribed complete rest; her rear leg is in a plaster cast, so there'll be no herding or solo walks for that old gal for quite some time. Given the peace and tranquillity in Verity's pitch, it's the perfect place for Floss to begin healing.'

I notice their eyes flicker and widen. Is it my imagination, or has a whole other conversation just occurred?

'I'll head back to the office, so shout if you've got questions,' Ned says, before offering me a bright smile and swiftly exiting the reception's rear office.

'Boy, he made me jump,' says Jemima, the second we're alone. 'I hadn't realised how deeply I was focusing until he barged in.'

'Hardly a relaxing awakening, was it? Never mind. It proved to you how beneficial the technique can be, which is good news.'

'I know, but surely that can't be good for your nerves; I feel tense and tetchy now,' says Jemima, easing herself from the chair. 'I'd best crack on with this. Thank you, Autumn, catch you another time.'

'Certainly will! We can try again when Ned isn't about.' I give a chuckle for fear of offending her.

'Too right. We might want to think about somewhere quieter next time, like the ballroom. I don't think we'd be disturbed.'

'Sounds great, a couple of chairs and a five-minute break.'

'That's a plan! See you later.'

In seconds she's gone, retracing Ned's footsteps across the tiled hallway.

Chapter Twenty-Eight

Pippa

'Don't start your act with me, Pippa!' says Levi, once our weekly lunch is under way. 'You might be able to fool some of the people some of the time, but I've seen the other side of you.'

I baulk at his accusation, pursing my lips.

'Did Callie tell you?' I ask, unpacking my cheese sandwiches from their brown paper wrapping.

'Not directly, I overheard her telling Jemima whilst I was helping Mungo out at the gallery. There's a charity scarecrow event being planned and he wanted ... anyway, less of that! With a flick of a switch you act like a loose cannon, you put up a fight, become defensive and lash out, hoping people will leave you alone. You need to start being you, Pippa.'

'Do you know how hard that is, given their opinion of me?'

He shrugs. 'Why did you do it this time?' he says, tucking into a ham and mustard roll.

'She started it!' I snap. I'm narked by him implying that I'm guilty of pretence.

I shift uncomfortably in my seat. The spotlight under which he's placed me burns a little brighter, and I resent his tone of interrogation. I shrug, hoping that will be enough to satisfy his curiosity.

'Don't give me that. Why?'

'I was grumpy and running late after a long day. Callie was silently goading me as I walked back and forth. Wrong time, wrong place, I guess.'

Levi shakes his head; he's not going to let me off the hook.

'Nah, you're better than that, Pippa. You've made a real effort in recent weeks, by taking on this delivery round, appearing cheerier, and chatting with others – then you let yourself down by ranting at Callie.'

'I bet she took great delight in telling Jemima?'

He gives a hearty nod, before taking another bite of his lunch.

'Did she mention anything other than my rudeness?'

'Nope.'

Typical Callie, get your version of events in first but forget to mention the vital detail: selling Nanna's engagement ring.

'And don't you think I might have had a reason?' I ask him.

'There's always a reason, Pippa.'

Do I . . . or don't I? Levi's making out he'll understand, but I can hardly retract the information if he doesn't. He and Jemima are close friends, we're becoming closer friends, so I'm bound to lose out if he doesn't take kindly to my explanation about the injustice of Callie's secret sale.

'Come on, out with it.' Levi stares at my profile, while I pretend not to notice and eat my lunch.

I switch my focus slightly. Can I risk ruining what is slowly developing between us? I wouldn't accept such remarks from anyone other than Levi; I can trust his judgement.

'It's like being the family cuckoo. I belong elsewhere but was deposited into the family nest whilst their backs were turned. Everyone has fed me, nurtured me, but deep down they aren't entirely sure if I belong amongst them – if that makes sense?'

'Sadly, yes. So, what's your plan for breaking out of this little-cousin syndrome?'

I hesitate, cautiously eyeballing him before answering. 'Do my own thing. My biggest test is how to handle others who have previously hurt or misjudged me – and still do, on occasion!'

My generous nature will take them by surprise, and I'm half

expecting them to reject the true me as an imposter after all these years. Can a cuckoo ever fit in and be accepted for who they truly are?

'Just do it. Be yourself and show them what you're made of.'

'I don't feel like I have a choice. I need to develop a sense of belonging or I'll remain the cuckoo for evermore.'

'You're stuck in an act, Pippa; you deliver what others expect of you. I know the other side of your nature – the generous, caring and sensitive side.'

I pull a 'nonsense' face.

'You can't deny it. I've seen it.' His tone is adamant.

I swallow before speaking. 'When?'

'All the time.'

He's simply being kind to bolster my confidence.

'Don't you believe me? I taxi certain retired folk back and forth throughout the week to various appointments, family visits and shopping trips. I always chat to the older clan, as they sometimes don't see many people in their average week.'

I'm nodding; I do likewise on my rounds. But where's this going?

'Recently, I've been hearing more and more about a certain bread delivery woman who's been doing kindly odds and sods each week – some of which she's hidden from her bosses, and even prearranged – making life a little easier, brighter and generally more pleasant for others. Any guesses who that could be?'

'No,' I say curtly, my cheeks colouring suddenly.

'Well, Archie thinks she's an angel for saving him a fortune in wasted bread,' says Levi, with a chuckle. 'And that's definitely the right way into any old geezer's heart.'

'It's called common sense in my book,' I say, ignoring the heat radiating from my cheeks.

'Sure is, I'm not knocking it.'

'And the other half doesn't go to waste. I—'

'I know. Nothing is wasted on your daily routes.'

I crease my brow, indicating my confusion.

'Nancy Crabtree buys the other half further along your route. She tells me every week whilst driving her to Archie's for lunch. "Fresh, crusty and worth every penny," she says.'

My crimson cheeks blush a little more, if that's even possible. 'Saves wasting it,' I mutter, embarrassed to be the topic of a conversation. Then it dawns on me. 'They know each other?'

'Sure. I'm not speaking out of line when I say the crafty buggers worked the deal between them.'

'While letting me think it was my idea?' I ask, shocked at their shrewdness.

'Archie thought it might take a few weeks to work on you, but apparently not. A matter of minutes, wasn't it? You ought to show this side of your character a little more often.'

I shake my head as tears spring to my eyes. I feel overwhelmed, knowing that people have actually complimented me.

'Phuh! I knew all along; the older generation always think they can pull the wool over my eyes,' I say, trying to subtly wipe away my tears whilst elaborately scratching my nose. Both sides.

'Are you crying?' he asks, playfully nudging my elbow in a poor attempt to cover his alpha-male embarrassment, caused by my emotional display.

'No!' I retort, scratching my nose for good measure.

'You big softy,' adds Levi quietly.

'What's that supposed to mean?' I say, looking straight at him, purely to show I'm not crying. Well, not now.

He begins to nod, not the reaction I am expecting. 'As if you don't know? You're one big bundle of contradictions. You might fool some but not me; I see right through you. You let others think you're a pain in the arse, when in fact there's a warmth and depth that you rarely show your family. Because that's easier, isn't it? Easier to have them be mad at you, constantly complaining about your antics, than to let them in and allow them to see the real you.'

I stare straight ahead, biting my lip in a poor attempt not to cry again.

Levi continues, 'But where's that going to get you in the long run, Pippa?' His question lingers in the space between us, hovering somewhere over the handbrake and the gear stick. 'Are you listening?' he asks, when I don't respond.

I nod, unable to speak for chewing the inside of my cheek, curling my toes and focusing on the road ahead. He takes it as an invitation to continue.

'You've already admitted that Jemima's a pretty decent sort.'

How much did Callie repeat to Jemima?

'Yep, birds of a feather usually flock together,' I mutter.

'Too right. She's one of my dearest friends and I don't see why you'd judge her so harshly, seeing as we get along so well.'

'Do we?' I tease, screwing up my empty sandwich wrapper.

Levi flinches at my question. 'Yep, we do. Despite you being as prickly as hell when it suits, mardy at times, and downright infuriating at other times.'

'And you're Mr Bloody Perfect, are you?' I say, turning to face him.

'Of course!'

Silence descends as we both openly smirk at the honesty of our exchange.

'What?' I say, noticing his lingering gaze.

'What?' he playfully repeats.

'This,' I whisper, without hesitation or regard for the consequences.

My face draws near to his and his inclines to meet mine as our lips gently brush against each other's. I've never acted in this manner before, but if Levi wants the real me, the complete truth with utmost honesty, then I need to show him, without fear or fuss.

His bottom lip lingers on mine, a soft side-to-side sweeping action develops, causing my nerves to jingle throughout my body. We're barely touching, like a whisper of a kiss. Such a tender gesture, which is tantalisingly playful yet so instinctive as we savour this moment, together. The rest of the world falls away, nothing else exists except us. This feels like the most natural thing in the world, as if we've done this a million times before and plan to repeat it a million times again. His breath warms my cheek, his stubbled chin gently scratching mine as his palm lifts to slowly drift into my hairline, cradling my head. As the anticipation builds, our affectionate gesture increases in movement and pressure until our heads tilt, our lips connect impatiently, and our passion takes hold, unleashing our true feelings.

Autumn

'Such a beautiful ballroom!' I exclaim, as Jemima closes the large double doors behind us.

The grace and beauty of this ballroom puts some cruise liners to shame. I suppose the manor was built in a time of decadence, which is reflected in every detail – be it the flooring, the panelled walls, and especially the ginormous chandeliers.

'This is one of my favourite things about this room; look how the sunlight throws abstract shapes on the wooden floor.' She points to the effect, a short distance away.

'Is the flooring sprung?'

Jemima shrugs. 'I assume so. We had dancing and bagpipes in here at New Year, but I don't know for certain, given its age. Ned might.'

I walk across the room adding a bouncing step to each stride.

'If it is, you could think about offering or hiring this out for dance classes – it would be a fantastic space to use for ballet or ballroom dancing lessons.'

'Just imagine that!' Jemima's eyes light up with delight. 'I can see it now: tutus and ballet slippers parading about, and a piano over in the corner.'

'Exactly. Would Ned entertain such an idea?'

Jemima peers at me from under her dark fringe. 'Ned is always open to any ideas. He'd backed himself into a corner with the financial burden and heritage of this place; he couldn't see the wood for the trees, but now he'll mull over any ideas which promote using the space for a practical and productive venture.'

I'm lost in a world of my own; there's so much potential here. 'In addition to dance classes, could I suggest maybe yoga and relaxation sessions? I'm sure a local teacher would be dying to claim such a beautiful space.'

Jemima nods and smiles in agreement.

'But first, let's drag over a couple of chairs and finish where we left off earlier.' I'm in desperate need of a quiet five minutes of contemplation and slow breathing.

'Yes, quickly – before Ned rudely interrupts, bringing us back to reality with an unceremonious bump.'

'Or we could arrange a third chair and invite him to join us?' I suggest, suppressing a giggle. 'You said he could do with lightening the load for a few minutes.'

'Now that, even I would pay good money to see!' teases Jemima, selecting the nearest chair and settling herself, eager to make a start.

Chapter Twenty-Nine

Thursday 3 March

Natalia

It's just after seven o'clock on a bright but chilly morning. I turn left, heading for the cobbled courtyard, and am surprised to find an array of people lined up outside the alpacas' overnight stable: Dottie, Mungo, Isla, Jemima, Callie, Levi. Great! Being sociable with this particular herd is the last thing I need so early in the day! I stride across, attempting to make eye contact with Dottie, but the crafty minx averts her gaze, suddenly finding the cobblestones of intense interest and ignoring my approaching figure.

'Need I ask whose grand idea this was?' I say haughtily, knowing full well that I sound decidedly prickly, made worse by my slurring.

I'd been led to believe we'd be a small party of three. Given the frantic wing flapping of Crispy duck, as he marches around the cobbles, he hadn't been informed either.

'Morning, Natalia,' calls Jemima, as the others chorus a greeting with varying degrees of cheeriness.

It appears I might not be alone in lacking enthusiasm for this early morning jaunt.

'Now that we're all present, I'll begin. We're going to treat this morning as a practice run, so I'd appreciate your full attention as I'd hate anything untoward to occur.'

I glance around the group; there are seven of us, all togged up in sturdy boots, warm clothing and colourful beanies; this is a slight oversight even before we start, as there are only six animals.

Jemima continues, 'We're going to follow the protocol as if you were paying guests. I'm sure you'll be delighted to hear there is a hot breakfast awaiting our return, although the guest package is actually for afternoon cream tea in The Orangery. I figured you wouldn't want bannocks and clotted cream this early in the day. Isla has kindly offered to lead today's session. Over to you.' Jemima gestures towards Isla, who beams before taking hold of the metaphorical baton.

The stable door has the upper section pinned open, enabling the alpacas to nosily view our gathering from their straw-strewn haven.

'Morning, folks, I'm Isla. I'll be your lead guide for today, with additional assistance from Callie, so should you have an issue or a question, please refer it to either of us, OK?'

I dutifully nod alongside the others, turning to view Callie when her name is mentioned. This reminds me of school trips as a child, when we'd stand stock-still until permission was granted to find a partner and sensibly walk in crocodile file.

'I need to run through some basic health and safety rules,' says Isla, 'then I'll introduce you to one of the boys, giving a brief demonstration and a little information about the species, before you are paired up with your special walking buddy. Can everyone hear me OK?' she asks, scanning the group and receiving a series of nods. 'Do say if you can't and I'll turn the microphone up a little way.'

I hadn't realised she was wearing a mic and portable speaker; she sounds perfectly clear to me.

Isla spends the next few minutes reading out a list of our names, politely smiling as if she'd never met us before, then checks our footwear and suitable attire. It all seems very formal but her bubbly tone, light humour and eagerness settle the group's nerves.

'Perfect, everyone's present. So let's meet today's chosen male, Karma ... Callie, if you wouldn't mind,' says Isla, gesturing towards the stable door, which slowly opens.

I hadn't noticed Callie disappear inside whilst the register was taken. She slowly exits the stable, leading the fawn-coloured alpaca, my favourite.

'And this, ladies and gents, is our boy Karma. He's five years of age, a happy chappie, as you'd expect from his name, but he doesn't like to be away from his mates for too long, so can I ask that we all stand quietly while I give you a little lesson about alpaca anatomy.'

I'm impressed. I know Isla keeps a Shetland pony but the way she handles, touches and manoeuvres this animal is skilful, especially as the alpacas are such recent arrivals. She turns him, walks him, lifts his feet, shows his toothy grin and calms him, as if she's spent her life amongst these animals. Karma stands proud and affectionately nuzzles her shoulder every now and then, the perfect model.

'As you can see, they are calm, quiet animals, so we need to respect their wishes and walk alongside them confidently but not in a boisterous manner; they don't respond well to harsh treatment, so please be gentle but firm at all times.'

I get that; I have similar principles myself.

I'm intrigued as to how the next hour will pan out. But I'm also anxious in case I'm given a feisty alpaca who wishes to run, pull or even misbehave.

'If you could make a line, you can collect your walking buddy from Callie,' says Isla, gesturing towards the stable door.

I'd happily take Karma, but Isla swiftly hands his rein to Jemima. I queue behind the others who, one by one, are each handed a lead by Callie and informed of a name: By The Grace

Of God, This Too Will Pass, Be Happy, Let It Be. And finally, I reach the front of the queue with one alpaca remaining inside the stable.

'I'm not sure this is a good idea with my arm,' I say, before adding, 'I haven't any strength on that side.'

'It won't be an issue, I promise you,' says Isla quickly.

'Here you go, Natalia. This is your beauty, Carpe Diem ... though we tend to call him Carpe. Enjoy,' says Callie, handing me the knotted rope attached to a full-grown, alive and potentially kicking russet-coloured alpaca.

'Thanks, I think.' I feel overwhelmed by his name alone. If you'd shown me a list of names, I'd have chosen him. It hadn't occurred to me when watching them in the paddock that they'd have such unique names, let alone distinct meanings. Carpe simply follows my lead; no pulling, fighting or refusal. 'We are going to get along just fine,' I whisper, calmly leading my boy away from his stable to join the others milling around the stable yard.

I fondle his fluffball head, so soft and fleece-like, I can just imagine a ball of yarn crafted from such a mop of hair.

'Guys, if I can remind you before we make our way under the arch. Please shout if you have any issues, any questions or any difficulties. The purpose of today's walk is for you to learn about these wonderful creatures and have fun bonding with nature during this fabulous experience,' says Isla, stroking the nearest alpaca, held by Levi. 'So, off we go! Follow me.'

Isla leads us through the stone archway and along the drive running the length of the fenced pasture.

'You might notice a slight pulling as we near their enclosure. I'm sure each animal recognises where they spend the majority of their time, but if you can hold a firm rein until we are past, they'll soon realise this isn't their usual morning walk but something a little different.'

As if on cue, Carpe Diem begins turning towards the entrance gate of his daytime pasture. I give a little tug to align his head with the designated route ahead.

'They're not daft, are they?' calls Mungo, attempting to steer his black alpaca past the gate.

'Certainly not, simply creatures of habit,' calls Isla, from the back of the pack. 'Keep walking, folks, we are heading towards the far end of this driveway before taking a left turn towards the wooded terrain.'

A sense of calm descends as my pace matches the rhythmical stride of the alpaca. We rub along, gently bumping hips every now and then, much like the rest of the pack. It feels therapeutic to be coupled with an animal that has a free spirit but which chooses to remain beside me, without fear or flight. I've often wondered if Magnus' Floss can sense my current vulnerability whilst I regain my strength. Can Carpe sense the exact same – my need for protection within this herd formation?

I linger at the back of the pack, behind Levi whose alpaca, Let It Be, appears to be shoulder-barging his herd buddies in order to win a place at the front. It's far easier than walking Ned's dogs; they used to pull on their leads, whereas my alpaca simply follows the route I take without fighting, baulking or snagging his rein. He's so well behaved, I almost forget that, apart from the rein I'm holding, the animal is totally free from restraints and is choosing to plod beside me rather than gallop ahead to join his mates.

Autumn

'Hello, can I help?' I ask, as two women enter the entrance hall, surveying the grand staircase and stunning chandelier.

Both look startled when I speak up from behind the reception area.

'Sorry, we've never been here before. We have an appointment with Mrs Campbell for ten o'clock. Emma Harrison and Grace O'Neill,' says the blonde lady, her cheekbones as delicate as porcelain.

I reach for the appointment book and find their details, neatly written in Jemima's handwriting: dance instructors.

'If you'd like to take a seat, I'll inform Mrs Campbell of your arrival.' I gesture towards the row of elaborate hard-backed chairs positioned a short distance from the counter, either side of an oversized antique ginger jar.

Both women instantly follow my instruction and settle down to wait, taking in the tartan swathes, rich burgundy fabrics and heavily carved wood of the entrance hall.

It takes Jemima a few minutes to appear. She descends the staircase, her beaming smile instantly putting her guests at ease.

'Good morning, I'm Jemima Campbell. Thank you for coming at such short notice.'

I watch as she heartily shakes hands with each woman and they duly repeat their names. The blonde woman is Grace, her friend clearly Emma.

'If you wouldn't mind following me, we'll get started. Would either of you like a drink? Tea, coffee?'

I hear a murmured reply from each before Jemima turns in my direction. 'Would you mind organising two teas and a latte, Autumn?'

'Certainly,' I say instantly; anything to please.

'We'll be in the ballroom, thank you,' says Jemima, before leading her two guests in the direction of the double doors.

Chapter Thirty

Pippa

'Pippa, could I have a word, please?' asks Ned, appearing at the rear of the Bread Basket as I remove the last wicker bread trays on my return.

'Yeah, sure,' I say, spinning around at the sound of his voice.

Ned steps up on to the vehicle to join me. I'm not sure if I'm expected to stop what I'm doing, but I give him my full attention anyway. He looks decidedly uncomfortable, as if unsure how to proceed. I've been here long enough to know that Jemima tends to conduct the staff tête-à-têtes, should anything personal need discussing.

'We've received a written report that you took a friend along on your round the other day. Jemima is sure the person is quite mistaken, but I thought it best to ask,' explains Ned, surveying Rolly's interior as if completing an unannounced inspection.

'Nope.' Instantly, I know which day he's delicately referring to. And, I'm not about to discuss it.

It didn't go any further than a passionate kiss which, I'll admit, but only to myself and Levi, wasn't entirely a surprise. I suspect it's been on the cards for a little while, given our growing attraction to one another. And our reaction afterwards, giggling like a couple of teenagers, confirmed that theory. If I have to, I'll deny everything; it was just a brief lunch break and not the entire delivery round. I won't betray Levi, not after the kindness he's shown me. I'm not prepared to throw him under the mobile Bread Basket simply to save my own skin.

'Aren't you going to ask when?' Ned eyes me cautiously, as if reading my body language.

I shrug. Unless my dashcam has swivelled around, recording the interior of the vehicle, all will be good as long as I stand my ground. 'It makes no difference. Unless it's the one day you insisted Callie come along for work experience, then they're wrong.'

'Last Tuesday?' His tone is questioning; he's not convinced.

I need to up my game. I pull a nonplussed expression, coupled with a head shake, keeping my gaze level with his. I'm not wavering. I refuse to budge an inch with my adamant manner. Levi wouldn't discuss such a private moment with anyone, I know that for certain. So what are the chances of Callie's friends spotting us and then her writing a letter to stir up trouble?

'OK. Jemima said if you wished to read the letter for yourself, you can go to the office.'

'No, thanks. Whoever has taken the time to put pen to paper has wasted their effort and ink – which is a shame, but . . . who knows what motivates some folk to cause drama?'

Ned waits for a split second before responding. 'I see. OK, thanks for that. If anything comes to mind, just let me know,' he says, eyeing me cautiously.

I'm not convinced that he's convinced.

'Sure. But I can tell you now . . . someone's trying to stir the pot, that's all.' I might have wavered between boss-speak and family-in-law speak, but either way I've survived his interrogation.

He lingers for a second before openly admiring Rolly's interior.

'It's looking very clean and tidy in here, Pippa,' he says, gesturing to the stacking units and countertop.

'I try my best,' I say, hoping to send him on his way on a positive note.

'Well done!'

'Cheers.'

I busy myself the second he steps down from the Bread Basket; I want to show that I'm not bothered or flustered by our little chat. From the corner of my eye, I spy Ned giving me a backwards glance, as if checking.

Autumn

'Was your earlier meeting productive?' I ask, unsure if I should mention it or not.

'Absolutely. I was going to run a proposal past you, since you planted the initial idea regarding the ballroom,' says Jemima, browsing the data on occupancy rates on the neighbouring computer screen. 'I invited them to view the ballroom with the potential of hosting weekly dance classes. They practically squealed with delight on viewing the available space and suggested either Highland dancing or traditional ballroom lessons. What do you think?'

'Me?' I'm flummoxed by her question; surely my opinion doesn't count?

Jemima nods, encouraging me to speak.

'I think the locals, and especially the tourists, would be interested in the traditional reels as one-off sessions but, given the popularity of programmes such as *Strictly*, I think there's more scope for weekly ballroom classes.'

Jemima hangs on my every word, her expression thoughtful. 'I never thought of that. Most tourists are only here for a short time, a fortnight or so, whereas weekly classes need continuous attendees, otherwise they'll fold after week three.'

'The craze to learn traditional ballroom dancing is still popular; it's a highlight of Saturday night TV for most people. Don't we all envisage ourselves twirling a tango or mastering the paso doble at one time or another!'

'You're right. You've hit the nail on the head, Autumn. We need to cater for the masses – popularity equals success. Ned did suggest you might want to start a weekly yoga and meditation class too. I said I wasn't sure if you'd be willing or not . . .' She pauses, taking in my shocked expression.

'Wow! I never saw that coming. I last taught yoga over ten years ago, to earn a little extra on the cruise liners. Yes, of course, I'll happily organise and teach a weekly class.'

'We'd just need to buy the right equipment: some mats and a decent sound system. Have a think about feasible dates and times . . . and let me know. I've definitely found the introduction to meditation beneficial.'

'Thank you. That's made my day – I'll come back to you about public liability insurance and such like.'

I'm buzzing, this will give me something to sink my teeth into, benefiting me as well as others. I know Jemima has appreciated the few sessions we've completed, but to suggest that I teach weekly sessions is amazing!

'No worries, take all the time you need.'

Natalia

'How did you find it?' asks Pippa, the second our drinks are delivered to the table in The Thule.

'Surprisingly enjoyable, to be fair, and far easier than I'd imagined. Cheers!' I clink my glass against hers, mainly in appreciation that she's invited me out. A busy bar, a quiet table and the change of scenery have given a definite lift to my spirits – and no disrespect to Dottie, but a younger companion whose conversation I'm badly in need of. 'Were you not interested?'

'I bailed like the saddo that I am, but I asked Levi if he'd step in for me; I couldn't face it,' she says, grimacing.

'Alongside your Callie?' I say, my words continuing to slur.

Pippa nods, but refrains from commenting further. From comments I've overheard between Dottie and Jemima, I gather there's no love lost between them.

'She knows her stuff alright,' I tell Pippa. 'Both she and Isla gave a running commentary about the alpacas, their habitats and behaviour throughout the ninety-minute walk. I was knackered by the time we came back around to The Orangery for our hot breakfast.'

'She'll have honed her skills and knowledge, I don't doubt that. But I couldn't play along; it's not for me.'

We sip our drinks before I break the silence. 'Levi seems lovely.'

Earlier, Mungo had hinted to Dottie that there seemed to be something blossoming between the pair.

Her expression changes in an instant. 'Isn't he just? It's early days, but still, I'm punching above my weight for sure.'

'No, you're not!'

'I'll admit it, I am. He is genuinely the nicest guy you could wish to meet. He has manners, values, morals – the full package – with the unexpected twist that he listens when you speak the truth. Seriously, the man is a human lie detector!'

I grimace, unsure if that's as good a thing as Pippa's making out.

'You can say exactly what you're thinking and he doesn't take offence or rile you for being totally honest.'

I raise an eyebrow.

'Stop it! He's not as he first seems.'

'He comes across as being pleasant and kind – but a human lie detector? Really?'

'Yes, really. At first I thought "gift of the gab", being a taxi driver, but there's more to him that that. He's a true friend, a genuine sort; he has other people's interests at heart. I can see why the likes of Dottie and Jemima love him so much.'

'Err, don't talk to me about Dottie; she's incredibly kind, but she's doing my head in.' I grab my drink and take a large swig, only to find Pippa intently staring at me. 'You haven't heard the half of it!'

'The lady has made it her mission to p-practically single-hand-edly restore your h-health,' stammers Pippa, her eyes agog.

'Tell me about it – there's nothing she won't do. She means well, but it's all a bit much when you're used to being independent.'

'Did the doctors say what caused the stoke?'

'Probably a horrible combination of things. They found I have high blood pressure, but the shock of finding out Ned was married must have sent it sky-rocketing without my realising it. And I was just a ball of stress and anxiety, feeling rejected, my whole life plan in tatters. In hindsight, it's not such a shock. But I never thought this would happen to me, Pippa ...' I pause, having slurred my way through such a lengthy explanation. The inconvenience of not being able to express myself as fluently as I once did is the ultimate frustration.

'Of course you didn't. And it must feel ironic that, given your history with Dottie, she's the one you've found yourself relying on.'

'Yes! She hated me with a passion.' I smile, recalling our many barbed conversations.

'And yet you still ran the gauntlet, risking her disapproval with each visit. Brave soul.'

'Exactly, she didn't deter me. It's no wonder she pushed your Jemima forward in my absence.'

'Come off it – as if!' Pippa shakes her head in disbelief.

'Seriously, she did! Dottie's as good as told me so during our many hours together.'

'For what reason – to continue to exert her influence and power over Ned? I've not always been our Jemima's biggest fan, but she's got more backbone than to allow Dottie to rule the roost.'

'There's more to Dottie Nesbit than she makes out. She's a

strong old gal and, with Mungo by her side, those two can do no wrong.'

'Hardly! They're just two adorable crumblies who are enjoying their final years doing what they love.' Pippa gives me a coy smile, before slugging back the remains of her wine and quickly adding, 'Anyway, less chatter about Dottie. I want to hear what happened between you and Lachlan.'

My heart sinks; I thought that had been brushed under the carpet, thanks to my recent trauma. I empty my glass and gesture towards the waiter, asking for another round.

'Come on, out with it,' she says, digging for salacious gossip.

'There's really nothing to tell; it was what it was.'

Pippa seems disappointed by my lack of recall; it's not that I'm holding back or being precious about my private life. More that those few hours spent with him now represent the final hours of this woman being the woman I once was. And remembering her – living life to the full, so carefree and vibrant – seems like a distant memory, which hurts like hell.

The waiter arrives, delivering two large glasses of Pinot Grigio.

'Thank you,' I say, before returning my focus to Pippa.

'Are you aware that he chased Isla for a while, before getting himself into deep water with the law?'

'No, he didn't mention that.'

'Aha, lady. You spill the beans first, then I'll fill you in on his backstory,' teases Pippa, raising her glass to mine. 'Cheers.'

'What's there to tell? We met in a bar, he came back to the hotel with me, we stupidly pinched a set of room keys – and the rest, as they say, is history.'

There's so much I miss about my former life right now; this, at least, is one piece of history that I'm more than happy to leave behind me.

Chapter Thirty-One

Saturday 5 March

Pippa

'I didn't expect to see you here!' says Jemima through the fencing.

She has spied me, trowel in hand, shovelling compost into tubs, as she passes Levi's allotment. She's already tended her own plot, plus Dottie's.

After returning from a morning spent at the local laundry, sorting my life for the coming week, I'd dashed down to accept Levi's Saturday afternoon invite. A welcome change from my regular family commitment.

'Nor you – I don't know how you find the time, with your workload,' I say, standing up, conscious that my last visit to her plot had been under the cover of darkness, and somewhat underhand. 'Checking on Ned's beehives, were you, as well as your own chickens?'

'What's the saying? "If you want something doing – ask a busy person"? It is how it is. I walk down most mornings to let my chickens out, but usually it's before anyone else arrives.' She blushes, as if she's concealing something, her gaze flickering towards Levi. 'Ned comes on the mornings I can't . . . I mean, don't attend.'

'It's non-stop for the pair of you, but the effort must be paying off,' adds Levi, standing up to join our conversation.

'Definitely. We couldn't ask for better. The locals and tourists have embraced both the hotel and the gallery's artists, so it's a win-win situation – each venture complements the other.'

'I bet Dottie stops me tomorrow, asking after your where-abouts,' I jest, foolishly attempting to keep the conversation flowing, but without putting my brain in gear.

'Really?' asks Jemima.

'Oh yeah, she's clocking you left, right and centre at the minute. You're definitely on her radar, and there's no end to her questions. Seriously, I've started to dodge her when she's dusting the banister on your landing.'

I sense Levi flinch rather than see it.

Jemima's mouth drops open. 'Surely not?'

'You bet. I can't scurry past her without another round of the Jemima quiz. You know what she's like, she loves to keep a check on everyone and everything – her current obsession only ever revolves around you though.'

Jemima's expression instantly turns serious.

I ramble on, ignoring her body language. 'Honest. She's caught me leaving our morning meeting for the last three weeks. If I didn't know better, I'd suggest she might be earwigging at Ned's office door, before collaring me to ask additional questions as I come down.'

'Well, as harmless as that may be, I'd rather you didn't report back to her on my actions or whereabouts. If friends need to know where I am, they can ask me and not snoop about behind my back!' she says, her tone sounding sharp, which is unusual for my cousin.

'She means well,' says Levi.

'These elderly dears have little to keep them entertained,' I say, attempting to lighten the mood. 'Though she's done a fabulous job of nursing Natalia.'

'You know what Dottie's like, Jemima – she's into everyone's business before they are. She doesn't mean any harm, simply filling her days playing matriarch amongst the allotment plots,' says Levi, shuffling his feet.

Jemima looks truly miffed. 'I'd rather folk kept their beaks out of my business, thank you – matriarch or otherwise.'

As swiftly as she delivers the sentiment Jemima is off, striding along the turfed pathway heading for the car park and the walled gateway, towards home.

'What's up with her?' I ask, staring up at Levi.

'Who knows? But I doubt Dottie will cease with the questions any day soon.'

'Exactly. Jemima actually looked upset at the very mention of it.'

'Mmmm, not the reaction I was expecting. Though probably not your finest hour, spilling the beans about Dottie's constant questioning.'

I can't argue, Levi's got a fair point.

'Maybe not . . . but see what I mean about my family? They're as tetchy as hell when it suits.'

We exchange a puzzled glance, before craning our necks to view Jemima's retreating figure gathering pace along the pathway.

Natalia

'You don't want me to wear nail varnish?' I say, showing Isla and Melissa my fresh manicure of pillar-box red, which Dottie carefully painted for me earlier. I feel glamorous for once, despite the fact that it is half past six on a Saturday evening, and my only invite has been to come to an empty Orangery.

'Not really. The catering profession tends to insist on nails being bare and clean, in case the polish chips off into the food. It's hardly hygienic,' says Isla, touching her pinned hairnet subconsciously, as if proving a point.

'The photographs need to be professional in every aspect,' adds Melissa, tinkering with her camera equipment and tripod.

She is positioned directly in front of the countertop laden with baking paraphernalia. It's the first time I've seen her since my stroke. I'd thanked her profusely for sending me the whiteboard and pen, which had been a godsend a few weeks ago.

'I can't imagine publishers considering the proposed submission otherwise,' she explains.

I'm stumped by this assignment. 'I see,' I say, pronouncing each syllable slowly, as I say everything slowly nowadays to combat the slurring. 'These photographs aren't the final images then?'

'No,' says Isla, looking dubiously towards Melissa. 'These shots are my suggestions . . . or examples, to show how the step-by-step method might be portrayed. My cookery book isn't being published until November, to catch the Christmas sales market. I believe the publishers will use their own foody photographers for the final published images.'

Ah. That explains why I was asked to do this favour.

There's a weighty silence.

'I imagine Jemima has nail varnish remover. Shall I fetch it?' asks Isla, glancing nervously between us.

I nod. Melissa follows suit on seeing my response; you'd think a pregnant woman would rest, given half a chance. But she's at that blooming stage, looking a picture of health, and she carries it well, with her tall willowy frame.

I assume this will become a regular occurrence in my new life; everyone waiting for me to react and then, and only then, responding with their emotions held carefully in check. I presume they are trying to be sympathetic to my new condition, thinking I need space and time to adjust. But more importantly, I suspect they are trying to keep me on an even keel, because God forbid if I lose my rag at one of their suggestions; I might have another full-blown stroke, which could be the end of me. It feels as if they're pacifying me, agreeing with everything I say purely to avoid a scene or another medical emergency. I wish to God that somebody would have the backbone to disagree with me, say, 'No, Natalia, hang on a second, that is out of the question!' Will I never hear strong opposition ever again, for fear of the consequences?

Isla swiftly departs in search of Jemima and her bottle of nail varnish remover. I can't imagine it'll be much cop; cheap super-market stuff, costing no more than a quid, but still, it shouldn't do too much harm. How my nails will look without a coat of polish is a whole other matter, but I doubt Isla will think to ask if the boss's wife has a bottle of clear nail varnish.

I struggle to remove the bright red varnish on my right hand; Dottie applied a double coat plus top coat this morning. I try my hardest not to leave any residue on my cuticles and surrounding skin. But when your fingers don't work like they ought to, it's not easy.

What I hate the most about my new life is the constant obser-vation and scrutiny. I wouldn't be offended if Melissa or Isla offered to help; the task would be done in half the time. Instead, they stand and stare, observing my every mishap, tremble and shake, without a word being uttered.

It's frustrating more than humiliating. When I think of the times I've removed varnish in seconds, without thinking! Now I have no choice but to concentrate on every tiny movement, cursing my poor dexterity.

After twenty minutes – twenty minutes, I ask you! – I'm free to continue. My bare nails are now pristine and clean.

My hands are in the centre of Melissa's camera shot. Isla has placed a bowl of dry ingredients on the countertop. I simply need to position my hands in a manner that suggests action: stirring, mixing or sieving. I gently rest my left hand on the side of the beige mixing bowl and pick up the balloon whisk with the other, holding it above the pile of dry ingredients.

'Hold it there,' mutters Melissa, peering into her view-finder camera screen and depressing the button with her thumb. 'Nearer, but without touching the ingredients.'

I follow her instructions. I'm unsure whether to laugh or cry; have I made it back to modelling, or am I a long way off returning to my chosen career path? I'm fully aware it is my hands that are the star attraction here. I can't imagine my lopsided smile will ever be booked for an assignment, so I need to make the most of my greatest asset, though I'll need to fudge the capabilities of my left hand until more movement is recovered. For now, resting on the side of a mixing bowl is the limit of what I can do. Only time will tell what my capabilities will be. To think I used to model for the highest-paid jobs in the cosmetic world, and now my world has come to this ... a photo session for a cookery book by an unknown bakery chef! I want to cry!

Within minutes, Isla has removed the original bowl and replaced it with an identical one containing a mixture to which I assume the milk and eggs have been added. My task is to hold a balloon whisk protruding from the beige gloop, demonstrating the next step. I don't even know what bake this series of shots is creating. I imagine it to be a cake, but no one has said. Maybe they think my neurons can't cope with such an overload of excitement!

The final image will focus purely on my hands. The exclusion of my face seems poignant, as if my features are being rejected because of the stroke. Why is that bothering me today? I modelled nail polish for years, not caring that my face was never photographed.

When I think of the locations I have been flown to: Bali,

Malaysia, India, Costa Rica. The list of exotic assignments is endless, yet here I am behind a café countertop in Shetland. Not the trip I'd imagined in so many ways. Dear Lord, let the ground open up and swallow me whole now. Right. Now. I feel as if I'm nothing more than a glorified shop dummy, with a false arm and ridged fingers. Ironically, a sniping comparison frequently thrown at models from people outside the industry; I never accepted the insinuation that we're nothing more than clothes horses with blank expressions.

How am I ever going to earn a living now? My assignments as a model have dried up, and my mobile hasn't rung for weeks. I can only assume that word has got around the industry and nobody is calling to enquire if I'm available for work. Who needs to hire a model with a lopsided smile for a hand cream advert, when there are thousands of willing young beauties out there with perfect smiles and excellent cuticles.

'Excellent, Natalia. Now the next shot is spooning the mixture into tiny cup cake cases. Is that something you can do?' asks Melissa hesitantly, rubbing her baby bump.

I shrug. Until I try I'll never know. Isn't that the mantra of life?

Isla appears with a baking tin that she's already filled with decorative paper cases. I'm to spoon a dollop of cake mixture into some, and Melissa will capture the task partway through. Coordination is going to be the name of the game here. Part of me wishes to ask Isla to fill the tiny cases, and I'll simply hold the used spoon in place, but how feeble does that sound? Dare I try? Can I perform this seemingly simple task? I pick up the offered tablespoon and attempt to scoop a measure of cake mixture and deposit it within the frilly paper case. Can I heck! The beige dollop drops off the spoon, spilling over the edge of the paper case, smearing the metal baking tray and ruining the pristine arrangement. Much like this stroke coming out of the blue and ruining my existence.

'Don't worry, accidents happen,' says Isla, grabbing the baking tray and attempting to wipe away my mistake with a paper serviette.

I look away, embarrassed, unable to watch. A wave of self-loathing rises from my stomach. If I can't complete the simplest of tasks, how will I survive living on my own, functioning as an independent woman and venturing back into the world of work?

'Let's take a break, shall we? Have ten minutes to chill, grab a coffee and come back for the final shots. There's no rush for these pictures – they'll take as long as they take,' says Melissa, breaking the silence, as she drags her tripod stand backwards, away from the counter.

Crash!

We all freeze at the sudden noise of breaking pottery.

'Oh shit!' mutters Melissa.

Isla and I lean over the countertop to view the large broken vase with its scattered dried flowers and ornamental grass, which she's knocked over in her hasty retreat.

'Isla, I'm so sorry.'

'Welcome to my world,' I mutter, attempting to offer her a sympathetic smile, knowing how awkward she feels.

The vase lies in eight broken pieces amongst a smattering of smaller chips.

'It was an accident, Melissa – don't fret,' adds Isla, finishing her task with my baking tray.

'I'll replace it, I promise.'

'Phuh! There's no need. The dried flowers were only a temporary measure until Dottie could supply fresh delphiniums from her allotment. I'll order a replacement vase tomorrow,' says Isla, waving aside Melissa's offer.

'Please don't. I'd like to mend it,' I say, sensing an opportunity the others won't recognise.

'I'm a ceramics teacher, and I say good luck in mending that!' says Melissa, pointing at the broken vase.

'I'd like to try, and that's what matters to me,' I say, more to myself than the other ladies.

Chapter Thirty-Two

Wednesday 9 March

Pippa

'Morning, Dottie,' I say, emerging from a sales meeting in Ned's third-floor office. There's a definite spring in my step as I approach her position; not that I have any intention of sharing my secret.

'Morning, Pippa, good meeting?' Her piercing blue eyes glisten with curiosity as her yellow duster glides along the wooden banister.

'Yes, the usual, but . . .' I glance towards the office, to find Jemima leaning against the door frame.

What's with her? I pause in my answer, causing Dottie to look up from her polishing duties. Her gaze follows mine to where Jemima is watching us both.

'Mmmm, I seem to have upset someone,' I remark, 'though Lord knows how.' Unless my cousin is still miffed about our allotment conversation, when I mentioned Dottie's constant questioning. In which case, I'd best not let on to Dottie that I've let the cat out of the bag.

I descend the first few steps of the staircase, removing Jemima from my eyeline, before Dottie speaks in a low voice.

'I doubt anyone, or anything, could upset that one at the minute, lassie.'

'What?'

'Sssssssssh,' mouths Dottie.

What is going on around here?

'Married life suits her well, don't you think?' whispers Dottie.

'Who?'

'Jemima.'

I instinctively stand on my tiptoes to view the corridor through the banister rail, only to find the office door is now firmly closed. It's one thing to answer Dottie's questions, but I don't wish to get caught – or be accused of gossiping. If I stay too long, I risk her wheedling my news out of me, and then I'll kick myself for sharing. I want to savour my excitement, enjoying that warm fuzzy feeling, relishing my first date with Levi for a little longer, if possible.

'Yeah. Suits her just fine,' I say, eager to return to my work.

'Did you see her out and about over the weekend? A peerie bird told me you were at the allotments, helping Levi.'

Does anything ever go unnoticed or slip Dottie's attention?

I stop mid-step, turning back to view her properly. She's statue-like, her yellow duster resting on the gleaming banister, her can of polish clasped in the other hand.

'I did. Levi asked if I would help him to plant his hanging baskets, despite the weather being too cold to display them anywhere other than inside his polytunnels.'

'Right. So are you one for hanging baskets then?'

'I am, actually.'

'Levi's never planted hanging baskets any other season,' Dottie retorts, giving the banister a rapid polish as if rubbing in the details.

'Is that so.' Duly noted. 'Well, he'd grown plenty of petunia plugs under glass, so we planted up four hanging baskets.'

'Mmmm, interesting.'

I should leave the conversation and be on my way, but Dottie's comments intrigue me. She's an expert at this game; I've watched her on numerous occasions. It's as if she's silently plotting whilst doing her polishing. Her master plan is to ask a series of leading questions which will tease out a response from her unsuspecting victim, without them realising they've given her the information that she's truly after. Oh, I'm on to you, Dottie! The question is . . . do I play along?

'What made you ask about Jemima?'

'I was wondering if she'd visited the allotments whilst you were there? That's all.'

'She did, as a matter of fact.'

'Do any digging, did she?' Dottie's arm rhythmically works the surface of each banister post, her gaze averted from mine.

'No.' One point to me.

'Weed her crazy paving?'

'Nope.' Two points to me.

Dottie looks up after my second short answer. I can play the yes or no game as well as anyone, which I know she hates; you learn very little information when the responder doesn't elaborate.

'What then?' she asks, her brow furrowed.

Hat trick!

'She tended her chickens and then headed over to your plot, actually. I take it she borrowed Ned's keys and was doing something with the bees.'

Dottie's watery blue eyes widen, as big as saucers. She lifts both hands to her mouth with a look of delight.

'That duster probably shouldn't be near your face when it's been used,' I say.

But Dottie doesn't seem to care. 'Oh, lovey, how long was she there for?'

'Err, a few minutes. She didn't use his wood smoker or wear his protective veil – but then she didn't lift the roof of the hives either. She definitely did something with them before leaving, though, as she was standing very close to the hives.' I'm taken

aback as Dottie suddenly comes to her senses, snapping out of
her pose of wonderment.

'That's good to hear. And nothing more, she did nothing
more?'

'No. She left immediately, after a quick word with us.'

Dottie's head is almost bouncing in a frantic nod.

'Dottie, are you OK?'

'Me? I'm fine, lovey. In fact, I've never been better.'

I'm half expecting more questions about the hanging baskets,
but she appears to have rapidly moved on. She's no longer interested in me and Levi, which is slightly disappointing.

'OK, then ... Catch you later, I'm just heading out on my
rounds,' I say, continuing my route down the stairs.

'That you will, lovey. Mind you nurture those baskets good
and proper, otherwise Levi won't be bothering next year!' she
calls after me as I turn on to the lower landing.

She's a crafty one. She makes everything sound innocent, yet
deep down there's a hidden message in every comment. Wait
till she finds out that Levi and I are going out for a quiet drink
tonight! Boy, will she have questions.

Autumn

'I'd be flattered if I were you,' says Nessie, as I linger in the forge
on my lunch break.

'I am. It started off as a way of managing my own stress
throughout the day. Then I taught small classes of six, almost
private sessions, whilst on board ship. But the question is ... can
I juggle doing my job here, plus teach yoga on a larger scale?'

'What's your gut telling you?' asks Isaac, from the far end,
sitting at his workbench and tucking into his sandwich box.

'Well, that's just it. Being the kind of person I am, I'm

overthinking it all. Will anyone sign up? Will there be huge classes of attendees in the first few weeks, then they'll deplete to disappointing numbers after constant no-shows? Or will I ruin my own enjoyment by taking this on? I said yes straight away, but now I'm concerned it might take up too much of my time.'

'Only you can answer those niggles,' says Nessie, forking rice and beans from her Tupperware box.

I shrug. It's a no-brainer if I'm going to ruin my own sense of well-being by taking on a class to support others. I can do without constant stress, the weekly anxiety, and even the negativity of others questioning what I'm doing if numbers decline. That's what happened on board, where numbers and interest fluctuated so much. I need like-minded people who are open to trying the techniques, rather than bombarding me with questions and complaints, thus ruining our yoga or relaxation sessions.

'I'm scared.' The real reason slips from my lips before I have a chance to check it.

Both Nessie and Isaac stop eating, stare at me, then glance at one another.

'I don't think that's her intention. Jemima thinks she's being helpful by offering you the opportunity. She's not one to be pushy or controlling; she's not that kind of boss. If you don't want to do it, she won't make you,' says Nessie, putting her lunch box down and reaching for my hand.

'I know that, she's been lovely. It's me. I don't want to let the Campbells down, because everything they do is a success, but likewise I don't want to bog myself down when I've struggled to see my sister or keep to arrangements in recent weeks. I might come across as confident in my work, but then I trip myself up unexpectedly. I don't want these sessions to become the final straw that breaks the camel's back.'

'Take it step by step, then. Offer a six-week course where the attendees have to pay up front for the block booking. That way, if the classes are half empty, or issues arise for them or you, you're only obliged to complete the six weeks. If it's a success, you'll have the chance to renew the block bookings. Use the limited duration as a safety net for you and the attendees,' suggests Isaac, before continuing with his sandwiches.

'Surely that's worth a try,' adds Nessie, eyeing me cautiously.

'I'm liking that suggestion, thanks, Isaac.' I instantly feel less anxious about taking on a new addition to my weekly work-load. 'Right, after interrupting your lunch break, I shall mosey back across to the manor house and jot down some ideas before chatting with Jemima. Thank you.'

I go to make a move but Nessie holds me fast by the hand.

'You need to treat these hands, you know.' Her gaze is locked on my scaly raw knuckles and reddened skin.

'I do. I have creams and things,' I say, embarrassed by her scrutiny.

'Why don't you ask Dottie for a hand massage – I hear she's introduced Natalia to the wonders of sweet almond oil, as a means of improving circulation in her left arm. It might do the trick for you too.'

'I doubt it, though Natalia has complimented her several times, she finds it so relaxing.'

Nessie releases my hand and gives a polite smile.

I wave farewell and am about to leave the courtyard when a beautiful sight catches my eye. Lying on the cobblestones in front of Verity's Yarn Barn is Floss, sprawled out and sunning herself. And, nestled between her paws, lies Crispy duck, eyes closed and sleeping.

'You pair need to be careful, you'll be giving Jemima ideas for opening a pub,' I snort, shaking my head and imagining the new Dog and Duck of Lerwick suddenly springing to life.

I cross the cobbles, head under the stone archway and back towards the hotel's entrance.

Nessie and Isaac have got a point; I need to break it down into small chunks, to allow my confidence to grow. It's been so long since I taught a yoga class. Who says it'll fade to nothing like my on-board classes did, all those years ago? I'll probably kick myself after the first session, wondering what I was worried about. But first, I definitely need to address my unsightly hands.

As I reach the hotel steps, I spy Natalia walking beside the alpaca field. Her head is low, her shoulders drooping and, given her demeanour, I suspect she's crying. I stop and stand, not wanting to stare, but I wouldn't for the world ignore someone who needs a kind word. Isn't that what Nessie and Isaac have just delivered to me?

I saunter over to where she's stopped to lean against the wooden fencing. She gives me a sideways glance as I approach: she's weeping. Standing beside her, I slip my arm around her shoulders to deliver a warm embrace. She nestles her head on to my shoulder. I let her cry.

No words are necessary as we stand together and watch the alpacas gleefully frolic around their paddock.

Chapter Thirty-Three

Thursday 10 March

Pippa

My head is banging. My stomach swirls each time I move. I've run to the bathroom four times between sipping my morning coffee and two bites of my buttered toast.

'I am never drinking again,' I mutter, for the umpteenth time this morning, as I brush my teeth.

How am I going to hold this together on today's delivery route? If I puke in my own lap it will serve myself right for being stupid on a work night. I don't want to recall how many drinks I downed whilst out with Levi. Worse still was the mixture of cocktails and wine consumed – it never works for me, so why did I think it was such a good idea this time? Yes, I was nervous, but that's no excuse. I should know better at my age. Levi stuck to an alcohol-free night and seemed to enjoy our chat, so why couldn't I?

I was that drunk last night, I dropped my key on the carpet after I locked the door. How ridiculous! Hello, irresponsible Pippa is back! When I've tried for weeks to develop a new, improved version – the be-myself-come-what-may Pippa. In a matter of three hours, I reduced myself to the alcohol-binging, kebab-eating monster of yesteryear. I don't even like garlic sauce, so why I insisted on smothering my late-night snack with it is beyond me. I found the half-eaten remnants of my foolishness on my chest of drawers this morning.

I swill my mouth out and check my complexion in the vanity mirror. My eyes look bloodshot, with dark circles underneath, and my skin has a waxy glow despite a dab of powder.

If I can successfully dodge Jemima, Isla and Callie for the entire day, I'll have run the gauntlet. Ned won't be a problem; he rarely speaks to me. I bet he wouldn't know a hung-over woman if I marched into his office and openly announced my stupidity amidst the sales figures and 'wastage' log.

If I can dig deep and put on a bubbly persona in the company of others, not throw up in their presence, and take a very slow and steady drive around the villages, I'll be fine.

Won't I?

I strap myself in and turn the ignition key, firing Rolly's engine . . . and hesitate. I shouldn't be doing this, I really shouldn't. Loading the wicker bread trays was a job and a half, as the pretence that I was all happy and smiley took it out of me. I glance at the three bottles of water and packet of digestive biscuits lying on the passenger seat. It might look like forward planning, but surely they represent my awareness that what I'm about to do is totally wrong. Unethical, in fact.

I'm hung-over. They'll throw the book at me if have an accident. But what options have I actually got?

I glance up at the third-floor office window. I can envisage Ned, Jemima and Isla sitting around the meeting table, busily discussing matters of the day. It would be easy to march upstairs and explain. It would be, could be, should be; but I'd be in for it, if I did. I'd probably be sacked, demoted to work alongside Callie in The Orangery, which I wouldn't complain about – given the way I feel – if it was her day off. But as it isn't, I won't be going there.

Why did I allow this to happen? I've worked so hard in recent weeks at turning over a new leaf, showing people my true colours, and yet I've failed myself in this ridiculous situation. If I come clean and am honest, I can already hear the remarks being fired at me: 'Typical, Pippa does it again', 'What did you expect, she never gives it her all?' or 'It was only a matter of time before she messed up!' I've been so stupid.

I've no other choice. Despite my actions being socially and morally unacceptable. I'll play it safe. Drive slowly for the entire day, and take no chances; perform extra checks at every crossing or junction, and no squeezing through tight gaps. I'll take regular breaks, hydrate as quickly as possible, and this will be another life lesson. No excessive drinking on a school night!

I swiftly put Rolly into first gear and slowly pull away, driving under the stone archway with my hands positioned at 'ten to two' and using all my mirrors like a learner driver on their test day.

I trundle along the driveway. I'm doing good. My headache is thumping, my mouth is dry, but I no longer feel sick. Though my stomach is somersaulting; but that's a reaction to what I'm doing, not the alcohol content.

There's a lone figure standing beyond the gates, watching the traffic go by. Good Lord, if this is Lachlan still pining for Isla after all these months, I'll send her a quick text as a warning. He should be ashamed of himself after his ... A wave of guilt rises within me. Am I not doing the exact same thing, in a slightly different manner? Didn't he drive off in a temper, the night of the Yule Day celebrations, wheels spinning for good measure, thinking all would be OK and he'd arrive home safely? A dangerous bundle of hot rage, fuelled by emotion and having possibly consumed a dram or two of something strong during the fête. With tragic consequences for dear old Niven.

As I near the entrance gates the figure turns around: Levi.

My wave of guilt disappears faster than warm bannocks on a cold day in Shetland.

I draw alongside, lowering my driver's window. He turns and opens my door wide.

'Out you get, lady,' he says, his brow furrowed, gaze averted, avoiding mine.

'What?' I'm surprised by his instruction and tone.

'I said, out yee get!' His voice is firm but not unkind.

I don't move, but pull on the handbrake.

'You're not fit to drive so, now you're clear of the gallery and the bosses, we can switch seats. Either jump down and walk around, or budge over the handbrake into the passenger seat.'

I don't argue with his steely expression. I undo my seat belt and slide over the seats, lifting the bottled water and biscuits as he jumps in, slamming the door closed.

'Provisions, I assume?'

'How do you even know?'

He stares at me whilst securing his seat belt. 'I take it you can't remember getting home last night?'

I settle myself, not daring to answer but flicking through my memories: the pub, the cocktail bar, large kebab, extra onions, extra garlic sauce – I think. Urgh, garlic sauce. My memories falter, much like a Sky dish in a thunderstorm when the reception ceases.

'Err . . .' I'm stalling but there's nothing more. 'I woke up in bed.'

Levi indicates and pulls out into the morning traffic, glancing sideways at my last remark. He waits a few minutes, working his way through the gears on reaching the main road, before saying, 'Fully dressed, though, weren't you?'

My mouth drops wide. How the hell?

'Seriously, you haven't a clue, have you?'

'I must have flopped into bed and pulled the quilt over me. I can sleep for Scotland, some nights.'

'Nope. Though you can stick to your version, if it makes

you feel better. I drove you back to the hotel, but when you couldn't even open the tradesman's entrance door – because of the step aerobics class you were performing on the doorstep whilst waving your key in every direction but the lock – I opened it for you. You then, and I quote, said, "Bingo! I'm in," before crawling along the kitchen floor towards the staircase to your landing. That's when you collapsed, announcing that you'd prefer to sleep there than attempt to move any further.'

I slide down in my seat under the weight of sheer embarrassment.

'You even pulled a tea towel from the range to use as a makeshift pillow.'

It sounds like me. I close my eyes. I daren't look at him as I ask, 'Did you actually put me to bed?'

'I did. I assumed the locked bedroom was yours; all the others, barring one, were open to view as we moved along the landing. I didn't turn your bedroom light on or anything, so you can save your blushes; the bathroom light was enough to see by. I dropped you in the bed, removed your shoes and threw the quilt over you. I fetched you a glass of water from your sink and kipped in your armchair until five o'clock, checked you were still OK, then let myself out. Locking your door and posting the key underneath, I might add – you should have found it this morning.'

'My God, yes ... I wondered why it was there!' I exclaim, jolted by his explanation.

'So you won't be protesting about having a driver for the day, will you?'

'Thank you, Levi. It was stupid of me.' I am hot with shame. 'I had a few drinks when I was getting ready to meet you,' I admit awkwardly. Knowing I can be honest with him, but wishing I didn't need to be.

'The prospect of going out with me that bad?' Levi asks wryly.

'No ... no, not at all,' I murmur. 'I was nervous ... and yet excited – the situation simply got the better of me.' I've probably blown my chances of a second date.

He throws a quick glance my way and clears his throat. 'It might be my day off, but I'll do you a favour. I don't know what the hell you were thinking, loading up and pulling away as if you're feeling tickety-boo ... given the state you were in, I'm surprised you woke up in this world.'

I feel utterly reckless. He's right, every damned word is bang on. I should have called in sick, but no, I go and stupidly act as if nothing is wrong.

'You're absolutely right to be angry with me. I have no excuses, other than I was desperate for us to get along outside work. I wanted you to see the real me, dressed up nicely and enjoying myself, rather than being het up with nerves.'

'You'd best take more care on our second date then, otherwise I'll be wondering what I'm getting myself involved with.' He shakes his head but delivers me a cheeky wink; clearly very forgiving of my idiotic behaviour.

Levi swiftly navigates the town centre traffic, heading out towards Gulberwick. He gives a nod, accepting my explanation, but I can see the cogs are whirring.

I sit back, grateful that I have such a close confidant in my world. And desperately hoping that I haven't disappointed him again, this time beyond repair.

'Drop me off here, I'll walk back home,' says Levi, pulling into Lerwick Manor's driveway. 'Switch seats and no one will be any the wiser.'

He hasn't mentioned my misdemeanour for the last six hours; instead, he has calmly and quietly driven me about the route, helping out where he could and being jolly to the customers. Having company has made for a pleasant day, until my brain remembers the reason why. I know I was foolish. Would I have made it all the way around the villages today? Or called it quits if it proved too much? I'll never know, thanks to Levi.

'Are you sure?'

'I'm sure. I suggest you unload as quickly as you can and get yourself off to your room – you still look slightly green around the gills, Pippa.' He jumps down from the driver's seat and stands in the open doorway as I slide across the seats. 'If you need anything dropping off, just call, OK?'

I feel humbled by his kind gesture; I don't deserve his support. I've totally messed up and shown myself to be lacking in moral fibre.

I nod, too choked to speak.

'And Pippa, I suggest we keep this little incident between us, OK? I've a feeling others won't be so understanding,' he says, slamming the driver's door closed.

I swiftly lower the window, not wishing to be deprived of his company.

'Thank you,' I mutter, before adding, 'I won't forget this, Levi.'

'I believe you, even if thousands wouldn't.' He steps back, giving me a brief wave as I pull away. 'Call me if you need anything, OK?'

I nod, quite overcome by his generosity and the day's events.

Natalia

I stare at the figure before me. Framed by the mirror's fancy gilt edge, my naked body is unchanged in many ways: form, weight and posture. A body that I was once so proud of: a figure to die for, topped with a mane of thick blonde hair, and blessed with graceful, fluid movements. I could wear what I liked, do as I pleased and always looked good doing it.

My healthy body with which I have earned my crust over

the years, admired time and time again, wherever I was sent for modelling assignments.

I'll admit it's a strange way to earn your money. People assume you're an airhead, lacking in intelligence or personality, but I'm neither. I'm me. I believe I've stayed true to my values in life. I'm not afraid of hard work; honesty and integrity are my backbone, and the trappings of status and power which others rely upon have never interested me.

My future has always been within my control. But now, I'm not so sure.

I've made considerable progress in recent weeks, thanks to the constant care received from Dottie and the hospital's out-reach teams. My initial fluttering muteness has been replaced by a slurring voice which I've grown accustomed to, my overall weakness has given way to a healthier energy, and my previously sky-rocketing blood pressure is now under control.

But still my journey continues, day by day.

I stand lopsided, staring at the reflection, attempting to hide the one limb I've purposely not included each time I've used this mirror, for nearly a month. My body and most of my face are exactly the same as before; my left arm is severed by the mirror's bulky frame.

It's the sliver of reflection denied that I need to address.

I rock towards the right, allowing my left side to join the rest of my body, freshly showered and moisturised, not yet dressed.

Instantly, my perception changes; my gaze fixates on the imperfection. The lack of health, life and energy which mars the rest by hanging like a pendulum, without purpose or function. I'm guessing that it represents roughly five, maybe ten per cent of my body, and yet it will be the first thing strangers, photographers and lovers will notice.

Already I've seen people stare before swiftly looking away, trying to hide their reactions when they spot the uncontrollable droop to my lopsided smile or the careful repositioning of my hand, permanently tucked inside my left pocket or resting on my lap. And these are people who know what I've been through; imagine the untold conversations with acquaintances who haven't seen me in several weeks. The hot-shot photographers, the other models and the agency bosses, who all think they know what they're getting when they book Natalia Muir for an assignment.

Can I survive in an industry fuelled by perfection, when aspects of me clearly signal a difference? Will they accept this new kintsugi vessel with her additional strand of gold?

I look myself in the eye, direct and honest, and I see that the woman before me is crying.

I need to be brave and take steps towards my future, whether that is within the industry I love, or elsewhere.

Chapter Thirty-Four

Saturday 12 March

Autumn

I wake an hour before my alarm. I find the cold side of the pillow, in a poor attempt to drift back off. But it doesn't happen, because my mind is already racing to plan the day ahead. Will I be working an extra shift like yesterday? Will Hannah turn up for her late reception shift? Will I be given time off in lieu? Or will my extra hours be absorbed into the ether of salaried overtime – like all the previous occasions?

A full night's sleep would have been great, especially as my rota covers the breakfast shift, which is rarely a quiet one. As much as the kitchen staff now know the menu, and the guests know the morning routine, the breakfast shift always needs assistance from reception. And that's what I can do without this morning. I need everything to run like clockwork, leaving me to oversee the covers, smile at guests and enjoy a welcome start to a Saturday morning. Instead, I'm bound to be dashing up and down stairs carrying trays for room service, retracing my steps with forgotten items, or delivering newspapers which have arrived late. And that's assuming no staff are off sick or arrive late.

Did I pass on the telephone message about the installation of the picnic tables to Ned? Did I return the pinking shears I borrowed from Verity? Did I confirm my dental appointment for Tuesday? And that's without organising the scarecrow festival. There still remain a few unselected names in the cloth bag; this spells potential disaster, as not everyone will be involved, which is likely to cause offence and disappointment on the actual day.

I've been awake for all of five minutes and already my brain is bamboozled by a set of imaginary scenarios which haven't even occurred, yet I'm firefighting each one from beneath my duvet. This is ridiculous. This isn't supposed to happen. When it happened last time, I ended up leaving my position on the cruise liners and seeking work elsewhere. I don't want to leave the Campbells. I know where dry scaly hands, pockets full of debris and a racing mind will lead me if I don't take action and look after myself. My drive for perfection will consume me and I'll end up becoming a slave to the inner me who relentlessly strives to be the best version she can possibly be. And then, when push comes to shove, I'll crumble as my body and mind remind me in a pretty unglorified manner that I'm simply human, like everyone else. All work and no play makes Autumn a dull gal. Actually, from experience, I know that it's far worse than that. It makes me a gibbering wreck who has walked away from her last two jobs, unable to cope with the build-up of pressure and self-imposed tension that I, and only I, demand of me. A superhuman quest which ends in self-sabotage when my health plummets and I belatedly recognise how poorly I actually am.

I pull the duvet up to my chin, as if straightening the situation and taking control. I need to revert to the basics: food, sleep and structured work. No more pushing the boundaries, covering for others and allowing my OCD world of perfection to pull me under and drown me. I need a timetabled, structured day which enables me to work, rest and play and be a happy lass. Because if I don't, I'll return to those dark cloudy days of struggling to cope, and eventually resigning from a job I love in order to save my mental health from suffering any more.

I stare at the stippled ceiling. I need a plan.

Step one: speak frankly to Jemima.

Step two: meditation.

Step three: get some fresh air.

I rerun the three steps in my mind; it sounds like a start.

Natalia

I'm enjoying the peace and quiet of the library, with Floss lying at my feet. It seems selfish not to collect the poor mite from The Yarn Barn for a gentle walk to the paddock and back while Verity is busy working. Though today, she's followed me into the hotel, which I won't complain about; Floss is good company, she doesn't interrupt my thinking. We're currently two of a kind, both awaiting our recovery.

I look up to find Jemima hastily approaching; I've no doubt she'll be giving me the usual pep talk that everyone else seems to offer so freely. I don't move or attempt to avoid her gaze, merely wait until she reaches me.

'Afternoon, how are we today?' she asks, standing beside the study table, her tone brisk and bright. She's staring at the broken pottery of The Orangery vase, spread out on the newspaper before me.

'Good, thank you. You?' My words still slur together as if linked. I watch the flicker of concentration as Jemima deciphers my speech.

'Good, good. I thought you'd be outside enjoying a bit of fresh air. Not that it's stuffy inside, but you know ... it gets stuffy inside.'

She's tripping over her own sentences, conscious of every word she utters, for fear of offending or upsetting me. Our manner has changed considerably since our chat at the carp pond; we're unlikely ever to be the best of friends, but still, a mutual respect has developed.

'I went for a walk earlier, I wanted to make a start on mending this vase,' I say, gesturing towards the broken pieces.

'The pattern and glaze are beautiful, but surely it's too difficult to mend, with so many splinters?'

'It is, but I believe I have all the pieces. Isla was good enough to carry them over in a box. Isaac, the glass blower, has provided me with glue – and Verity from The Yarn Barn has supplied my companion,' I say, as Jemima smiles at each item in turn. 'I have all I need. Give me an hour or so, and I might have something resembling a vase. It'll never be watertight, but then dried flowers and ornamental grass don't demand such necessities.'

'Do you need a helping hand?'

I glance up on hearing the question. There's a pause before she continues.

'Sorry, that was tactless. I meant it in a kindly way, I wasn't referring to your . . .' Jemima blushes profusely at her error.

'I know, you were offering your time rather than your working limbs,' I say, enabling her to calm down and regain control after becoming flustered.

'I simply wanted to offer my assistance, that's all. Everyone seems to be doing their bit for you, helping your recovery, and I appear to –' she sighs deeply whilst finding the right word – 'avoid you, for fear of upsetting, offending you or hindering your progress in some way.'

I nod. 'I'd noticed that you keep your distance – it really isn't necessary. My focus is on regaining my strength and ensuring my progress continues. I appreciate that you and Ned both have your own lives to live. You've been incredibly generous in allowing me to remain here, close to the hospital and my outreach team. You don't need to feel uncomfortable; this is your home, not mine.'

Our eyes meet as we both understand the depth of my final remark. I'm simply being honest, not malicious.

'If you want to pull up a chair, please do so; I have no objections. Isaac said this glue was strong but incredibly messy, so I'm armed with tissues just in case.' I select the nearest piece of pottery and gently place its broken edge against another large piece, as a test fit. They match perfectly, despite the ugly crack between them.

Jemima hesitates, as if replaying my invite in her mind, before responding. She gently draws the nearest chair from beneath the table and settles herself, making sure she leaves Floss plenty of room to lie at my feet.

It takes much longer than I imagined to mend the broken vase. I'm all fingers and thumbs with the glue, and it's impossible to hold the pieces together with only one good hand, so I appreciate Jemima's assistance. The process is slow and laborious but, piece by piece, the broken pottery begins to take shape.

'Have you any idea when you'll return to work once you're home?' asks Jemima as she holds two aligned pieces together, waiting for the glue to dry sufficiently.

'Not really. The modelling agency want to hold fire on my unsigned contract. I can't say I blame them. There's no point signing me if they can't find me suitable assignments. My portfolio will look somewhat different from now on. I can refer back to the old images but I'll never resemble that model again, will I?'

Jemima slowly nods.

'There's no point pretending in my industry that looks don't count, because they do! When was the last time you saw a product, let alone beauty cosmetics, being advertised by a model who'd suffered a stroke?'

'Honestly, I can't name any,' Jemima admits. 'Can you?'

'Nope. It'd take a huge effort to convince the industry other-wise. Let's be honest, selecting me for an assignment would be a huge gamble for any company or photographer. It would be make or break for a product brand – and pretty controversial.'

'It would be more realistic as a representation of the public they're selling to,' adds Jemima, holding her pottery piece per-fectly still as I gently release my grip on my own piece.

'True, and given that I potentially represent thousands of people a year, old and young, from all backgrounds and cultures, who will suffer a stroke, I probably shouldn't be hidden away from modelling the products they will continue to buy. But it won't happen, will it? I don't know that my agency have ever employed anyone other than physically able-bodied people for modelling shoots; it's what the high-paying brands expect.'

Jemima frowns, adding, 'Well, maybe you shouldn't be hidden away.'

I let go of the piece I'd been tentatively holding: it's secure, the glue has held.

'But I am. Or rather, I will be for evermore, until social atti-tudes change and people living with disabilities are accepted more frequently as models. I'm not going to hold my breath for that day to arrive.' I select the next pottery piece, testing its position against our partly repaired vase.

'Have you the fight in you to change it?' she asks, glancing up through her dark fringe, watching me cautiously.

Her words ring in my ears. It's an honest question, with a challenge attached. Modelling is all I've truly known. Have I the strength to fight for my right to remain in my chosen career? When I got upset viewing my body the other day, I hadn't thought of others out there in society but had focused entirely on my own limitations, the aspects of me that now look so different. But I'm not alone in this; there are potentially thousands of others who are affected too.

I rest the selected piece back on the table and stare at Jemima.

'I could try ... I could make enquiries whilst I'm still recuperating.'

'That would be a start,' offers Jemima kindly.

Instantly, the idea blossoms within me, with a burst of energy and life that nothing else has aroused in recent weeks. My gaze rests on the repaired cracks of the pottery vase, half reconstructed on the table before us. It might not be true kintsugi, using molten gold, but together we've resurrected this vase for a second life. Maybe Jemima's suggestion can do the same for me?

'I could. I should at least try. Why should I slink away and retire from modelling purely because of my stroke? I shouldn't. I'll still buy and wear make-up – I've used cosmetics and products every day since leaving hospital.'

'You have, Natalia. Dottie's mentioned it several times in passing. It's probably given you a sense of normality, if nothing else, during this difficult time.'

'That's what I'm going to do.' I feel my determination growing. 'I'll start by calling in a few favours from photographers I've known over the years. That's it ... I'll show them what I can do.'

Pippa

This is not my usual shopping spree, I confess. I'm more of a jeans and jacket kind of girl than diamonds and glitz. I can't remember the last time I purchased a pair of earrings, let alone browsed for something a little more glamorous. But here I am, outside the antique jewellery shop, perusing their window display for a certain sapphire engagement ring.

I feel self-conscious, standing here staring at the sparkly goods displayed in the spot-lit window, but the thought of entering the shop is daunting. The fact that I'm on the hunt for my nanna's ring ups the stakes for me; I'm furious that Callie was only given £800 for a piece which is irreplaceable in our family.

I'm not expecting the owner to be a cheapskate, more a shrewd businessman who knows value when he comes across it. My nanna's engagement ring was on her finger for more than six decades before her untimely death. What Callie was thinking is beyond my comprehension. The ring is probably long gone, being loved by its new owner, but it's worth a try if nothing else.

The door chime sounds as I enter. Inside, the shop is dark and fairly claustrophobic; I feel confined by the display cabinets, each crammed with velvet cushions and sparkling gems.

'Can I help you?' asks the man, his tweed jacket bursting at the buttons across his rotund frame.

'I'm browsing for a sapphire ring,' I say, gesturing towards the window. He probably saw me loitering outside.

'Old or modern?'

'Old . . . preferably.'

'For yourself?'

I nod. I feel like a fraud but I don't want him to know what I'm really after. I want to see if he still has the ring, and then I'll go from there.

'Sapphires are such lovely stones . . . often overlooked, you know, nowadays as everyone is chasing diamonds!'

'That's why I thought I'd consider it . . . take a look anyway,' I bluff, hoping he hurries up and shows me the desired ring.

He collects a large set of keys from the countertop as he speaks. 'If you don't mind waiting, I'll fetch a particular pad of gems which I think might interest you.'

'Sure. I'll wait.'

Autumn

'Autumn, I'm free now. Did you say you wanted a quiet word?' asks Jemima, popping her head inside the reception area.

'Please.' I look up from my desk, grateful that she's come looking for me. I'm OK but there's a definite emotional wobble going on deep inside, now the moment to talk has arrived. Hannah had shown up surprisingly early for her reception shift so there's no issue regarding covering reception. 'I'll need to make a quick call over the radio and then I'll be free.'

'Is the office OK?'

'Could we walk and talk instead?' I ask, gesturing towards the main entrance.

'Sure, that's a great idea. Let's head out to see the alpacas.'

We haven't even reached the top of the stone steps before I begin; she won't need to dig below the surface or prise this conversation out of me.

'Putting it plainly, I'm not feeling great; and that was highlighted yesterday when Hannah missed her shift duty again. I do all I can to make myself available in case of emergencies, but I recognise the signs, and last night I felt dreadful, empty in fact. I know how this story ends if I ignore my own needs. In such a short time, I've allowed my hands to become red raw, my sleep is being disrupted, and I'm spending an unhealthy amount of time at work. I think because my room is onsite, I can't clock off properly, you know?' My delivery isn't great; my words tumble out in one long stream. The important thing is that I air my concerns, rather than swallowing them down and finding I'm pushed to my limit.

We reach the wooden fencing of the alpaca enclosure and watch as they frolic and play.

'Absolutely right, Autumn. I couldn't agree with you more.

I'm grateful to you for being honest and upfront with me. I fully appreciate where you're coming from. The very reason I stayed with the allotment association was because of my own experience with anxiety, and the way it affected my life both at work and at home. I was totally drained and, like you said, feeling empty and wiped out.'

'That's exactly it. I hold my hands up. I've taken on more than I should – and this is the end result.'

'Rest assured that Hannah has been spoken to regarding her conduct; she's had an earlier appointment with Ned. How can I make things a little easier? Would you like me to assist with any of your duties, or maybe take over the organisation of the scarecrow festival?'

'No, that isn't necessary. I simply need to stop working around the clock, covering unexpected shifts, and take time to pursue some leisure activities. It's my nature to be a people pleaser, taking on more tasks than I should, trying to accommodate everyone's needs, but it has to stop before I burn myself out . . . again. I agreed to teach the yoga classes because I know the benefits for those who are signing up. I'm looking forward to starting them; the class environment will provide a welcome release from stress for me too. And then there's my sister . . . I need to make a concerted effort to stick to our plans, rather than cancelling arrangements because of work issues.'

'I agree. You need a balance in life, Autumn. Maybe now's the time to press the reset button and address what's brought you to this point. Sounds like you're creating a sensible plan with which to move forward in the coming weeks. Can we catch up in a week's time? I'd like to know what you've implemented and how it's going,' asks Jemima.

Instantly, I feel relieved. She listened, she fully understood my dilemma. She made it so easy for me; that alone makes a difference.

Chapter Thirty-Five

Tuesday 15 March

Dottie's diary
Blood pressure: 124/83 – a vast improvement from the 172/110 recorded on her admission to hospital. Aspirin – who'd have thought it so special! She's looking perky; my daily nursing is working a treat, but there's a long way to go. Natalia's yamse for my home cooking – she can't get enough of my tatty soup or bannocks.

Pippa

'Pippa!'

I turn around on hearing my name called while I'm closing Rolly's rear doors. I look around the side of the vehicle, expecting to see a last-minute customer wanting a loaf. Nothing.

'Pippa . . . over here,' comes the weak yet forceful voice.

I turn towards the row of cottages, to see a front door wide open and a bedraggled figure in a towelling dressing gown, with her belt tied over her giant bump, clutching the doorjamb for support.

'Melissa!' I jog over to her garden gate. She looks in great discomfort.

'Any chance of a lift to the hospital?'

'Bloody hell, of course . . . here.' I open the gate and semi-jog along the pathway.

'Little one's too eager and has caught us off guard by about two months,' winces Melissa.

'Is there anything you need to bring?'

'My suitcase . . . it's right here.' Melissa opens the door a little wider, allowing me to squeeze past and collect the prepared case.

'Stay there, I'll take this to Rolly and then come back for you, OK?'

Melissa frantically nods through a clenched-teeth grimace, which I assume suggests a contraction. I can't remember the last time I moved so fast, scurrying from front to rear doors and back to Melissa's side.

'Where's Hamish? Is he anywhere near?'

'Fishing. Gone bloody fishing with his lads. I've called him and he's heading back into shore, but I need to go now. I could have called Levi but . . . well, you know . . . it d-didn't seem fair or r-right,' she stammers as she comes through her window of pain.

I remain schtum; she's got a point. Levi would help anyone, but it might get Hamish's back up to think another man has been the knight in shining armour on such a family occasion. It's not a topic we lingered on during our Tuesday lunch breaks, but Levi openly admitted that he and Melissa had become somewhat closer than allotment buddies during last summer. He hastened to stress it was before Hamish returned home from the Gulf of Mexico and his job on the oil rigs. I'm not the jealous type; Levi's life before me is exactly that. And who am I to judge?

'I think I might have left things a little too late, hoping that Hamish would get back here in time.'

'Hey, hey, don't go there, lady! I'm employed for one type of delivery only. Rolly isn't functional for any other, do you hear me?'

Melissa shakes her head, suggesting she's not in control of what happens from this point on.

'Have you got your keys?' I ask, sensing she won't be returning without a swaddled bundle.

'On the radiator shelf,' huffs Melissa, pointing inside the hallway.

Again, I squeeze past her bulky frame and grab her key ring. 'Is that everything?'

She gives a nod, a look of relief dawning on her features.

'I'll drive as smoothly as I can, but are you ready to rock and roll in Rolly?' I slam the front door, secure the lock and offer Melissa my arm to lean on.

'I hope you aren't expecting the honour of a namesake ... because Rolly Robins would be an unfortunate label in life,' jests Melissa, as she takes fairy steps towards her waiting chariot. 'Almost verging on cruelty!'

'How ungrateful are you?' I retort jovially, conscious that my strides need to be halved if this is to work. 'Not only will you be delivered in style but I'll let you choose a bakery treat for the journey.'

'I'll give it a miss, thanks.'

It feels like it takes an age for me to manoeuvre Melissa into the passenger seat; the step doesn't help, and the door frame doesn't provide adequate handholds for her to grip on. It makes sense why all previous patients were wheeled in through the rear doors. And as for the seat belt, well, that proves to be a whole other issue. I never thought I'd get up so close and personal to Melissa's rear end whilst she struggles to find and secure the metal tab in its holder.

Eventually, I turn the key in the ignition, secure my own seat belt ready for the off.

'Comfortable?'

Melissa bursts out laughing. 'As comfortable as I can be in this situation.'

'Fair enough, I promise I'll get your bun in the oven delivered safely from this doorstep to the hospital's.'

Melissa rewards me with a contorted smile. I suspect she's putting a brave face on for my benefit. I hate to think how much is happening to her body right now.

I indicate, pulling away from the kerb, dearly wishing I had a radio on which to play soothing music. From the periphery of my vision, I can see Melissa sporadically tensing and bracing herself as I navigate the lanes. It can't be comfortable. How great would it be to have wheeled out the disused trolley? I'm trying my best to drive as efficiently as I can, alternating between speedy Lewis Hamilton style and learner driver snail-pace mode. I can't work out which is best; additional speed but a slightly bumpy ride, or much slower and taking far longer but with a smoother drive.

The traffic is busier than usual – which is typical on the one morning I have a special delivery. Any other day at this time, I'm free to drive at my own pace and not adopt this stop-start action due to road works, snarled junctions and the slowness of unusually wide loads. Melissa is continually moaning in a soft self-soothing manner, all the time sliding lower in her seat, as if the upright position is uncomfortable. I'm trying to rein in my imagination; I refuse to be a 'headline hero' and deliver this baby. I'm determined to avoid being pictured on the front page of *The Shetland Times* proudly holding my namesake 'baby Pip' and explaining how I parked on a traffic island and swiftly delivered a baby on the wooden counter surrounded by the best artisan bakes from the gallery. To be honest, the very thought gives me the heebie-jeebies!

Hearing Melissa's groaning intensify, I'm wondering at what point I should transfer her to the rear of the vehicle, given the difficulty of manoeuvring her into the passenger seat initially. I'm fighting the urge to suggest it, as it seems one step nearer to me being more hands-on than I would choose! Another consideration is that, apart from brown paper, sticky labels and my serving gloves, I have no useful equipment – I imagine that metal tongs would be a no-no!

My right foot presses the accelerator pedal a tad more firmly.

Imagine if I can arrive like they do in the films! Roll up to the maternity entrance, midwives greeting us with a wheelchair and, after the quickest hand-over in medical history, off Melissa goes to meet her baby. As for me, I can take my time driving back to the gallery homestead and recover my nerves en route. It brings me little comfort to reflect that Levi would have been a much better option in this situation, despite Melissa's misgivings. He would remain calm throughout, probably produce a medical kit from his taxi's rear boot, alongside an emergency cradle and oxygen tanks, taking full control of whatever situation developed.

Melissa's increasing groaning brings me back from my thoughts. I'd best do a round of questions, to reassure her that I'm doing my bit.

'Are you OK?'

'Urgh!' replies Melissa, her knotted features grimacing.

'Don't you start pushing!' Which is not what I meant to say, but my brain isn't in gear: I wasn't bred for pressure such as this. I baulk at my error but Melissa doesn't react, so maybe she didn't hear me.

I don't trust myself to ask further questions, so I do the only thing which springs to mind: sing.

Maybe the thought of Levi's calmness influences my actions, but I don't care, whether I'm tuneful or not – I'm singing!

The first few lyrics of 'Here Comes The Sun' leave my lips, which brings Melissa back to reality.

'Karaoke . . . *great*!' she mutters, sending me a mutinous stare from the passenger seat, her knees braced against the dashboard and her hands clutching at the upholstery. I eyeball my dashcam in fear that it'll be dislodged, fall from its mounting and record the first front-seat delivery in this vehicle. I focus on my lyrics in a poor attempt to offer something soothing for her pains.

The traffic isn't kind as I make my way back into Lerwick.

It feels like a TV challenge where celebrity commentators give a running account of my progress. Melissa's soft moaning has turned into wailing, and I can't ignore it much longer; my dulcet tones are being drowned out by her solo vocals. My left hand reacts without my brain engaging in the process; I accidentally flick the 'forbidden switch'. The secret one which the MacDonald brothers made Levi promise he'd stay schtum about. Instantly, Rolly's engine grille plate lights up like a Christmas tree, with a fetching neon-blue strobe signalling to all and sundry.

As if by magic, the traffic separates like the Red Sea before Moses, peeling away to left and right as I put my foot down and navigate a swift route through the middle. Rolly might have lost his ambulance colour palette, but I doubt anyone can read our logo and strap line at this speed! They might query why a beige bulk without the recognisable Battenberg pattern is being given the right of way, but I'll be long gone before they can note my registration plate. I've never been a professional driver, can't even brag about go-carting, but I instantly quit my singing, which feels good in itself, and focus on the empty road ahead.

This is bloody marvellous! The adrenalin is flowing, my heart rate is pumping. I might shirk the idea of midwifery duties, but I'd certainly contemplate those of a Formula One driver. Though I pray the local police aren't cruising the area in pursuit of speeding vehicles; they won't believe their eyes if they are!

Likewise, on passing at speed, I note that my waiting queue of customers at my next planned stop turn in unison as I whizz past as if an emergency bread delivery were the name of the game for today's special.

Melissa has her eyes firmly closed, which I'm grateful for. I doubt she's clocked my speed dial nudging towards the maximum speed for these roads.

Never have I been so grateful to see the Gilbert Bain hospital looming before me in the distance, but I'm not out of the woods yet. I have no hang-up about parking in the cross-hatched section in front of the main doors, alongside the other parked ambulances. They might have a different paint job to Rolly's but his outline matches exactly. I'm sure it feels like coming home to be amongst his old mates.

'Wait here!' I say to Melissa, as if she had other plans. Her expression is twisted in agony and she's panting like a dog on a summer's day. 'Sorry, I'll be . . .'

'Just go!' she screams.

I dash from the Bread Basket into the entrance foyer to find a smiley lady on the phone behind reception. She continues to talk whilst acknowledging me, but her call doesn't end. I jig about, reinforcing my impatience, but it makes no difference. She continues to explain the procedure regarding visiting times, without any sign of hurrying; no clipped sentences or cutting short her stream of instructions in order to answer my obvious needs. Does she not sense I have an emergency occurring out the front?

Finally, she replaces the handset and welcomes me warmly with a 'good afternoon'. I don't answer her, but launch straight into a disjointed account of Melissa . . . her baby coming . . . groaning and much panting. The smiley reception lady takes her time. I want her to rush, kick it up a gear, but no, she's as calm and methodical as a priest.

'If you'd like to return to your friend, I'll send the porters out to you, OK?'

'Yeah, sure . . . you can't miss us – an ambulance which looks like a giant bread roll,' I say, before dashing out to rejoin Melissa, who appears to be in much discomfort.

I don't bother relaying any messages, I'm not sure she can hear me. I grab her small suitcase and stand inside the open door, praying the porters will get a move on. It feels like hours before two men arrive with a wheelchair to support and assist Melissa.

I stand back and watch in awe as they gently manoeuvre her from the passenger seat – which is no mean feat, given the height of the drop from the vehicle on to the tarmac.

'Here are her belongings,' I say to a porter, handing over the suitcase before turning to Melissa. 'And here are your door keys.' I pop them into the top of her handbag. 'I'll let the folk at the gallery know the news and, err, take care now . . .' My sentence fades as I run out of pleasantries, hoping to convey concern rather than the intense relief I feel that she is no longer my concern.

'Thanks, Pippa, I'll let you know.'

'All the best, whatever flavour it is.'

'It's a boy, we already know that,' she mutters, her eyes clamped shut with pain, as the porter swivels her chair around, heading for the entrance.

'I stand a good chance of Rolly gaining a namesake then?' I reply, eager to be gone.

'Could you move your vehicle from this designated area?' says the second porter, carrying the suitcase.

'Sure, but . . .' I was about to explain my emergency but he doesn't wait to hear my reasoning, simply strides after Melissa in her chariot.

I trundle back towards the gallery, with the majority of my bread stocks still on board, planning and rehearsing what I'll say to the Campbells. I'm sure they won't have an issue when they hear the full story involving Melissa.

I pull into the cobbled courtyard, half expecting everyone to be gathered to provide a hero's welcome, but they're not. It's your usual Tuesday routine: a couple of artists milling around, making the most of a customer-free day, and Crispy duck completing his litter-picking duties.

I'm in two minds whether to speak to Isla first or head straight for the third-floor office before unloading. My indecision doesn't last too long, as the green-painted door of the manor opens and Ned strides out. He looks like a man on a mission, his head held high, his brow creased, his expression stern. What's worse is he's heading in my direction.

Chapter Thirty-Six

Autumn

'What the hell are you doing?' screeches the voice behind me, causing me to jump out of my skin.

My hands judder, dropping the opened can and nearly cutting my fingers on the jagged edge of the open lid.

'Bloody hell, Dottie!'

'Bloody hell nothing, Autumn. What are you up to now?' She appears at my right elbow, staring at the countertop, and takes in the sight of me with a bowl, a sieve perched on a Pyrex jug and the fork clutched in my hand.

'The new guest, a Miss Hamilton staying in the Whalsay Suite, would like . . .'

'Alphabet spaghetti?' she wails, piercing my eardrum.

'No. Alphabet spaghetti drained from the sauce and without the letter "O",' I correct her, staring at the tomato sauce currently draining, drip by drip, into the jug. I daren't look up for fear of seeing her expression.

'For the love of God, what is this world coming to?' She scowls, before adding, 'And the likes of you are encouraging their fanciful whims by kowtowing to their sodding wishes.'

I can't correct her, so I remain silent. I grasp the handle of the sieve, giving it a shake to help the draining process along. I would like to stir the contents with a fork but daren't, in case I smush or break the delicate lettering.

'Are you out of your mind?' asks Dottie, after a moment of silence.

Again, I don't answer her.

I am a professional. I am dedicated to my role. My enthusiasm knows no bounds. I will go to any lengths to meet guests' expectations, ensuring that every visitor to the hotel has the experience they were dreaming of when booking their stay. My reward will be a positive review and even a return booking.

'Autumn, did you hear me?'

'Mmm-hmm.'

'So, what's it to be?'

'A plate of alphabet spaghetti minus the sauce and the offending letter,' I reply, not lifting my gaze.

'And how much are you charging her for this whim?'

I don't answer.

Dottie swiftly continues, 'Because I don't remember this nonsense being included in the room service tariff.'

She reaches for my hands, as if that'll stop the process. Her digits fold around mine, providing a contrast in age and appearance. The unexpected gesture shocks me, even more so when she squeezes and her warm gesture feels alien to me. I can't remember the last time I allowed another person to comfort me; I'm usually the one delivering a much-needed hug or supportive gesture rather than receiving them.

'Autumn, please.'

I stop shaking the sieve, resting it on the lip of the jug. 'What do you expect me to do then? Refuse such requests? Disappoint guests by fobbing them off? Or call Ned each time for authorisation?'

Her watery blue eyes meet mine. 'I'd expect you to be polite, thank the guest for their call to reception, whilst mentioning there will be a surcharge for such tasks to reflect the amount of time devoted to meeting sir or madam's request. They'd soon quit with this stupidity if it was costing them fifty quid an hour. We can all dash about like silly fools for the benefit of others, run ourselves into the ground attempting to please them; enough is never enough for some folk.'

I bite my lower lip. I want to cry. I'm torn between delivering the goods and knowing that every word she says is correct. I simply can't stop, it's almost an addiction, a need to please which is now costing me more than time and energy . . . it's draining me.

'I suppose now you'll pick out the offending letter?'

I give a nod; my mind is in turmoil as to whether I should continue or not.

Dottie gives my hands a quick squeeze before releasing them and grabbing the fork from my clasp.

'Give it a bloody good shake then, lassie – otherwise we'll be here all day!'

I fight the urge to cry. She doesn't approve, I can't imagine her ever saying yes to such a request, but she's prepared to help me, thus ensuring I succeed in pleasing another guest – and that means the world to me.

I wiggle the sieve, causing the spaghetti to slither and slide, while Dottie hooks the letter 'O' each time one surfaces from the jumble of letters.

It takes ages; far longer than I expected. Eventually, I'm satisfied that there's not a single 'O' remaining in the sieve. I've checked and rechecked the squiggly orange mass which has repeatedly moved like a weird anagram – one which I can't imagine the producers of *Countdown* will ever adopt.

'Dottie, can you pass me a white plate, please?' I ask, having checked and rechecked one final time.

'No toast?'

'Nope.'

'Not even cooked?' she asks, grimacing at the thought.

'She simply asked for a can of alphabet spaghetti drained of juice and without the one letter.'

'She sounds like a weird sort to me, lassie. Mind you stand back from the door when delivering it.'

'Dottie, you do say the funniest things.'

'Phuh! The likes of this is the funniest thing I've ever seen in my eighty-odd years.'

'Mine is not to question why,' I mutter.

'Next time, ask her – purely to provide me with a bloody good laugh.' She chuckles, before asking, 'And what's to become of these?' Lifting the bowl of discarded 'O's.

I shrug nonchalantly.

'It looks like an orgasm in a bowl,' chuckles Dottie. 'Don't tell me it doesn't!'

My mouth drops wide at the very suggestion; I'm not used to this saucy side of her nature.

Pippa

Ned opens my driver's door before I have a chance to remove the ignition key, let alone climb down.

'Perfect timing, Pippa. Can you explain why I've had the local police pay us a visit this afternoon?' He stands in the open doorway, his hand still grasping the handle, and glares at me. Now I haven't seen Ned when he's annoyed, but I doubt it gets much scarier than this.

I have two choices: either kowtow to his rudeness and explain in detail straight away, or have my own fun.

'Excuse me,' I say, my tone as sickly sweet as I can muster, gesturing that he's blocking my route to climb down.

Ned releases the handle and shuffles back a few steps.

I step down on to the cobbles, taking my time, as is my nature when someone ruffles my feathers. I shouldn't do it, but I can't help myself.

I make my way along the side of the vehicle and around to the rear doors. Ned follows like a loyal puppy, his brow furrowed in frustration at my attitude. I unlock and pin each door wide, taking my time, much longer than is usual for the simple task. Again, I shouldn't be acting up; I can't help myself.

'Are you going to answer?' asks Ned, his voice stern but calm, befitting an employer not a family member.

'Mmmm, in a second.' I step up inside and begin releasing and stacking my wicker bread trays, moving them into the middle section, as I always do when emptying the van for the day. I daren't look up; I imagine he's seething at being kept waiting.

He shifts his stance, glances across the yard before returning his attention to me as I methodically remove each wicker tray. I sense how this conversation will go and can pretty accurately picture the previous exchange he must have had with his wife regarding my actions. What they don't know is the truth.

I can almost hear their remarks before I'd returned. 'It's Pippa, what do you expect?' or 'I knew this would happen – she never adheres to rules or responsibility' – it's always the same old story where family are concerned. They think they know everything before I've had a chance to explain. They've assigned me a family label and expect me to meet their lowly expectations. Of us three cousins, Jemima's seen as the quiet, sensible one, Callie's the reliable older one – when she truly isn't – and then there's me. I'm simply the odd one out. The one who can't be trusted, the daredevil who screws it up, time and time again, or so they think. I get that I have form, and there's plenty of history and memories kept alive amongst our family.

Well, this time, I have news for all of you. She who laughs last, laughs the longest!

'Could you hold these, please? As you can see, they're pretty full – I haven't sold as much as usual today.'

Ned's eyes widen at the sight of my wicker bread trays – virtually full. He's baffled by my behaviour. I bet he's wondering if he should have tackled me or sent Jemima to complete the task. I have no doubt she's watching from the third-floor window. I might give her a hearty thumbs-up as I step down from Rolly and close the rear doors.

Together we grab each end of the stacked bread trays and head towards The Orangery. Not a word is said as Ned wrenches open the glazed door, allowing me to enter first.

'What the hell have you been up to?' Isla's harsh attitude fades as Ned follows behind like the back end of a strange wicker pantomime horse.

'Hi, Isla,' I smile, breezing past her and leading the way to the rear kitchen where this load can be stashed and sorted. Or binned.

Isla's mouth drops open, as I expected it would.

'Two coffees, please, Isla, when you're ready – we'll use the rear table for a little chat,' instructs Ned, as he passes her position.

It's not that I'm enjoying the attention, or the mystery created by my current silence and wayward behaviour, more that some folk need to learn a lesson in life. There is always a reason! I'm going to continue to play it cool, listen to what he has to say in our 'little chat' – which I can't believe he is going to hold in full view of the other staff in the corner of The Orangery. Though, he's been thoughtful enough to order coffee – which will give me something to occupy my hands as he talks.

'An explanation is in order, Pippa,' says Ned, choosing his seat, a wing-back armchair, at the rear of The Orangery, once the returned stock has been carefully unloaded.

I hesitate in taking my seat; the soft couch or the padded recliner? The rebel within me wants to slouch in the recliner and tilt it back full length, though it may be a tad disrespectful. I opt for the couch and slide my coffee mug on to the low table. And wait, while Ned stirs his coffee, takes a sip and clears his throat.

'In the last hour, we've had numerous complaints about today's delivery route. Now, I expect the odd criticism, now and then, but even the police have dropped by regarding your driving. Apparently, you've been racing through traffic, ignoring customers waiting at our designated spots, and the police claim you've used a blue emergency light – which I find farcical.'

'Yep.' I nod, taking on board his every word.

Ned's eyebrows twitch; he wasn't expecting *that* reply.

'You're admitting to this slapdash approach, knowing full well that the gallery's logo is plastered across the side and anyone witnessing your erratic driving can easily report you?'

'Yep.' I lean forward, pick up my mug of coffee and take a sip. I shouldn't be acting up like this, but I'm sick to death of the folks around here assuming they know me inside and out. Well, they don't. And it's my family who are showing the least respect, despite blood being thicker than water.

Ned's gaze falters and focuses at something beyond where I'm sitting. I turn to see Dottie entering The Orangery. She gives a weak smile in our direction before heading for the counter. Obviously, everyone has heard of my antics and has passed judgement. I swiftly turn back to focus on Ned.

'As I was saying, the phone has been ringing off the hook for the last hour; complaint after complaint has been made by passing drivers, pedestrians and local shop owners. Poor Isla arrived in my office with a handful of notes, all of which outline your ludicrous driving. And as for the police visiting ... that never looks good for a company, Pippa.'

'Guilty as charged. I've probably broken numerous speed limits. I don't think I was caught by any mobile cameras, if that's what you're worried about. I have charged past numerous queues of eager customers waiting for a bread delivery ... and I have absolutely no remorse in relation to my actions.' I take a long sip of my coffee.

Ned's eyebrows react as I expected; they shoot up into his greying hairline quicker than me accelerating away from the local hospital.

'Though I didn't jump any traffic lights, which I could have if I'd wanted, so I did show some respect to other road users.'

'Pippa, how can you sit there and blatantly admit that you drove like a fool, thrashed our vehicle at speeds beyond the legal limits, and still expect to keep your role?'

'Because it was all in the name of a good deed.'

'A good deed?' A vein at Ned's temple begins to pulse.

I can see he's frustrated by my attitude, my answers and possibly my steady stare. Jemima's much better at handling staff discussions, but on this occasion – given our family connection, I assume – he's drawn the short straw.

'Yep, a good deed. And if I had to do it all again tomorrow, I would.' I need to stop, tell him the truth, but I've waited a long time for this moment.

Ned takes a swig of coffee, buying valuable thinking time. He probably wants to fire me on the spot, if that's allowed by employment law. Or he's planning how he can save face and call Jemima to attend to her difficult cousin.

I hear The Orangery's door open behind me, see Ned's gaze flicker and his head slowly turn, as if tracking someone approaching our corner.

'Excuse me,' says Levi politely to Ned, appearing at our table and addressing me. 'Are you OK, sweet?'

I quickly nod before he continues.

'Can I say, full marks to you, Pippa. I've just heard and, although I realise you might be having a serious chat here, I wanted to say well done! Sorry for interrupting, Ned.'

'Cheers, Levi,' I say, a coy smile breaking across my features, knowing he's inadvertently broken our cover by addressing me so attentively.

Ned does a double take between me and Levi. He's not up to speed, but he'll be there any second.

'I'm glad I did what I did. I was telling Ned the exact same thing. I'd do it again tomorrow.'

'I'm sure there'll be good news sooner rather than later, but just to let you know I've taxied Hamish up to the hospital too. Thanks, catch you later.' Levi plants a kiss on my cheek and swiftly departs.

Ned tilts his head in a questioning manner.

I slowly sip my coffee. 'Yeah, sorry about this, Ned. You didn't ask but Melissa, the ceramics lady cum art teacher, she's pregnant, though you probably know her from the allotments . . . she called me over whilst I was on my delivery round and she needed to get to hospital pretty sharpish as the baby was coming. Apparently, he's incredibly early.'

'The baby was coming?'

'Yep. I thought you wouldn't mind if I diverted my route just this once and did her a favour, rather than leave her home alone waiting for an ambulance. It might be unconventional, but surely a delivery is a delivery, though I'm grateful that I didn't actually have to deliver the bairn. My knowledge is limited to the hot water and towels usually called for in old Hollywood movies! And sorry for using the blue lights, but it seemed apt in view of Rolly's former role with the NHS.' I fall silent, sit back and let that sink in. My gaze never leaves his. I'm living dangerously, but what the heck, this lot deserve it!

I'm not expecting Ned to apologise; bosses rarely do. I realise

I've dropped the MacDonald trio into hot water regarding their conversion job, but that's their issue not mine.

Ned scratches his head, gives a few short sharp nods and finishes his coffee in one gulp. 'Well, glad we got that cleared up. In future, could I ask that you're mindful of others in relation to traffic laws and . . . well, never use the blue lights again.' He stands up as he delivers his final words, collects his empty mug and sidesteps our table. 'I'll bring Jemima up to speed and we'll say nothing more on this matter. Mmmm, yes . . . blue lights . . . Thanks.'

'Sure.' I don't move an inch.

I haven't finished my coffee yet so have no intention of jumping up as if I've been dismissed by the boss. I shouldn't, but I feel quite smug. Not for doing what I've done, but more that everyone thought I'd been a badass maniac out on the road and jumped to the wrong conclusion, and I've proven them wrong. I'll linger. Callie can clean the neighbouring table if she wishes; I won't be bad-mouthing Ned to her. I've owned up to my mistakes in the past, but I've got a damn good heart when I'm allowed the chance to show it. Melissa didn't hesitate in calling me across, did she? Others are too quick to jump to the wrong conclusion about me.

Apart from Levi, of course.

Chapter Thirty-Seven

Friday 25 March

Natalia

It took over a week for me to pluck up the courage, but I had little else to do, except bite the bullet.

'Hi, Natalia. Long time, no see!' cries Marston, entering the library. I've arranged for him to be shown in courteously by Autumn. Our plan has worked; his leggy stride delivers him to me in seconds, before he greets me with a quick peck on each cheek. There's been no need for me to move from the couch.

I speak slowly in an attempt to articulate my words clearly and combat the slur. I can't hide it, it's now part of the new me.

'How fabulous of you to come! I've missed working with you so much,' I say, half expecting his gaze to drift to my arm, conveniently positioned in my lap.

'Boy, what a place to be staying. I got goose bumps as we were approaching the airport, seeing a landscape filled by beautiful heather – I'm itching to start exploring locations for some photo shoots. I imagined the only thing I'd see would be a thousand and one Shetland ponies but this place . . . is something else.'

I'm thrilled to hear his enthusiastic response; it's the infectious energy I've missed in recent weeks – and on this occasion it's apt, given the beauty of the surrounding scenery.

I gesture towards the opposite chair and Marston quickly

sinks into its cushions, his eyes roving the high ceiling and stately mantelpiece.

'Relatives of yours?' he asks, his gaze returning to me after he's taken in the room.

'Not quite, more friends,' I say, feeling slightly guilty.

'Nice! And we'll be allowed the full run of the hotel and grounds?'

'Sure, though there are guests staying on certain floors, and particular rooms are pretty busy during breakfast and evening mealtimes, but otherwise . . . a free run.'

'Fantastic, so what are you thinking?'

I'm about to answer him when Jemima enters the library carrying a tray.

'I thought you'd like a pot of coffee,' she says, carefully delivering the tray to the nearest table and proceeding to pour two cups. 'Milk? Sugar?' I'm grateful. She's trying to make my meeting as easy as possible; I've been dreading the handling of a heavy coffee pot.

'Thank you. Milk, two sugars, please,' answers Marston, taking in her appearance: her fleece gilet and walking boots are not typical serving attire. He repeats his appreciation as Jemima hands over his drink.

'Thank you, Jemima.' Her gaze meets mine and a gentle smile adorns her lips. She knows, she understands my gratitude.

'Anyway, as I was saying, what angle are you aiming for?' asks Marston, the second the library door is closed.

'Ah, now that's very particular, let me explain.'

It takes all of fifteen minutes for me to retell my tale of woe, albeit avoiding the inclusion of Ned Campbell.

'And so, as you can see, I've been bestowed a gammy arm which has a mind of its own and is currently choosing to slumber its way through each and every day!' I crack a lopsided smile before falling silent.

Marston's gaze is firmly fixed upon my left arm and has been throughout my explanation. I sit back and sip my coffee. I'm expecting a brief wait while the news sinks in, but not the lengthy silence which follows.

'Natalia, darling, what can I say! We've worked together for many years and you know, as well as I do, that contracts, assignments and agencies are never forthcoming when . . . if . . . I mean . . . look, you know what this industry is like . . . as shallow as a puddle in a heatwave. You know where I'm coming from, sweetheart.'

I sip my coffee. This was my biggest fear. A trusted friend reacting in this way, rejecting the very idea on which my whole future is pinned, without any appreciation of what is at stake here.

'It's an arm. The rest of me is bloody perfect. It's just this one little bit that has decided to play up, but I can assure you it behaves itself in company and won't distract by not complying. In fact, given the difficulties I've previously had whilst modelling for you, it'll probably play its role far better than the rest of me, which could never keep still.'

Marston puffs up his cheeks and exhales deeply.

'It's a lot to ask, but please think about it. In a world that recognises inclusion, I'd like to be included! Why shouldn't I continue to model? It's been my career since leaving university – I might not have reached the heady heights of the catwalks and runways of Paris and Milan, but I've earned my crust in front of your lens many a time.'

'Mainly for products, though, Natalia.' His tone sounds apologetic.

'What's the difference? How many times did I need both hands for the products I modelled?' I peer at him over the rim of my cup. His crumpled brow tells me he's going to need some persuading. 'I've already completed a photo shoot for a cookery book. What about knitwear? There's plenty of scope around these parts for pattern modelling, household appliances or furnishings, even my beauty contacts with nail varnishes – look, my hand isn't withered. It simply doesn't work as well as it used to.' Putting down my coffee cup, I quickly pick up my left hand to show him.

Marston's gaze drops to inspect the inside of his coffee cup.

Instantly, I recoil at my own behaviour. I'm verging on begging, which I shouldn't have to do; I'm a capable, beautiful human being, brimming with experience and enthusiasm.

'Marston, I can do this!' My voice is a whisper as I fight back my tears.

His doleful expression says it all. I watch the deep gulp he takes before choosing his words of rejection carefully.

Suddenly, this entire meeting seems shamefully awkward for us both, sitting in silence in a hotel library, but more importantly, for anyone in society who doesn't fit the expected norms of those like Marston who'd prefer to see only physical perfection and beauty portrayed within glossy magazines and on advertising posters.

Pippa

'Pippa!' calls Jemima, her eyes on stalks and her mouth gawping, spotting me as I cross the cobbled courtyard.

'Yes?' I say, clutching a wrapped gift, trying not to squash the blue ribbon decoration.

'You look ... who'd have thought peacock blue was so becoming on you?' she asks, looking me up and down, as my long cotton dress gently billows in the evening breeze.

'I'm meeting Levi. We're off to the maternity ward; Melissa and Hamish want us to meet baby Noah. We aren't allowed any cuddles, as he's in the Special Care Baby Unit, but they've assured us we can see him through the glass partition,' I say, watching her taking in my appearance. 'Afterwards, Levi's surprising me with a dinner date for two.'

'How lovely! Sorry, I'm so used to seeing you dressed like a skater girl in your jeans and bomber jackets that this –' she gestures up and down my frame – 'is a dramatic make-over. It suits you.'

'Thanks. Is there anything else?'

Jemima seems as taken aback by my question as she is with my appearance. 'Nothing. Except give our love to Melissa, Hamish and baby Noah. I still find it amazing that he weighs no more than a couple of bags of sugar! Anyway, we hope to see them soon, but I understand the first invites are for the special people who were urgently called upon to help.'

'Cheers. I've bought him his first Dinky toy. It's an ambulance which Isaac has repainted beige to match Rolly,' I say, waving the wrapped gift, before striding towards the stone archway beyond which I can see Levi's car waiting.

'Evening, Pippa, you look lovely,' says Levi, as I close the passenger door and settle in beside him to receive a gentle but welcome kiss. 'Are you ready?'

'Evening, Levi. I certainly am.' I adjust and secure the seat belt.

Levi continues to beam from our brief interaction in full view of his friend, after which he turns the key in the ignition and we pull away.

Framed by the stone archway, and with Crispy duck scurrying around her feet, Jemima stands and stares after us. Her cogs will be churning, there's very little doubt about that; hopefully, Jemima will be thrilled that Levi's found someone who cares about him – just as she has.

'How fabulous is this?' I whisper, leaning into Levi's warm embrace.

We're standing entwined before an ancient window of Scalloway Castle, watching the fiery sunset beyond.

'I'm thrilled that you're enjoying the surprise. That's all I wanted,' he replies in a soothing tone, as his warm breath tickles my earlobe.

We'd both taken delight in viewing the tiny baby in his perspex crib, complete with monitoring attachments and surrounded by bleeping machines. Melissa and Hamish showed their appreciation of our customised gift and we managed to prise ourselves away when tiny Noah became crabbit, demanding his feeding time.

'Thank you, it's the perfect end to a fabulous evening.'

'Not the end yet! I have much more planned. First we're having pre-dinner drinks downstairs in the vestibule and vaulted kitchen, and then I'm treating you to dinner, by candlelight, in the Great Hall.'

'By candlelight,' I softly repeat.

Levi's arms tighten around my nestled frame, and I press my shoulders backwards into his broad chest. I'd never have believed that friendship could blossom into something more substantial, but ours has provided a foundation of trust and honesty which I've never experienced before. And now, our understanding of each other feels like a blessing as we move towards a deeper connection, confirming a newfound comfort within each other's world.

'Did you notice the Latin above the entrance door, inscribed on the lintel?' asks Levi softly.

I shake my head. I was too taken aback by the incredible ambience created for this one-night dining experience to notice any inscription.

'It translates to read: "That house whose foundation is rock will stand, but will perish if it be shifting sand."'

I allow his spoken words to settle deep within me before answering.

'Strong foundations – that'll suit me nicely,' I say, turning within his sturdy embrace to gaze up at him.

His chin lowers, his breath brushing my cheek, before he whispers my name. My chin lifts and his lips find mine and I'm lost to a world made for us. I never dreamt that I would find anyone who saw me as me. The real me. Who willingly looks past my flaws to embrace the woman I am, right here, right now, in this stage of my life. Someone who prefers to accept my past mistakes, rather than raking them up only to ruin our present or future time together. A man I can believe in, and one with whom I feel a sense of true belonging. If the truth be known, I breathe differently in Levi's presence – which tells me everything I need to know.

Autumn

I hear the approaching footsteps so glance up from my admin tasks to view Natalia and her guest crossing the hallway, heading back towards the entrance. There's an icy expression on her features while his backbone is ramrod straight. I can't help noticing the uncomfortable distance between supposed friends. I continue with my work, but listen, concerned, to their parting conversation.

'Let me know what you think. I'm happy to meet up tomorrow and we could take a drive around the local area; I'll show you the sights and some of the locations that I was thinking of,' says Natalia. Her voice is buoyant but her features suggest something else.

'I'll get back to you, Natalia. Lovely to see you again. Take care.' He pecks her cheek before gently rubbing her upper arm and swiftly exiting the main doors.

Natalia stands motionless as the door closes. Her shoulders are now as rigid as his were. I'm expecting her to turn at any second and say something, but she doesn't; she simply continues to stare at the closed door.

'Natalia?' I call softly, not wishing to intrude.

She doesn't answer or move.

'Natalia, are you OK?' I slip out from behind the reception counter, crossing the hallway to where she stands, frozen in position. I sidle around her to view her stricken face, which is tear-stained and pallid. 'Hey, what's happened?'

Natalia slowly shakes her head, her watery gaze meeting mine. 'What's the point in trying, when all anyone will ever see is my broken limb – and not my potential? I'm finished, Autumn. It's over.'

I'm lost for words. My arm snakes around her shoulders, pulling her in close as her shoulders quiver and angry tears erupt. I don't understand another word she mutters as I escort her through reception and into the rear office, settling her in a chair.

'It was humiliating. I begged him to take photo shots of me promoting absolutely *anything*, purely as a means of getting his name next to mine on a photo tag. I shouldn't have to do that, Autumn. My previous career and work ethic should speak volumes, but not now. When I think of the times Marston asked *me* to do *him* a favour, just so he could peddle a new shot to his contacts, and now, when the tables are turned, he baulked at the very idea of using me as a model. Physically flinched, he did.'

I listen; it's the only practical thing I can do for her now, apart from supplying hot tea.

'How the hell am I supposed to support myself if I can't work . . . with this?'

It's my turn to flinch as she gestures to her left arm.

'I'm not about to become some charity case and hide away for evermore. Can you imagine how difficult my life is going to be now? I've totally lost my independence and my ability to support myself, all due to this . . . and this!' She gestures first to her lopsided smile and then prods her left arm, which is resting on her lap.

'Natalia, please stop. I can't possibly imagine what you're going through, but why succumb to the attitudes of others? Responding and treating your own body in such a negative way is unacceptable. Look at how much progress you've made in recent weeks. The first time I saw you, when you'd just returned from the hospital, I never imagined holding a conversation with you. I couldn't understand a word you said, but now I hardly notice the change to your voice. As for your facial features and arm – there's been a vast improvement there too. You have no idea where your continued progress will lead you, in a month, or even a year's time.'

She rolls her eyes in annoyance.

'Stop it. I'm being honest and fair. You should be celebrating your progress – not prodding at your arm like that, as if it were wooden and useless.'

'It might as well be, for all the good it does,' she says disdainfully.

'I disagree. You tell that to someone who's lost a limb, or suffers from paralysis with no movement from the neck downwards. I understand that adjusting to the changes in your life isn't going to happen overnight. But, Natalia, you are lucky to have a body and mind able to move and function. What is it you said? Five per cent of your body is lame? Maybe you should be overjoyed that ninety-five per cent isn't! It's a case of majority rule – and you need to take back control, rather than allowing others, especially the likes of that guy, who you'd previously trusted, to condemn you to a smaller life than the one you're willing to fight for.'

There's a glimmer of light in Natalia's steady gaze; I've touched a nerve.

'It might be tiring, but you're going to have to fight for everything that you want from this point onwards, Natalia. Before this happened, things may have fallen into your lap, excuse the pun, but now, you'll need to do battle to achieve exactly what you want. No more batting your eyelids, swishing your mane and relying on your looks to attract attention. It's back to the basics of life, with hard graft.'

Natalia sits back, her gaze still steady and strong, as that initial spark of life takes hold.

'You're right. I need to forget about my old contacts. Assume that they're all of the same closed mindset. I need to get my own assignments, build new contacts and find paying work from elsewhere.'

I'm nodding frantically, hoping each movement is encouraging her to stoke the fires deep within.

'Right, I'd best get to it then!'

I'm taken aback as she stands up, pushes the chair under the desk and wraps me in a bear hug.

'Thank you, I needed that.'

'Don't thank me, you got there . . . you said it.'

'I did and, what's more, I'm going to show the likes of Marston Brookes exactly what I'm made of.'

Chapter Thirty-Eight

Tuesday 29 March

Pippa

'Jemima, can I have a word?' I ask, as my stomach knots with nerves. I've tried to bide my time all morning, knowing she is busy, but the moment has arrived and there'll be no going back once I start to explain.

'Are you OK?' she says, clearly noting my anxiety.

'Not really.' I'm conscious that our conversation has the potential to upset her for the rest of the day, but it's necessary.

'Somewhere private?'

I nod.

'Come on, let's go to the library, Ned's busy working in the office. We won't be interrupted at this hour of the day.'

I don't utter a word on our walk from the courtyard, though Jemima glances sideways at me several times. She holds the library door open, allowing me to pass through before closing it behind us.

'Take a seat. I'm all ears . . . though I'm a little concerned.'

'Me too,' I say, settling into the nearest armchair, feeling the oppressive air of the shelved books surrounding us.

She sits waiting for me to speak. I don't know how to begin. I've practised this in my head several times this morning, but every time it ends up as a garbled rant, consisting of sparse details with a few facts thrown in for good measure. I got teary at one point, which didn't help matters.

'I'm going to start talking. Sorry if this causes you distress or upset; it's not meant – and certainly not from me, for once.' I see her dark eyebrows twitch. 'It's about Nanna's engagement ring.'

'OK,' she says, instantly baffled.

'There's something I need to tell you. Remember when Grand-dad's apartment at the Happy Days complex was cleared after the funeral and I came to see you at the allotments, miffed that Callie had already asked for an item without thinking about the two of us?'

'Sure. Nanna's sapphire engagement ring.'

I'm trying to lead her to work this out, rather than bowling her over with the harshest of facts.

'She received it after Grandpop's death—'

'No. She *asked* for the ring, she wasn't given it or bequeathed it, Jemima,' I interrupt her.

'Yes, I believe she did ask.'

I realise how snappy and tense I sound, so I take a few breaths before continuing. 'I was furious that she should have been so brazen, without even asking either of us if we wanted it. Remember?'

'I do ... though we agreed that neither of us specifically wanted it,' says Jemima, recalling the sequence of events correctly, which pleases me.

'OK, I'm glad you remember.' I feel calmer now she remembers our chat from last April. 'I think we assumed that, since she was the eldest granddaughter, then maybe it felt right?'

'You can't be too sentimental about these things – hardly right to chop it into three purely to satisfy the other two.'

'That's right. You said that Granddad had left you enough memories, and I said jewellery wasn't my thing; it was the sheer brazenness of her not even asking us that annoyed me.'

Jemima is nodding in agreement; so far, so good.

There's no good way to say the next sentence, so I blurt it out.

'She sold it!'

'What!' Jemima's horrified expression is worse than I expected. I nod. 'Yep, she sold it almost immediately.'

'How the hell do you know that?'

'She told me when we argued, a few weeks ago.'

Jemima sits back in her chair, her eyes flickering in annoyance and her brow deeply furrowed. 'Are you sure?'

I nod again.

'Well, I'll be damned! Here's me saying I didn't want it ... when I would have gratefully accepted it, if offered. I was trying to be generous to you both, but my God, if I'd thought for one minute that she would ever sell it ... I would have jumped in and made a case for either of us to keep it in the family.'

'I remember you saying that Nanna loved it, and for that reason alone you would have liked it, but you graciously allowed her to have it because you had your legacy.'

'The legacy and allotment definitely coloured my viewpoint ... but to think she sold it.' I watch as her eyes well up and she frantically blinks back the emotion.

'I realise that we're not as close as some, but I thought it best you knew the truth.'

'And she actually admitted all this to you herself?'

'We were arguing. I felt she'd encroached on my territory again.'

Jemima frowns as if not following my meaning.

I shouldn't dredge up the past, but it's so deeply entrenched in how our lives have unfolded, so I quickly add, 'Like switching jobs to become a waitress here. And then, aeons ago, when she always overshadowed everything I ... *we* did as little kids.'

'That wasn't our intention in taking Callie on, Pippa, but still, I understand where you're coming from.'

'The thing is ...' My nerves flare annoyingly in my stomach; I don't know how she'll take the news. She'll probably think I'm lying. I shouldn't feel daunted by the prospect of talking openly to a relative. I need to say it and be done. She'll deal with the facts as she must. And Callie needs to answer for her actions. 'I've found the antique jeweller she sold it to.'

'You have?'

I nod awkwardly, reaching into my jeans pocket to feel the tiny sealed packet.

'Don't ask – it hasn't been easy. Would you believe she sold it in town for eight hundred quid?'

'Are you joking? That's peanuts, given the size and quality of the sapphires. How much are they asking now?'

'Two grand.'

'No way! Having paid Callie a measly eight hundred. Does she know?' asks Jemima, the colour draining from her features.

I shake my head as my fingers grip and retrieve the packet from my pocket.

'Here,' I say, offering it to her. 'I think it's only right that you have it.' My words falter as emotion clogs my throat.

'What's this?' she asks, taking the brown envelope before peeling opening the seal.

I don't answer. She'll find out soon enough.

Jemima tips the engagement ring out into her open palm, before staring at me in horror. 'Pippa!'

'I want you to have it. I believe Nanna and Granddad would have wanted that too. I know she's the eldest but, given the way she's acted and how she's tainted its memory, I'm not going to offer it back to her. She doesn't deserve it.'

'But why?'

'Why did Callie sell it? You'll need to ask her. Personally, I think it's unforgivable. We should have been asked before she parted with it.'

'I agree, though I'm curious as to how she'll justify her actions.'

'She doesn't know that I've retrieved it from the jeweller. I'm not planning on having that conversation with her, to be honest; it's no business of hers.'

'Pippa, have you paid for this in full?' She slips it on to the tip of her index finger and gently twists it from side to side with her thumb, allowing the light to catch the precious stones.

'Yep, I have. I managed to knock him down by a hefty chunk when I gave him the whole story about our grandparents' deaths, which Callie had accidentally forgotten to mention. His final asking price was fifteen hundred ... it was a case of pay it or lose it for ever.'

We sit motionless, for what seems like an age, as our emotions ebb and flow between us. I don't ever remember sharing such a moment as this with anyone in my family.

'Are you OK?' I ask finally, after a lengthy pause, filled only by our sniffing and deep sighs.

'A bit overwhelmed to think she could part with Nanna's jewellery and not mention it.'

'Seems heartless, doesn't it?'

Jemima nods. 'But I can't take it, Pippa. Here.' Jemima extends her finger, offering me the ring back.

'I don't want it. I never have. I bought it back, as it belongs within our family and no one else's. Granddad would want you to look after it for the rest of us.'

'But you've paid ...' Jemima prevaricates, slowly retracting her outstretched hand as a fat tear trickles the length of her cheek.

'The money doesn't matter, not to me,' I say, knowing I've made the right decision.

'Ah, Pippa, come here,' cries Jemima, springing up from her seat to wrap her arms around my shoulders. 'Thank you so much, I'll treasure it!'

I start to cry, encircled in the warmth of her embrace; a swift action, filled with affection, which finally erodes the boundaries created since our childhood.

'Don't cry, Pippa ... the secret isn't a secret any more. You can breathe easy – you did the right thing.'

I try to speak, but I can't, as another wave of emotion takes hold. Jemima has no idea how much her words mean to me; I did the right thing. If I could explain, I'd apologise for all the stupid stuff I've done to her: the damaged pumpkin, the looted honesty boxes and the constant sniping. But more importantly, I'd tell her how much I admire her as my older cousin.

Chapter Thirty-Nine

Thursday 31 March

Pippa

'And who have we here?' asks Mungo, looking me up and down as if I were a prize parsnip, clipboard in hand, denoting his status of 'high-chief-ticker-of-list' at the entrance door.

'It's me, Mungo. Pippa.'

'I mean what act are you supposed to be? Twiggy? Suzi Quatro? It's a seventies-style karaoke, so you're probably one or the other.'

I look down at my sequinned strappy dress and ponder his faculties. Surely biker leathers and a tousled hairdo would suggest Suzi Quatro; I can't imagine her music agent ever suggested a slinky sequinned number with heels. I take in his appearance: a knitted cardigan, a clean shirt with his usual corduroy trousers. Allotment attire is hardly seventies fancy dress, Mungo!

'No.' I take the clipboard and pen from his clutches and write down my chosen act, plus the song title which I've learnt off by heart. It's taken all the self-belief I possess to prepare and dress for this event; I can do without hearing a wayward comment which might knock my confidence and send me traipsing towards home and my skater-girl look.

Mungo's greying eyebrows shoot up to his hairline as I return his clipboard. He can comment all he likes once I'm inside The

Orangery. Who'd have thought this would be my first hurdle of the night?

The flashing retro lights and stipulated fancy dress of the evening make it difficult to recognise anyone. There's a mixture of excellent hired costumes mingling with home-made outfits amongst the masses. Thankfully, I spot Elvis within seconds. Levi's sparkling white jumpsuit with bejewelled collar and belt steals the show; every gem twinkles and shines like a walking glitter ball.

'Hi,' I say, sidling up alongside him, knowing that his enthusiasm will be sky high when he sees me in character.

'Don't tell me, don't tell me!' says Levi, stepping backwards to take in my full-length appearance. He'll never guess in a month of Sundays, but I'm not about to ruin the fun. 'Mmmm, you're not Tina Turner or ... sorry, I'll need a clue. Obviously, my seventies knowledge doesn't include ...' His head tilt is meant to prompt an answer.

'I'm not saying.'

'Are you joking?'

'No, it's a secret. I've signed in. You'll find out who I am if I get selected to perform onstage.'

'Seriously, tell me ... whisper?'

'No, Levi. I'm happy with my choice so ... let's see what happens. Drink?'

Levi looks me up and down, giving a beaming smile, raising the back of my hand to his mouth in a gallant gesture before tucking it under his arm, not caring who sees us together as a couple.

'You look sensational, whoever you are. This way, my lady – it'll be my pleasure to accompany you to the bar.'

Levi cuts a path through the bustling crowd as we manoeuvre between Jemima's version of Kate Bush, standing behind the Bee Gees – who I assume are the MacDonald trio under all that facial hair – and, eventually, line up at tonight's makeshift bar behind Kaspar, dressed as Rod Stewart complete with a blond mullet wig, a tartan football scarf and his usual yellow waders Sellotaped to his legs, creating drainpipes.

Never in my wildest dreams did I think I'd be on Elvis's arm queuing behind Rod Stewart waiting for a large glass of wine!

'At least I've made an effort – unlike Mungo,' I say, surveying the bustling crowd.

'He's come as Val Doonican. He's even stashed his props in the rear kitchen, just in case he is called upon to sing,' corrects Levi. 'I'm the poor bugger who's been nominated as his stagehand if the circumstance arises.'

I recognise the singer's name, though I can't recall any of his songs.

'In that case, I'm tempted to bribe Ned in order to secure him a performance onstage,' I jest.

'You wouldn't dare!' retorts Levi, breaking into a laugh. 'If he suspects it's you, he'll pay you the same honour, so be careful.'

'Mmmm.' It might prove worthwhile.

'You don't seem unnerved by that possibility, Pippa. Are you up for it, if you're called to sing?'

'Yeah, I think so . . . it's now or never.'

'Nah, I've scratched that from my repertoire.'

It takes me a minute to catch on to his Elvis joke.

'Very clever. Please don't spend the night dropping song titles, because you're spoiling your own fun by repeatedly asking – now wait and see,' I tease, knowing it's killing him.

'And if you don't get called up?'

'Maybe you'll be invited to a private performance of our own!' I say, giving a cheeky wink, much to Levi's surprise.

I mingle in the crowd, avoiding anyone whose fancy dress I can't genuinely name. I get that it was way before my birth, but still, I have no idea who they're supposed to be from the chosen era.

I watch as Ned makes his way onstage, clearly depicting numerous nameless game-show hosts, in his tuxedo and cummerbund. I suspect he's not a fancy-dress kind of guy in reality. But this could be his best Engelbert Humperdinck impression, who knows! That's the problem with being the boss; you need to be seen to join in and yet not undermine the respect others have for you. Pretending to be Freddie Mercury in a sequinned one piece with your chest and torso revealed to the world is not the look I imagine Ned is chasing – unlike the chap being added to Mungo's door list. Oh my God, it's Isaac!

Ned gently taps the microphone, the DJ lowers the background music and the audience turn in unison to stare at the large karaoke screens aligned with the spot-lit stage.

'Ladies and gentlemen, thank you for coming and hopefully participating so heartily at tonight's charity event, the first of two celebration days for us here at Lerwick Manor. Tomorrow's event is a fun-filled family day, so please bring your little ones and explore the grounds, the allotments, our alpaca paddock and our brand-new sculpture park. All proceeds from both events will be equally divided between two very worthy causes in our local hospital. Firstly, the Special Care Baby Unit where a certain tiny baby is currently fast asleep in his crib. And secondly, the Stroke Outreach Team who have helped a close friend of ours in recent weeks.'

Ned pauses for a second, swallows and takes a breath before continuing. 'So please dig deep into those pockets, any loose change will be gladly welcomed in supporting others. Now, I believe Mungo is our talent scout for the evening, and his able assistant will be randomly selecting the order of artists. Remember, you won't all be selected to perform, so please, no backroom tantrums or antics commonly seen in the seventies.

There'll be no smashing guitars onstage, hurling whisky bottles or trashing hotel bedrooms if your name isn't called!'

There's a titter of laughter from the surrounding crowd. I notice that Natalia, seated nearby, doesn't flinch, though I don't think it was a dig at her. Personally, I'd give my eye teeth to see Mungo throw a strop in his cardigan and corduroys. Dottie would give him what for if he dared to show her up in public.

'So, without further ado, let's get proceedings under way with our first performance, from the one and only Elvis Presley!'

Ned's spotlight cuts, the intro music begins and the circular white light traces the steps of the King, climbing onstage. My heart leaps. Gone is the burly, blokey walk I recognise as Levi's; instead, the strut and exaggerated mannerisms of an icon grace our presence, centre stage. His wide stance, the gyrating hips, the lip curl – he's got the lot, as well as a deep singing voice. I'm instantly star struck.

Within seconds of the opening line of 'Suspicious Minds', the audience are singing along, swaying back and forth whilst surging forward for a closer look. If Levi wished, he could give up the day job of taxi driver and don his glad rags each night as an Elvis impersonator, though the amount of work he'd actually find here in Shetland wouldn't feed him for a week.

This is going to be a hard act to follow; no one is going to want to be the next superstar act under the spotlight!

When the lyrics end, Levi graciously declines the audience's demanding chants for 'More!'

'Thank you very much, but maybe later,' he says, doing an Elvis thrust and a final windmill arm to complete his act. 'Now, I do believe our next act tonight is the unforgettable Val Doonican.'

The audience provide rapturous applause for the newcomer as the stage lighting is temporarily lowered. I look around the assembled crowd, searching for a glimpse of the next performer, relieved it isn't me, as Elvis jumps from the stage, cutting a distinctive figure as he dashes through the crowd. The stage remains pitch black; there's a slight movement, highlighted by the DJ's retro lights, which I assume is our next act getting into position. There's an excited buzz amongst the waiting audience, as if we've all forgotten within ten minutes that it's us, the locals, dressed up for the night and not the actual celebrities appearing onstage.

'Excuse me. Mind your head,' says Elvis, returning to the stage and holding a wooden rocking chair above his head, before delivering it to the darkness and what seems to be an empty stage. The crowd bunch forward, giggling and laughing like excited children at a pantomime, as a hand reaches out from the depths of the stage and retrieves the rocking chair.

When the spotlight returns, we're greeted by Mungo, cardigan and all, sitting centre stage, gently rocking back and forth. As he begins to sing, the crowd automatically sway in unison, and I join in. Within minutes, Levi's strong arms wrap themselves about my frame and his nose nuzzles my right ear lovingly. 'You look utterly fabulous, tonight. I wanted you to know that, whether you get to perform onstage or not,' he whispers.

I turn around, snuggle into his tight hold and thank him with a proper kiss. He has no idea just how much his words of encouragement truly mean to me.

Autumn

I drift amongst the swaying crowd, checking that everything is in place, everyone has what they need, and urging the waiters to collect empty glasses as they go. It has been one hell of a long day – a long few weeks, actually – but seeing the smiles, the charity buckets filled with change and the array of celebrity costumes filling The Orangery, it's been worth it.

'Autumn, how are you?' asks Nessie, drinks in hand, returning from the bar.

'I'm great, thanks . . . just keeping an eye out, checking all is well, you know how it is with these things.'

'I do. It's been a huge success, you must be thrilled – and the Campbells are chuffed to bits!' she whispers loudly, combatting the noise from the MacDonald trio/Bee Gees 'oooooooing' incessantly onstage. She doesn't wait for a reply, before continuing, 'But how are you really? Are your hands any better?'

I instinctively curl my fingers, hiding them from view, but she's not stupid. I'm grateful that hers are clasped around a wine glass and a pint of Guinness, otherwise she'd be reaching for my hands and chastising me for sure.

'Yes, kind of . . . getting there . . . better than they were last week,' I say, attempting to bluff my way through. But why? She's a friend. She cared enough to ask after me. I change tack. 'Actually, they're as sore as hell and red raw. I've had a chat with Jemima about how I'm feeling. She's been an angel in trying to support me these past few weeks to separate work and play, so things are looking up.' Never before have I had a boss who genuinely cared about my ongoing welfare like Jemima does; nothing has been too much trouble in recent weeks. She's cajoled me into sticking to my weekly plans, be it visits to my sister's, preparing for the yoga classes, covering extra shifts, or simply a kind word in passing. I'll still have the occasional slip-up and feel bogged down, but generally things are improving for me.

Nessie nods encouragingly, before saying, 'Living on site can't help. I imagine it's difficult to say no when you know there's a hotel emergency three floors below you?'

'Exactly, I have wondered if it was a wise move after all.'

Nessie's eyes widen. 'I'll tell you what . . . I heard on the grapevine that a certain cottage might be available to let in a matter of weeks if a certain couple decide to move in together. Now, that might be worth considering?'

'Really? You've heard that?'

'Absolutely, I think an announcement is fairly imminent from Magnus and Verity . . . if you get my drift. In which case she won't be needing to rent Harmony Cottage for much longer.' Her nodding head becomes quite comical as she drives home her point.

'Ah, I see, interesting. Purchasing together, or a move to a big rambling family farmhouse nearby?'

'The latter, definitely the latter, as there are his aged parents to consider – which is a massive step, as Verity's roots are in the Midlands. So that's worth considering. And, remember, I'm related to the giant of a man, so I'll put a good word in for you.'

'Thank you, I'll have a serious think because . . . yeah, that sounds perfect,' I say, grateful for her kindness.

'And, in the meantime, you know where we are.'

'I do, and you'd best take those drinks over, otherwise your Freddie Mercury may think you've been lost in a time warp,' I say, letting Nessie drift off before Isaac comes looking.

'Hello, lassie, who are you supposed to be?' asks Dottie, peering at me through a rather fuzzy blonde wig perched atop a sparkly gold dress.

'Hello, Dottie, I'm not dressed as anyone in particular, just myself.'

'Best way to be, lassie. I'm supposed to be Barbra Streisand but I look more like Miss Piggy from the Muppets in this get-up,' chuckles Dottie.

'I think you look beautiful, regardless of the get-up. Are you enjoying yourself?'

'I am. Did you see Mungo singing as Val Doonican?'

'I did, very tuneful. I'm impressed.'

Dottie nods erratically, as if she can't quite hear me over the stage music, so I let her slip by on her way to keeping Natalia company. She's been an absolute trooper, the way she's tended to Natalia's every need and supported the local hospital's outreach team with her physio care. She genuinely has a heart of pure gold, and all of us – the allotment association, the artists at the stable gallery and the staff of Lerwick Manor hotel – we're so lucky to have her around to share our joys and sorrows.

Pippa

'Our next performer has come all the way from Wales ...' announces Ned over the sound system, from the side of the stage.

I hear a murmur of 'Tom Jones' and smile; I needed a little notice to gain some composure before the true artist is revealed.

'Let's hear a big Shetland welcome for Miss Shirley Bassey!'

The audience turn, frantically looking around in a quizzical fashion, trying to work out who's who and what's what.

Ah, that'll be me then!

I hitch up my sequinned hemline and ease my way through the crowd towards the stage. Thankfully, on arriving the spotlight has been lowered, so not everyone sees me stumble up the steps on to the stage before Elvis quickly offers me a helping hand. How can I dress elegantly for once in my life yet fall on to the stage like a baby elephant at a watering hole?

'Excuse me, ladies and gents ... a little hush would be welcomed,' soothes Ned, as Elvis passes me the performer's microphone.

My stomach is rolling like the North Sea. I'm convinced the audience can see it in such a sheer dress. My opening bars of music begin, but I'm not ready, so I miss the first line of lyrics. The music continues while I turn around, hoping to read the next line of lyrics off the screen. I'm now off kilter with my practised act; I can't carry off a flawless performance like Levi did, which throws me. They'd pressed play before I was ready. I was still thinking about the size of the crowd, the sea of faces before me, the dramatic arm gestures required to carry off a convincing Bassey stance.

'Can I start again, please?' I ask, totally out of character, just plain old Pippa.

I see the audience shake their heads and tut, as murmured comment lifts from the sea of bodies before me. I get it, they were prepared to give me a chance as Miss Bassey, but now I've ruined the illusion by snapping back to real life as Pippa. 'Typical Pippa,' they'll be thinking, always messes it up. Always comes across as the 'big I am' then fails to deliver the goods. I know what they're thinking, but I'm determined to prove them wrong, once and for all. I might not be wearing a Bassey wig, or be dripping with diamonds, but I've made an effort with this act. I've exfoliated my skin to be blemish free and polished; I've been studying this woman's dramatic poses in the mirror for hours. So I will deliver the very best Shirley Bassey – if it kills me!

The backing music stops, as requested.

'Ladies and gents, if we could have a little quiet please, while Miss Bassey composes herself . . . are you ready?' asks Ned.

Levi blows me a kiss from his position behind the music system. I jokingly catch it; knowing nothing else matters as long as I have Levi's steadfast support.

This time, I'm ready. This time, I forget where I am, forget the crowd before me, forget my history, their history, and focus purely on hearing that first note, and then . . . I belt it out. I hear the gasps, I see the front row of wide-open mouths and the looks of utter surprise which turn into an admiring acceptance that this girl can actually sing. For five minutes and thirteen seconds I perform 'This Is My Life' as I've never sung it before, in the exact manner of the great star herself. And when I'm done, there is absolute silence. That too is what I wanted. Just one chance to show people they don't know everything about me. They can't predict my talents or flaws based on what they've heard in the past. I'm me, and they've just witnessed a whole other side of *moi*.

Natalia

From the comfort of my armchair, strategically positioned not far from tonight's makeshift bar, I watch the evening's proceedings; everyone is happy and smiling. And singing. I can't complain; they've made me feel very welcome, despite me being an outsider of sorts.

Sitting here, I can't help but admire my repaired kintsugi vase standing proudly by The Orangery's entrance, now complete. Gold paint has been applied as mock molten gold, highlighting each glued crack, and I've refilled the vase with an abundance of dried flowers and colourful ornamental grass. A symbolic reminder of how far I've come on my personal journey since arriving here in February.

I chose my shamrock-green dress, which I'd kept for a special occasion, so it seems fitting. I've answered to 'Blondie' all evening, but that's a lie. I haven't a pocket in this dress to accommodate the dead weight of my left arm, so have chosen to remain seated all night. I've had plenty of fly-by visitors, drink in one hand and buffet plate in the other, asking how I am. Dottie has checked up on me every thirty minutes; I half expected her to pull her blood pressure machine out of her handbag and insist on a 'little reading', just to be sure. Thankfully, she hasn't. Autumn has dashed back and forth to my table with snippets of info and chat, using it as her base camp for her large glass of vino, which I've happily babysat, speaking up whenever keen waiters approach and ask 'Is this done with?' in an overenthusiastic attempt to collect dirty glasses. Verity, Nessie and even Melissa, who popped in for an hour, have come across to me, ensuring I've had a constant flow of company and a full glass. Though my favourite visitor sits beside me, her muzzle resting on the padded arm of my chair, her wet nose sporadically nudging my left hand, requesting another ear tickle – delivered with my right hand, of course.

They've had a decent turnout, which is cause for celebration. I'm relieved that not *all* the locals showed up though. I wasn't relishing the idea of facing Lachlan again, having heard of his horrific misdemeanours from last September, when fate handed us both a lesson in life. Not that I'd switch places with him, given the impending court case and assumptions from the locals that he's going away for a fair while. It's one thing to share a lustful night, knowing there's nothing in it, but to hear there might have been an element of revenge towards Ned Campbell and young Isla, now that's another head screw. Though I'm yet to have a conversation about the suite he trashed when left to his own devices. And as for lying about his age, that simply gives me the 'ick' each time I recall his lie. Never mind, you live and learn!

'Natalia, can I get you a drink?' asks Pippa, dashing by on her way to the bar.

'I'm fine, thank you, though come here a second.' I beckon her to come nearer so I can whisper. 'You, ya cheeky minx, should have spilt the beans a little more about you and the lovely Levi instead of acting so coy! How did you contain yourself on our night out? You hardly said a word, yet now look at you both!'

'I know, it was pretty early days then, and I didn't want to say too much, just in case . . . you know how it is.'

'I certainly do. Enjoy getting to know him, don't rush it, but make sure you know exactly where you stand!'

We both giggle before she continues on her way.

Floss nudges my hand again, in want of attention. Like me

she's healed well, but the rhythmical movement of her limbs as she walks has been interrupted by a definite clunk to her rear leg.

'You are a beauty, Floss,' I say, as her doleful gaze meets mine. 'If only you could talk, I wonder what wisdom you'd share.' Her long eyebrows flicker in response. I might get a dog; she's been good company, a constant listener and, with her own woeful injury, a patient friend. I smile, yeah ... I'll get a dog when I go back home.

Home. It seems like a distant memory. I've extended my two-week stay unexpectedly, though deep down wasn't that my intention all along? I chuckle. Yep, it certainly was, but for very different reasons. The idea of home suddenly feels right. Home, my own place, seeing my family, my own belongings and, hopefully, renegotiating the life I left behind to catch a flight to Shetland. Boy, how much has changed.

Ned and his microphone cut through my thoughts.

'Folks, there's just half an hour remaining, so what's it to be? Is there anyone who hasn't sung who wishes to? Let's open the floor, any song, any era. No, Levi ... you're done for tonight – Elvis has officially left the building!' There's a roar of laughter from the happy crowd.

I shift in my seat. Floss eyes me warily, questioning my actions as if she senses my thoughts.

'It'll be fine, you watch,' I mutter, before yelling aloud. 'Me! I'm up.'

The crowd turn and a sea of faces greet me as I awkwardly rise to standing.

As I walk cautiously through the crowd, I'm conscious that this is the most alcohol I've had to drink in months. My footing is fine, my good hand steady, and my slurring might go unnoticed – after all, plenty of others are currently slurring their speech too!

On reaching the stage, I find Levi waiting by the steps to give me a helping hand, for which I'm grateful.

'What do you want to sing?' he asks, gently guiding me at each step.

'I've only practised one song,' I say, before whispering the title into his ear. I observe him gulp and clench his jaw before the briefest of nods. 'I'll sort it. Take the mic and ready yourself.'

I'll need to be ready. I haven't practised once without ending in tears.

I stand before the stage microphone, avoiding eye contact with anyone in particular. I've no fancy dance moves, no dramatic arm movements – nowhere to hide, in fact, and nothing to fill the awkward silence as I view the expectant crowd, eager to hear the intro and recognise my choice.

I see their instant reaction, rather than hearing the intro myself, as the first few piano notes are played, but I'm ready with the opening line and join in seamlessly with Christina Aguilera's 'Beautiful'.

There's not a dry eye in the house as my closing lyrics fade. I discreetly wipe each cheek with the back of my hand, step away from the mic and smile.

And now I'm ready for home. My home.

Chapter Forty

Friday 1 April

Pippa

Ned taps the microphone head, causing the speaker system to boom, as is his habit on such occasions. The bustling chatter fades to silence, with people craning their necks to get a better view as we gather in the newly installed picnic area between the alpaca paddock and the driveway's sculpture park.

'Ladies, gentlemen and little ones, welcome to Lerwick Manor on this glorious spring afternoon. Can I say a huge thank you to those who attended last night, I'm sure you'll agree we all had a fabulous time and were thoroughly entertained all evening! We raised a wonderful amount for our two good causes – and today, we'd like to do exactly the same. Remember, every penny will be going to the Special Care Baby Unit and the Stroke Outreach Team of our local hospital, which means we as a community all benefit from your kind-hearted generosity.'

'So, back to today . . . and I'm reliably informed that the local schools have just broken up for the holidays so the youngsters aren't bunking off en masse, so I'd like to invite you all to enjoy our glorious grounds. You're welcome to visit the alpacas, see the scarecrow parade on the adjoining allotments, take afternoon tea in The Orangery or the Lerwick Manor Hotel, and browse the gorgeous gifts created in the gallery. And when you need a quiet moment, please take a few minutes to admire the talents of our resident blacksmith, Wednesday Smith, who was commissioned to create, especially for this estate, the beautiful sculpture park you see beside us, here by the driveway, and which over time will complement our woodland nature walk. So, without further ado, can I ask Nessie to join me as we unveil the first of her five sculptures: Time.'

There's a pause while Nessie nervously makes her way to centre stage beside Ned. She puts a hand out to grasp the giant white drape, which she's been panicking about all morning, worried about it blowing off in the wind.

'Nessie, would you do the honours, please,' says Ned, passing her the microphone.

She won't be happy about being the centre of attention; she might look fearless, with her shocking pink hair, but I know different.

'It gives me the greatest pleasure to have crafted each piece for this exhibition. The commissioned theme was "things we waste" and I believe I've been able to capture the essence in each piece. I hope you enjoy each sculpture and view it as a gentle reminder of what's precious. I feel honoured to have completed the commission. The title pieces exhibited today are: "love", "breath", "effort", "resources" and . . .' She grabs the corner of the billowing drape and tugs it free to reveal . . . '"Time"!'

The air is filled with cheers and worthy applause as the huge metal sculpture catches the afternoon sunlight on its polished surface.

'Thank you, Nessie . . . I'm sure it will be appreciated for years to come. Well done!' says Ned, retrieving his microphone. 'Ladies, gentlemen and children, please enjoy your afternoon. And remember, dig deep, as today is for two very worthy causes. Thank you.'

Autumn

I shot through the allotment's entrance gate, like a racing whippet after a rabbit, hoping to be one of the first to arrive. How wrong I was! The car park is jam-packed with parked vehicles and allot-menteers, all eager to view the scarecrow parade for themselves. The level of secrecy has been tighter than at Fort Knox! I've given up asking what ideas folk are implementing; my casual enquiries have been met with numerous scowling expressions and pretty harsh refusals to indulge my curiosity. No one is discussing their plans, for fear of a third party pinching the best idea ever! Now, I'm going for gold against the best; I needed to arrive an hour ago to beat this crowd.

I'm praying that everyone who selected a secret scarecrow name has adhered to the rules and produced something in the name of their inspiration, otherwise it'll be embarrassing if there's an odd-one-out who doesn't have a replica namesake created in straw.

I can't say I've visited the allotments regularly in recent weeks – which maybe I should have done, given my central role supporting this charity event – but my understanding is the allotments are set out in a figure-of-eight shape. So I select the nearest pathway and begin to walk, perusing the entries before me. Immediately, I'm shocked at the sight of mannequin heads on spikes, army camouflage nets suspended from metal poles, and the littering of white plastic chairs almost everywhere you look. Thankfully, I soon come across immaculate allotment plots with trimmed edges, neat rows and water butts standing to attention like tubby soldiers. And there, standing beside the locked gate, is the first scarecrow I've spotted. A male, with a rather large pumpkin for a head, dressed in a checked tartan shirt, with a suitcase suspended from each straw bushel depicting arms. Is it Levi? An interpretation of his porter's duties at the hotel? I'm unsure but hope no one's offended by my assumption.

'Hey, Autumn, have you seen the Dottie scarecrow?' calls Isaac, doubling back when he spots me in the throng of visitors.

'No, am I heading in the right direction?'

'Sure, a bit further up – you can't miss her,' he instructs, his arm tightly wrapped about Nessie's shoulders as they walk ahead.

I'll be thrilled if that's the case, because I'm still unsure if I should have allowed Mungo to cheat the odds and select the only ticket he wanted. But if he's done her proud then who am I to argue?

'Hi, Autumn, have you just arrived?' asks Melissa, meandering amongst the families.

'I have. How's the little one coming along?'

'He's getting stronger and bigger by the day. He's a gutsy little thing where his food's concerned, so fingers crossed he'll be home in no time,' she says, a big smile adorning her face at the very thought of her tiny boy, not so far away in the Special Care Baby Unit. 'I hate leaving him but Hamish insisted I come today, even for a short while. I was quite overcome with emotion on the way here. But how could I resist, knowing that Jemima and Ned have arranged a charity event in honour of the hospital's baby unit as a thank you? Hopefully, the money raised will help other tiny babies who arrive a little early, just like our boy!'

'I'm sure we'll collect more donations from today's event to help others in similar circumstances,' I say, proud to have emptied the brimming contents from last night's karaoke buckets. I make my way through the crowd as it moves at a snail's pace, viewing every element of every allotment plot through their wire fencing. Me, I simply wish to see the array of scarecrows. Especially Dottie's likeness, if it is a bit special.

It doesn't take long before I pass a plot with an actual wooden front door, which seems baffling, and suddenly find myself greeted by not one but two scarecrows, arm in arm, staring straight at me. One with the widest straw hat I have ever seen. The brim extends past the shoulders of the scarecrow, which is dressed in a tweed skirt and a flowery blouse; her straw bushel arm is linked to a taller, slender figure in a glamorous skin-tight red jumpsuit, her flowing blonde locks blowing in the gentle breeze. Her left arm ends abruptly, poking into her pocket. Instantly recognisable as Dottie and Natalia – though what she'll think of this is anybody's guess. I'm sure she'll see the funny side, but still, it might come as a bit of a shock.

'Autumn, what do you think?'

I turn at the mention of my name, to find Jemima standing behind me.

'I recognise who they are! I hope they're not offended?'

'No. Mungo ran the idea past Natalia before adding her in. She's helped Kaspar on his allotment in recent days, so he thought why not include her as part of the scarecrow parade?'

'A buy-one-get-one-free combo, as such!' I say, relieved that Mungo has had the sense to inform her, or ask.

'Did you see the dedicated bench as you passed?' she goes on to ask, gesturing back the way I came.

'No. I don't know my way around these plots, so I'm unsure where I'm going or what I'm looking at.'

'Here, this way, I'll show you.' Jemima leads the way back a couple of plots or three, and there beside the locked gate is an ornate wrought-iron bench. At first, the metalwork looks simple and painted plain black, but when I focus on the details, I spot a row of metal trowels for an armrest, then a row of hand forks creating a second armrest. On closer inspection, I see that a couple of decorative wheelbarrows provide the seat section, with a sturdy backrest made from long-handled rakes, welded together with struts which imitate bamboo canes, supporting a rambling rose. A miniature tartan cap is slung on the back-corner post, as if awaiting its owner's return. How touching!

'Did Nessie create this?' I ask, blown away by her imagination and craftsmanship.

'She certainly did. It's dedicated to our dear friend, Old Bill. He passed away last September and we wanted something as a commemoration of his life's work here on the allotments. Where better to put it than outside his old plot, where you can take a breath before continuing your walk down to the car park.'

'Wow, what an honour in a tight-knit community such as this.'

'It certainly is. Though I'm not so sure of my scarecrow! Look . . .' She points to the one we've just passed in our haste to view the bench.

I look at her creation. There's a duck-shaped corn dolly at its feet, which I assume is Crispy duck. I take in the rest; at first it doesn't make sense, but then the penny drops, with a resounding clang. Before me is a rather rotund scarecrow, tiny in stature and dressed in maternity dungarees, with the largest stuffed belly imaginable.

'Are you . . .?' I don't finish my sentence before Jemima begins to beam, and her smile confirms it: pregnant. 'Well I never!'

'Come off it! You must have guessed – everyone else has. I've been the talk of the estate for the last few weeks as I traipse back and forth talking to the bees.'

I frown; I don't get it.

'It's tradition to tell the bees any news first, before others . . . it's supposed to bring good luck from the other world. Admittedly, I was eager in telling the bees that we were even trying for a family, which led Dottie to wrongly assume I was already pregnant. But now I am. It's very early days but now severe morning sickness has kicked in so soon, making me feel utterly wretched, there's no chance of hiding the fact for the usual twelve weeks before announcing.'

'I never knew that. And no one said.'

'Surely Dottie dropped enough hints?'

'Not to me, she didn't. Well, congratulations to you both, that's fabulous news.' I quickly give her a tight squeeze. 'And to think, you were helping me through my troubles when you might not have been feeling so great yourself.'

'No worries, I'm here to support the staff all I can. The morning sickness has knocked me sideways, I must admit, but the meditation you taught me has come in very handy, a saving grace in recent days,' says Jemima, with a chuckle. 'Not that Ned's volunteering to join me anyday soon.'

Pippa

'Jemima, have you seen Natalia this afternoon?' I ask. I've been searching the allotments and manor grounds, looking for her.

'I believe she left this morning, Pippa – the key for the Unst Suite was left on the reception counter, alongside an allotment key she'd borrowed from Kaspar,' says Jemima, pulling a sad face and tilting her head.

Typical Jemima, showing care and attention towards others, even in difficult circumstances.

'Ah well . . .' I say. 'Though I doubt she had a bill to settle – did you mutually agree that, weeks ago?'

'Pippa, you are cheeky!' says Jemima, with a giggle. 'Besides, that's none of your business – family or otherwise. It's strange, but Natalia and I found a mutual respect for one another along the way; I'd have liked to say goodbye and wish her well.'

'I've got a funny feeling she did that last night!' I say, putting my arm around Jemima's shoulder.

'Given the reaction she received from the audience, I believe you may be right, Pippa.'

'Anyway, less concern for others and more for yourself. I hear that congratulations are in order, with the pitter-patter of tiny feet coming your way!'

'Yes, we're thrilled to bits – a December baby, or so we've calculated.'

I'm overcome with joy to see how happy she is, despite looking slightly washed out and pale. I sweep Jemima into my arms and squeeze her tight; it feels wonderful to be included in her family news. Who'd have thought, at the beginning of the year, we'd ever overcome our differences? Not me! 'Your dad is going to be chuffed to bits when he learns he's to be a grandpop!'

'Believe me, we debated whether to say given that it's so soon and he's living on the mainland. But it's only fair if others know, so we've already told him – and yes, he was over the moon with the news,' says Jemima.

'So, after today's event, it'll be feet up and rest for you,' I say, knowing Jemima could never let someone else take over her role.

'Are you joking? As of tomorrow, I start helping Dottie and Mungo plan for September's annual Allotment Festival. There's no rest with those two about; they keep me on my toes, that's for sure.'

'You love it, and you know it!' I chide, giving her a quick squeeze before I head off in search of Levi. 'Can I assume you won't be submitting an entry in the giant pumpkin category like last year?'

'Phuh! There's no fear of that – I'll have enough to do nurturing this little pumpkin, this year,' says Jemima, gently tapping her stomach.

Epilogue

Saturday 3 September
Lerwick Manor's annual Allotment Festival

Pippa

On a gloriously warm afternoon, the date expertly chosen by the allotment's committee back in April, I wander from the enormous beer tent, glass in hand, making my way across the crowded driveway of Lerwick Manor. On the far side of the driveway, I'm greeted by a sea of locals and tourists, mingling amongst a posse of dedicated allotmenteers who are crowding around the front of the second marquee, listening to the Allotment Association's prize-winning vegetable announcements.

Sidestepping my way through the gathered bodies, I smile and nod to various people, all huddled in friendship groups, eagerly listening or awaiting certain categories and prizes. I spy Nessie, the blacksmith, snuggled arm in arm with Isaac, the glass blower. Verity, the Yarn Barn knitter, leans against her giant of a man, Magnus, as dear Floss lies obediently at his feet. And jubilant new parents, Melissa and Hamish, rhythmically jiggle a pushchair containing a sleeping baby Noah.

'Excuse me ... sorry ... thank you,' I repeat at intervals, squeezing between the gaps in the swelling crowd. I finally spot the trio I'm looking for: Levi, a radiant Jemima complete with her neat bump, and Dottie, whose wide-brimmed straw hat forces her to stand a little distance away from her neighbour, for fear of taking Jemima's eye out. I sidle up, snaking my arm around Levi's middle, giving him an unexpected squeeze.

'Hey, babe, where have you snuck up from? We looked for you earlier,' he says, bending to plant a gentle kiss upon my forehead. His blond hair grazes my face before he straightens, causing my skin to tingle with excitement. We're still very much at the loved-up stage, where we frequently commit PDAs regardless of who is around. I'm hoping that never changes for us, but all relationships evolve over time.

'Just chilling, and taking in the scenery, that's all,' I say, exchanging a welcome smile with both Jemima and Dottie.

They acknowledge my arrival, before reverting their attention to the proceedings on the main stage. I crane my neck to see between the shoulders of the crowd, and make out Ned and Mungo, onstage with microphones in hand, alongside three prestigious-looking judges, all presenters belonging to *Gardeners' Question Time* or some such radio programme – or so I'm led to believe by the excitement drummed up on their arrival at the hotel, earlier today.

'Dottie's just won her twenty-third First Prize for her delphiniums,' whispers Levi, gesturing with a nod.

'Congratulations, Dottie,' I silently mouth, not wanting to interrupt her enjoyment of the awards, but happy to share her good news.

She wrinkles her nose up and gives a little giggle, as if she were surprised. I doubt anyone from the allotment community, let alone Shetland, would expect to take that spot while she's still entering her bouquets.

'Ladies and gentlemen, our next award is for the category of hanging basket,' announces Ned, his voice booming out across the crowd, thanks to the powerful speaker system. 'Mungo, if you'd do the honours, please?'

'Thank you.' Mungo's microphone creates an ear-piercing

wailing noise before he continues. 'A glorious new category, introduced by our committee to encourage the smaller individual projects within our gardens. I'm proud to announce that the second prize is awarded to Kaspar ... Kaspar ... well done, Kaspar, mate!' Mungo stutters and stammers on seeing Kaspar's surname displayed on the announcement card. The noise of the crowd's appreciative applause, wolf whistles and chanting masks Mungo's embarrassment.

'Every time. Someone needs to learn how to pronounce it before next year!' mutters Jemima, stifling a giggle.

'We all know who he means, though, lassie,' adds Dottie, the voice of reason. 'How many Kaspars do we have around these parts?'

I remain silent, watching as the one and only Kaspar meets and greets the line-up of judges, before collecting his prize certificate, his red satin ribbon and posing for the obligatory photograph. Once the stage is clear, Mungo continues.

'First prize in our prestigious new hanging basket category is ... Levi Gordans,' wails Mungo, his excitement getting the better of him. 'Ah mate, I'm chuffed for you.'

'Oh my God, you didn't tell me you'd entered those!' I shriek at Levi, attempting to push him forward to collect his prize.

'You go, Pippa! It was your hanging basket I entered, not mine,' he answers in a hushed tone.

'Sod off. I'm not going up there. You go!' I argue, as the surrounding crowd turn around to view our double act beside a bemused Jemima and Dottie.

'Come on, Levi, son. Don't be shy now!' booms Mungo's voice over the speaker system.

'Go, Levi, she'll not be convinced,' ushers Dottie, knowing that many more categories and prizes need to be awarded.

Levi takes Dottie's advice and strides off through the crowd towards the stage, much to my relief. I'm hoping to God he doesn't get disqualified; he can't prove that I did plant that particular basket. After much applause, chanting of his name, and a hearty handshake with each judge, Levi returns armed with his bounty of goodies: a certificate, a blue satin ribbon and his prize voucher.

'Stop it, I can't look at you for laughing. Please don't ever do that again; I nearly died at the thought of you insisting I go up there. Never in all my days!' I say, before taking an interest in the goodies he holds.

The awards continue for a fair amount of time, but after much cheering, the handing out of numerous prizes, and hearty applause for countless names and faces, the categories run dry.

'Well, I suppose that's the end of that for another year!' says Dottie, her watery blue eyes twinkling enough to cause her to dab them with a handkerchief.

'Shall I get a round of drinks in?' asks Levi, gesturing towards the beer tent.

'You can, but its orange juice for me and this little one,' says Jemima, rubbing her bump proudly.

'Of course,' agrees Levi, enjoying his friend's look of contentment. 'Is it a glass of Mungo's beetroot wine for you, Dottie?'

'A large one!' corrects Dottie, always quick to rectify errors.

'I'll have a soft drink, please – I'm selling ice creams in a little while,' I add, before we watch him head off across the driveway.

'Have you seen Callie?' asks Jemima, glancing around us at the milling crowd.

'Yep, she's over there, standing with Autumn, Isla and Tabitha from the gallery's soapery.' I watch as Jemima locates them and observes the relaxed group for a moment before speaking.

'She's never mentioned Nanna's engagement ring, you know. I haven't ventured to ask her, for fear of hearing something I can't forgive or forget.'

I shrug. 'There's not much I can say on the subject, other

than I'm glad I retrieved it, and I'm pleased to know it's safely in your possession.'

'I'm intrigued, though,' muses Jemima, watching the quartet of ladies a short distance away.

'Levi would say that she must have had her reasons. He always says that about folk,' I add, unsure if I'm convinced in Callie's case. 'Maybe she didn't want to leave it in a jewellery box for ever and a day, maybe not. I'll never know.'

'Do you care?'

'Not really. Levi's taught me to live and let live. I steer clear of drama by not associating with her. I've realised that I can't change the past, but I need to protect my future, so I rarely interact with her nowadays.'

'Letting bygones be bygones then?' asks Jemima, glancing at Dottie, possibly wondering how much she knows.

'Nah, more a case of letting cuckoos be cuckoos,' I say, before a giggle escapes me on seeing Jemima's deeply furrowed brow. 'Nothing . . . forget it, just a private joke between me and Levi.'

'Pippa, there you are!' calls Ned, fast approaching us through the crowd.

It's sweet how he gives Jemima a peck on the cheek, and her bump a gentle pat, before continuing to speak.

'Pippa, we know how you don't like being the centre of attention, so we didn't call you up on to the stage but . . .' Ned begins to rummage inside his jacket pocket and retrieves a sealed envelope.

A brief glance is exchanged between him and Jemima, after which she shakes her head, before he turns to face me. Dottie starts to smile whilst looking over Jemima's shoulder.

'Technically, this is a separate business not associated with the allotments, so it wasn't fitting to announce it or call you up on to the stage, but we . . . Jemima and I, that is . . . voted you our "employee of the season". So, to show our appreciation, we'd like to present you with this. A little gift . . .' says Ned, falling silent.

'Our way of saying thank you for all you've done since taking on the mobile Bread Basket. Whether it's your dedicated effort, helping others, or assisting within the community . . . you've handled each task perfectly, and we wanted to show how much we appreciate it,' adds Jemima, her gaze twinkling as much as Dottie's.

The envelope dangles in the space between me and Ned.

'Here, take it and enjoy, Pippa,' he says, nudging it towards me.

'Thank you, I'm quite taken aback.' I grasp the envelope, slide my finger under the seal and find a cheque made out to me for a total of £2,000. My eyes widen and my jaw drops on seeing the amount.

'This is too much for such . . .' I pause, as the amount and the hidden sentiment make sense. I shake my head, before adding, 'Sorry, but I can't take it. Honestly, I can't.'

'You can and you will,' says Ned. 'There's more than enough there to cover a recent expense, with a little extra for you to enjoy being our first nominated "employee of the season".'

I feel overwhelmed. I know it makes perfect sense: a reimbursement of the cash I forked out for Nanna's ring, plus a gift. But deep down I don't need them to do this for me. I'm happy to have helped save the sapphire ring for future generations.

'Please, it's the least we can do,' says Jemima, gently patting my hand as she does with her baby bump.

'Look what I've got,' says Levi, returning with a tray of drinks, and catching us by surprise.

We all turn, expecting his announcement to be our drinks, but he's holding an open letter.

'Here, take it, Dottie,' he says, lifting his thumb to free the paper from his clasp around the tray edge. 'It was addressed to the hotel, so Autumn opened it with this morning's post.'

Dottie gingerly takes the letter, and peers closely.

'Without my glasses, I can't read that,' she says, abruptly. 'Here, Jemima.'

Levi hands out the drinks, one by one, apologising to Ned that he's left empty-handed.

'It's from Natalia!' says Jemima, glancing at Ned before continuing to read.

Dear Dottie and Co,

I'm hoping this letter finds you all happy and healthy. I pray today will be the day of the Lerwick Manor annual Allotment Festival. I've checked on the website for the correct date, but one can never be quite certain of the postal system.

Having attended in previous years, I know how hotly the various categories are contested! I'm hoping that Dottie has retained her first place for the fresh bouquet with her stunning delphiniums – I'll be shocked if she hasn't. I'm imagining that you're all sauntering around the lawns, terraces and gallery, sipping beetroot wine and enjoying the sunshine.

I just wanted to say a huge thank you to you all for the love and kindness shown to me on my last disastrous visit. Not the great return I'd planned or hoped for, but a visit which has changed my life for ever. I'm writing this letter whilst sitting beside the swimming pool of The Royal at Atlantis, in the Bahamas. I didn't sign my contract with my former agency – they withdrew the offer, despite negotiations – but no fear, I have a silver lining. Tomorrow I'm booked for a promotional assignment, modelling cosmetics for a New York agency who Marston has previously worked with. Turns out he did have a conscience, after all, so he put me in touch with them soon after I arrived back home in Edinburgh. The directors are keen to demonstrate an inclusive ethos in relation to their advertising and products, so my career continues to progress.

Talking of progress, my speech continues to improve, as long as I slow down and focus on the pronunciation. My facial features are fairly unchanged whilst the dexterity in my left hand continues to improve gradually.

Who knows? If my career continues to flourish, I might drop by on an unexpected stopover, whilst jetting between countries and modelling assignments, to enjoy more sunny stays at the Shetland hotel!

Love to you all,

Natalia xx

'That's lovely to hear,' says Jemima, folding the letter in half and passing it to Dottie. 'I bet she's missing you a treat!'

'She will be, but she won't be missing my blood pressure machine quite as much!' chuckles Dottie, a mischievous smile adorning her features as a little tear springs to the corner of her eye.

Acknowledgements

Thank you to my editor, Kate Byrne, and everyone at Headline Publishing Group for believing in my storytelling and granting me the opportunity to become part of your team.

To David Headley and the crew at DHH Literary Agency – thank you for the unwavering support. Having a 'dream team' supporting my career was always the goal – you guys make it the reality!

Thank you to my fellow authors/friends within the Romantic Novelists' Association – you continue to support and encourage me, every step of the way. A special mention for Bella Osborne, Alison May, Janet Gover and Christie Barlow – always a writing retreat or a text message away, throughout the longest of lockdowns!

Special thanks to Kathryn Jenkinson, Sophie Penrose, Rebecca Hibbins, Joanne Hall and Beth Harsley – 'five star' friends who always provide the smiles and laughter at get-togethers. And Paddy Cheshire, a shining example to us all, bless you!

A heartfelt thank you to the Shetlanders for providing such a warm welcome whilst I holidayed in Lerwick, Shetland – who would have thought that this little girl's dream of visiting the top of the weather map would result in a series of books!

Thank you to my family and closest friends, for always loving and supporting my adventures – wherever they take me.

Unconditional thanks to the A&E medical team at the George Eliot Hospital who, in July 2021, 'allowed' me to experience an

ECG and a CT scan at short notice, and definitely unplanned. Plus, the dedicated Stroke/TIA Clinic team in the Felix Holt Ward who assessed, and double-checked my assessment, to give me the all-clear – thank you! Be it a life experience or personal research – nothing is ever wasted in my line of work, as proven.

And finally, thank you to my wonderful readers. You continue to thrill me each day with your fabulous reviews and supportive emails. I'm truly humbled that you invest precious time from your busy lives to read my books. Without you guys, my characters, stories and happy-ever-afters would simply be daydreams.

Curl up with the new feel-good read for
the holiday season from Erin Green!

a Shetland Christmas carol

Order now from

REVIEW

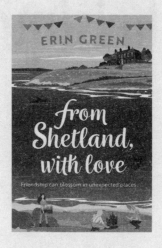

from Shetland, with love at Christmas

Spend the holiday season in glorious Lerwick!

Available now from

Taking a Chance on Love

The perfect feel-good, romantic and uplifting read –
another book from Erin Green sure to warm your heart.

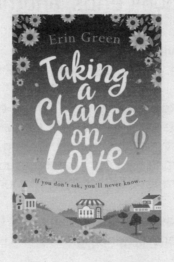

Available now from

REVIEW

Bookends

When one book ends, another begins...

Bookends is a vibrant new reading community to help you ensure you're never without a good book.

You'll find exclusive previews of the brilliant new books from your favourite authors as well as exciting debuts and past classics. Read our blog, check out our recommendations for your reading group, enter great competitions and much more!

Visit our website to see which great books we're recommending this month.

Join the Bookends community:

www.welcometobookends.co.uk

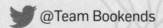 @Team Bookends  @WelcomeToBookends